Marry Me Forever

Starry Hills
Book 3

Kayla Chase

Mythical Lake Press, LLC

This book is a work of fiction. Names, characters, places, and incidents are either the product of the writer's imagination or are used fictitiously, and any resemblance to actual persons, living or dead, business establishments, events, or locales is entirely coincidental.

Marry Me Forever

Mythical Lake Press, LLC

Print Edition

Cover Art by Laura Hoak-Kagey of Mythical Lake Design

ISBN: 979-8891560130

Also by Kayla Chase

Starry Hills

Want Me Forever

Stay With Me Forever

Marry Me Forever

Trust Me With Forever (2024)

Reader Note

This book contains thoughts, memories, and discussions about childhood bullying and the death of family members. I hope I have treated these items with the care and consideration they deserve.

Chapter One

Nolan

I never thought I'd propose marriage at a children's birthday party. And yet, as I scanned the room looking for my potential bride, I was going to do just that.

Oh, not in front of everyone. Because my proposal wasn't to a woman I loved and longed to spend my life with. No, it was all part of a plan. One that would hopefully get my ex-girlfriend to finally move on and stop telling the world we were engaged.

And considering Wendy Webster and I were both movie stars, it wasn't exactly a private spat I could solve easily. After months of my ex sending her fans to harass me and ask when we were finally going to tie the knot, I'd had enough.

If only I could find the woman I wanted to make my deal with, then maybe I could finally enjoy my niece and nephew's birthday party.

I was just about to ask my sister, Abby, where her friends were when the person I was looking for entered the room—Katie Evans.

She was short and curvy, with pale skin and long auburn hair. While her jeans and dark green sweater were nice enough, it was her smile that made her stand out. Well, her smile and the ever-present gleam of mischief in her blue eyes.

Katie made a beeline for my eleven-year-old nephew, Wyatt Wolfe. After she whispered something into his ear, the usually shy, reticent boy hugged her. Curious, I walked over and stood next to Wyatt's dad and my oldest brother, West, who asked, "How did you do it, Katie? I thought no one wanted to play soccer around here."

Katie grinned and patted Wyatt's shoulder. "Oh, it wasn't that hard. I know everyone lives or dies by little league in Starry Hills, but after asking around, I discovered a lot of kids want to try playing soccer too. You can thank Rafe Mendoza for that."

I noticed West's girlfriend, Emmy Mendoza—Rafe's younger sister—tense. West wrapped an arm around her and murmured something in her ear. And when Emmy smiled up at him, jealousy rushed through me.

I envied him not only finding someone who loved him but also the fact that Emmy was close with my brother. West had left when I was in high school and had only recently returned to town. To say our relationship was strained was an understatement.

Katie's voice snapped me out of my head. "And guess who offered to sponsor your new soccer team, Wyatt?"

I frowned and tried to catch Katie's eye to remind her of our agreement to keep it secret, but she ignored me.

She gestured toward me. "Your Uncle Nolan!"

Wyatt smiled at me. "Did you really, Uncle Nolan?"

"Er, yes. I started a production company and thought they could use the publicity."

Wyatt shook his head. "I don't think that's the reason you did it, though."

"Why do you say that?"

"I'm eleven, not five. I know you're really famous, Uncle Nolan. You did it for me." Wyatt hugged me, and I patted his back as he added, "Thank you."

Over the past eleven years, I had only seen Wyatt and his twin sister a handful of times—both because of my busy schedule and West living far away. But I promised myself that I'd try to get to know Wyatt better from now on. His sister, Avery, too.

I ruffled his hair. "No problem. Just save me a seat at your games, and I'll try to go when I can."

Wyatt released me. "Of course, Uncle Nolan. And now I need to tell my friends. They won't believe it." He looked at his dad. "Can I go now?"

West nodded. "Go on, then."

"And I'm going to rub it in Avery's face, too!"

Before West could say a word, his son dashed off to find his friends.

Katie caught my eye and smiled. "See? I told you it'd be the best birthday gift ever."

This is the woman you need to make a deal with.

I should ask Katie to chat for a minute. I could even use my team sponsorship as an excuse.

But as my heart pounded and palms sweated, I knew I needed a little more time to prepare. Being outgoing and spontaneous wasn't my thing.

"Yes, it was a good idea," I replied.

After nodding at my brother and his girlfriend, I quickly walked over to my aunt.

Aunt Lori was short, with dark hair liberally streaked with gray, and dark brown eyes that could see into your soul. Or so my siblings and I always said growing up.

She took one look at me and clicked her tongue. "Why are you nervous?"

I looked around the room until I found Katie laughing with Abby, Emmy, and their other friend, Amber King. "Just some work stuff."

"Hmm. I think you're lying."

I resisted smiling. Because Aunt Lori *always* knew when I was lying. It'd been a hell of a thing to deal with growing up.

Aunt Lori sighed. "It's that witch again, isn't it?"

Since evading her question would only draw more attention to me—and I didn't want her to guess what else I was keeping from her—I shrugged and answered, "Yes."

"I get why she wants you, lad. I do. You're successful, attractive, and sweet. And no, don't try to say you aren't. Your tall height and rugged jaw won't ever fool me. But why does that woman want to all but bully you into marrying her? Wouldn't that be disastrous? It's clear as day you don't love her."

My aunt had married the love of her life young—my Uncle Tim—and had lost him young too, when he died during the Gulf War. She took marriage very seriously.

I sighed. "You know that, and I know that. But Wendy cares more about outward appearances and status than actual feelings and relationships."

"And since you're the most in-demand movie hero at the moment, she sees you as a trophy."

I grunted. "There are plenty of other male lead roles she could pursue, ones who would want to share the spotlight with her."

She replied, "Hmph. You're the most beloved by the public, and you know it."

I shrugged. I'd learned long ago that fame and fortune could be a double-edged sword.

Aunt Lori patted my arm. "Have I told you lately how proud I am of you, Nolan? And not just me, but your siblings as well. Your parents probably would've plastered your movie posters all over the walls, uncaring that it didn't tie into the winery, if they were still with us."

Not wanting to go down memory lane—their deaths had fractured my family in so many ways—I changed the subject. "I'll be here for Thanksgiving."

She narrowed her eyes at the sudden shift but then shrugged. "I knew you'd come."

"Oh, really? Even though I told you I'd be in South America shooting an action-adventure film?"

"Even then. Because you've never missed a Thanksgiving or Christmas, and I doubt you'd start now."

It'd been a near thing a few times. But despite how busy I was, I was determined to have two days a year to myself. Two days where I wasn't the world-famous Nolan Drake and could simply be the small-town boy Nolan Wolfe.

From the corner of my eye, I noticed Katie exit to the back porch. This was it—my chance to pitch my proposal.

"I see someone I need to catch up with, Aunt Lori. I'll find you later, before I leave, okay?"

"You'd better. If I don't get my goodbye hug, I'll get spicy with my emojis again."

I groaned dramatically, simply because I knew it'd make my aunt smile. "Not the overheated one. Or the peach. Just stop. Please."

She patted my arm. "Then make sure you say goodbye to me, and you'll be spared."

I placed a hand over my heart and bowed my head, as if I were some knight of old. "As my lady wishes."

Aunt Lori snorted. "Go on with you, then. Use that charm on someone who isn't related to you and can appreciate it better."

After winking at my aunt, I slowly made my way to the back door and slipped outside. Katie stood by herself, near an open fire pit, and stared up at the darkened sky.

The moonlight caressed her face, softening her features a little. Her expression was pensive, as if silently asking the moon about some life-changing decision.

Stop it. You're just delaying things. Get on with it.

So I walked up to Katie Evans, the woman I planned to ask to fake marry me, and hoped she'd say yes.

Chapter Two

Katie

It shouldn't hurt that even my closest friends had expected me to do something outrageous instead of thoughtful for the twins' birthday party, and yet it did.

Oh, I knew everyone expected me to be silly and outgoing and to do things most people found embarrassing. I'd been doing it for years, ever since middle school, in fact.

And yet, that wasn't all of who I was, not even close.

Needing a break, I walked out to the porch for some fresh air. I stopped in front of the fire pit, needing some warmth against the chilly October night, and stared up at the moon.

Ever since I'd been a little kid, the moon and stars

had calmed me. Something about the patterns I could make from the stars, or how constant the moon was with its cycles and shapes. No matter how hectic my life was, the moon would always be there, right on schedule.

As I scanned the stars, looking for new patterns—not the actual constellations—someone walked up to me. I mentally sighed. It looked like my quiet time was over.

I pasted a smile on my face and turned to find Nolan Wolfe studying me.

He was tall with dark hair, like all the Wolfe brothers. Muscled, too. More so than Beck, but not West; Nolan was somewhere in between.

Although why he was here on the porch, staring down at me, I had no idea. Maybe he was mad at me for revealing his sponsorship of Wyatt's soccer team. But really, once the uniforms were delivered, everyone would've seen his company's name anyway.

I waved. "Hi, Nolan. Did you get lost?"

He blinked and shook his head. "No. I wanted to talk with you."

Since we'd mostly texted about the sponsorship, it was weird he wanted to chat in person. Unlike the younger Wolfe siblings—Abby, Zach, and Zane—I never hung out much with Nolan growing up. We weren't exactly friends. "Talk with me about what? Did something go wrong with the soccer uniform orders? Or the coach we hired? Or any of the equipment?"

"No, no, that's all good. Not even my assistant could find a loose end to tie up, and she's the queen of finding that kind of stuff."

Not wanting to risk hearing how Nolan thought I

was some scatterbrained woman or something, I said, "Then just spit it out. You know I don't like to beat around the bush."

He smiled, and maybe it was the flickering flames from the fire, but my heart skipped a beat at how handsome he looked.

I quickly pushed that thought aside. This was Nolan, after all. The boy who'd constantly had his nose in a book. One who'd always told me to stop bugging him whenever I asked him to play with me.

The one who'd left town and broke his sister's heart.

Not to mention he's a world-famous movie star and is miles out of your league.

"Well? What is it?"

Nolan cleared his throat, checked to see no one was about, and then lowered his voice. I had to lean closer to hear him say, "I have a problem that I hope you can help me with."

"Now that sounds interesting. What is it?"

He cleared his throat again and tugged his shirtsleeves down. The untucked dress shirt really did emphasize his broad shoulders.

Be good, Katie.

"First, promise to hear me out before you laugh or run away."

"Hmm. That sounds intriguing. What, are you going to tie me up, whisk me off to a love nest, and do dirty things to me?"

As soon as the words left my lips, I regretted it. Because this was *Nolan*. Not some random guy on a tour of my family's dairy farm that I would hook up with later.

Thankfully, he ignored my teasing and leaned down to whisper, "You've heard about the rumors from my ex, right?"

I frowned. "You mean the ones about you being engaged? Yes, I've heard them. But Abby says they're all bullshit and that woman is a superficial, vindictive cow."

He sighed. "I don't like to talk shit about people in general, but yes, she is. No matter how many times I confront her and say we're definitely *not* engaged—nor will we ever be—she won't listen."

I tilted my head. "Then why does she keep pushing that you are? I mean, she's just as famous as you. She could get anyone." I realized how harsh that sounded and added, "Er, you're definitely a catch yourself, of course. But there are plenty of other big fish in the sea, ones who might actually *want* to marry her."

He shook his head. "You don't know Wendy like I do. Whatever she wants, she gets. It's always been that way, ever since she was a child. Her parents were actors as well, and she had her first starring role as a teenager. And, well, not many people have said no to her before."

"Until you."

Nolan grimaced. "Apparently. If it was just her I had to deal with, I could handle it. However, she constantly asks her fans to pester me with questions—such as when I'm finally going to set a date, where we're going to tie the knot, when am I going to give her the perfect ring, etc."

"Do they think random comments are going to make

you instantly love this Wendy person and agree to marry her?"

"I don't know. But it's not just random comments, either. I receive a lot of angry videos, including more than a few death threats."

I'd never thought about this side of being famous—dealing with random people on the internet. "Oh, Nolan. That sucks."

"More than that. It's getting dangerous, too. Recently, one of Wendy's fans went after some paparazzi that said I'd never marry Wendy. They retaliated by destroying their cameras and setting their car on fire."

"Holy shit."

"Exactly. And just when you think the bad press would make Wendy stop, she distances herself from what she calls 'crazies' and tries another tactic to pressure me."

"And no one listens to you?"

He shook his head. "No. While Wendy and I are both in-demand actors, she's cultivated a huge online following, one that I don't have. Anything I say goes on deaf ears without fans and followers to spread the word."

"And to think I used to complain about having to take pictures of my family's dairy farm for social media." I crossed my arms over my chest. "The police won't help you?"

"There's nothing to tie Wendy directly to me. I can stop certain individuals and report them, but that's about it. I worry soon she'll hit me where it'll hurt most—by threatening my family and the winery to try to force my hand. And I refuse to let that happen."

The Wolfe Family Farm and Winery was run by two of the Wolfe siblings—Beck and Zach. Aunt Lori—we all called her that—helped them too.

And even if Nolan had left Starry Hills as a teen to pursue his acting career, he'd always cared for his family. He'd also tried to help them over the years by investing, but the Wolfe family was stubborn to a T and had always refused him.

To even think about this Wendy woman threatening the Wolfe family made me angry, and I asked, "So then what's your plan to deal with your ex? She's the problem you need help with, I assume. But I'm wondering how I factor into it all?"

"Well, this is the part where I need you to listen and not instantly run away."

I searched his gaze, trying to figure out what the hell he was talking about. But the man had always been good at hiding his feelings, and tonight was no different. "Fine, I promise not to run away. Now, start talking."

He crossed his arms over his chest—muscles straining against his somewhat impressive biceps—and I did my best to focus on his words and not his body.

"From what I remember of the family dinners you ate with us and what I've heard from Abby, you've always wanted to travel and see the world. Is that still true?"

"Yes," I said slowly, wondering what that had to do with anything.

"Good. Then in exchange for helping me out with

my Wendy problem, how would you like a six-month, all-expenses paid trip?"

I blinked at his offer. "Hold on for a second. Back up. What is it I need to do, exactly? Because if you think I'm just going to say yes and give you carte blanche, you're crazy."

He leaned down, his breath tickling my ear, and it distracted me a moment before he said, "Here's what I'm asking: pretend to be my fiancée for six months, Katie, and that trip is yours."

I stepped backward so I could see his face again. But no, his expression was serious. He wasn't joking. "What? Why in the world would you ask me to do that? We barely know each other."

Not to mention no one would believe it.

As I debated simply leaving—despite my promise—he put up a hand as if to stay me. "Don't run away yet, Katie. Let me finish. Please."

At his desperate expression, my curiosity grew stronger. "Okay, fine. But make it quick and get to the point."

Nolan nodded. "It's simple—if I have a public fiancée, then my ex can't keep saying we're engaged, and I think she'd lose interest after six months."

"And if she doesn't?"

"I think she will. She doesn't like to be out of the spotlight, and she'll try to find someone else to latch onto. Maybe. I'm like 90 percent sure."

Not iron-clad odds. Still, I was more than curious now. "So, let's say this works, and she moves on. Then what happens?"

"Well, at the end of the six months, you can dump me, give any reason you like—although I hope it's not because I cheated—and then I'll pay for your trip. Anywhere you like, with no spending limit. You can even use my private jet, if you want."

"You have a private jet?"

The corner of his mouth kicked up. "Out of everything I just said, that's what you focus on?"

"I-I..." I took a deep breath and tried to wrap my head around everything. Because this was like out of a movie or a book or something, and it was definitely not the norm for my routine, boring life.

Part of me wanted to just scream yes and do it. The public persona I'd crafted for more than a decade would definitely do that.

But my rational side hesitated. I needed to know exactly what my role would entail and then decide if it was worth the risk of angering millions of Wendy's fans on social media. Millions who'd be far meaner than the bullies from my childhood.

Not wanting to think of the Mean Girls of Starry Hills, I asked, "Using your jet would be a definite bonus, but I have questions. Lots of them."

He gestured to the bench by the fire. "Let's sit and ask me anything you like."

I did, and Nolan sat beside me. Even with a few inches between us, I swore he radiated heat. Heat that most definitely didn't come from the fire.

Had I ever noticed that before?

Get a grip and focus. This is too important. Not wanting to look at Nolan and suddenly realize he had sexy eyes or something, I stared at the flickering flames of the fire and asked, "What are the requirements? Where would I need to be seen? What would I need to do? And what about this ex's fans? I can't imagine they're going to be super nice to me."

From the corner of my eye, I saw Nolan thread his fingers together and hang them between his widespread legs in a very male pose. "Dealing with her fans will be the hardest part, I won't deny it. But if you say yes, I'm going to do everything within my power to protect you as best as I can, Katie. My assistant is good at keeping the trolls away via blocking and deleting. She can also help with your social media, too. I can't guarantee she'll catch every little thing, but it does help. Trust me, hiring her for that, among other things, was one of the best decisions I ever made."

"Then why not ask her to be your pretend fiancée?"

Crap. Why had I said that? I wanted that trip, didn't I?

Nolan snorted. "Jenn is married. Happily. To a woman."

"Oh."

"Yes, 'oh' is right. She's been out a long time and the press would see right through it, even if she wasn't married."

I finally made myself look at Nolan again. "Why me, though? I'm not an actor, Nolan. And everyone would see the truth before too long."

His gaze met mine, and I resisted a shiver. "I think you're a better actor than you'll ever admit, Katie."

My heart thudded. Surely he hadn't figured it all out. It'd taken some of my closest friends years to do so.

But as his eyes searched mine, it almost felt as if Nolan Wolfe could see into my very soul, could ferret out all my secrets, and knew I didn't like always playing the outrageous court jester.

As I scrambled on how to reply, he spoke again. "I have faith you can do this, Katie. And if you want to do a trial run here in Starry Hills first, we can. If my family and yours can buy us dating, then the world should, too."

"Wait, you plan to keep this from your family? Even Aunt Lori?"

"Most especially Aunt Lori. I need the world to believe this is real, and while my aunt can keep secrets most of the time, she isn't great when it comes to keeping them within the family. She'd tell my siblings, and then who knows what would happen. No, to everyone but you, me, my assistant, and my lawyer, we'd be engaged for real."

I bit my bottom lip and tried to imagine fooling my best friends, my sisters, my brother, and even my parents. Well, my parents would be the easiest, truth be told, since they were desperate at this point to have any of their children get married.

But Emmy, Abby, and Amber were my sisters in all but blood. We'd been that way since we were children and had formed the BFF Circle.

Could I really keep this from them?

And was I really contemplating saying yes?

Nolan reached out a hand, touched my arm, and it eased a little of my tension. He said, "All I ask is for you to take a few days to think about it. Please. And just know that if you agree, then I promise to help you every step of the way, protect you any way that I can, and pay for anything you might need to attend events and the like."

Not even the promise of a high-end shopping spree would distract me from my biggest question. "I still don't understand why you're asking me to do this, Nolan. I mean, there are probably thousands of other women out there who could not only do this better, but keep it secret without blinking an eye. So, why me?"

He tapped a hand against his thigh. "Well, the reason I asked you is because my family trusts you. Which means I trust you. And..."

I searched his eyes. "And what?"

"And I think you're a little like me, in that you love Starry Hills but also want to see and experience the world beyond." He turned more toward me. "I want to give you that chance, Katie. I'd rather make the dreams of someone close to my family come true instead of doing it for a stranger."

I really looked at Nolan for a second and wondered if he'd always been this thoughtful and considerate. He'd left Starry Hills for his first big role in an indie film at eighteen and had rarely been back much since.

Which made me wonder—who was he really, apart from my best friend's older brother?

Nolan stood and put out a hand to help me up.

I shook my head. "No, I want to sit here and think a little longer about your proposal. When do you need an answer?"

He lowered his hand. "The week before Thanksgiving. If you say yes, we need to get everything figured out before we attend Thanksgiving at my family's house as boyfriend and girlfriend."

Wouldn't that be a surprise? "And if I have more questions?"

"Text me anything, anytime. I can call, too."

I stared up at Nolan and tried to imagine fake dating him. Holding his hand, kissing him, and snuggling against his side—all those little things couples did that if we didn't do them, it'd raise eyebrows.

However, doing those things wouldn't be a hardship, far from it. Really looking at Nolan, looking at him as a man and not my friend's sometimes annoying older brother, I could admit he was sexy. And the shy smile of his always made me wonder what he was thinking. Not to mention he was far kinder than the assholes I'd dated over the last few years.

Not that we'd be dating for real, but still.

"I'll think about it and give you an answer soon."

He nodded. "Thanks for not running away and screaming."

I smiled. "You forget that I'm a tour guide. Once people are tipsy and full of cheese, some love to overshare. Like, really overshare. TMI doesn't even register." I shuddered. "I've heard and seen things I'd rather forget."

He frowned. "Your brother should do a better job of looking out for you."

"Kyle does fine, I promise." I sat up a little taller.

"Besides, I'm a grown-ass woman. One who isn't afraid to knee someone in the balls if they try to cross a line."

He grunted. "You still shouldn't have to deal with that kind of stuff."

"Nolan, it's fine. I'm fine. I promise."

He studied me, as if trying to read my mind. In this, at least, I was truthful. While I may never have the chance to face my childhood bullies and stand up to them, I sure as hell tried my best not to let others walk all over me as an adult.

He blew out a breath. "I still don't like it, but I won't say anything else about it. For now. If you end up agreeing to my plan, I will protect you. So be prepared for it."

Maybe if some other guy said that, I'd hate it. Because maybe they'd be overbearing or treat me as a weak, helpless woman, or some other such bullshit.

But Nolan tended to be protective only when needed. Or, at least, that's what I remembered of him looking out for Abby when we were all kids.

He gestured with his head toward the patio door. "Well, then I'm heading back inside. But remember to ask me any questions you have, okay?"

"Okay."

Nolan nodded, gave me one last, long look, and went into the house. I returned to watching the flames, trying to get my head straight.

I'd probably have more questions later, for sure. But was I really considering this? Ready to upend my life, lie to my friends and family, and face the wrath of Wendy Webster's fans?

Maybe. Yes, maybe. If I didn't seize this chance, I might never see the world beyond a few states in the US.

Not only that, but I had a feeling that I'd never really figure out what I wanted to do with my life if I didn't see what the world had to offer beyond Starry Hills.

Pretending to be engaged to Nolan for six months wouldn't be the end of the world.

Would it?

Chapter Three

Katie

Me: So what if someone figures out your plan?
Nolan: They won't.
Me: Just because you say it won't happen doesn't mean it'll work out that way.
Nolan: I have faith in you, and I have faith in me. That's enough.
Me: What about my family? I can't just abandon them when I feel like it. They rely on my awesome tour guide skills.
Nolan: I'll hire someone to help when you're gone. And they'll be the best.
Me: What, an actor who owes you a favor?

Nolan: Something like that. It should help your family's dairy, though, and give them some free PR.
Me: You're full of secrets and plots, aren't you?
Nolan: Not usually.
Me: And how much PDA will there be?
Nolan: Whatever you're comfortable with. Although kisses and holding hands would make it more believable. I can even come up with a backstory, no problem.
Me: Are you treating this like your next movie?
Nolan: I'm afraid to answer that.
Me: Fine. Last question: Will your family hate me after this?
Nolan: No. Never. Once I explain how it had to be authentic, they'll forgive you. I'll make sure to take all the blame.
Me: Why?
Nolan: Because you're more important to them and to Starry Hills.
Me: Why would you say that?
Nolan: It's the truth.
Me (typed but deleted): But don't you realize how much your family loves you?
Me (actual reply instead): I'll do it. Just don't get mad at me if this fails.
Nolan: I won't, I promise. And here's what we need to do...

A few weeks later, on the day Nolan and I would meet for our first "practice session," I tried my best to smile at the obviously drunk couples wolfing down the cheese at the end of the tour. After touring the dairy farm and the cheese making areas, I always took them to a room where they could try my brother's world-famous cheeses, paired with Starry Wolfe wine. Most visitors were polite, asked relevant questions, and then either ordered something, took a flyer about our online shop, or simply thanked me and left. Sometimes I got a tip, sometimes I didn't, and then I went on to the next group.

However, today had been pure hell. Even though this was the final tour of the day—the last one before we closed for the Thanksgiving holiday—the somewhat drunk couples had been loud, crass, and had nearly wandered off to "go at each other country-style" in a barn.

The last one I'd nearly let them do because rolling around the hay wasn't all it was cracked up to be. Hay poking your ass or lady bits was brutal.

And now? One of the women sat in a cushy chair and promptly passed out.

Oh, for fuck's sake. I understood enjoying a vacation, but a person needed to know their limits.

I eyed the husband, but he was drinking more wine and ignoring his wife.

And then he turned toward me and smiled. "Maybe you can wake up my wife with a kiss?"

I pasted a smile on my face when I really wanted to

knee him in the balls. "As tempting as that is, it's against company policy."

"Oh, come on now. I won't tell. And it'll make our tenth wedding anniversary that much more special. Especially since I've always had a thing for chubby girls in bed." He gave me a once-over. "You'd be a firecracker, wouldn't you?"

I clenched my fingers into a fist. My uncle, the sheriff, had warned me that I could only hit someone in self-defense and not for simply being a dick. I forced out, "We're about to close, and I think it's time I called you a cab."

He stumbled toward me, and I took a step back. "Now, now, we have another ten minutes left to enjoy the wine and cheese. You don't want me to leave a bad review, do you?"

I hated when people threatened one-star reviews to get their way. Fortunately, my brother's fame in the cheese world protected us more than other small-time places, so I shrugged. "If you want to leave a bad review because I care about your safety, then I'll chance it."

He frowned. "I'll do it. And I'll tell our wine and cheese club about it too. No one will want to order from you any longer."

I somehow kept a smile plastered on my face. "I hope it doesn't come to that. Nevertheless, I need you to wait in the reception area until the car arrives."

He stumbled toward me until he was about a foot away. Since my back was against a wall, I couldn't put more distance between us.

Crap. Well, at least if he came close enough, I could punch him and claim self-defense.

The man sneered. "You're being a bitch and ruining our vacation."

Okay, that was enough. "This is the last time I ask you to head to the reception area. Otherwise, I'll call the sheriff and you'll be arrested."

I wasn't sure with what, but my uncle could probably think of something.

The stumbling man walked over to me and before I could act, he tossed his wine at my face.

I blinked, stunned, and wiped the worst off my eyelids and cheeks. *What the hell?* In all the years I'd been doing this, no one had ever thrown wine in my face.

It was on now.

I was about to take out my phone and call my uncle when a familiar, low voice came from the doorway. "You have ten seconds to get through the door and sit your ass down in the reception area or I'll be forced to make you."

Nolan Wolfe stood in the doorway, his eyes burning with anger and wearing the most menacing expression I'd ever seen. So much so I blinked again. But nope, it was him.

Then the unruly man flipped him off, and Nolan strode over, grabbed his shirt, and tugged him toward the doorway. "Come on, before I call the sheriff."

The other couple had been watching it all with their mouths open, but the woman pointed a finger at Nolan. "You're that movie star, aren't you?"

I did my best to get the other, more cooperative

couple to the doorway. "No, no, but he does get that all the time. He's my neighbor."

"No, I'm sure I'm right—that looks like Nolan Drake."

Nolan didn't even blink as he got the unruly guy through the door and dragged him toward the reception area. I didn't hear what they said, only muffled shouting.

Thankfully, the other couple went on their own, wanting a better look at Nolan. That left me with the passed out woman in the chair, the one with drool currently dribbling down her chin.

Some days I wondered why the hell I still did this job.

Sighing, I went over and gently shook her. She jumped and blinked up at me. I said, "Time to leave, Jean. Your ride will be here soon."

She nodded groggily, and I half-pulled her to her feet. Walking, on the other hand, proved more difficult, even with her arm around my shoulders. Just as I tried to think of how the hell I'd get her to the reception area, Nolan appeared again.

He murmured, "The reception guy is watching that bastard."

I nodded, wanting to ask more but knew it'd have to wait. Nolan helped me get the woman to the reception area. Her husband was nowhere to be found, thank goodness. And before long, Nolan had all of them packed into the cab and on their way.

He walked over to me and took me in. "Let's clean you up."

The thought of Nolan caressing my face, my neck,

and my chest with a warm washcloth sent a rush of heat through me.

I quickly jumped back. "No, just give me five minutes. I'll meet you outside."

And then I ran, my cheeks burning. Both from thinking of Nolan washing me and from embarrassment. Because of course, the one time someone threw wine in my face, Nolan was there to see it.

It doesn't matter. He's not your real boyfriend. Just think of the trip you get at the end of this agreement.

Right, that's what I'd do, think of my grand tour.

Besides, a little embarrassment was nothing compared to the full-on hatred I'd soon face from his ex's fans. Life was bound to get worse, much worse, before my sweet reward at the end.

Today was just a little training in the making. With that thought, I hurried into my room and cleaned up.

Chapter Four

Nolan

Aunt Lori: What time will you get here? <plane emoji>
Me: Tonight, like the other ten times I've told you.
Aunt Lori: <tongue out emoji> I want exact times, Mister. I rarely get to see you, and I need to make a schedule.
Me: Not a schedule...
Aunt Lori: Hey, I even have "sibling bonding time" penciled in. <surrounded by hearts emoji>
Me: You promised not to meddle in our lives.
Aunt Lori: What? I'm not meddling. I'm just ensuring you get quality family time. <angel emoji> Emmy and

Sabrina will be your sisters soon enough, and you need to get to know them better. <heart emoji>

Me: You don't know that for certain.

Aunt Lori: Oh, when it comes to love and marriages, I'm excellent at spotting what'll work or not. <monocle emoji> I was right about West's first wife, wasn't I?

Me: I have a plane to catch. I'll let you know when I get there.

Aunt Lori: You better. Something was off at the twins' birthday party and I'm determined to figure out what. <pensive emoji>

It took a lot to get me angry. Online trolls, borderline stalker fans, or even my brothers trying to piss me off when we were young—I could handle all that.

But when I saw that dickhole abuse Katie by throwing wine and insulting her, it took every bit of restraint I had not to clock him and kick his ass to the curb.

Did she have to put up with that shit on a daily basis? If so, why didn't her family get her help or have stricter rules about customer behavior?

As I waited for Katie to get changed, I paced in front of my car. What I'd witnessed today paled in comparison to what would happen once our engagement became public, true. But she still shouldn't have to put up with any kind of crap like that. And for as long as she pretended to be mine, I was determined to help her in all aspects of her life.

For a start, I needed to make her time at work easier and safer. I doubt she'd just let me hire someone at my expense. But I could hire some security, even secretly, if I had to. There was no way I'd let her suffer that kind of abuse again.

"Nolan."

I jumped and spun around. Katie stood a few feet away, her arms crossed, and standing tall. Whatever embarrassment she'd felt earlier had vanished. A good sign, given what we were about to start.

After clearing my throat, I said, "Hey, Katie. Are you still up for going out?"

She nodded. "The sooner we head out, the better. It's a bit of a drive, isn't it?"

Even though I wasn't in Starry Hills that often, I had a house and car nearby, for when I visited. My family didn't know about the house, but I'd told Katie. I thought we could use it as a base of operations. "Yes, up in the hills. Come on. I wouldn't put it past Aunt Lori to have spies everywhere and already knows that I'm here."

I went to the passenger's side and opened the door. Katie frowned, but then slid inside. I jogged over, hopped in, and started the car. As soon as I pulled out onto the main road, I asked, "Isn't there a rule against drunks being allowed on the tours?"

"Yes. But they seemed fine at first. I guess some people are just better at hiding it. It's not the worst group I've ever had, though. Not by a long shot."

I glanced over at her, but Katie's gaze was firmly out

the side window. "If you weren't working for your family, what would you be doing?"

She remained silent for a few beats, and I focused on the road. Eventually, she replied softly, "I don't know."

"Not at all?"

"I sometimes get ideas, but then they never really pan out. I tried community college, but it didn't really fit. I've tried a variety of jobs for my family's business, and the tours are the only thing I'm really good at." She shrugged. "So that's what I do."

I stole a look at Katie's profile. Her cheeks were slightly pink, as if she were embarrassed. Wanting to distract her, I blurted, "I came into acting by accident."

She looked at me. "What do you mean you got into it by accident?"

I let out a long breath. Talking about myself was rare, but if Katie was to be my supposed future wife, she should know something about me. "A teacher noticed how well I recited plays during class in high school, and she suggested I try out for a local play they were putting on for the Summer Star Festival."

"Hmm, I was still in elementary school and don't remember much, but wasn't it something to do with Alice in Wonderland?"

"Yes. I was the Mad Hatter. I was nervous as hell, too. But it wasn't long after my dad's death, and I liked the escape of becoming someone else for a short while. After the performance, I asked my mom for acting classes, kept studying and trying out for parts, and devoted everything to becoming the best."

"More because you enjoyed it, or because it gave you the chance to escape the real world?"

I tapped the steering wheel. I could deflect and change the subject. *No.* This was something my ex would know and might test Katie on. "Both, about equally, I think."

"And do you still use it as an escape?"

"Most of the time."

She turned more toward me. "What about you? If tomorrow you had a clean slate and you could do anything you wanted, what would it be?"

I shrugged. "As much as I enjoy acting, I like producing more. Maybe one day, I could try my hand at being a director, too."

"Hence the production company. It's like your first step to branching out."

"Yes." She fell silent a few beats, and I added, "Ask me anything, Katie. Neither of us has seen much of the other since we were kids, and it's important to get comfortable around one another."

"Anything?"

"Sure. Although I always hold veto power."

She smiled. "Now I want to test you."

"Then do it."

"Okay, then. You're super rich, aren't you?"

I blinked. "Um..."

"Oh, I'm not a gold digger or anything. I promise not to fall in love with you. But if you *are* rich, then you really can do anything you want to, huh? I know having money comes with issues too, but it also opens doors."

Even though her words weren't anything I hadn't

heard before, they hit a nerve. My wealth was a bone of contention with my family.

Push it aside. Katie has nothing to do with your relationship with your family.

Since I didn't want Katie to be intimidated by the fact I was actually a billionaire—I'd invested wisely over the years—I merely answered, "I probably could do anything I wanted to and never work again. But the thought of never working or having some kind of purpose seems empty to me."

She muttered, "I wish I could figure out my purpose." I opened my mouth to ask more, but she beat me to it. "So given the drama with your ex, have you considered bowing out from your acting gig? Maybe she'll give up then if you're not as famous."

I shook my head. "I'm not ready to quit acting just yet. And even if I were, I wouldn't do it to run away from Wendy."

"Right, that cow. Which is why I'm here in the first place." She tapped her hand against her thigh. "You said you'd tell me more about today's meeting and 'lessons' in person. So, start talking."

Grateful for the distraction, I replied, "Well, Thanksgiving is in a few days. And if we're to fool my family, we need to practice being a couple."

"Is this where you say we're going to have kissing lessons?"

I blinked. "What?"

"You know, where we kiss to try to get the kinks out. Everyone's different. Maybe you like to slobber all over a woman, and I should prepare myself."

I growled. "I don't fucking slobber."

She laughed. "Or maybe you're the type to clash teeth repeatedly, until you accidentally knock one out."

"Katie."

"Or, wait, I know! You bite too hard, draw blood, and secretly turn out to be a vampire."

"I'm not a vampire. I was just in the sun."

"Well, some vampires can be in the sun. I didn't check, but do you sparkle?"

"I don't fucking sparkle."

She laughed again, the sound reverberating in the car, and I couldn't help but smile. That sound could brighten anyone's day.

Katie clapped her hands. "Too bad, because that would've made you even more famous. And the next thing you know, guys would stop copying your haircut and would start applying glitter makeup to be just like Nolan Drake."

I nearly ran a hand through my hair. "I don't ask people to copy me."

"No, but it happens. It's kind of a compliment, in a way. And it's better than them sending you clipped toenails in the mail, right?"

"What in the hell are you talking about now?"

"Well, I'm sure you've had superfans figure out how to get packages to you."

I glanced at her. "I think you've watched too much TV."

"Books. I read a lot of books. Mysteries and romances, mostly. I can feel like solving crimes one day and then have the best imaginary sex of my life the next."

"Pardon?"

"I like books with sexy times in them. Why more guys don't read them and really learn how to make a woman orgasm, I have no idea."

At the word "orgasm" I imagined Katie's flushed face staring at me as I licked between her thighs.

Stop it, Nolan. Sex wasn't part of this deal. A few kisses, yes. But sex? Most definitely not.

"This is where I live."

I turned down the long, private road and drove up to the top of a large hill. My house soon came into view.

It looked more like a big cabin, complete with a log facade, and giant glass windows everywhere to let in the sun and take advantage of the views.

Katie said, "Wow. It's beautiful. And you've never taken your family here? Why?"

I parked the car. "I don't want to talk about it."

After disembarking, I rushed over and opened Katie's door. Once she slid out, she looked up at me. Had she always been so short?

"Well, I think you should bring your family here, no matter what they think. You've earned your success, Nolan. Don't hide it."

Ignoring her words, I gestured toward the front door. After frowning at me, Katie walked, and I followed. Sometimes my assistant came up here with me, but not this time. So I unlocked the door and Katie rushed inside, all the way to the massive wall of windows at the back.

"This is breathtaking, Nolan!"

The view of the valley below never got old. "You should see it at sunset or sunrise."

"I can only imagine."

I couldn't look away from the pure joy on her face. Something as simple as a beautiful view completely entranced her.

I wish I could still be that way. But years in Hollywood and shooting films around the world had taken its toll. Enjoying the little things was hard when merely getting a cup of coffee meant constant paparazzi and people asking for selfies—and not in a nice way, but threatening me if I didn't comply.

Not wanting the outside world to intrude on my sanctuary, I pushed aside those thoughts, cleared my throat, and walked across the open space to the kitchen. "Did you want something to drink?"

"Water's fine."

I filled a glass from the fridge dispenser and brought it over. "We don't have much time, Katie, since my family is expecting me for dinner. So we should probably talk and get started."

She sighed, glancing out the big window again. "I know." She met my gaze again. "But even though this place isn't that far from Starry Hills, it almost feels like a vacation to me."

"When was the last time you took one?"

"I never took one on my own, only for family camping trips or renting a cabin on Lake Tahoe with the BFF Circle. I can't afford to go anywhere else, and besides, my family needs me."

It was on the tip of my tongue to ask why they didn't pay her more—Starry Evans cheeses were extremely popular among the Hollywood set, meaning her family's dairy had to be doing well—but she took the glass of water, gulped down half of it, and then turned to face me.

"We'll have plenty of time to talk later. For now, just kiss me already."

I blinked. "Er, what?"

She put down her glass of water. "I did some research and saw that you've always been affectionate with your past girlfriends. So if this is to be believable, well, we need to look like we kiss all the time. So, best to get it over with and figure out our style."

I wasn't fond of "getting it over with," as she put it. But it made sense.

My gaze moved to her mouth. Her full bottom lip begged to be nibbled, and I could only imagine what those full lips would look like wrapped around my cock.

Wait, no. Not my cock. Public kisses? Yes. Sex of any kind? Not required.

Although just imagining kisses with Katie stirred my dick, so I took a second to think of cold showers, the stifling heat and humidity of the jungle, and finally the change in cameras over the last twenty years.

Once I had myself under control, I replied, "Are you ready?"

She raised an eyebrow. "No dramatic line? Something along the lines of, 'Ready for me to rock your world, baby?'"

The corner of my mouth kicked up. "What decade

do you think we live in? Which one do you want? Because if you want me to pretend we're in an old-timey movie, we'll be pressing our lips together like we're trying to crack a nut between them, and nothing else." I lowered my voice dramatically. "And that's definitely not my style, baby."

She giggled, and I smiled. Besides my family, few people knew I could be funny sometimes. Mostly because they wanted the sex god movie star full of charm and smolder, which wasn't the real me.

Hanging out with Katie, who merely saw me as her friend's older brother, was rather...nice.

Nope, don't go there.

She replied. "Well, this fake engagement of ours is kind of a movie production, right? Or a TV show? So we could be in any decade, really. Preferably one where we kiss with lips and tongue."

Like where I use my tongue to lap up your sweet honey?

I resisted readjusting my cock, mentally told myself to get a grip, and focused on the conversation. "Hmm. That gives me a lot of leeway. But do you really want to have giant hair and wear the fancy, poofy dresses from the 1980s?"

She made a face. "No, thank you."

I laughed. "You say that, but I imagine wearing a corset for a period piece would be a hell of a lot more uncomfortable."

She muttered something I thought was, "Then I'd look like an overstuffed sausage," but before I could confirm, she placed a hand on my chest.

The light touch of her fingers sent heat rushing through my body, and it took more mental images to keep my dick from getting hard.

Had I always been this drawn to Katie Evans? No, I didn't think so. Her treating me like a normal guy must be the reason my imagination and desires were going into overdrive.

Plus, after so many years of never really being seen, just this brief experience was intoxicating.

Katie leaned in, her heat and scent making the cock situation even more difficult, before saying, "Just kiss me already, Nolan."

I cupped her cheek, stroked my thumb against her soft skin, and my heart raced a mile a minute.

Was I nervous? *Yes.* But why? I'd kissed various women and men for past roles. This shouldn't be any different.

And yet, as I stared into her dark blue eyes and watched her pale cheeks turn pink, I very much wanted to kiss her. Just because.

So I lowered my head and pressed my lips to hers.

Chapter Five

Katie

My heart thudded so hard I was surprised Nolan couldn't hear it. Standing so close to the man, I couldn't help but feel his heat and breathe in his scent—a mixture of woodsy and pure male.

Hell, it was hard not to lean in and press my nose to his chest. Had he always smelled so good?

Focus on playing the role, Katie. Nothing else.

After all, I'd steered the conversation to our first kiss, wanting to avoid talking about why I still worked for my family. I wasn't about to admit my long list of failures to a man I barely knew.

And yet, I was all for kissing him. I tended not to date really tall guys because I was so short. But with

Nolan, even if he towered over me, I kind of liked it. He made me feel...safe.

Which was ridiculous. Helping me with one drunk asshole didn't make him my bodyguard, or anything.

Then he leaned down and time slowed, almost as if Nolan was giving me the chance to back out.

Always a gentleman, like all the Wolfe brothers were.

But once his lips touched mine, I forgot about his brothers. Something snapped inside of me. Heat surged, and suddenly I wanted to be closer to him. Much closer.

So I pressed my front against his hard body. Even through our clothes, my body was on fire, in a good way. For a beat, I wondered what it'd feel like to rub my nipples against him. Would he have chest hair?

How would it feel to have him suck and bite one?

But as Nolan's lips moved, everything else faded away. His lips were gentle at first, caressing, letting me get used to him. Then his tongue seamed my lips, and I opened with a groan.

As his tongue twined with mine, I reveled in his heat and taste and the way he claimed my mouth. Shy, quiet Nolan Wolfe knew how to fucking kiss well.

Then his hand on my cheek tilted my head for better access, and soon the kiss turned even hotter. Licks and nibbles and strokes. And unlike with some kisses, it was as if we each knew what the other would do or wanted, and every time Nolan groaned into my mouth, wetness rushed between my thighs.

Then his phone vibrated in his pocket, and Nolan broke the kiss. For a few beats, we stared at each other, breathing heavily. No doubt Nolan's stunned expression matched my own.

I'd never been kissed like that before in my life.

I almost wanted to say Nolan felt the same way, judging from his expression. But then again, maybe it'd all been an act?

Then all too quickly the moment ended, and he took out his phone as he retreated several feet. I fanned myself, closed my eyes, and tried to get my body under control. My voice, however, wasn't as steady as it could be when I asked, "Who is it?"

"My aunt. The gossip tree must be in full swing because she wants to know why I went to your family's place before seeing her."

With one last deep breath, I regained some semblance of composure and opened my eyes. "Well, that's easy—just say you needed to place a cheese order for New Year's or something like that. Maybe for a grand party. After all, you usually don't stick around after Christmas, so it's totally believable."

I slapped a hand over my mouth because that sounded critical.

He shrugged. "Well, it's true. I always spend Thanksgiving and Christmas in Starry Hills. But usually my agent or assistant makes me go to some big New Year's Party for connections and exposure."

Removing my hand, I walked closer to Nolan. "But judging by the use of 'makes me,' you don't really want to go to them, do you?"

"Not really. I don't know if you remember, but parties and stuff were never really my thing."

"And yet, you have to do them—and big fancy premieres—for your job."

He put his phone down and rubbed his hands over his face. "Yes. That's the only reason I ever agreed to go out with Wendy in the first place. You see, my agent suggested she could put in a good word for an upcoming role. She wanted a handsome man on her arm, and I needed to make a connection. It seemed a win-win at the time."

"Did you get that role?"

"No. And it was the first and last time I took dating advice from my agent, John."

I sat on a stool at the kitchen island. "So let me get this straight—your agent is named John and your assistant is Jenn. Right?"

He leaned on the counter, close to me. It took everything I had not to ogle his shoulders or stare at his mouth, or even reach a hand out to see if he had late-day stubble on his jaw.

Somehow, I focused on his reply instead. "Yeah. My lawyer's name is another one you should probably know. Her name is Tina, and she's Jenn's wife. They met by working together on something for me."

"That's adorable. Kind of like in a movie—two overworked employees bonding over their demanding boss."

"I'm not—"

I shook my head. "I'm teasing, Nolan. Diva is the last word I'd use to describe you."

"Thanks?"

"You're welcome. Now, before Aunt Lori starts her emoji-filled text harassment, we should hash out some last major details. Especially if you're taking me to Thanksgiving. You didn't say it was me, just that you were bringing a date, right?"

"Well, since you hadn't said yes when I RSVP'd for the dinner, I thought it was safest."

"Did you have a backup plan?"

"Not really. I don't have a long list of women I trust to do this with me."

He'd said he trusted me before, and yet, hearing it again softened my heart a little.

Before I could do something stupid, like reach over and pull him close for another kiss, I cleared my throat and said, "They're going to ask about our backstory. You said you'd write one, and it was too long for texting, so let's hear it."

"Just a second."

He walked away, toward a door on the far side, and I couldn't resist looking at his ass. Yep, firm and round and probably biteable, just like I'd thought.

Strange how I'd never noticed him in that way until recently. Nolan had always just been Abby's big brother, the one nearly seven years older than us. The famous movie star that all the students in high school had begged Abby to bring to a dance.

And he did go to prom, as dates to all of us in the BFF Circle. We'd all been dateless and had vowed to dance with each other. But once the famous Nolan Drake had danced with each of us in turn? Well, to say we became the envy of the school was an understatement.

Even the bullies I'd managed to avoid for most of

high school had started harassing me again.

Nolan strode back into the room, and I banished my bad high school memories. I was twenty-six—nearly twenty-seven—and hadn't seen my former bullies in years.

He held up a binder. "I typed it all out and categorized it with color-coded tabs."

After he placed it in front of me, I opened the binder and smiled. "Organization was always your thing."

"Hey, it saves time. And be careful with this—the media would die to get their hands on these documents."

"Of course, I'll be careful." I flipped through and scanned the summary:

Two childhood friends reunite at a family party. The movie star who longs to be normal, and the small-town girl who never saw him as more than her friend's annoying older brother. But some wine and conversation around a flickering fire soon changes everything...

I met Nolan's gaze. "Staying as close to the truth as possible, aren't you?"

"The easiest way to keep lies straight is to do just that."

I closed the binder. "Are you sure you want to do this, Nolan? It's a rather big lie to tell your family."

He shrugged. "They'll understand. Eventually. Besides, Beck and West are busy with their girlfriends. Zach is busy with his new traveling sales-type job. Zane is who the hell knows where on assignment. And Abby... well, Abby has secrets of her own that she won't share."

I knew a little about them, but not the whole truth. Some asshole had manipulated her and broke her heart. But no matter how much Amber and I tried to get her to talk, Abby would always brush it off and say she'd get over it soon.

But since she'd given up her dream of teaching as soon as she returned to Starry Hills, after initially accepting a teaching contract, I sensed the two were related.

I said, "I'm still worried they won't forgive me."

Nolan leaned over and took my hand. His was so much bigger and warmer than mine, and I couldn't help but squeeze his back as he said, "I'll make sure they know it was all my idea and my fault. They won't hate you, Katie. I promise."

I bit my bottom lip and searched his blue eyes. It was crazy, but I believed him. Almost as if Nolan always kept his word, if at all possible.

And considering he'd kept some rather ridiculous ones to his sister and me throughout our childhood, he should be able to carry this one off too.

I nodded slowly. "Okay. I'll go through the binder before Thanksgiving and memorize as much as possible. And don't worry, I can get out of my family's dinner provided you promise to see them at Christmas. It's always a bigger deal for my family, especially when it comes to decorating. I mean, you really don't want to know how many blow-up creatures my dad has collected in the after-Christmas sales over the years."

I shuddered dramatically, and Nolan chuckled as he removed his hand. "I'm curious now. While I see my family every Christmas, I usually have to go right back to L.A. or my latest shoot and don't get to see the decorations around town."

"Oh, they can be amazing, Nolan. Maybe you can see some this year."

Crap. There I went, inviting him to do things as if I really were his girlfriend.

But Nolan merely nodded. "Maybe I can. Hmm, should I bring a new inflatable for your dad as a Christmas present? Does he have that giant dragon wearing a Santa hat yet?"

Groaning, I shook my head. "No, and he'd love it, even if it'd drive my mom nuts. She would say dragons aren't very Christmas-y."

He raised his eyebrows. "I didn't realize there was a firm list about what is okay for Christmas or not. I mean, I've seen skeletons wearing Santa hats before."

"That's probably because of *Nightmare Before Christmas*. However, there hasn't been a famous Christmas movie or special about a dragon yet." I smiled at him. "Maybe that could be a project of yours —to make dragons a part of Christmas traditions. I mean, you do have Drake as your stage surname, after all."

Nolan grinned. "That's quite the challenge. And we'll see. I'm always looking for new script ideas..."

He stopped talking, and I narrowed my eyes at him. "Wait, have you written any movies or TV shows before? Because I've never heard anything about that."

"That's because I use a pseudonym. For acting, I use Nolan Drake. For scripts, I use Jeremy Stone."

"Your father's name and...?"

"Stone was my mother's maiden name."

"To honor them both."

He nodded and glanced away. "Yes." He cleared his throat and looked back at me. "Provided we can keep this up—and you don't want to call it off and run away—until Christmas, I'll get him the inflatable and we can visit with your parents." He came closer and held out a hand. I took it. "And we can start with this baseline: we'll be the couple who holds hands in public but maybe doesn't have kisses as heated as earlier. Agreed?"

Him just mentioning kisses made me remember his heat and taste and the feel of his hard body against mine.

I wanted that again. Desperately.

And yet, I nodded. "Got it."

He released my hand, and I nearly snatched it back. "Let me drive you back, and we can use the time to work out some more details for Thanksgiving."

And far too soon, we were back in the car. The drive back to my family's dairy was strictly business, with no talk of PDA or kisses, but only the made-up backstory and some superficial knowledge. Apparently, Nolan didn't like cranberry sauce or brussels sprouts.

Just as Nolan drove away from my parents' house, my eldest sister, Cassie, pulled up in her car. With a wave, she exited. "Was that Nolan Wolfe? He's back in town?"

"Yes." Taking a deep breath, I decided it was time to get the ball rolling with my family. "He came to see me."

"Why?"

"Because we're dating."

Cassie blinked, and then again, her mouth moving with no sound coming out.

Eventually I patted her shoulder and said, "Yes, yes, I know—it's unbelievable. Yada, yada, yada. But it's true, I swear. Now, let's head inside. I need to butter up Mom before letting her know I can't attend Thanksgiving since I'll be going to Nolan's place as his date."

Cassie finally closed her mouth and searched my gaze. My older, no-nonsense sister would be the hardest to fool.

Eventually, she shrugged. "If you say so. Now maybe Mom will stop pestering me about my breakup and focus on you and your love life for once."

"She's not still nagging you about dumping that winery owner, is she?"

Cassie rolled her eyes. "Yes. I think she's so desperate for her over-thirty daughter to get married that she's willing to overlook a little thing like him cheating on me."

I hooked my arm through Cassie's. "You definitely deserve better, Cassie. And just how big of a distraction do you want me to be? If it's extreme enough, maybe you'll owe me one."

Cassie raised her eyebrows. "Owe you? What about sisterly love and doing it out of the kindness of your heart? Or maybe repaying me for some of those favors you promised when you were a kid and I never collected on?"

I stuck out my tongue. "Fine. We're even. And who

knows, my news might even put me in Mom's favored status."

Which had never really happened before. Oh, she tried to love us all equally, but kids could tell favorites. Always.

Cassie shook her head. "Kyle's always been the golden child, though. I swear, he can do no wrong in Mom's eyes."

"Kyle has his faults, and one day they'll catch up with him, I'm sure. For now, you can help me plan the best way to tell Mom about me and Nolan. I want to make it dramatic. It's hard to make Mom speechless, but I'm going to try."

As my sister and I put our heads together, I started to enjoy this fake dating and soon-to-be engagement thing.

My sister seemed on my side. And I'd barely uttered the words before my mother hugged me and started talking about wedding bells.

I did feel a little guilty about when I'd have to tell her Nolan and I were finished.

Think of your trip. Yes, maybe I'd meet some hot, smart, kind guy on my travels.

More than that, I needed the trip for myself. To maybe figure out my life. To finally stop wondering what if and start making plans.

And by the end of the day, I was more confident about pretending to be Nolan's girlfriend. But the true test would be Thanksgiving.

I was both eager and anxious for it to arrive.

Chapter Six

Nolan

Katie: Are you sure about this?
Me: Yes, surprising my family will be the best option.
Katie: I think you just didn't want them to interrogate you for days alone.
Me: Maybe. You've never suffered Aunt Lori's interrogations before.
Katie: The world-famous movie star is afraid of his nearly retired-aged aunt?
Me: Yes. Sometimes. We all are. <horror face emoji>
Katie: <laughing emoji> I definitely need to learn Aunt Lori's secrets. As a fellow short person, I could use the tips.
Me: You're not that short.

Katie: Says the six-foot-something guy.
Me: I never noticed your stature. Your personality is always front and center.
Katie: Wait, are you saying I'm too much or over-the-top?
Me: Er, no...just lively.
Katie: And lively is good?
Me: Yes. I'm jealous, actually.
Katie: <laughing emoji> Jealous of me? Why?
Me (typed but deleted): Because you charm strangers in a way I never could.
Me (actual reply instead): You have access to Kyle's cheeses whenever you want...
Katie: <tongue out emoji> You're the worst.
Me: But you're still coming to Thanksgiving, right?
Katie: Yes. I want that trip, and be prepared for the bill. It won't be tiny.

I parked outside Katie's house on Thanksgiving Day and debated whether or not I should go inside. Her family was beyond excited—her mom was even planning a wedding even though we were only "dating" right now and not yet engaged—and I had a feeling that once I set foot inside their house, I might not leave for days.

But as soon as I saw Katie exit the front door, I promptly forgot about her family.

She wore a dark blue dress that hugged her breasts

before flaring out and dancing around her hips and down her legs, to just above her knees. The amount of cleavage on display made my mouth water.

I wanted to run my tongue through the valley before tugging down her dress and taking her nipple into my mouth. Then I'd grab her full hips, press her soft belly against me, and claim her mouth until I knew she'd be nice and wet. That way I could run my hand up, play with her pussy, and make her come as she dripped down my hand.

Katie opened the car door, and I mentally cursed at where my thoughts had gone. I definitely needed to be more careful, or I'd show up for Thanksgiving with my dick at full mast.

As she slid inside, I said, "You should've let me open it for you."

"You were too busy staring at my boobs, so I didn't hold my breath."

I frowned, trying to think of how to reply. But she beat me to it. "Don't worry. I'm used to it. I got my first bra in second grade and to this day my best friends make a game of tossing shit into my cleavage. It's no biggie."

Despite her words, I sensed she wasn't so casual about it. "Does Abby, Amber, and Emmy know you don't like it when they toss crap into your tops?"

She shrugged one shoulder. "They would stop, if I asked. It's not them I mind so much—we all tease each other about something. But it was brutal when some of the girls made fun of me as a kid. And these days, I just have to be careful with what I wear on the tours."

"You shouldn't have to be careful, though."

She patted my upper arm. "You're sweet, Nolan. But I'm a grown-ass woman. I'll be fine."

I growled. "First, the drunk on the tour. And now this? Does no one in your family look after you?"

"How would they in this case? Do you expect them to be constantly on alert and act as the boob-watching police? Because do your siblings step up to form a wall when you take your shirt off, to shield your glorious muscles from the world?"

"I rarely take my shirt off."

She rolled her eyes. "You deal with the paparazzi and rabid fans, and I deal with lechers and skeevy guys. A few women, too." She shrugged. "It is what it is."

I couldn't change the world, but I could do something for Katie. "Well, whenever you're with me and you feel uncomfortable—because of me or someone nearby—tell me. I'll try to do better or take care of it."

As I maneuvered back to the main road, Katie said, "What, do you have a high-class security team and with a nod, they make people disappear?"

"Not quite that extreme, but close."

"Do you really have a security team?"

"At my house, yes. One woman snuck onto the property a year or so ago. And now with my ex stirring up shit with her fans? I have to be careful."

"It's a double-edged sword being famous, I think."

I glanced at Katie and then back to the road. "Most people say I'm ungrateful when I bring that up. So I stopped trying."

"Surely your family doesn't think that."

I sighed. "Maybe, maybe not. I'm not as close with my family as the rest of them are with each other. So I don't really talk about my problems with them, if I can avoid it."

"Why do you set yourself apart like that, though? I get how the age differences between you, Zach, Zane, and Abby probably made things difficult as children. But Beck's only three years older, right? My eldest sister Cassie is six years older than me, and once I was out of high school, we became best friends. Did something happen between you and Beck?"

I'd talked more about myself with Katie over the last few weeks than I had with anyone since probably high school. And yet, I didn't want to change the subject like I usually did. "I was closer to Beck and West when we were little. But after our dad died..."

She finished for me. "West ran off with that woman, and then Beck took over the winery and became head of the family."

"Yes. Beck didn't have time to hang out with me any longer, and my other siblings were so much younger that it was hard to do more than play games with them. So I kept my own company, and between my books and my acting, I found ways to distract myself."

I expected her to ask *why* I had wanted to do that—and discuss the death of my dad and later my mom—but she rearranged the skirt of her dress and said, "Well, I know West and Beck are hanging out together more now. And I'm sure if you asked them to go to The

Watering Hole, they'd jump at the chance to drink with their younger brother."

The Watering Hole was the bar for locals, off the main road, to give us all a break from the tourists. "Maybe later. For now, I need to focus on the problem of my ex, and then I can try fixing things with my brothers."

"I don't think you need to fix things so much as get to know each other as adults."

"Easier said than done, when our lives are so different."

Not to mention that both Beck and West had refused my help out of stubborn pride. I wanted to help my family as much as the rest, but somehow my way of doing that—usually by offering money—was a no-starter.

Forget about that for now. Thanksgiving is one of the few happy times a year with your family. Just enjoy it.

I pulled into the back parking lot of Wolfe Family Farm and Winery, where my family lived, and turned off the ignition.

After dashing out of the car and around to the other side, I opened the door and put out my hand. As soon as Katie placed hers in mine, a thread of electricity shot through my body and memories of our earlier kiss rushed back.

The kiss where I'd wanted to strip her naked and claim more than her mouth.

But then she shivered, and I squeezed her hand. "You're cold."

"Sometimes you have to suffer for fashion and to make a statement."

I tried to shrug off my coat, but Katie merely threaded her arm through mine and tugged. "Let's just hurry inside. I want to make an entrance."

We walked toward the door. "With my family? Why? You've known them since you were born."

"Well, yes. But you're the hot, sexy movie star, and I'm, well, I'm just Katie Evans. I need to up my game."

I stopped walking and turned to face Katie. I cupped her cheek and made her look at me.

The uncertainty in her eyes killed me. "Here's how I see it—Katie Evans treats me like a normal guy, which makes her the best of the best. Irreplaceable, even." I stroked her cheek with my thumb and murmured, "You look beautiful, Katie. I don't think I said that earlier."

She opened her mouth, but Aunt Lori's voice carried through the air before Katie could reply. "Wait, is Katie this mystery date of yours, Nolan?"

I reluctantly released Katie's cheek, and we both walked toward Aunt Lori. "Yes, Katie's my girlfriend. We didn't tell anyone at first so we could figure things out on our own. But we're serious, and so I thought I'd surprise you with the news."

Aunt Lori studied my face for a few seconds before smiling. "Well, Katie's always welcome here." She smiled at Katie. "You're looking lovely today, dear. Makes me wish I had a fancy dress like that."

Katie smoothed the skirt. "I got lucky and found it at the thrift store, Aunt Lori."

"Don't tell anyone that, dear. Just own it, as if you bought it on Rodeo Drive."

As soon as we entered the hallway, my niece and

nephew barreled toward us. Avery hugged me. "Uncle Nolan! Did you bring me that autograph like you promised?"

I pretended to think and tapped my chin. "Autograph? Well, I can sign something for you later."

"No, not yours! Oh, you're amazing. But you promised to get Kane Williams' autograph!"

Kane Williams was a teenage actor I'd worked with the year before, for a superhero movie. Avery had a little crush on him and had squealed when she found out I knew him. "Oh, *that* autograph. I have it, but you're not getting it until after dinner."

Avery put out her bottom lip. "Really?"

My brother West walked up and put his hands on Avery's shoulders. "Yes, later. And stop pretend-pouting. We talked about that." West nodded at me. "Hey, Nolan." His gaze moved to Katie. "Katie, what a surprise. I didn't think my brother was your type. But then again, I never saw myself with Emmy until this year, so anything's possible."

I growled. "West, be nice."

Katie gave me a warning glance before replying to West, "Maybe all the BFF Circle members are destined for unique stories. But I discovered Nolan is my type, after all."

Part of me wished her words were true. However, I knew they weren't.

My only sister, Abby, joined us in the hall. Her eyes zeroed in on Katie's arm wrapped around mine. She blinked at me and then Katie. "Wait, what? You're dating Nolan, Katie?"

I nodded and answered before Katie. "Yes. What does everyone find it so hard to believe? I'm a world-famous movie star, for fuck's sake. I'm quite the catch."

Aunt Lori clicked her tongue. "Yes, we know that. But, well, usually I sniff out these things sooner."

She studied us for a few beats. *This is it.* The first real test.

I silently hoped Aunt Lori would buy our deception.

Katie still had her arm in mine and squeezed me gently. She said, "How about we go help with any finishing touches for dinner? I promised Beck to help with decorating the table."

Avery spoke up. "Yes, let's! The sooner we eat dinner, the sooner Uncle Nolan can give me Kane's autographed picture! I want to hang him on my wall. It'll annoy Wyatt, and I can't wait."

She dashed off. West smiled, shook his head, and followed his daughter. Aunt Lori maneuvered between Katie and I, forcing me to release her, and my aunt said, "You're going to share your love story over dinner tonight, right?"

I sighed. "Really? Shouldn't it be more about what we're thankful for, and you bugging Beck and West over when they're going to get married?"

Aunt Lori sniffed. "I do that several times a week already. No, tonight is all about you and Katie, lad. I know you don't like the spotlight once the cameras are off, but we're family. And if you think I don't want to learn how yet another of my nephews convinced an amazing woman to date him, then you don't know me at all."

Katie snorted, and I glared. But before I knew it, Aunt Lori had me down the hall and folding napkins into fancy shapes. She didn't ask me questions one-on-one, but I knew the hardest test of Katie's and my farce was coming. Soon. If my family didn't believe us, then no one probably would.

Chapter Seven

Katie

Cassie: Good luck.
Samantha: From me, too. Aunt Lori will probably ask for a wedding invitation during dinner.
Me: I know how to butter up Aunt Lori. Have fun with Mom, though.
Cassie: Ugh. She has been talking about wedding plans ALL DAY.
Samantha: Which is why I was out tending the cows most of the morning.
Cassie: You're the worst sister ever.
Samantha: You mean the best. You hate anything to do with the dairy. I saved you the trouble.
Cassie: <tongue out emoji> I wouldn't have to do it,

anyway. I'm a nurse, remember? I have my own job.

Samantha: Dad still would've made you help. But I saved the day. You can kiss my ring later.

Cassie: <middle finger emoji>

Me: lol. I'm both glad and sad to miss dinner with the two of you.

Samantha: If you're tired of Nolan already, I'll take your place AND him. Rawr.

Me: <eye roll emoji> That's not how it works.

Cassie: Enjoy! Although you're going to miss me asking Kyle about that woman he saved from the fire at the diner. I'm going to make sure Mom thinks there's something there. <demon emoji>

Samantha: Oooh, we need to talk more about this. Have fun, Katie. You're going to miss something amazing. Kyle doesn't squirm often.

Me: I can't wait to hear all about it. <heart emoji>

As soon as Abby slowed our pace to let Aunt Lori and Nolan get ahead and disappear into the dining room, I knew what was coming. "Just go ahead and ask me."

Abby stopped and faced me. "Why didn't you tell me about you and Nolan?"

"Given how the media tries to ferret out the smallest gossip about Nolan, it seemed safest to test out the waters in secret. I'm sure you understand that, right?"

Abby searched my gaze. "Maybe. But you're going to be his ex's biggest target now. It won't be easy."

While I secretly worried about how bad it'd get, I kept my doubts to myself. "I know. But hopefully she'll get tired of Nolan ignoring her and move on. I mean, how desperate do you have to be to want a guy clearly dating someone else?"

"Oh, Wendy Webster doesn't like being denied anything. She's famous for that. And to her, Nolan is merely a trophy. One she wants."

The thought of Nolan being boiled down to an object, wanted for his fame and not the man himself, made me want to punch something. "Well, she can bring it. I'm not a rich movie star, or some social media darling, but I'm no wilting flower. She won't say anything that I haven't heard before."

"Katie, it's going to be a million times worse than what you went through with those bitches from elementary and middle school."

While I knew Abby was merely looking out for me, it still hurt. She didn't believe I could stand on my own two feet. "I can handle it, okay? You asked for some space after the Douchebag Disaster in San Jose, and we all left it alone. In return, all I ask is for you not to harp on about Wendy Webster, okay?"

She searched my gaze. "I just hope you know what you're doing, Katie. I'd love for things to work out between you and Nolan, and we could be sisters for real. However, I don't want you to get hurt or shattered in the process."

Abby had been hurt so many times in her life—by

her dad's death, her mom's battle with cancer, West abandoning his family, and Zane joining the Navy SEALs and pretty much doing the same thing. Then the guy who broke her heart last year had been the worst, making her want to shift her lifelong dreams and become someone I didn't really know any longer.

Because of that, I softened my voice and put an arm around her. "I'm made of tough stuff, Abby. Besides, I'm one of the few people who can embarrass Aunt Lori. I think that proves my mettle, above all else."

Abby smiled. "She did blush when you asked about that book you gave her."

I waggled my eyebrows. "I think the four guys sharing the woman in the story was her limit."

We stared at each other and broke into laughter as we remembered Aunt Lori trying to work out the positions of all the guys in certain scenarios. I wish we still had time for the sexy book club, but life had gotten in the way.

After hugging Abby, I released her. "I'll fill you in later, with everyone else at dinner, so I don't have to repeat myself."

She sighed. "And because you're dating my brother, I can't ask for the juicy details. Why can't you all find and love guys not related to me?"

"We can't choose who we fall for. And I look forward to whispering with Emmy and comparing notes."

I wagged my eyebrows, and Abby mimicked throwing up.

With a laugh, we made our way down the hall and

into the dining room. Part of me regretted the fact I'd never get to compare notes with Emmy. After all, sex wasn't part of the deal with Nolan, no matter how curious I was about how he'd be in bed.

As soon as we entered the room, Emmy—Emilia Mendoza, another BFF Circle member—and Sabrina O'Connor—Beck's girlfriend from San Francisco who'd moved to Starry Hills earlier in the year—came right up to us.

Emmy asked first, "Is it true about you and Nolan?" I nodded, and Emmy clapped her hands. "This is so exciting! I've thought for a while that you two would be amazing together."

I frowned. "You did?"

Emmy nodded. "Of course. I know the Wolfe family a little better than you since I grew up with them from the age of ten. And Nolan always had a soft spot for you."

Abby blinked. "What the hell are you talking about?"

Emmy replied, "Katie often sought out Nolan when we were kids and would try to get him to play with us. He never really did, and we all thought he hated us. But then when we were eleven, and the Secret Santa came up...don't you remember, Katie?"

A vague memory flashed into my mind of opening a present and revealing a book Nolan had been reading a few months earlier. "Nolan bought that book for me?"

Emmy raised her brows. "He never told you?" I shook my head. "Well, it was him. I overheard Nolan asking his mom and Aunt Lori to take him into town to buy it. The exchange stood out to me because the book was over the dollar limit, but Nolan argued that he'd pay the extra amount."

I still had that book—*The Hunger Games*. "I was surprised to get it, but really happy. I'd read the back cover copy months before and asked to borrow it from Nolan. He said no because he didn't want me to drop it into the bathtub like the other book he'd lent me."

He'd remembered all that. Why? I would've sworn he viewed me as an annoying pest back when I was eleven. Of course, I could've been distracted by other things, like my hellish life at school.

Abby snapped her fingers, garnering my attention. "I remember that gift now! We all ended up reading *The Hunger Games* and even tried making our own bows."

I looked at Sabrina, who wore a puzzled expression. I explained, "Our bows all sucked, big time. They were basically branches with twine, and they didn't work. At all."

Sabrina smiled. When I'd first met her, she'd been a little stand-offish, something to do with her shitty past. But the more time she spent with the BFF Circle, the more she let down her guard. "I only ever saw the movies, and by that age, I didn't have time for stuff like that."

I tapped my chin. "Hmm. Well, then you have some catching up to do. I'm sure we can come up with something absurdly childish to do together. Just give me some time."

Sabrina asked, "Should I be worried?"

Abby and Emmy said, "Yes," at the same time I said, "No."

We all laughed, and Nolan came up behind me. As soon as he put a hand on my waist, my laughter died. And when he pulled my back against his front and held me close? I struggled to think about anything but his hot, solid body touching mine.

He even caressed my waist with his thumb, back and forth, oh-so-slowly, and each pass shot straight between my legs.

Sabrina nodded. "I can see it now."

Nolan leaned down and nuzzled my cheek. My skin heated, and I mentally cursed. Since I had pale skin, everyone in the room would notice how he affected me.

And it was no act.

Warning bells rang inside my head, but I ignored them.

He said, "I heard my name and decided you've had enough time to talk about me."

Emmy replied, "We were talking about the Secret Santa gift you gave Katie all those years ago."

"How did you know it was me?"

Emmy rolled her eyes. "Please, you Wolfe siblings are never as sneaky as you think you are."

West came up and put an arm around Emmy's shoulder. "Oh, we have a few tricks, love. Ones you haven't figured out yet."

Beck also arrived, took Sabrina's hand in his, and grunted. "I knew almost everything that went on inside this house, once I took over." He looked at each of us in turn. "I know most—if not all—of the skeletons in the closet."

Abby rolled her eyes. "Stop trying to be scary, Beck. You fail at it, big time."

He scowled, but Sabrina lightly elbowed him in the ribs. "You're a big softie for your family, Beck. Don't even try to deny it."

"Maybe." Beck nodded toward the table. "It's nearly time to sit down. I need help carrying things from the kitchen. Right now, Avery, Wyatt, and Aunt Lori are attempting to do it, and I'm a little worried."

West tugged Emmy with him. "Come on. Wyatt's more and more often trying to prove he's an adult at eleven, and it doesn't always end well."

Abby said, "It's always the quiet ones you have to watch out for. Which, in addition to my nephew, includes more than half my brothers."

Nolan chuckled behind me. "By that logic, I'm the quietest. So maybe you should sleep with one eye open." He pointed his forefinger and middle finger at his eyes, at Abby, and back again. "I'm watching you."

Abby gave him the middle finger. "You may be the quietest, but you're the least scary, by far. Not even that famous smolder will get me to do your bidding since I'm your sister."

I turned my head to look at Nolan's face. "Oooh, you should do the smolder."

His eyes turned heated, and I bit my bottom lip, reminding myself that it was all an act.

He said huskily, "I'll give you a private show later, baby."

Abby made retching sounds. "If he has a nickname for you and is talking about private shows, that's my cue to leave. Come on, Beck. Put me to work."

Soon Nolan and I were alone. I expected him to release me, but he kept his arms around my waist and propped his chin on top of my head. Closing my eyes, I reveled in our farce. No guy had ever been so sweet with me in the past. Even if it wasn't real, it made me realize my choice of going after the bad boys had been misguided.

There was something to be said about nice guys. Especially if my dreams of what Nolan could do with his hands and tongue turned out to be true. Then he wouldn't be such a nice guy in bed. Which would be perfect.

Stop it, Katie.

I had no idea how long we stood like that—as if we both wanted to make the moment last a little longer—before his phone vibrated in his pocket. Repeatedly.

He sighed. "I need to check that. There's only one person who'd try to call me on Thanksgiving, and it won't be with good news."

I reluctantly stepped away, and Nolan released me. I turned to watch as he answered his phone. But he moved too far away for me to hear anything.

His expression, however, went from irritated to downright furious.

Then he looked at his phone, tapped it a few times, and he growled. "What the fuck?"

I sidled up to him and asked, "What is it?"

"Wendy and her damn Thanksgiving message. Here, you should read it. Prepare yourself."

After giving him a wary glance, I took his phone and scanned her social media post. By the end, I was speechless.

Nolan took his phone and asked, "Are you okay, Katie? I promise none of it's true." He waited, but I still couldn't believe what I'd just read, and he added, "Just talk to me, baby."

When I could finally string a few sentences together, I said, "How does she even know about us already?"

He placed a hand on my back and rubbed it in slow circles. "I wouldn't put it past her to have people watching me." He paused and then softened his voice. "Do you want to back out? I'd totally understand. Her hatred and vitriol shouldn't be your problem."

The most hurtful paragraph from the post came back to me:

My darling Nolan recently signed a deal to be the spokesperson for that trendy weight loss program—you know the one. He's so dedicated, as usual, and to help advertise the deal, he even found a fat woman to be his temporary girlfriend. After the New Year, he'll dump her and has finally agreed to set a date with me. Keep an eye out! Two lucky fans will win a trip to my wedding.

I hadn't been picked on like that since I was a teenager, and a mixture of emotions swirled inside me—anger, insecurity, irritation, pity, and sadness, both at her and for myself.

Rationally, I knew it took a mean and really insecure person to throw shit like that around. And yet, all those years of being bullied came back to me, along with the pain.

Tears even pricked my eyes, but there was no way in hell I'd cry in front of Nolan Wolfe.

So I said, "I just need a minute. Make excuses to your family? I'll be back before dinner, I promise."

And with that, I ran through the hall and to the door that connected with the reception area at the front, used for the winery customers.

I found a bench along one side, sat down, and put my head in my hands. Wendy's words had brought back the taunts and tricks and pure hell the Mean Girls of Starry Hills had put me through.

It shouldn't bother me any longer. It really shouldn't. After all, I was a grown-ass adult. I'd learned to be outgoing and how to flirt. How to make people notice me for something other than my body, and it'd worked for so many years.

However, I didn't think being outrageous would solve this problem like when I'd been younger.

Or could it?

Being outrageous without crossing the line into bitchy would be difficult. I never wanted to become a bully myself, even if I thought someone deserved it. Wendy Webster most probably did, and yet I didn't want Nolan to suffer because of my actions. I was supposed to be helping him, not making it worse.

After taking a deep breath, I lifted my head and nodded to myself. I would think of a way to handle Nolan's ex.

He'd warned me from the beginning about how she would be mean and horrible and try to make me cry. Well, I wasn't about to let her win.

And now that I knew what kind of shit she'd throw my way, I could better focus and figure out a plan.

Chapter Eight

Nolan

Jenn: I've already started on damage control.
Me: It can wait until tomorrow. Enjoy your Thanksgiving.
Jenn: Oh, don't worry. Tina and I live to irritate that woman. Besides, it's better than spending time with my uncle and him saying how nice it is for his niece to have such a "good roommate." She's my wife, FFS.
Me: You could've come here. I invite you every year.
Jenn: I know. But it'd break my mom's heart if I didn't come to Thanksgiving. Anyway, Tina's started on the statement, and we'll post it everywhere once it's done. What do you want to say about Katie?
Me: Just that she's my girlfriend, we were childhood

friends, and there is no weight loss program deal. The bigger announcement will come soon enough, but I won't do it now because of a knee-jerk reaction.

Jenn: You shouldn't have to do any of this at all.

Me: We've discussed this.

Jenn: I know, I know. I can't wait to meet this Katie in person, though.

Me: Soon. She'll need a friend in L.A. If she still agrees to continue with this shit show.

Jenn: Just use that hidden charm I know is there. <winking emoji>

Rage didn't even begin to describe how I felt about Wendy's post. I'd expected Katie to become her target, had even warned her about it, but the words Wendy had written were beyond cruel.

I trusted Jenn and Tina to handle the official response. However, right now, Wendy could wait. I needed to find Katie.

Yes, she'd asked for space. But the thought of her suffering alone, because of me and my problems, didn't sit well.

Not to mention I wanted to let her know she could end this now, even in front of my family, if she wanted.

So I followed her and found her sitting on a bench in the winery's reception area. She had her fingers clenched into fists, a determined expression on her face.

It was a hell of a lot better than earlier, when I thought she might cry.

As I approached her, she finally noticed me and I asked, "Are you okay? I couldn't let you suffer Wendy's bullshit alone."

"I won't lie—what she said hurt. But I'm not about to let her win."

Since Katie didn't stand, I sat next to her. "Now that you've had a little time to let it sink in, tell me truthfully—do you want to back out of our deal? Because Wendy will become even worse once the news of our engagement breaks."

Katie laced her fingers together, undid them, and then put them together again. "I know she will. And it won't make her words any less hurtful. But at least now I'm prepared for her level of meanness and bullying."

"Katie."

"Just let me finish, Nolan." I nodded, and she continued, "However, it tells me that she must be a petty person who doesn't have much love in her life. Sure, she might be rich and pretty and have a legion of fans. But does any of that really matter if she's so full of hatred and ugliness inside? It makes me think she's unhappy."

"Maybe. But I think it's more the fact she's just shallow." I ran a hand through my hair. "It didn't take me long to realize that her public persona—which had been much nicer before I broke up with her—was just a front. In reality, she wants a handsome guy she can control, to do her every bidding. Someone to look nice next to her in photos, to further build up the facade of a perfect life, but one who doesn't get to have anything his way." I paused, and before I could think better of it, I added, "Like most of the world, she has an image of me in her head and expected me to match the fantasy of Nolan Drake instead of wanting the reality that is Nolan Wolfe."

Katie placed a hand on my arm, and I looked at her. She searched my eyes and said, "Well, I don't know Nolan Drake very well. But I mostly like Nolan Wolfe."

"Mostly?"

"Well, you are annoyingly tall."

The corner of my mouth kicked up. "Being tall is a negative? That was out of my control, you know."

"Try being barely over five feet and see how you feel standing next to a veritable giant. It gives a girl a crick in the neck."

"We're sitting right now, though, and are nearly eye-to-eye."

She put a hand to the top of her head and moved it over in a line to hit my nose. "I'm still shorter."

I wanted to say she could sit on my lap and we'd be about the same height. It'd be perfect for kissing her soft lips again as I rocked her against my cock. Perfect for me to grab her ass and pull her close, and maybe make both of us come with our clothes still on.

Shifting in my seat, I looked away from Katie's tempting mouth. "Well, if you want to continue this deal, then I'll have to be Nolan Drake sometimes. Remember how I said I'm always convinced I need to go to a New Year's event or party?" She nodded. "It's the same for this New Year's, and that would be our first appearance together in L.A." I met her gaze again. "And I won't lie—it'll be nerve-racking and make you the focus of a good chunk of the world." I took one of her hands in mine and gently squeezed. "Since repeatedly asking if you want to do this will get annoying, I'll ask just once more. And after that, you'll simply have to tell me if you want out at any point. And if so, I promise there will be no hard feelings. So, are you ready to face your family for Christmas and then the world for New Year's?"

Katie sat a little taller. "Hell yes, bring it. I'll win them all over, easy peasy."

I smiled and brushed a stray strand of hair off her cheek. "Well, then we should probably head back inside and deal with my family."

"You make it sound like you're going to confront a firing squad or something."

I shook my head. "It's not that bad. But usually I can avoid too much notice at Thanksgiving. I'm pretty good at keeping quiet and only cracking a joke when it really makes an impact. But tonight, we're going to have tons of questions and teasing and who knows what else."

Katie shrugged. "I can take it. After all, my mother is already making wedding plans."

I blinked. "Wait, what? We're not even officially engaged yet."

"No, but none of her children have gotten married yet, so she's champing at the bit. I mean, my brother is the same age as Beck, so she's been waiting a long time. Of course, it's kind of fun being the youngest and supposedly the first one to get married. It was a surprise for my mother."

"Why?"

Katie shrugged. "I've briefly dated a lot of guys over the years. Ones I knew I didn't see a future with. I guess it was part of me trying to figure myself out. My mother, on the other hand, just saw it as me making bad decisions."

I suddenly disliked Katie's mother for thinking so little of her daughter.

Placing a hand on my thigh, Katie said, "It's her way. She loves me, I know it. And if I proposed moving to Australia tomorrow, she'd support me. But part of the way she shows she loves us is to be critical of everything."

"It's so different from my mother. She was usually sweet, unless we got into trouble. Then she took no prisoners and gave lengthy lectures." I smiled at a memory of my mother having a go at Beck. "By the time she finished, we'd agree to anything to get away. It worked really well, for whatever reason."

"She was always nice to me. And she made the best pies in all of Sonoma County. Just don't tell my aunt that, or I'll never hear the end of it."

I chuckled. "I promise." Wanting to change the subject from mothers—it was still hard sometimes to talk about mine since I missed her so much—I said, "Back to us and our long-term strategy. We'll have to decide exactly when we want to announce our engagement. But not yet." I stood and offered a hand. "Today, let's just eat too much, play some games with my family, and pretend the rest of the world doesn't exist."

She placed her hand in mine, and I tugged her up.

Katie stumbled against me, and I steadied her with my hands on her waist.

We stared at one another, pressed as close as we could get with clothes on, and my heart raced as my dick hardened. Katie was so fucking beautiful, and soft, and she smelled so good that I wanted to eat her up.

Everywhere.

Then someone cleared their throat loudly. The voice was Zach's. "Here are the lovebirds. I finally get back from my trip, and you weren't there to greet me. That wasn't very nice, was it?"

Katie backed away from me, and I wanted to growl at being interrupted.

Thankfully, Katie had better manners than me and said, "You're here all the time, Zach. I saw you less than a week ago. If anything, you should've been here to welcome Nolan home." As I turned to face my younger brother, she took my hand. "You're not as happy to see Nolan as I am, of course."

Zach snorted. "I heard about you two dating. At this rate, are all my brothers going to end up with someone with the BFF Circle?"

Katie wrinkled her nose. "Considering Abby is a member, and she's your *sister*, that's just gross."

"What the hell are you talking about? Of course I didn't mean Abby. This isn't some weird-ass book where siblings hook up with each other." He shuddered in revulsion. "No. Just, no."

Katie shrugged. "If you meant Amber, then you should've just said so. Although, if you've finally noticed her, you're too late, by the way. Amber started dating someone a couple of weeks ago."

Some unknown expression flashed across Zach's face, but it was gone before I could blink. "Well, good for her. I always said her stepmom works her too hard, and she should live a little. Now, are you two coming? Aunt Lori said to drag you to the table, if needed. Although how I'm supposed to drag two people, I don't know. I'm not Superman, or anything."

I snorted. "And here I thought you were some sort of superhero or god, given your cockiness most days."

Zach flashed his middle finger. "Says the movie star god. Now, come on. While I love traveling, I definitely miss Beck's cooking when away. I don't know what I'm going to do if I ever move out of here."

My youngest brother walked off, and we followed. Once I was pretty sure Zach was out of earshot, I whispered, "Is Amber really dating someone?"

While the news seemed innocuous on the surface, Amber had been in love with my brother since middle school. Pretty much everyone had known that fact, except for Zach. And even then, I wondered if he'd known and pretended not to, even if it was a dickish thing to do.

Katie whispered back, "Yes. Things got strained between Zach and Amber earlier this year. Whatever happened gave her the kick she needed to look elsewhere. Because if Zach can't see how amazing Amber is, then he doesn't deserve her."

I nodded. Amber was the quietest of the BFF Circle,

and the one I knew the least. However, as kids, Amber and Zach had been thick as thieves.

The entire situation only reinforced how little I knew about my siblings these days. "I think I'll try to go to the bar with my brothers and Abby tomorrow. I don't have to go back to L.A. until the day after."

Katie squeezed my hand. "I think you'll have a blast. And I promise, the BFF Circle won't make an appearance. Although last time we went at the same time as the Wolfe siblings, it pretty much set things in motion for Emmy and West. Who knows what would happen next time?"

What indeed.

But then we entered the hallway and were in the dining room before either Katie or I could say anything else.

And both of us stopped in our tracks as we noticed the new addition to the group gathered around the table —Rafael "Rafe" Mendoza. He was Emmy's older brother, a world-famous soccer player, and had once upon a time been best friends with West.

And now that West was dating Rafe's sister, Rafe wasn't happy about it. Or so West had told me.

Katie whispered, "I thought he couldn't make it?"

"Well, he must've found a way."

Aunt Lori spoke up. "Yes, yes, Rafe's here, too. The more the merrier, I always say. It just gives me more people to tease with embarrassing childhood stories. Who remembers the time Rafe and West thought it'd be fun to toss cow pies at each other? And then they had to hose down naked outside because neither of their moms would let them in otherwise because of the smell?"

West grunted. "You were only visiting then, and you still remember that?"

Aunt Lori nodded. "Of course. You were about seven or eight? And Beck then kept chanting, 'Cow pies, cow pies, cow pies' over and over again. Eve then made cow pie cookies, and neither of you would touch them." She smiled. "It's hard to believe it's been nearly thirty years since then."

Eve was my mom, and a memory rushed back to me. "Didn't she make those every year for a while, until she realized none of us would eat them?"

Aunt Lori replied, "Yes." She glanced at West and then at Rafe. "And now look at the pair of you—great strapping men who scowl too much."

Both Rafe and West's brows furrowed at the same time, and everyone laughed, breaking the tension.

With a hesitant smile, Rafe sat down next to his sister. I then helped Katie into her chair and took my place beside her.

Once everyone was sitting—Katie was to my right and my niece Avery to my left—Aunt Lori lifted her wine glass. The adults did the same, and the kids raised their sparkling cider.

Aunt Lori said, "It's been quite eventful since the last Thanksgiving, but mostly in a good way." She nodded at Sabrina and Beck, then West and Emmy, next at Avery and Wyatt, and finally at Rafe. "While our family isn't quite complete, I know Zane will be here in spirit. To another great year and wishes for it to be even better!"

We all cheered and sipped our glasses. It hadn't escaped my notice that Aunt Lori had left me and Katie out of her "big changes" observation.

Which meant she didn't quite believe us.

We'd just have to work on it.

But as we dished out dinner—the game my family often played with getting the best cuts of meat was forbidden for holidays—and went around to say what we were grateful for, the outside world and my ex and the pressures of the press all faded away. With the exception of Jenn, Tina, and Zane, everyone I cared about was in this room.

And later, as I caught Katie's eye and we smiled at each other, I thought maybe this year was a little better for reasons I was afraid to admit.

Chapter Nine

Katie

Me: So we're still on for the Christmas Market tomorrow?
Nolan: Yes, barring last-minute emergencies. I'll fly in tomorrow morning and, fingers crossed, be there on time. I might be a few minutes late.
Me: Are you sure you want to come? I know you've been rehearsing for the last week or so for your project in the new year.
Nolan: Of course I'll be there. It's part of the Next Step.
Me: If you're sure...
Nolan: I'm going to be there, Katie. You've been teasing me about the drama at your house. I definitely need an

update in person. Texts aren't the same. And you hate phone calls.

Me: Not true! You're always too busy, and you want to call at like 1 a.m. I work on a dairy farm. That's nearly time to get up.

Nolan: <tongue out emoji> Fine, country girl. We can work out a phone schedule in person, too. Texting takes too long.

Me: Says the old man.

Nolan: I'll show you old the next time I see you...

Me (typed but deleted): I hope you mean in bed.

Me (actual reply instead): If you can catch me...

Nolan was late. He said he might be, but as I stood near the giant Christmas tree in the center of the Starry Hills Christmas Market, I paced and fidgeted and did my best not to constantly check my phone.

Texting with Nolan since Thanksgiving had been fun. And I had been bummed that the only time he seemed to be able to talk on the phone was when I was fast asleep. I knew this was all fake, and yet I rather enjoyed talking with Nolan. I didn't feel the need to constantly be entertaining or outrageous or plaster a smile on my face like I did for my job.

I could just be...me. And that was rather addicting.

And dangerous. *Don't fall for him for real, Katie. You*

have just under five months to go and then you're supposed to dump him.

But until then, he was still mine.

As I tried to pack away my excitement so Nolan wouldn't think I was clingy or needy or something, I heard some familiar female voices from the other side of the tree. Voices that had haunted my dreams as a kid.

"I saw her in the parking lot earlier. I still can't believe Nolan would want her, of all people."

It was Kristina Smith, one of the three Mean Girl bullies from my school days.

I'd often dreamed of being able to put them in their places as an adult. And yet, I couldn't seem to move from where I stood and continued to eavesdrop.

Another girl, Lydia Johnson, said, "I think Wendy Webster was telling the truth—he just needed a fat girlfriend to help promote his latest deal. Because why would he pick chubby Katie Evans over a goddess like Wendy Webster? No one would, that's for sure."

I clenched the fingers of one hand into a fist. And yet, I still couldn't make my mouth work or feet move. The third woman who'd terrorized me as a child, Jordan Miller, said, "I'm sure she smells of cow shit and Nolan has to put some kind of scent under his nose just to be around her."

The women laughed, and Kristina spoke again. "I hope he pays her well enough. It's not like she'll ever amount to anything and will probably die in Starry Hills. Gah, I'm so glad I married well and moved away. Even this market seems like a shit hole compared to the ones I visited in Germany last year."

Jordan said, "But your mom is sick, and our moms are close, so we had to come. It might be her last Christmas."

"Which is why I lowered myself to coming back here. Maybe we can find Katie at the market and remind her of how we were such good friends back in the day. Give her some of the same teasing. That would make this visit almost bearable."

Lydia spoke up. "I even have this mulled wine I can spill on her."

Kristina said, "And I have this awful crepe that I don't even know why I bought. I could bump into her and rub it down her front."

Jordan snorted. "Maybe I should hit up a food stall too so I can add to the disaster masterpiece. Wasn't there some kind of melted cheese thing they had? And make sure to snap a picture of Katie afterward so we can share it with Wendy. Could you imagine if she saw it and replied, or even shared it?"

A low, male voice filled my ear. "Do you want me to help put them in their place?"

I glanced at Nolan. Had he heard everything?

My cheeks burned, but just his touch on my arm helped calm me down a little. I whispered back, "I guess so."

He put out a hand. "Then come with me."

After I took it, he tugged me to the other side of the tree. As soon as we were in sight of the three women, he pulled me against him, cupped my cheek, and said, "Kiss me like you mean it, baby. I've missed you."

For a second, the heat and yearning in his eyes threw

me off. Then I remembered where we were and who watched and how he was an actor. So I gripped his coat, stood on tip-toe, and he closed the distance.

As soon as Nolan's mouth crashed down on mine, everything else faded away. He was warm and smelled delicious, and the way he held me against his body made me feel precious.

His tongue demanded entrance, and I opened, moaning as soon as his tongue found mine. He flicked and licked and tangled. And I met him stroke for stroke, needing more, much more, but knowing it would never go beyond kissing.

Except when his hard cock pressed against me, I couldn't resist rubbing and torturing him. His moans and groans and the intensity of his kisses drove me just as crazy. Before I knew it, he lifted me up, and I instinctively wrapped my legs around his waist. Somewhere in my mind I knew I was in public and that people were watching. Hell, they'd probably be taking a video, and it'd be all over the internet within the hour.

And yet, I couldn't care less. I wrapped my arms around Nolan's neck, ground more against him, and my heart raced as I grew wetter and turned on. It wouldn't take much more to push me over the edge.

Nolan's possessive hands on my ass rocked me against his cock. With a moan, I got lost in his kisses and hard chest, and for a short while, imagined this was my life—a boyfriend who couldn't get enough of me, didn't care who knew it, and could nearly make me come from kisses and a little friction, all with our clothes still on.

Someone yelled, "Nolan Drake, look here!" and Nolan broke the kiss.

Rather than looking around, he laid his forehead against mine and we both tried to catch our breaths. He stared into my eyes, but I couldn't read his expression. I guess he'd stopped acting.

It was on the tip of my tongue to ask what he was thinking, but I held back.

Instead, I finally murmured, "You didn't have to do that."

He hugged me closer. "We'll talk about it more later. What do you want to do now, Katie? They're still watching."

All of my earlier nerves and insecurities had vanished. I replied softly, "Put me down and follow my lead."

"Anything you want, baby. I'm here for you."

I smiled at his words. However, as soon as my feet touched the ground, I turned to face the three women who shouldn't have any power over me. And thanks to Nolan, I was in control and no longer stuck reliving old memories.

I walked over to Kristina. Nolan followed me and stopped by my side. I nearly took his hand, but decided I needed to do this for myself. "Hello, Kris. Do you really have nothing better to do than call me fat and want to throw shit at me? I mean, I know a pair of eleven-year-olds who wouldn't even do that kind of stuff."

Kristina blinked a second and then narrowed her eyes. She gave me a once-over. "Well, the first is certainly true, Katie. Oh wait, what was it that we called you? Oh, that's right—Fat Kat. I'll make sure to let Wendy know about that name and the whole world will start calling you it too."

Nolan growled, but I put up a hand. Anger churned my belly, but it was better than fear or tears. "I won't ever resort to name calling, but there are plenty of facts I could bring up about you. Your sister was drunk at the bar one night and let a few secrets slip out..."

Kristina took a step forward. "Try it, Fat Kat. You'll lose in the end."

It would be so easy to call her a name and cross the line, to become a bully and spill the secret of how one of her children was fathered by someone other than her husband.

But I couldn't do that to an innocent child. However, there was another piece of information I knew, something that would only affect Kristina. So I whispered for her ears only, "I know you paid someone to take the SAT for you. You know, the score that got you into Stanford, where you met your husband? Don't you sit on some alumni board or something like that? Imagine what they'd say if they learned the truth."

Kristina paled a little before her cheeks turned bright red. "My grades got me there, Fat Kat. Try it. My husband is a powerful lawyer, and you won't stand a chance."

Nolan touched my hand, and I glanced at him. He raised his eyebrows in question.

He wanted to help me. And maybe it was crazy, but I trusted him. So I nodded.

Nolan leaned forward. "I know better lawyers. Ones

who can ferret out any kind of secret, too. Mess with my woman, and you'll regret it."

I took his hand without thinking, and Nolan threaded his fingers through mine. As he squeezed gently, I felt a little calmer. So I said, "Just go back to your life, Kris, and I'll do the same. You've always hated Starry Hills and called us a hole-in-the-wall town. So just go and leave us alone."

Kristina opened her mouth, but Jordan stepped forward and whispered something. Both women noticed all the people watching and more than a few cell phones pointed in our direction.

Kristina said, "Watch your back, Fat Kat. That's all I'll say."

With that, the three women left. Nolan tugged me away from the crowd until we found a quiet corner next to the Starry Wolfe wine booth. Zach waved, but at our expressions, he frowned. Nolan made some gestures to his brother—probably some kind of secret Wolfe brother code—and tugged me behind the booth, which hid us from view.

Nolan ran the back of his fingers against my cheek. "Are you okay, baby?"

He'd called me that a lot today. I'd laughed at ridiculous nicknames in books before, and yet, when Nolan said it, I rather liked it. The term made everything more intimate.

Which we needed, if everyone was to believe our lie.

I replied, "Yes. Before you came, I was frozen in place, my head stuck in the past. So, thanks for your help and backing me up."

The corner of his mouth kicked up. "Don't make it seem like a hardship. Any man who gets to kiss you is a lucky man indeed."

"We're alone, so you don't need to keep up the pretense, Nolan."

He traced my cheek with his forefinger, and I resisted a shiver. "I'm telling the truth." I opened my mouth to tell him to cut it out, but Nolan spoke before me. "Let's put that aside for now. From what I could tell of the conversation, they bullied you as a child?"

"Yes. I got boobs early and resisted a bra—I was still a kid—and that made me a target. And since I gain weight on my lower body, they always made snide remarks about the size of my thighs and ass." I shrugged. "It hurt more as a kid than when I was a teenager. But by the time I was in high school, with Emmy, Abby, and Amber at my back, the Mean Girls went and found someone else to terrorize."

My best friends had been furious when they'd learned about the bullying. I'd kept it a secret from them for years, not wanting to burden them. Plus, I'd always thought that one day, I'd be able to stop it myself.

Which, in retrospect, had been fucking stupid given how I'd needed help even as an adult.

I noticed Nolan was preternaturally still, his jaw clenched, and asked, "What's wrong?"

"I wish I would've known sooner. Maybe I could've stopped it earlier."

"While sweet, you left Starry Hills at eighteen, and I was twelve. By that point, we rarely saw each other because you were busy starring in movies and TV shows."

"What about your sisters? Didn't they want to help you?"

I bit my bottom lip for a few seconds. "Later, Cassie and Sam promised to have my back if I needed it. But no, I didn't tell them until after high school. So they had no way of knowing."

He searched my gaze. "What else are you hiding?"

That I want to kiss you again, strip you, and moan as you come inside me.

"Nothing, really. However, after the display in the market, you're going to have another fire to put out. I'm sure our make-out session will be all over the internet by now."

He studied me. "You're changing the subject."

"Because I don't want to talk about the past any more today, okay? Let's just focus on the future and, more importantly, our plan. Is today still the day? Or do we need to rethink it?"

Nolan and I had agreed to be vague when it came to our fake relationship details. That way, fewer people could guess what we were up to.

However, he knew exactly what I was talking about. "No, we'll go ahead, as planned." He took my hand. "Provided you're up for it, of course."

"Yep. The sooner, the better. Maybe this next step will make your problem go away for good."

He shook his head. "You're far more optimistic about that than me, baby. We'll see how it goes." He pulled me forward until he could put his free hand on my hip. "But let's have a little fun at the market before we take the next step, okay?"

I tilted my head. "Why? I'm sure it's nothing compared to the bigger ones in SoCal."

"Southern California has many advantages—warmer weather, beautiful beaches, and some of the best restaurants in the world. However, Starry Hills has one thing that it doesn't."

"Which is?"

"Home. This is home, no matter how often I'm away. There's something about the rolling hills of the vineyards, everyone knowing my name—my real name, not my stage name—and how much fun I have spending time with you."

I searched his gaze at that last line. He had to be acting. Right?

Zach popped his head around the corner. "Are you two okay? I finally had a break from visitors and wanted to see what was up."

I stepped back, and Nolan released my hand before answering, "I think we have everything under control. Right, Katie?"

"Yes. I just ran into some girls from high school and rather wish I hadn't."

Zach raised an eyebrow. "The Mean Girls again? I told you before and I'll tell you again: just tell me and Beck, and the two of us and Kyle will protect you."

"No, no, that's okay. Nolan was amazing, anyway. His fame can be super helpful at times."

Something crossed Nolan's expression, but it was gone before I could blink.

He cleared his throat. "Well, we're off to wander the market. Is there anything you want?"

Zach nodded. "Yeah, if you see a present for Aunt Lori from all of us, then get it. She's hard to shop for, unless it's a tacky tourist mug, and Beck and I haven't been able to come up with any ideas."

"Of course. We'll stop by your booth again before we leave and let you know if we find anything."

Zach studied us again and then smiled. "Thanks. Now, I'd better go back to my duties before Beck gets word that I abandoned my post, even if it's for a worthy cause."

With a salute, Zach disappeared.

Nolan offered his arm. I threaded mine through it and said, "You're the only guy I know who does that."

"What?"

"Offers your arm like an old-timey gentleman."

As we walked back out into the market proper, he replied, "All of us Wolfe brothers have our own little acts of being a gentleman. I don't know how that happened. My mom tried to instill them in all of us, but not everything stuck."

Eve Wolfe had died nearly five years ago now. "Your mom was always the best, though. And not just because she let Abby have more sleepovers than any of the other parents."

"Are sleepovers the measure of a good mom for young girls?"

I rolled my eyes. "There's no uniform measuring stick."

Nolan grinned. "Well, whoever fed us the most was usually the best for me and my brothers."

"Boys and their food, I swear. Does that still work?"

"Naw. For certain roles, I have to stick to strict diets to add muscle or keep it off. It's definitely one of my least favorite parts of my job."

"I never thought of that. But you were pretty beefed up for that superhero movie, so that must've taken some work."

"Saw it, did you?"

"Of course. I've seen all your movies."

Okay, I hadn't meant to let that slip.

His eyes turned curious. "Even the awful ones? Even *Bigfoot's Hunt*?"

I smiled. "That one was pretty horrible, I'll admit. The story was way over the top, and the dialogue was super cheesy. You had to know that from the script, so why did you take the role?"

He shrugged one shoulder. "Well, it was early in my career, and I sort of took whatever I could get. There was one positive from it, though—I realized horror movies weren't my favorite to act out. After the Bigfoot sequel, I never did another horror flick."

"So what is your favorite kind, then?"

"Hmm. I like historical ones. Or comedies. Although I rarely get roles for the latter."

"I would think that at this point in your career, you could turn down anything. And with your production company, couldn't you make the movies you want to star in?"

"It's complicated." He stopped us in front of a Glühwein stall—German mulled wine. "We can't come to this market and not get some Glühwein."

"Is that allowed? Drinking from the competition? I mean, your family owns a winery."

He lowered his voice. "What they don't know won't hurt them."

Nolan winked, and I laughed. "Imagine the fall-out if they discovered this particular secret too."

He lightly bumped his hip against me. "Planning to blackmail me over it?"

I tapped my chin. "Hmm, maybe. Imagine the headline: Movie Star Snubs Family Winery."

After pulling me to the side, away from the stall, he leaned down and nuzzled my cheek, promptly making me forget about anything but the scruff of Nolan's jaw and his woodsy scent and his heat.

He murmured, "Maybe you need a bribe to keep it a secret, then."

I was about to say I was only teasing when Nolan cupped my cheek and moved his head until his lips were a few inches from mine.

His breath caressed my mouth as I asked, "What kind of bribe?"

As he continued to stare into my eyes, his mouth so close to mine, my heart raced and wetness rushed between my thighs. If he used kisses as bribes, I'd take as many as he'd give me.

He said, "As a kid, you always loved marzipan from this market. If you still do, I'll brave them in exchange for the mulled wine."

I did my best to hide my disappointment—kisses

would've been better. *He already gave you quite a show earlier. Don't get greedy, Katie.*

Clearing my throat, I replied, "I still like marzipan. But I'll admit stollen has become a bigger favorite in the last few years, ever since a new family moved here with the best recipe."

"Stollen and Glühwein it is, then. Maybe we should have the cake-bread-thing first, to soak up the alcohol."

"Why, is the big-time movie star a lightweight?"

"Wouldn't you like to know?"

"That sounds like a challenge, Mr. Wolfe."

"Maybe it is, Miss Evans."

After staring at each other for a few beats, we both laughed. I spoke again first. "Let's have the wine now and we can save the stollen for later. But I wouldn't be against trying some marzipan tonight."

"You drive a hard bargain, but I think I can swing that. Come on."

Nolan ordered the German mulled wine. I sniffed and was bombarded by a multitude of spices. I sipped slowly and then drank some more. "It's better than I thought it'd be."

After savoring a sip, Nolan asked, "What were you expecting?"

"I don't know. Mulled wine hasn't been my favorite in the past, but this seems okay."

"Okay?" He placed a hand over his heart and looked wounded. "You're killing me here."

I giggled. "Oh, now you're just being silly."

A little boy of nine or ten stopped next to Nolan and stared up at him. The boy asked, "Are you Nolan Drake from that superhero movie? The one where you fly and can smash boulders with your fists?"

Nolan leaned down and braced a hand on his thigh. "I am. Did you like it?"

"Oh, it was great. I liked all the fighting and the big group of friends. Although..."

"Although what?"

"Your powers kind of sucked."

I bit back a laugh, and Nolan's lips twitched. "Which ones did you like better?"

"The teleporter. I mean, how awesome would it be if I could just think of where I wanted to go, and I'd be there?"

"Well, you'd have to be careful not to end up in a wall or in the ground."

"Oh, I wouldn't do that. That's a rookie mistake."

At the boy's matter-of-fact tone, I pressed a hand over my mouth to keep my laughter at bay.

Nolan nodded. "I agree. Now, did you have another question? Only one more, because I'm here with my girlfriend and I promised we'd visit more stalls in the market."

The boy turned to a woman behind him. "Mom, can you take our picture?"

The woman was vaguely familiar, but older than me, so I couldn't quite place her. "You need to ask permission, Owen. We don't take pictures of people who don't want it, remember?"

Owen turned back to Nolan. "That's my last question—can we take a picture together?"

Nolan handed me his empty glass. "Of course."

After Nolan posed with the boy, the boy's mother thanked him, and they walked away, he turned back toward me. I said, "That was nice of you."

He shrugged. "I like talking with kids. It's the women telling me they want to see me naked in the supermarket that I tend to run away from."

"You still buy your own groceries?"

"Sometimes. If I wear a hat, usually people won't recognize me. And I like people-watching. It gives me inspiration for characters I could play or write about."

"So, are you doing that tonight? People-watching?"

He gently touched my cheek. "I'm mostly focusing on one person tonight."

"Oh."

His gaze turned tender, and my heart skipped a beat. It would be so easy to lean in, stand on my tiptoes, and pull him down for a kiss.

Nolan cleared his throat and offered his arm again. "At any rate, I think it's high time we find some treats, hunt down a present for Aunt Lori, and give everyone a show. Well, another one."

I nodded, trying to ignore the disappointment swirling around in my stomach. "Of course. Let's get this show on the road, then."

And as we walked down the aisle of booths, I leaned more against Nolan's side. If nothing else, I wanted to make the most of the time I had with him. Maybe if I were lucky, I'd find another guy like him.

As if there would be another man like Nolan.

Stop it, Katie. I could do all the exploring and dating and sex I wanted on my big trip. All my energy should go toward playing a besotted fiancée and not wondering what it'd be like to have Nolan as my own.

The next step in our arrangement was the proposal, and I wondered when and where he'd finally do it. Even if it would only be for show, it would be my first one. And I was definitely nervous.

Chapter Ten

Nolan

Zach: If you need me to be your backup, just say so. Those bullies left Starry Hills before I knew what they'd done to Katie.
Me: Thanks, but we're good for now.
Zach: I'd say more than good, judging by the video that's already online. Who knew my quiet brother had it in him?
Me: I do...okay.
Zach: Stop being modest, Nolan. And hey, if you really love me, maybe you'll set me up with one of your famous friends? Purely as a business opportunity, of course.
Me: <eye roll emoji> Sure. And the sky is pink.
Zach: I'm offended. Truly offended. But just think

about it, okay? Your video ads for the winery have been a huge help, but I want to take Starry Wolfe wine to the next level. To do that, I need connections.

Me (typed but deleted): You could've done that already if you'd only taken my help earlier, when I offered to invest.

Me (actual reply instead): I'll see what I can do. Now, leave me alone. I'm on a date.

Zach: Don't do anything I wouldn't do. <winking emoji>

As I guided us toward the marzipan stall, a mixture of emotions churned inside me. I was still pissed as fuck about those women and what they'd intended to do to Katie. For most adults that age, they'd be beyond that petty crap. And yet, I knew firsthand that reaching eighteen years old didn't mean people automatically behaved better.

At times, some of the private and direct messages people had sent me in the early days of my career still haunted me. Behind a keyboard, people truly had no shame or boundaries.

However, I had fame and money to help protect me. Katie didn't. Even so, she seemed determined to tackle everything by herself. Oh, the BFF Circle helped when they could, but I still wondered *why* Katie shouldered so much alone.

Even though I should turn on the charm and get the proposal scene staged, I couldn't help but blurt, "Who do you confide in? I mean, really confide in about your troubles?"

Katie raised her brows. "Who do you confide in?"

"Mainly my assistant and my lawyer."

She looked back toward the line of craft and food stalls. "I have my friends, but I'm closest to my sister, Cassie."

"And yet, I sense you still hold back from them all."

She swung her free hand, and then finally squeezed my arm in hers. "Yes. And before you ask why, it's complicated."

"Which means you don't want to talk about it."

"Maybe later."

If I were really her boyfriend, I'd probably push her.

However, I had to remember it was all an act. Yes, we had to prove we were a couple to the world, but that was it. Soul-bearing hadn't been part of the deal.

Even though I wished it had been.

Since we were at the marzipan stall, I decided to drop it. For now. Because I burned to figure out Katie Evans, no matter what it took. Which was probably a huge fucking warning bell, but I ignored it.

Katie released my hands and oohed over the marzipan display. "Look at all the little creatures! And ones made to look like food! This year seems more amazing than the last."

I caught the seller's eyes, and he nodded at me. I'd arranged a few things on my way to meet Katie, which was why I'd been late. "Which is your favorite?"

"Oh, that's a hard question. I like both the penguins

and the reindeer. Although the fruit ones are pretty, too."

"Order whatever you like, baby. It's yours."

She smiled at me. "You're going to spoil me, aren't you?"

"Every chance I get."

Her voice softened. "Thank you, Nolan. You don't have to, you know."

I leaned closer and whispered for her ears only, "I want to, baby. I promise." I leaned back. "Now, take your pick."

As Katie made her selections, I moved to the far side of the stall and took my special order from the owner. He winked and then went to ring up Katie's treats. Once she had them all packaged up, I stood in front of her, with one hand behind my back. "Did you get everything you wanted?"

"Oh, probably too many. But it's Christmas time, so I don't care. I'm treating myself."

I took the package from her hands and passed it to the stall owner. Katie's brows came together, but once I kneeled on the ground, her mouth dropped open.

My heart raced inside my chest. I was an actor, for fuck's sake. This performance should be easy.

And yet, I'd always dreamed that my one—and only —marriage proposal would be to the woman I loved.

This is necessary. If it gets Wendy off your back, that's all that matters.

Clearing my throat, I moved my hand in front of me. A little marzipan box made to look like a present sat on my palm. "We grew up together, Katie. And for so long,

I didn't notice you. I was a fool, of course, to waste all those years. But ever since reconnecting with you this year, and spending so much time with you, and falling in love with you, I knew I'd found my person—the woman I wanted to spend the rest of my life with." I lifted the lid of the present to reveal the ring inside. "Will you do me the great honor of becoming my wife?"

For a second, Katie merely gaped at the ring inside the box. I offered it up toward her, and she snapped back to the present. "Yes, Nolan. Of course I'll marry you."

I removed the ring, set the box aside, and slid it onto the fourth finger of her hand. The dark blue sapphire twinkled under the Christmas lights.

I stared at the ring on her finger, and a sense of rightness and possession and something I couldn't name rushed through me.

Katie tugged at my shirt. I pushed the feelings aside and stood. I didn't waste time hauling her close and kissing her.

Without thinking, I pushed my tongue into her mouth and groaned. I licked and stroked and reveled in her taste and heat. My hands gripped her hips, and I wanted to move them to her ass, to rock her against my already hard cock, and finally hear her sweet cries or moans or whatever sound she made when she came.

Fuck, I burned to feel her warm, soft, naked skin against mine.

Cheers rose up around us, and Katie broke the kiss. After giving me a shy smile, she held up her hand and shouted, "I'm engaged!"

People took pictures and a familiar face came up to

us—the blonde-haired, blue-eyed form of Amber King. "Oh my gosh, Katie! I didn't know things were this serious!"

Katie smiled at her friend. "A girl has to have some secrets."

Amber shook her head and then hugged Katie. "I'm so happy for you, Katie. So happy. First, Emmy getting engaged right after Thanksgiving and now you! Something must be in the air."

Her voice sounded wistful, but I didn't know Amber well enough to ask her about it.

Katie gave her friend a one-armed hug. "Your day will come, Amber. After all, you were the one with all those Barbie weddings when we were kids, pretending it was your own."

Amber's smile looked forced. "Maybe. But enough about me. Can I share the news with Emmy and Abby? Or do you want to share it first yourselves?"

Katie looked at me, and I said, "Since it's still pretty early, I thought we'd visit our families tonight and tell them in person."

Katie shook her head. "Prepare yourself. Mom probably won't let you out of her sight for days."

Amber laughed. "Your mom can be rather enthusiastic."

"That's a nice way to put it," Katie drawled. "Let's visit your family first. That way, if it's late, it'll limit my mom's gushing and planning."

"Whatever you want, baby."

Amber sighed. "And he calls you baby."

I raised an eyebrow in question, and Katie explained,

"She's always wanted a guy who has a cute pet name for her. When it comes down to it, Amber's a hopeless romantic."

Amber's pale cheeks burned bright pink. "No more than anyone else. But I have to get back to my family's stall." She hugged Katie again. "Congrats Katie! I can't wait to hear more about it."

With that, Amber waved and hurried down the aisle.

Even though the show should be over, I took the hand wearing my ring and kissed the back of it. "I hope you like it."

"Of course. I love sapphires, but how did you know?"

I waggled my eyebrows. "A guy has his secrets."

Namely, my sister Abby had helped me pick it out.

"Well, good job. But if we're to hit both families, we should get going."

As she took her marzipan order, I said, "We'll stop and pick up some stollen on the way out."

"You really are spoiling me, aren't you?"

I wanted to say someone should. But instead, I merely nodded and placed a hand on the small of her back. "Come on. I'm sure there will be questions, and we should prepare ourselves."

In addition to the stollen, I spotted a great gift for my aunt and bought that too.

Soon we were on our way back to my family's house and getting our story straight. And the whole time, I kept stealing glances at the ring on Katie's finger.

Chapter Eleven

Katie

Abby: Congrats! <party popper emoji>
Me: Wait, how did you hear about it already?
Abby: Well, I knew it was coming. But it's all over the Starry Hills social media group.
Me: Sigh. I guess privacy is a thing of the past.
Abby: Nolan's pretty good at being discreet, for the most part. But I think he wants people to know about your engagement. Like, he's so smitten he wants to show you off!
Me: I guess.
Abby: What have you done to my friend? The one who'd boast about her boyfriend and how she planned to take L.A. by storm?

Me: I'm just tired and trying to celebrate with my fiancé before facing you all.
Abby: <tongue out emoji> Don't "celebrate" too hard. If you arrive with sex hair, I'm going to throw up.
Me: Hey, Nolan's sexy. <overheated emoji> I can't help it if you don't notice since he's your brother.
Abby: He kind of looks like my mom, so ew.
Me: You look like your mom as well. So does that make you "ew" too?
Abby: <middle finger emoji>
Me: <blowing a kiss emoji> Love you back.

As soon as we were in the car, I couldn't stop staring at the ring on my finger. The dark sapphire was set with white gold and not so big as to get in the way. "Thanks for not putting a boulder on my hand. I'm not strong enough for that."

Nolan had been quiet for a few minutes and started at my voice. "Well, Abby helped me pick it out. That's how I knew you liked sapphires."

"You didn't have to go to that much trouble, Nolan. I mean, a regular diamond would've been fine."

"According to Abby, you think diamonds are boring and lack personality. So why would I get it for you? Even if it's not real, you should have something you like. After all, you'll be wearing it for a while."

He tapped the fingers of one hand on the steering

wheel, and I tried to judge his mood. It was somewhere between nervous and frustrated.

Although what he was frustrated about, I had no idea. Still, I didn't like seeing him upset. So, without thinking, I laid a hand on his thigh and Nolan jumped. I nearly pulled it back, but he placed his hand over mine briefly and squeezed before taking the steering wheel again.

Since I enjoyed his rather firm thigh under my fingers, I kept my hand in place.

Even though I wanted to slide it up, up, until I could maybe determine the state of his dick. Would it be hard again? Or, could he control his erections like his acting?

Before I could imagine Nolan starring in a porno and me being his personal fluffer, I said, "Tell me what's got you so jumpy. And don't say nothing. Because while this may all be fake, we should at least be honest with each other."

His thigh muscle twitched beneath my hand before he replied, "I'm worried about Aunt Lori. I've never been able to lie to her before."

Since touching Nolan scrambled my brains, I removed my hand and sat back in my seat. "Well, it's not technically a lie. We are engaged for now, right? Neither of us will be dating anyone else, only each other."

He let out a slow breath. "It's still not the entire truth, is it?"

"We can call it off, if it's weighing that heavily on you."

"No!"

I blinked at his vehement answer. "No?"

He cleared his throat. "No, we've come so far, and I still have a lot of surprises in store for you. Aren't you the least bit curious to find out what they are?"

As I glanced down at my ring and the stollen and marzipan from the market, I replied, "You've already spoiled me enough, Nolan."

"Not even close. You deserve the moon, Katie, if you want it." He reached over and squeezed my hand before removing it again. "And you know what you have to do, if you want to stop."

I had to tell him I wanted out.

And yet, I didn't. Not just because Nolan supposedly had some more surprises planned for me, either.

Studying his profile, I zeroed in on his mouth. The mouth that could be quiet in groups but didn't have a problem talking with me.

A mouth that liked to kiss me like he might die if he didn't.

Add in his sweet gestures and stepping in to help me with the Mean Girls—but never overstepping and taking over—and a girl could get addicted to having that kind of guy as her own.

Was it so wrong I wanted a little more time with him?

To distract myself, I decided chatter would be best. "I'm looking forward to Christmas at my parents' house and that fancy New Year's party. I can't remember the last time I went to Los Angeles. Maybe as a teenager? We went to Disneyland a few times, but never north to L.A."

"I'll take you wherever you want to go, even Disneyland. Just not Magic Mountain."

"Why not? Six Flags can be fun."

"Promise me you won't laugh."

As he shifted in his seat, I did my best not to smile. "I promise."

"Well, when I was a kid, I threw up on one of the roller coasters. It was me and Beck and West with my parents—the others were too young, or not born yet, and had stayed with my grandparents. The whole time, my brothers badgered me to go on one of the upside-down rides. My dad asked me repeatedly if I was sure, and I said yes, but ended up getting sick. The only good thing about it all was that Beck and West sat in front of me and got the worst of it."

I laughed. "Sounds like karma. But you're not the only one to do something because an older sibling challenged you. Kyle and Cassie convinced me to go on Space Mountain before I was ready. I didn't throw up on the ride, but soon after, and I had to spend the rest of the day in our hotel room. Sometimes, older siblings suck."

"Agreed." Nolan glanced at me and smiled. "This is nice."

"What is?"

"Talking about childhood vomit stories instead of people asking me to take off my shirt. Or being interviewed about my love life and travel plans. Or, even why I don't let anyone tour my house."

"It's your house, so screw them. But I'm curious—are privacy concerns the only reason you don't want to give a tour?"

"No."

"Hmm, so there are other reasons. Aren't you going to tell me what they are?"

Nolan turned down the drive to his family's place. "It's better if I surprise you. After all, you'll be staying at my place in Malibu when you come down to L.A."

"I am?"

"You'll have your own room, don't worry."

Why did I suddenly feel disappointed?

Don't go there. Just keep him talking.

I shifted in my seat. "I'm going to constantly think and wonder what could possibly be in that house of yours. Do you have a sex dungeon? Because that could be fun. Or maybe you have themed rooms for your sexcapades. And hey, don't worry, I don't kink shame."

His lips twitched. "Maybe I have rooms of boxes and am a hoarder. Or, each of my hobbies has a room filled to the brim with supplies or knick knacks? Or maybe my house is completely empty except for a few rooms."

"I like the sex dungeon or kink rooms better."

Nolan laughed as he parked the car. "Those would definitely be good reasons not to give public tours. Because while you're open-minded, some people think if sex isn't missionary, it's weird."

"Hey, consenting adults can do whatever they want. I've read so many romances over the years that I have a stockpile of fantasies and scenarios I'm dying to try out with the right guy."

I nearly slapped my hand over my mouth. Why had I told Nolan that?

Nolan cleared his throat and was about to reply

when the back door of the house opened and Abby rushed out. She knocked on the car window. I opened the door, and she said, "You'd better hurry. Aunt Lori just heard about the proposal and if you don't give her the details, stat, she's going to drive even me insane, which is hard to do."

Saved by Aunt Lori, thank goodness.

I disembarked from the car, and Nolan was already there waiting for me. His gaze met mine and he nodded. "Ready, baby?"

"As much as I can be."

He took and squeezed my hand in reassurance, and we headed for the door. No sooner had we stepped into the hallway than Aunt Lori popped her head out of the living room entrance. "There you are! Now, come in and tell me everything. Because my friend texting me about your engagement was not how I'd hoped to find out about it."

I whispered, "See? I told you we should've called or texted first."

Nolan sighed. "I like doing things in person."

Abby stood nearby and snorted. "You know how Aunt Lori loves her emojis. You could've made an entire story out of them and made her happy."

Aunt Lori waved a hand in dismissal. "We're past that. Let's sit down, have some tea and coffee, and you can fill me in before your brothers get home."

And so we sat and recited the proposal, the buildup to it, and Nolan even gave me a few loving glances and kissed the back of my hand.

The entire time, I swore Aunt Lori watched us. Nolan was right—she would be the hardest to fool.

Since Nolan leaned against me, I could feel his tense muscles. I didn't like it.

So I yawned dramatically and said, "It's been a big day, Aunt Lori. And all I want to do is go home and share the news with my family."

Aunt Lori smiled at me. "Of course you do, child. And I'm happy for you both, truly." She paused to look at each of us in turn. "And I hope you know that you can trust me with anything."

Her words set off alarm bells inside my head. However, Nolan stood and took me with him. "We know, Aunt Lori. I'll be back later."

After saying goodbye to Aunt Lori and Abby—the others hadn't made it home, and the twins and West were staying at Emmy's place—we headed out to the car and got in.

I blurted, "She knows."

Nolan drove down the road. "Maybe, maybe not. Either way, she won't say anything."

I crossed my arms over my chest. "More than anything, I'm mad at your ex for making you do this. She's just a spoiled princess throwing a tantrum, and it's fucking childish."

Nolan shrugged. "I don't like her tactics, but something good has come out of this situation."

"Which is?"

He smiled at me. "I like spending time with you, Katie."

Smiling back at him, I uncrossed my arms. "I like

spending time with you too, Nolan. I'm sorry I called you boring when I was a kid."

He chuckled. "Hey, you were young. And for a kid, constantly reading and practicing lines might seem dull."

I shook my head. "I liked to read, too, so it wasn't that. I guess I was just frustrated that you mostly ignored me. And yes, I know you were nearly six years older than me and that was a much bigger deal back then. But still, Amber had Zach, and once Emmy moved in with your family, she spent a lot more time with Abby. And, well..."

"And you felt a little adrift."

"Yes. I knew my friends loved me, but I desperately wanted a friend of my own. One that would be special."

Although, why I was telling him this right now, I had no idea.

Except I was tired of constantly hiding parts of myself. Nolan liked that I treated him as a normal person and not a celebrity. And to do that meant lowering a few of my own inner walls. Not all, but some.

And this was something I'd wanted to share for so long. Not even the BFF Circle knew how I'd struggled with all the changes after the deaths of Emmy's parents and then the Wolfe siblings' dad.

Nolan finally replied. "I'm sorry I didn't notice you, Katie. But to be honest, I was also dealing with my own problems once my dad died. I just wanted to...escape. So hiding away in books or pretending to be someone else was how I coped. Because during those times, just for a little while, I could pretend to be a happy, normal guy."

He looked at me for a second. "But I notice you now, Katie Evans."

Part of me interpreted his words to mean he noticed me as a woman, one he wanted to be with for real.

But in reality, it probably just meant friendship. Still, I had to say, "And I notice you, Nolan Wolfe. That Drake guy is a stranger to me."

He smiled. "And how will your family see me? As the boy next door or as a movie star?"

"That, I don't know. But just the fact you supposedly want to marry me will be enough to cause chaos."

I sighed dramatically, and Nolan chuckled. "Don't worry, whatever may come, I can handle it. I promise."

He took my hand, squeezed it, and released it to turn onto my family's property.

"You say that now, but you've been to our yearly Fourth of July barbecues and baseball games. We're not a quiet bunch. Well, apart from my dad."

He raised an eyebrow. "Have you met my family?"

I snorted. "They're tame by comparison."

Once Nolan parked, opened my door, and we reached the front porch, the door opened and my mother clapped her hands. "Tell me it's true that I finally get a wedding and maybe some grandchildren!"

My cheeks burned thinking about the making of said children. "Mom, it's not a shotgun wedding. Sheesh."

My mother waved a hand. "I didn't say it was. But I have four children, FOUR, and not a one has gotten married, let alone had or adopted children. Not even a fur baby. I need someone to spoil."

Cassie appeared next to Mom. "If you're that desperate, then get a dog or cat."

"I would, if your father wasn't allergic. Maybe if you got your own place, you could get a cat and let me pet sit."

Cassie muttered, "I'm working on it."

My dad's voice bellowed down the hallway, "Come in or go out. You're letting the heat escape."

My mother ushered us inside and maneuvered between Nolan and me. "Now, Nolan, tell us all about your place in Malibu. I assume that's where you and Katie will be living?"

As my mother continued to interrogate Nolan—and my sister Sam asked about some movie stars—Nolan was polite and smiling the whole time.

Unfortunately, we didn't get any time alone again, not even when he said farewell. Once he'd left, my mother patted my cheek. "Good job, Katie. He was always my favorite of the Wolfe boys. And to think he invited us to stay at his house and let us use his private beach! The summer can't get here soon enough."

Except by summer, Nolan and I would no longer be together.

The thought of rarely seeing Nolan, let alone talking to him, caused sadness to rush through me.

Needing a distraction after the long day, I fetched some wine, a steamy book, and relaxed in a bath.

And the fact my dreams replayed all the steamy parts with me and Nolan instead of the characters from the book? Well, it was a fantastic end to the day, short of actually sleeping next to Nolan himself.

Chapter Twelve

Nolan

Me: Katie? Did you get my last message? You missed our phone call.
Katie: Sorry. I was passed out. I've been sick.
Me: Sick? What's wrong, baby? Tell me.
Katie: Nothing, just a cold. I'll be fine.
Me: Do you have a fever?
Katie: Yes. And my whole body hurts. But...
Me: At least tell me your family is looking after you.
Katie: Er...
Me: They aren't?
Katie: Well, they're visiting my aunt and uncle in Sacramento until Christmas Eve. I have so much family

that we have to do each side at different times for Christmas.

Me: And they just fucking left you there?

Katie: Calm down, Nolan. Cassie wanted to stay, but I told her not to. One of her old high school friends moved up there and she hasn't seen him in forever.

Me: I still can't believe they abandoned you.

Katie: They didn't! I'm not a kid, Nolan. But I'm tired and want to take a nap. So rage text all you want, but I'm going to ignore you now. Good night.

Later the same day as Katie's last text message, I pulled into the Evans place. The plane ride had helped to calm down my anger, but worry had replaced it instead. I'd interrogated my sister, who had said she'd stopped by Katie's place to drop off some soup. And yes, she was really sick. But no, she hadn't been able to stay because she was helping Emmy with a wedding. Not to mention Katie had told all the BFF Circle she was fine, and they didn't need to bother disrupting their day to stay with her.

Yet again, she was shouldering something alone. Katie Evans was indeed a stubborn woman.

I'd wanted to keep questioning Abby, but eventually she told me if I was so worried, to go check on Katie myself.

And so here I was four days before Christmas, in Starry Hills with a care package, and doing my best to keep my temper in check. Oh, I wasn't angry with Katie. No. But I still didn't think her family should've fucking abandoned her.

I debated ringing the doorbell, but didn't want Katie to walk around unnecessarily. So I tried calling her. She picked up on the fourth ring. "Nolan? What do you want?"

Her voice was scratchy and faint. I didn't like it. "I'm at the door and brought a care package. But don't you dare get up. Is the door unlocked? Or is there a spare key somewhere?"

"Wait, you're here? Why?"

Her voice sounded weaker, and I gripped the phone tighter. "I'm here to check on you. Tell me how to get in, Katie, or I'll have to break down the fucking door."

She sighed. "I'm fine, really. But to save the door, there's a key in a fake rock to the left of the porch, near the house."

I found it. "Where's your room?"

"Just leave the stuff downstairs. I'm all sweaty and gross. Trust me, you don't want to see me."

"Katie."

She sighed. "Fine, but it's your nose that will suffer. I'm at the top of the stairs, the third door on the right."

"I'll be there in a second."

I clicked End and unlocked the door. Soon I found the right room and knocked before turning the knob.

Inside, it was overly warm and smelled of camphor. I barely paid attention to the floral wallpaper or the giant map on the wall with pins in it. I walked over to the bed and my heart clenched.

Katie lay on her back, her eyes closed, breathing heavily. She was also far paler than normal. I placed a hand on her forehead and mentally swore—she was burning up.

Her eyes fluttered open, and at her unfocused look, I made a decision. After moving my hand to cup her cheek, I said, "You're not well, baby. Let me take you to the clinic."

"I'll be fine. I always heal pretty quickly. I just need some water and some sleep."

"You have a fever, you're sweaty, and you're having a hard time breathing. You need to see a doctor."

I set down the care package and looked around. Finding a throw blanket at her little desk, I picked it up and threw back the bedcovers.

Katie shivered. "That's fucking cold. Just let me sleep."

I took her hand. "If you're as well as you say, then squeeze my hand hard."

She tried, but there was barely any pressure. My stomach churned at how weak she was. What if something happened to her? What if she died from her stubbornness and I never saw her again?

No. I wouldn't let that happen. "You definitely need to see a doctor. I'm going to carry you to the car and drive you."

The fight went out of her—another bad sign. "Okay."

I helped her sit up and wrapped the blanket around her. Then I lifted her into my arms, and she leaned heavily against me, her head resting on my shoulder. I held her tight and kissed her forehead. "Come on. Let's get you better, baby."

I could barely hear her reply. "Nolan, I've missed you."

My heart skipped a beat. We hadn't seen each other in person since the day of the proposal. And as busy as I had been with my job, every night I had stared at my phone, wanting to talk to Katie. To the one person who wouldn't ask for juicy details about the actors I'd worked with that day. No, instead she'd ask if the food was better, or if the make-up artist had finally proposed to their partner, or about the little things that had happened during the day, as if it were any other job.

She was the only person who ever seemed to see *me* and not just my fame.

After kissing her forehead, I whispered, "I've missed you too, baby."

I carried her down the stairs and settled her into my car. The entire drive into Starry Hills, I kept looking at Katie. She was asleep; her face was really pale, and she kept shivering.

By the time I pulled into the parking lot of Dr. Washington's clinic, my nerves were on edge. Even more so once I had Katie in my arms again. As soon as I entered the building, I barked, "She's really sick and needs a doctor!"

The person behind the reception came over. "This isn't an emergency room. Should I call an ambulance?"

I readjusted my grip on Katie. "But Dr. Washington said she'd see emergency cases if they didn't require surgery. My fiancée is ill. Really ill. Please. I just want the doctor to see what's wrong. And the county hospital is so far away."

Katie murmured something incomprehensible, and I hugged her tighter against me.

The receptionist sighed. "Let me check with the doctor."

Since it was so close to Christmas and people were probably traveling or with family, the waiting area was empty. I whispered into Katie's ear, "Hold on, baby. Let's get you better. You've been dying to see what I got you for Christmas, and you need to be healthy before I can give it to you."

She said nothing, and my gut clenched.

The dark-haired, dark-skinned form of Dr. Washington rushed into the reception area. She took one look at Katie and gestured. "Follow me."

I complied and soon laid Katie down on a hospital bed. I didn't even get the chance to brush the hair off her face before the doctor motioned me aside. "Let me check her over. Wait in the chair over there."

Reluctantly, I obeyed and sat down in the chair. I watched as the doctor listened to Katie's lungs, checked her pulse, and took her temperature. By that point, a nurse had come in and was sent off on an errand.

Soon, they had Katie hooked up to an IV drip. I tried to stand up, but Dr. Washington gave me a look. "Stay there until I'm finished, or I'll banish you to the hall."

Nodding, I sat back down and watched the doctor work.

I hated being so fucking helpless. It seemed to be the story of my life. No matter what I suggested, my family always turned down my offers of help. All the Wolfes were stubborn, yes. But it fucking hurt when they kept declining money or other types of assistance from me. Beck letting me record videos for the winery had been my only victory.

And now there was Katie. Even if the engagement was fake, she should've reached out to me. Maybe even asked me to check on her.

Why did no one ever want to rely on me?

Rubbing my hands over my face, I told myself to stop the fucking pity party. I would do just fine and survive, as always. Right now, all that mattered was Katie getting well.

I had no idea how much time passed before the doctor walked over to me. As soon as I stood, I asked, "What's wrong with her?"

"I'm waiting on some tests to be sure, but I think she has both the flu and strep throat. One or the other is a lot easier to manage, but together they can be more dangerous. It's good that you brought her in because she'll need antibiotics for the strep. Plus, she's extremely dehydrated." The doctor studied me a second before asking, "How long has she been this ill?"

I ran a hand through my hair. "I don't know. I live and work in L.A., and we mostly text and call when we're apart. The last time we talked on the phone was maybe five days ago? Six? I've been busy with my job, and the days have kind of blurred together."

Dr. Washington nodded. "I get that. Well, I'd like for her to stay on the drip for an hour. In the meantime, I'll send her prescription out and it should be ready by the time you leave. Once you get her home, make sure she rests, drinks plenty of fluids, and takes the antibiotics until they're gone."

"Yes, Dr. Washington. Thank you."

"Just promise me one thing, okay?"

"Anything."

She raised her eyebrows. "Next time, don't shout at my staff like that. I know you were worried, but it doesn't make us work any faster."

I resisted shifting my feet. "Er, sorry. I promise I'll be a true gentleman next time."

Dr. Washington nodded. "Good. Then I'll go write that prescription. You can sit with her, if you like."

Once the doctor and nurse were gone, I pulled up a chair next to Katie's bed and took her hand. I brought it to my lips and kissed it. Seeing her unconscious and hooked up to the drip made one thing crystal clear to me —Katie had become more than a means of getting rid of my ex. She meant something to me, maybe more than I was ready to admit.

All I knew was that I wanted her as my girlfriend for real. The trick would be figuring out how to win her over, given my complicated life.

Chapter Thirteen

Katie

I blinked my eyes open to near-darkness. My entire body ached, my throat was on fire, and I felt as if I'd run twenty miles and promptly collapsed from fatigue.

I had a fuzzy memory of Nolan charging into my room and carrying me somewhere before I passed out.

But that couldn't be right, could it?

My eyes slowly adjusted, and I noticed I wasn't in my room. The walls were dark green, the bed was a lot bigger, and the window was in the wrong place.

As I tried to figure out where I was, I noticed someone sitting in a chair next to the bed, their head propped atop their arms on the mattress, snoring softly.

"Nolan?" I croaked.

He stirred, sat up, and blinked his eyes. He turned on a small lamp next to the bed. "Katie? Are you awake?" He placed a hand on my forehead and whispered, "Thank fuck. Your fever's gone."

Even though talking felt like rubbing sandpaper against my throat, I asked, "Where are we?"

"Shh. Let me get you something to drink first. I have a sports drink that should help you a little."

I wanted to say screw the drink and demand he tell me what was going on.

But then I tried to move, and it felt as if my limbs were made of stone.

Nolan returned with a cup and straw dangling over the side and set it on the nightstand. He said, "Let's get you up, baby. And then you can have some of this."

Too tired to protest, he had to haul me upright. I bit my lip to keep from groaning.

Once I was nestled against the pillows at my back, Nolan caressed my cheek. For a few beats, he merely stared at me, his eyes filled with...relief?

After picking up the glass, he put the straw to my lips. I took a few sips, the cool liquid soothing my throat a little, and I sighed. "Thank you. What happened? Where are we?"

He sat down on the bed, his hip against mine, and took my hand. "You were really sick, and I came to check on you." He explained about taking me to the clinic and the doctor's diagnosis. Then he added, "I brought you here, to my place, so I could take care of you."

"Nolan, you didn't have to."

He cupped my cheek. "Shh. Of course I had to. You're my responsibility."

"But—"

"No buts, Katie. It's okay to ask for help sometimes. Especially with me. For now, just let me be your nurse. You can consider it your Christmas present."

"What happened to my big surprise?"

He winked. Despite how tired and sick I was, it still made my heart skip a beat.

"I'm teasing you. Besides, I can't wait to see your face when you get your actual present. Although you can't have it until you get better, so that means you have to rest. Let me take care of you, baby. Stay here with me until you're stronger."

I should ask him to take me home. Being sick wasn't anything new, and my family would return in a couple days.

However, just sitting with Nolan and having him near made me feel better. Maybe staying at his place would speed up my recovery.

Plus, it'd be good practice for when I went to L.A. for New Year's and had to sleep under the same roof as him. Yes, that was the main reason I should stay.

Liar.

I replied, "Okay, I'll stay. But I draw the line at you helping me to the bathroom."

"Deal." He cleared his throat and then added, "Would you mind if I slept in here for tonight? Your fever just broke, and I want to make sure you won't relapse or get worse."

Imagining Nolan in bed with me made my cheeks

hot. "Well, it's not as if you're going to ravish me in this state, so I don't see why not."

He leaned forward. "You're still fucking beautiful to me, baby."

His words made my throat tighten. I so desperately wanted them to be real. But I knew they weren't. He probably was trying to cheer me up, nothing else.

"Katie?"

"Fine, you can sleep in here. Although if you get sick, you can't blame me."

"I rarely get sick, so I'll take my chances."

He knocked on the headboard—his bed was solid wood, with designs carved into it.

I smiled. "And yet, you still knocked on wood."

"Damn straight. I'm not taking any chances."

I laughed, but then quickly moaned. "Don't do that. It hurts to laugh."

"Sorry, baby. I'll try my best not to charm you off your feet. Which is probably easy, given I don't have Zach-levels of charisma."

"I like your type of charm. And you might not have Zach's outgoing personality, but you're sweet, Nolan." He made a face, and I added, "It's not a bad thing, I promise."

"If you say so. Women always seem to want the assholes or fixer uppers."

"Well, I like you just as you are, Nolan Wolfe." I couldn't hold back a yawn. "But as much as I want to keep talking, I'm tired."

He stood, retrieved a cool cloth from the side table,

and gently wiped my forehead, cheeks, and neck. I moaned in relief.

For a second, our eyes met and time slowed. No one had really ever taken care of me like this since I was a kid. And even then, no one had looked at me with such tenderness like Nolan was doing right now.

It would be so easy to fall for him.

Thankfully, Nolan broke eye contact to discard the cloth in the bathroom. Once he returned, he crawled to the other side of the bed—above the covers—and situated a blanket over him that he'd found somewhere.

If I wasn't so sick and smelly, I'd tell him to get under the covers with me.

Nolan leaned over, kissed my forehead, and whispered, "Sweet dreams, baby."

"You too."

And soon I fell asleep to dreams of Nolan holding me close in bed, his warm body around mine, and feeling safe and wanted and treasured in a way I'd only ever read about in books.

Chapter Fourteen

Nolan

Beck: You'd better get your ass over here for December 23rd.
Me: Why? I usually come over on Christmas Eve or Christmas Day.
Zach: Aunt Lori says it's a big surprise, one for all of us.
Abby: Not even I could get her to spill the secret, and I tried. Hard. But she's been texting a lot.
West: She texts all the time.
Abby: <tongue out emoji> This is different. No smiles or laughter, just furrowed brows. Almost like she's willing for something to happen.
Zach: Uh oh. That can't be good. She's not putting together a surprise wedding for West and Emmy, is she?

West: Fuck no. She'd better not. I want Emmy as my wife, but on her terms.
Beck: I doubt she'd do that. She's been gushing about Emmy and West's wedding date and their soon-to-be conceived children.
West: WTF?
Zach: <laughing emoji> Well, your super sperm got two kids at one go before. Maybe she's banking on that again.
Me: That's not how it works. <eye roll emoji>
Zach: Well, Wolfe family members are rather fertile. There are six of us. And even our Wolfe aunt in Sun Falls had five kids.
Beck: Then you be the Wolfe siblings with five or six kids. Not me.
Zach: Hell no. Five mini-me's running around would fucking drive me bonkers.
Abby: <laughing emoji> Zach will have ten. That's a nice even number.
Zach: <horror face emoji> Noooooo. Besides, wasn't Nolan the one who wanted all the kids?
Me: Since when?
Beck: Since that one night we went drinking a few months ago. You mentioned it. I hope Katie's on board with the plan.
Me: I don't remember any of that.
Abby: Katie loves kids. She's also really good with them. So you'd better get started, Nolan. <man feeding a baby emoji> You have that big house in Malibu to fill.
Me: What time do I have to be there on the 23rd?

Zach: Someone's changing the subject.
West: By 1 p.m. It's a lunch surprise.
Me: Fine. I'll be there. Maybe Aunt Lori's surprise is an arranged marriage for Zach.

Katie stayed at my place for only a day and a half before she demanded I take her home. She slept most of the time, so we didn't have time to talk or tease or even strategize about New Year's. However, I'd managed to sleep next to her both nights. I'd wanted to hold her in my arms, but kept my distance so she could get her rest.

However, just being there when she was vulnerable and her trusting me to take care of her had made me more determined than ever to be with her for real.

Although, as I pulled into the parking lot of my family's place, I pushed those thoughts aside. When it came to Aunt Lori, a surprise could be anything. One year for Christmas, she'd bought Victorian clothes similar to what you'd find in any of the *A Christmas Carol* movies and made us go caroling.

Granted, we'd all been younger back then and less likely to tell her no. Even so, the sky was the limit.

Since my family exchanged presents on Christmas Day, I didn't have to lug anything to the door. Before I could even knock, Aunt Lori opened it. "You're here! Finally."

"I'm two minutes late. I had to wait for a cow to cross the road."

"Yes, yes. Come in! You're going to love this, I promise."

She tugged me down the hallway and into the living room. I noticed everyone but West's little family had arrived and then did a double-take at the man wearing an arm cast. "Zane?"

My younger brother smiled. Even though he and Zach were fraternal twins and only looked a little alike, Zane had the trademark Wolfe dark hair and height. His eyes were hazel, and there were a lot more lines around them than I remembered. Plus, he now had a scar on his cheek.

I walked over, clapped his shoulder, and gave him a one-armed hug. "It's good to see you, brother." I leaned back. "But how?"

Zane readjusted his arm in a sling and maneuvered slowly into the armchair. "All I'm allowed to say is there was an explosion, I was hurt pretty badly, and I was honorably discharged."

I frowned. Zane had joined the SEALs at seventeen, and it had been his entire life for the past ten years.

Zach sat in the chair next to his twin. "It sucks, as I know how much Zane loved the SEALs. But hey, it means I might get to see my brother more than once every year or two."

Abby rolled her eyes. "Right, because seeing you is the only thing that matters in his life."

Zach grinned. "Damn straight."

Beck sat on the couch, his arm around Sabrina next to him. "Zane's going to stay here for a while, until he figures out what to do next."

Aunt Lori spoke. "And he still hasn't decided whether he'll stay in Starry Hills or not, no matter how much I ask."

Not wanting Aunt Lori to start guilt-tripping Zane, I changed the subject. "Just how hurt are you? Can you go out?"

Zane raised an eyebrow. "If you're inviting me to a party in L.A. or to ride motorcycles together, that will have to wait."

I rolled my eyes. "Do you remember me at all?"

Zane snorted. "Fair point. I can leave the house for short periods of time, if that's what you're asking. Even if Aunt Lori would rather chain me to this chair to keep me close."

"Only because I love you, lad, and it's been so long since we were all together for Christmas."

The doorbell rang, and Abby went to answer it. West, Emmy, Avery, and Wyatt entered the room.

West blinked. "Zane?"

Avery tilted her head. "The Uncle Zane I've never met?"

With Zach's help, Zane got to his feet and walked over to Avery. He put out a hand. "Zach says you're the princess of the manor. Nice to meet you, your highness. I would bow, except then I might fall over and not be able to get up. I'll need a rescue team."

He winked, and Avery giggled. "You're funny, like Uncle Zach."

The corner of Zane's mouth kicked up. "I try, but he's funnier." He turned to Wyatt. "And you must be my new favorite nephew."

Wyatt crossed his arms over his chest. "I'm your only nephew."

"I heard you like horses, which I love too. So you'll probably always be my favorite."

Zane winked again, and Wyatt smiled.

Emmy and West walked up to Zane. Emmy spoke up. "Zane. It's been so long! It's good to see you."

He hugged her, and then replied, "Long enough that you've fallen in love with my brother and want to marry the grumpy bastard."

Avery nodded. "She's going to be our new mom. And she's the best. She even has a swimming pool."

Zane chuckled. "Having a pool does tip someone over into greatness."

West rolled his eyes and then shook Zane's hand. "I forgot how annoying you are. Fuck, you and Zach together? I'm going to need a lot of ibuprofen. And whiskey."

"Bad word, Daddy," Avery scolded.

Aunt Lori jumped in. "Now that everyone's here, I can tell you the other part of my surprise. The six of you are going to The Watering Hole for a few drinks while Emmy, Sabrina, Avery, and Wyatt help me with last-minute cookie decorations." She glanced at me. "I'm sorry to hear that Katie still isn't feeling well."

"Me, too. She hasn't seen Zane in forever, either."

Sabrina stood. "Avery, if we hurry, we might be able to make those cookies you came up with a few months ago. Should we try?"

"Yes! Come on, Emmy. You need to learn how to make them, too. I already taught Sabrina."

Wyatt sighed. “Do I really have to help? I hate baking. It’s boring.”

Aunt Lori placed her hands on his shoulders. “You can help me wrap some presents, and then you can pick a Christmas movie to watch with everyone later.”

“Okay. I know just the one to annoy Avery. It’ll be great.”

Avery stuck out her tongue. “You suck, Wyatt.”

Aunt Lori made a shooing motion. “Now, go, the six of you. Try to get back by dinnertime so we can all watch the movie together. And yes, we all will. Don’t even think of trying to sneak off. Understood?”

We all mumbled, “Yes, Aunt Lori.”

No matter how old we got, some things would never change.

Zach slapped me on the back. “Come on, the car I ordered should be here soon.”

As I stood together with all my siblings for the first time in years, I wondered how the evening would go. I could loosen up a little with Beck, West, and maybe Zach. And Abby was good at keeping us all talking. But Zane? I didn’t even know who he was anymore.

Still, as we all piled into the van and headed to the bar, I decided to make an effort. “Since Zane hasn’t been around in a while, he can pick our first drink.”

Abby nodded. “Sometimes we do that, as part of our theme night. While we can’t have a full-blown one—complete with shirts or hats or what have you—you get to select the drink. Then we all have to have the same thing and can’t refuse. Oh, and you can pick the jukebox music, too.”

Beck drawled, "Just don't pick Starry Wolfe wine because we have that at home for free."

Zach sighed. "As if he'd do that. Seriously, Beck."

Zane smiled. "Same old Beck—offering sage advice, even if it's unwanted."

Beck flipped his middle finger. "This is the thanks I get for swaying Aunt Lori to let you join the SEALs."

"I forgot about that," I said.

Aunt Lori had been against it, mostly because her late husband had also been a Navy SEAL and had died far too young.

Zane said, "I'm still grateful for your help, Beck. But I tease you because you're my brother. And given my arm, you can't hit me, no matter how annoying I am. So I plan to take full advantage of it."

Beck raised an eyebrow. "I could still knee you in the balls."

West grunted. "And then I'd dump your ass into the horse trough, Beck. Again."

Zane asked, "Again? When did this happen? This is a story I need to hear."

As West told us about how he and Beck had gotten into a fight not long after West had returned to Starry Hills, some of the ease of our childhood returned. And as the night went on—Zane made us drink fruity, sweet cocktails all night—story after story came out. Most of them were from before Dad had died.

By the time we left, Zane wasn't as much of a stranger as before. He sat next to me on the ride home, and as Beck and Zach squabbled over something like always, Zane said quietly, "Congrats on your success,

Nolan. Even in my remote corners of the world, I tried to see as many of your movies as I could."

"Thanks. It's been a double-edged sword, but I'm still glad I took the leap."

"Yes, I heard about your ex causing problems. But you ended up finding love at home, huh, with Katie Evans?"

I couldn't judge his tone. "Yes. She sees me as a normal guy, and it's nice."

"She's pretty, too. And full of life. Are you worried about unleashing her on L.A.?"

Anger flared in my belly. "She's cheerful and playful and kind. Unleashing her makes Katie sound like some untamed animal. So watch your words, Zane. I fucking mean it."

Zane put up the hand of his uninjured arm, palm forward. "Woah, I'm sorry, Nolan. I didn't mean to insult her. She was just really outgoing in middle and high school. And from what I've heard, she can still be that way. Your ex will most definitely use it against her, too. You need to think of some contingency plans, in case things go south."

I studied Zane's expression for a few seconds. Sure, he could smile and joke like his twin. But there was something older, more mature, and even a little tired-looking about my younger brother now. His life as a SEAL had definitely changed him. I wondered what had happened to him over the last decade.

But if Zane were to share that with anyone, it would be with Zach and not me. "I know. And we're working on it." I paused and asked, "So, has the last ten years been one long backup plan after another for you?"

"Something like that. And if you need any help with strategy, I'm here to listen and analyze. I may not know all the ins and outs of being famous, but if you give me enough information, I can figure out just about anything."

"Thanks, Zane. I hope I never need your help like that, but I appreciate it all the same."

Zane nodded, and then Zach asked him when they could hit the town and look for women to flirt with.

I shared a glance with Abby, and she shrugged. It looked more and more like Zach and Amber's once close friendship would never be more than that.

As soon as we arrived home, Avery had us tasting cookies and then we all sat down to watch a movie—*A Christmas Story*. Avery hated it because she thought the boys made poor choices the whole time. It wasn't my favorite either, but sitting with my family, eating popcorn and cookies, all while Zach and Zane made wisecrack comments, reminded me of happier times.

If only Katie had been there, sitting in my lap, it would've been perfect.

Chapter Fifteen

Katie

Me: Bring wine with you. Lots of it. Today's going to get ugly.
Nolan: I'm scared now.
Me: Competitions in my family are vicious. Be careful or Kyle will challenge you to a fistfight to defend his honor, or something else ridiculously stupid.
Nolan: We're talking about board games, right?
Me: Or card games. But yes, it's that bad. And if anyone spots a cheater, watch out.
Nolan: Maybe me being there will calm things down.
Me: Sam had this boyfriend once, he had Thanksgiving with us, and he actually snuck off and broke up with my sister before dinner.

Nolan: Sounds like a loser, then.
Me: Be serious, Nolan.
Nolan: I won't run away, baby. I promise.
Me: You say that now....
Nolan: If nothing else, know that I always keep my word. I won't leave you, baby. Even if I have to fight your brother in a duel.
Me: What century is this?
Nolan: I can be from any century. It's kind of my job.
Me (typed but deleted): I wouldn't mind if you were a Highlander, tossed me over your shoulder, and whisked me off to your castle. Where you'd do extremely dirty things to me.
Me (actual reply instead): <tongue out emoji> Just don't be late.

I'd been a coward.

I had wanted to stay with Nolan another day. He'd offered to look after me, fetch whatever I needed from my parents' place, and do his best not to interrupt my beauty sleep.

But the better I'd felt, the harder it'd been to keep my distance from him and not do something stupid, like ask him to cuddle.

So I'd asked to go home. My family would be back later the day he dropped me off, and I really did feel better.

The distance also gave me time to reinforce my heart

and my lady parts. Nolan Wolfe was off limits. I needed to remember that.

Now it was Christmas Day, I was at about ninety-eight percent healthy and no longer infectious, and I currently held together a turkey butt while my mom stitched it together.

She'd been nattering on about weddings, and I'd kind of tuned her out. However, I caught her saying, "Maybe I should come move in with you for a few weeks after the wedding, to get you settled."

I loved my mother. But no matter how much—or even the fact Nolan and I would never marry—I wasn't about to let her think staying during a honeymoon was okay. "No, Mom. I mean, would you have wanted Grandma to stay with you right after you were married?"

"She came a few days after, in fact."

"And how did that go? For you and for Dad?"

"Well, your dad wasn't keen on it. But it made us rather creative when it came to sneaking off to have sex."

Since I was holding a raw turkey together, I couldn't plug my ears. "La, la, la, la, la, LA."

My mother rolled her eyes. "You wouldn't be here without me and your father having fun."

"Maybe. But I really, really don't want to hear the details. I like to pretend it's the 1950s and you have separate beds, like on some of the old TV shows."

"Why would I do that? Your dad is far too handsome, and it'd be a pity for him to sleep alone."

I groaned. "Can you finish the turkey so I can run far, far away?"

My mother clicked her tongue. "Katherine Ruth, grow up."

As I tried to think of a reply—my mother using my middle name meant she was truly annoyed—the doorbell rang. Cassie shouted, "I got it!"

Then I heard a squeal and smiled. Nolan was here.

As soon as he appeared in the kitchen doorway, I forgot all about my mother and her raunchy sexcapades. When Nolan's eyes met mine, I smiled wider. When the corner of his mouth kicked up, my heart skipped a beat.

I had it bad. Which meant I needed to be careful.

After we all said, "Merry Christmas," Nolan spoke. "Katie must be feeling better if she's helping with the turkey."

Cassie rolled her eyes. "Yes, because holding a turkey butt together requires vast amounts of strength."

I replied, "Well, Mom *does* overstuff it."

My mother shook her head as she cut the thread. "You love my stuffing, so stop complaining. And I can see you want some alone time with your man, so go. But the first game starts in twenty minutes. If you're not back in time, I'll send Kyle to find you. And do you really want your brother to see you half-naked?"

I'd just started washing my hands. "Mom!"

My mother winked. "I was young once. Now, go on. It's Cassie's turn to help with the pie crust."

Cassie waggled her eyebrows at me, and after drying my hands, I lightly punched her arm.

As soon as I reached Nolan, he leaned down and kissed me gently. "I'm glad to see you're feeling better, baby."

"Not here." I took his hand and tugged. I took him upstairs, to my room, and shut the door.

Nolan and I stared at each other, and the room seemed to shrink.

Then it dawned on me—I was alone with Nolan in a bedroom and I wasn't sick.

I leaned toward him, but he released me and put his hands in his pockets. A clear sign that the show was over until we were in front of my family again.

Pushing aside my disappointment, I leaned back against the door. "Did you have a nice Christmas with your family?"

Nolan shrugged. "It was good and yet weird at the same time. All six of us haven't been together since my dad died."

"And where did you fit into the group this time?" He raised his brows in question, and I added, "I mean, you always seemed apart from the rest once your dad passed. And thanks to Abby, I know you, Beck, West, and Zach sometimes get drinks together. However, did Zane change the dynamics?"

As soon as I finished, I knew I was getting into extremely personal stuff. The kind of things you might ask a boyfriend, but not a fake one.

However, as Nolan turned to the window, he answered, "Zane suggested they all come visit me in Malibu, and they all said yes. He's far more observant than he was when he was little. I think his time in the SEALs changed him."

"We all grow up and change a little, I suppose. But

that's good, right, that they want to visit you since you said they never visited before?"

He turned back toward me. "I suppose. Although you'll be there before them, provided you feel well enough for New Year's."

Nolan clearly didn't want to talk about his family visiting, so I didn't pursue it. Instead, I walked over to him. "I'm not on death's door anymore. I'll be fine."

He ran a finger down my cheek, and I leaned toward him. "I'm glad, Katie. I can't wait for you to stay with me in L.A."

His words had so many layers. "Why? So you can finally rub me in your ex's face in person?"

She might show up at the New Year's party, according to Nolan. But I wasn't scared. Mostly. Because I wanted to see her face-to-face.

He cupped my cheek. "No. I'm glad for other reasons."

"Other reasons, hm? And what would they be?"

"First, tell me, are you truly feeling better, baby? I need to know."

"I am. I promise."

"Well." His thumb stroked my cheek, and I nearly purred. "I think we should practice more before the party. And we need privacy. Like we have right now."

And he kissed me.

As soon as his lips touched mine, heat rushed through my body, and I pressed against him. As Nolan's tongue stroked mine, his hands went to my ass. He squeezed and lightly slapped and rocked me against his already hard cock.

I moaned and dared to grab his ass. His hard, round ass that I wanted to dig my nails into.

One of his hands moved further down my body, down, down, until he was inches from the hem of my dress. Then he froze.

I whispered, "Don't stop. Please, don't stop."

His mouth claimed mine again. His hand went under my dress until he finally brushed my clit. Even through my panties, his heated touch made me ache. I wanted more, so much more.

To encourage him, I maneuvered a hand between us and gently cupped his erection. Nolan moaned and then bit my lip. "Harder. Touch me harder, baby."

If I had any reason left in my brain, I would've stopped. Nothing good could come from this.

But between Nolan's kisses and his light caresses against my clit and pussy, I was beyond rational thought. I squeezed his cock, rubbed it, and he finally snuck a finger beneath the material of my panties and pushed inside me.

I cried out and arched against him. He whispered, "Tell me to stop."

"Don't stop."

"Then kiss me."

I did, claiming his mouth, stroking his tongue, and getting lost in his taste. I continued to squeeze and stroke his dick, and Nolan rewarded me by brushing my clit with his thumb.

I was close, so close. I tried to move on his finger, but he pulled out of me. I growled in frustration. "Don't tease me."

"I need to taste you, baby. Tell me I can."

Just the image of Nolan's head between my thighs made me even hotter. "Yes. Fuck, yes."

He maneuvered me toward the bed, kissing me along the way, and soon I sat on the mattress. He ran his hands up my thighs, down, and back again. I spread my legs wider.

Nolan's gaze burned into mine, and my heart raced as my core pulsed. This was finally going to happen. Here. In my bedroom. With Nolan Wolfe.

With a growl, he knelt in front of me and had just run his hands to my inner thighs when there was a knock on the door.

We both froze. The knocking continued, and my brother's voice came through the door. "You have one minute before I barge in. It's game time and you two need to come downstairs."

Son of a bitch. I shouted, "Go away, Kyle!"

"No. We can't start until you two come downstairs, and I have somewhere to be."

For a second, I wondered where the hell my brother needed to go on Christmas Day. But as Nolan stood, turned away, and ran a hand through his hair, my irritation at being interrupted notched up. "Fuck off, Kyle. You're a grown man. You can leave when you want."

He banged on the door, but Nolan spoke. "We'll be down soon."

I blinked, but Nolan kept his back to me.

And just like that, my body turned to ice. He probably regretted what we'd been about to do and wanted to get back in front of witnesses as soon as possible.

Closing my eyes, I took a few deep breaths. Kyle's interruption had been for the best. Crossing that line would've made things awkward as hell, for sure. And I still had months and months before I could break the engagement.

Since thinking about that day made me want to cry, I stood and smoothed my skirt. "Go down first, Nolan. I need to clean up."

"I need a minute."

My cheeks heated as I remembered his long, hard cock underneath my fingers. "Of course. I'm going to use the bathroom, so come out when you're ready."

Without another word, I fled the room and shut myself in the bathroom. Leaning my hands on the counter, I looked at my reflection in the mirror. My hair was mussed, my cheeks flushed, and my lips were swollen. Usually those signaled a good time.

However, for me and Nolan, it spelled out a possible disaster. Would he even want to keep up our fake engagement? Did he think I was just another fan throwing herself at him for his body, fame, or money? Even though it was more than that—because yes, Nolan Wolfe was extremely hot—he might not want the truth.

Namely, that I wanted Nolan as my own. For real. And not for a matter of months.

That wasn't the deal you made, Katie. You know that.

Even if he was turning out to be the boyfriend I never knew I'd wanted. Maybe even needed.

After a few more deep breaths, I tidied myself up and stood. I whispered to myself, "Time to pretend

Nolan didn't nearly make you come from his fingers and ask to lick between your thighs."

Yes, that would be the best plan—to pretend the last twenty minutes had never happened.

And so I went downstairs, smiling, and put up the cheery, outgoing facade I'd learn to use as armor as a teen. Nolan might not be a bully, but in a manner of speaking, he was a bigger threat to me than any of the Mean Girls of Starry Hills had ever been.

Chapter Sixteen

Nolan

Jenn: Everything's booked and ready to go. It was no easy feat, and I deserve a bonus.
Me: I already gave you a big Christmas bonus.
Jenn: But who else could coordinate what I did?
Me: Merry Christmas to you too.
Jenn: It's not over. I'm waiting for Wendy to ruin it.
Me: I hope not. Usually she goes silent for Christmas week to ski with her parents.
Jenn: Well, she hasn't said much since your proposal video leaked. But it's only a matter of time.
Me: Stop ruining the day. Go have fun with your wife.
Jenn: Go have fun with your...fiancée. Maybe naked. That would loosen you up.

Me: Why do I keep you around?
Jenn: Because I'm fucking awesome, that's why.
Me: I'll think on that.
Jenn: <tongue out emoji> Merry Christmas, Nolan. Have some fun and relax, for once.

As I stared out the window and got my dick under control, I could still feel how wet and swollen Katie had been for me. Then she'd basically offered herself up and just before I could finally taste her sweet pussy, her fucking brother had interrupted.

Yes, rationally, I knew the interruption had been a good thing. Our relationship wasn't supposed to go beyond kisses, after all.

But I'd never been so hard in my life. And when Katie had squeezed my dick through my pants? Hell, I'd nearly come right then and there.

With a sigh, I stared out the window and at the big milking barn in the distance. How was I supposed to face not only Katie, but her family now?

And what the hell was I supposed to do about sharing a house with the one woman I shouldn't touch? At least, until I let her out of the deal and asked her to be my girlfriend for real?

However, since I had plenty of time to think about things between now and when Katie would come to L.A.—if she was still coming—I pushed my desire aside.

I went into the hall, saw the bathroom was empty, and cleaned up. By the time I got downstairs, my erection was gone and my blood had cooled.

I found Katie's entire family in the dining room, sitting around the table, with some kind of board game all laid out.

Katie spotted me first and smiled shyly, her eyes uncertain. *Fuck.* I hated that I'd done that to her.

I sat down beside her and whispered, "We'll talk later, okay?" Once she nodded, I turned toward her brother. Who glared at me from across the table.

Kyle grunted. "Next time, take that stuff somewhere else. I'd rather not know that someone is defiling my sister."

Sam leaned forward. "Ooh, you were defiled, huh? You definitely have to share the details later."

Her other sister looked about to say something, but the dad of the family—Henry—whistled until he had everyone's attention. "Do you want to play or not? Because I'd rather sit in my new recliner and watch TV."

The Evans' mom—named Jody—patted her husband's arm. "Of course we want to play. It wouldn't be Christmas without board games."

I glanced down and saw it was *Wits & Wagers*, a game where someone asked a trivia question, you wrote down your answer, and then put it facedown to place your "bet" in a box. If you were right, then you got chips based on your wager.

Jody asked, "Have you played before, Nolan?"

I nodded. "My sister made me play this before."

Henry grunted. "Good. Then let's get started. And remember the rules—any arguing for more than twenty seconds means you lose chips. Do it a second time, and you're out of the game."

Katie whispered, "And you'll also have to do the dishes later."

Jody waved a hand. "Nolan's our guest, so of course he won't be doing the dishes. But the rule still stands for the rest of you." She rubbed her hands together. "Now, let's get started."

As the game went on, it was apparent how seriously the Evans took their games. There was little talking. And if I tried asking something once I'd written my answer, I was shushed and glared at.

Part of me wanted to win, but soon I thought it'd be more fun to be as ridiculous as possible. So when the question was, "How many inches tall is the Oscar statuette?" I wrote, "689 inches."

When I flipped it over, Cassie snorted. "That's more than 57 feet. I get wanting to display and show it off, but that's akin to building a temple like the Romans did back in the day."

Kyle's answer had been closest—13 inches instead of 13.5 inches—and he collected his earnings. "Didn't you win one of those, Nolan? You should've known the answer."

I shrugged. "Yes, I did, but it's in my closet somewhere."

Katie blinked. "You keep your Oscar in the closet? Why?"

"Well, it's nice and all. But I'm an actor because I

enjoy it, not because I need a statue to tell me how good I am."

Katie's mom waved a hand. "Stop being modest. I saw that film, and you were amazing in it. I never thought math could be exciting, but that movie made it so thrilling!"

The corner of my mouth kicked up. "Well, my character was working against the clock to stop a bomb that would've wiped out an entire country. It was always meant to be exciting."

Jody replied, "But to think it's loosely based on a true story!"

Kyle grunted. "Can we get back to the game already?"

I was nearly out of chips, and so I deliberately botched my next answer to get out.

Surprisingly, Katie had done the same thing.

She faced me and smiled. "Want to take a walk?"

After standing, I offered my hand. Katie took it, and soon we were bundled up and out the door.

But not holding hands.

I resisted reaching for hers and cleared my throat. "If you want to back out of L.A., I understand."

Katie stopped and turned toward me. "What are you talking about?"

"I, er, don't want you to think that I expect..."

"Expect what, Nolan? Sex?"

"Er."

She turned and started walking again. I easily caught up.

We walked in silence for a few minutes before Katie

let out a breath. "You weren't the only one who got carried away in my room."

"I know. But I don't want you to think you have to do anything beyond posing as my fiancée to get your trip."

She kept her gaze forward. "As long as we're together, we're going to keep thinking about it. I mean, it's clear we're both attracted to each other. So maybe..."

My heart rate kicked up. Was she about to offer what I thought she might? "Maybe, what?"

After letting out a long breath, she replied, "Maybe in L.A. we could get it out of our system. You know, once it's done, we'll think straight and can focus more on strategy. Especially since it'll be a long time before either of us can sleep with other people again."

Her words squeezed my heart. At the thought of other men seeing her naked and flushed, I wanted to hunt them down and tell these hypothetical men to stay the fuck away from my woman.

Get a grip, Nolan. Right, I needed to focus on her offer, lest she think I didn't want it. "Hey, look at me." Once she did, I continued. "You don't have to sleep with me, if you don't want to."

"Don't you want to?"

I could lie. But fuck that. I took her hand and nodded. "Yes. I dream about us naked together, baby. All the time."

Her cheeks flushed. "Oh. I, er, dream about you too."

Smiling, I pulled her closer until I could brush the hair off her cheek. "Care to elaborate? And see if we're dreaming the same thing?"

"What, like we're meeting up in dreams to hook up?"

I chuckled. "If that could actually happen, then I'd be sleeping most of the day. But, no, I want to make it good for you, baby. The best. Just tell me what you want, and I'll do it."

"Anything?"

"Well, just about. There are a few things I'd rather not try. One actor I know likes to play with knives and his partner enjoys it too."

"Oh, no, ixnay on the blood play, for sure. You naked and over me would be good. Maybe even..."

"Even what?"

She cleared her throat. "What you were going to do to me earlier, right before we were interrupted?"

Just remembering her hot, wet pussy around my finger made my dick hard again. "Oh, I'll definitely be tasting that perfect pussy of yours, Katie."

She blinked, and I mentally cursed. Maybe she didn't like any kind of crass or dirty talk.

Then she ran a hand up my chest and to the back of my neck. "And, well, I want to suck your cock sometime, too. If that's okay."

The image of her on her knees, taking my dick like a good girl, made me even harder. "Fuck, Katie. It's more than okay."

She smiled shyly and then backed away. I reluctantly let her go.

For a few beats, we stared at each other. The cool air made her cheeks bright pink, her eyes bright, and her dark blue coat hugged her every curve. Ones I wanted to caress with my hands and memorize with my tongue.

It was going to be a long few days until Katie came to L.A.

Which reminded me of something. "We'll do all of that, I promise, once you come to L.A. However, I still need to give you my Christmas present. But I can't do that until you join me down there. I know it'll be late, but I promise it'll be worth it."

"Nolan, you didn't have to get me a gift."

"I do. There will be more than one, actually. Because the first is something you'll truly want, and the second is something to show off to the world."

"Oh, of course. I didn't think of a gift for you to show off and make our story more convincing."

She bit her bottom lip, and I took a step toward her. "Don't worry, we can think of a public-facing gift from you later. But you do have a personal one for me?"

She smiled. "Still like getting gifts, do you?"

Not from everyone, but I really wanted to see what Katie had picked out. "Of course. Even if it seems like I have everything, it's the presents that come from the heart that I treasure the most."

After unzipping her coat, she took a rectangular present from an inner pocket and held it out. "Merry Christmas, Nolan."

I took it. It was the right shape and weight for a book. After unwrapping it, I stared at the title.

Katie asked, "Er, do you like it? If not, I can find something else. But it's just I remember you reading those books when I was little, and Abby told me which was your favorite, and..."

I closed the distance between us and kissed her. "I fucking love it, baby. Thank you."

She'd gotten me one of those Choose Your Own Adventure books I'd loved as a boy. My favorite, in fact—the one about the yeti.

She smiled at me. "You're welcome. And can't you give me a hint about mine? I mean, that's only fair."

I booped her nose. "Only that you'll love it. And the wait will be worth it. It's all set up for the night you arrive in L.A. So don't make any plans."

"Hmm, yes, let me see if I can fit you into my extremely busy schedule," she drawled.

I laughed. "Trust me, once word gets out that you're in town, you'll be getting all kinds of invitations." I paused, studied her expression, and asked, "Will you be okay accepting some of them? It would probably be weird if you ignored some of my recent co-stars or actor acquaintances."

She lightly patted my chest. "I'll be fine and look forward to meeting some of them. I'm pretty good with strangers, for the most part."

I hoped she was right. Because while I knew she'd had a lot of experience giving tours at the dairy, the crowd in L.A. was a whole different story.

Still, she took my hand, and we walked and talked about Christmas presents from our pasts. Any worries or doubts faded away as I enjoyed the calm before the storm.

Because here in Starry Hills, I could be merely Nolan Wolfe. But once I was back in Los Angeles, with my new fiancée in tow, the entire world would be watching us and privacy would pretty much be out the window.

Chapter Seventeen

Katie

Emmy: You and Nolan are going to take L.A. by storm, I just know it! <dancing emoji>
Me: We'll see. As long as I can avoid embarrassing him, I'll call it a win.
Abby: Now, don't start that! People love stories like yours—the famous movie star falls for the hometown girl. You'll be everyone's sweetheart.
Me: Not everyone's. Fans and his ex's followers will pick me apart.
Amber: If you ever need some backup, you only need to send word and we'll be there. We've got your back. <heart emoji>
Emmy: Hear, hear! It's been forever since I was down

there. Besides, I can use my brother's name to get us some good will. Maybe he has friends in L.A. who can get us into places.
Abby: It'd be better if Rafe actually stuck around and offered to help. Nolan's going to be your brother-in-law.
Emmy: Don't start that again. Rafe has lived in the UK for a long time. He's trying to balance his life between two countries.
Abby: You're way too nice. IMHO, he still has a lot to make up for. He needs to grovel.
Amber: It takes time, Abby. Be patient.
Abby: I've been patient!
Me: Forget about Rafe for now. And thanks for the offer, ladies, but I should be fine. I'll keep you posted. <heart emoji>

As I wheeled my bag out of the secure part of the airport, I searched for Nolan's assistant, Jenn Jackson. Nolan had a meeting he couldn't get out of but would meet me at some destination later today.

After glancing at the picture on my phone again, I finally spotted the tall woman with pale skin and red hair that had to be her. She saw me at the same time, waved, and wove through the crowd to reach me.

Once in front of me, she smiled and put out a hand. "I'm Jenn. Nice to finally meet you." I shook her hand and then she leaned in to whisper, "Come on, let's get you into the car before any of the paparazzi spots you. I've seen a few wandering around, asking questions about you, and I want to spare you their attention for as long as I can."

I tugged on the baseball cap Nolan had suggested I wear and readjusted my grip on my suitcase. "Okay."

Jenn waved a hand. "Follow me and stick close."

As I did, I noted how people seemed to move out of her way without even realizing it. Maybe one day I could be that confident and determined.

She typed on her phone as we walked, and eventually we reached the pickup area. A black sedan pulled up, Jenn opened the door, and the driver came to take my bag. After thanking him, Jenn and I got into the car and soon we were on the road.

Jenn tossed her phone into the cup holder on the door. "I think we managed to get away without being seen. If not, it'll be everywhere soon enough." She turned toward me. "You'll meet Nolan later, like I said. But probably not until after dinnertime. So you have two choices—I can take you back home, you can rest, and then go out. Or, we can go shopping and start getting the things you'll need here. I'd suggest the latter, if at all possible, so the alterations can be done in time for your New Year's gown."

I blinked. "Um, what?"

"Didn't Nolan tell you about our shopping spree? Sometimes I think he'd forget to eat if I didn't give him a schedule. At any rate, you need a dress for New Year's—something that will wow that cow and make her jealous."

"Do you know if she's going to be there? His ex? Nolan said he wasn't sure."

"I don't know. I wish I did, but we'll just have to assume she will be." She took out a black American Express card from her purse. "Which means using Nolan's card until we're too tired to shop any longer."

Seeing that rectangular piece of plastic only reinforced just how rich Nolan was. I sometimes forgot that, given how my gift of a children's book at Christmas had made him happy.

Or had he just humored me?

No. He'd loved those books growing up, and it showed I knew him, at least a little.

Trust yourself, Katie. If I was to enjoy my time here, then I couldn't let the glitz and glamor make me doubt everything. "Er, we can do some shopping. Although I have no idea where to start."

Jenn smiled. "That's where I come in. I know the perfect place to get a dress. There's this amazing vintage place that should have what we need. Quite a few of Nolan's friends, including my wife, have used it before."

A vintage shop in L.A., one that catered to the stars, sounded expensive. Really expensive. "I don't want to spend a lot of money, though."

"Why not? You could do your worst, and Nolan wouldn't even feel a dent. You do realize he's a billionaire, right?" I blinked, and Jenn sighed. "He didn't tell you. Of course not. He's far too modest. But he is, so don't sweat the costs. He wants me to treat you, and I plan to do so."

Nolan Wolfe, the billionaire. Why hadn't he told me? Did his family know?

But then I remembered him saying how they never allowed him to help financially and decided no, he probably hadn't shared it with them.

It was yet something else he kept hidden from those who loved him.

And even if helping Nolan with his family wasn't part of our fake engagement deal, I added some sort of reconciliation to my list of things to do before I took my big trip.

Jenn waved the credit card. "So, ready for some shopping?"

In the past, I'd been content to scour the thrift shops for finds. But while here, I needed to impress everyone and not embarrass Nolan. "Er, okay. Just..."

"Just what?"

"Just don't take me to those fancy stores that'll look down at me for not being a size zero."

Jenn rolled her eyes. "Fuck those people. Seriously. And don't worry, my wife is close to your size, so I know exactly where to go."

After she gave directions to the driver, I asked, "When will I meet her? Your wife? Isn't she Nolan's lawyer?"

She smiled. "Yes, Valentina Lopez is the lawyer to the stars, and one of the best in town, in my opinion. Although don't ever call her Valentina, as that makes her think of her great-aunt. Just call her Tina."

"Okay, Tina it is then. So how did you two meet? I only know the bare minimum."

And so Jenn told the story of how Tina had been late to a meeting, Jenn had taken her to task, they'd argued, and soon they'd ended up in a bathroom, making out. The rest was history.

I also learned that Jenn enjoyed traveling, and she told me about her recent trip to Thailand. The more she talked, the more my worry eased. I knew Nolan was a busy guy and couldn't be with me twenty-four-seven. However, I'd been afraid of being bored or lonely in L.A. But I liked Jenn. A lot.

When the car finally pulled up in front of a fancy vintage dress shop, my heart raced. I hated shopping. Finding something to fit a busty lady who also happened to carry weight on her lower body wasn't easy.

But Jenn smiled, told me to trust her, and soon she whisked me inside.

An hour later, the saleswoman finished zipping up the dress I'd picked out and gestured toward the three mirrors. "I'll leave you alone to look and decide."

Once she exited the dressing room and closed the door, I took a few deep breaths. On the hanger, the black dress had looked beautiful. It was an A-line dress that had shoulder straps, a deep neckline, and the skirt flared out from the hips.

However, even without seeing my reflection, I could tell the top didn't quite fit.

Stop being a coward.

After taking a deep breath, I turned and walked over

to the mirrors. The dress was beautiful and fit fairly well. However, since the shopping trip was impromptu, I hadn't worn shapewear like I usually did for dress-hunting. As a result, the bodice hugged every curve and highlighted every flaw and roll to the world.

It shouldn't bother me—I knew I'd look stunning once I had on the right undergarments. And yet, as I stood in arguably the most beautiful dress I'd ever worn, tears pricked my eyes. Some of the nasty messages from Wendy Webster's fans that had slipped through came back to me:

Nolan only picked you because of his weight loss company endorsement. Stop hurting Wendy and pretending he cares.

Are you pregnant? You definitely look it. And that's the only reason Nolan would pick you over Wendy.

Wendy is Nolan's soul mate. Stop being a selfish bitch and let him go. There's no way he could be attracted to you. Wendy's a goddess, and you're disgusting.

Closing my eyes, I willed my tears away. After all, this whole thing with Nolan was fake. Even if it were for different reasons than the ones the haters had said, they were right, to a degree.

Nolan wasn't mine to keep.

Someone knocked softly and then Nolan's voice came through the door. "Katie? I'm sorry I couldn't be here earlier, and Jenn should've waited. Regardless, let me in, baby. I want to see this dress Jenn talked about."

I ran my hands down my sides and replied, "I think I need a different one."

"If there's anything that I've learned from shopping with my sister, it's that sometimes you need a second opinion. Won't you let me in? Please?"

It was the please that did it. After all, Nolan would be buying whatever dress I needed. He should see it first.

"It's unlocked."

I kept my gaze on my reflection and avoided his eyes.

Nolan growled. "Fuck, you're so beautiful, baby."

I met his gaze in the mirror. At the heat and desire there, I blinked.

He then frowned. "Why are your eyes red? What happened?"

Shaking my head, I replied, "It's nothing."

Nolan came up behind me, placed his hands on my hips, and nuzzled my cheek with his own. "Tell me what's wrong. You're mine to protect, and I can't help you if you don't talk to me."

I tried to smile. "Yours to protect, huh?"

"You know what I mean. I'm not about to feed you to the wolves here." He squeezed my hips. "So, is it the dress? We can find another one, if you want."

"No, I love it. But it's just that..."

"Just what?"

I sighed. "Well, I didn't know we were going shopping, and so I don't have my shapewear on, and I started thinking about what Wendy's fans would say about me."

"Fuck those people." He pulled me back against him, against his hard cock, and he whispered, "You drive me crazy, baby. So much so, if I didn't think we'd get caught, I'd sit you down, toss up those skirts, and make you cry out my name as you came on my tongue."

I turned around in his arms. "Nolan."

He leaned his forehead against mine. "People like Wendy and her diehard fans will only ever see flaws—both in themselves and in others. But I don't want a fiancée who only feels better about herself when she puts down others. No, I want a woman who makes me laugh and knows I like books and doesn't try to mold me into something I'm not. And that's you, baby. You're the one I picked."

If only he'd picked me for real. "But you only have me for six months."

He leaned back and searched my gaze. As we stared at one another, Nolan's expression turned tender. Cupping my cheek, he murmured, "You're so damn beautiful in this dress, Katie. Trust me, I'll have to growl and glare at the others to keep them away."

He'd changed the subject, but I still smiled and decided a lighter mood was better. "Would you snarl, too?"

"Maybe. I have great teeth and should show them off."

He made a snarling face, and I laughed.

Nolan caressed my cheek. "There. Much better. Not as good as you crying out my name, but a close second." He stood back. "Now, do a little twirl for me."

"Twirl?"

He looked a little sheepish. "Yes. It's a fantasy I never knew I had, even if you're not naked."

I moved away, met his gaze again, and then lifted my arms above my head and twirled a few times, before slowing down and stopping. "Well?"

"It'd be even better if you were naked."

"Nolan!"

Maybe he'd been just like me, dreaming every night of when we'd finally sleep together. I eyed the bench, was tempted even, but ultimately decided I didn't want our first time to be in public.

Well, our first and only time.

Don't think of that now.

He reached for me, pulled me against his chest, and kissed me. Gently, slowly, and soon, I forgot all about my earlier insecurities. When he finally let me up for air, he said, "I wish I could take you home and strip you right away. But we have an appointment for your present."

"I thought Jenn said that would be later today?"

"I managed to clear my schedule and move it up. And since it's not something I can easily change to a different day, we can't cancel."

"Okay, now I'm more than curious."

He kissed me. "Let me help you out of this dress, and then we'll go. You can finish shopping with Jenn tomorrow."

He turned me around, nuzzled the back of my neck, and then ran his fingers from my neck, down the skin exposed by the dress, until he reached the zipper. Back and forth his finger went, just under the material, and I shivered.

I heard the zipper release, slowly. And as it exposed more of my skin, Nolan kissed each inch until he reached the bottom, not too far above my ass. His hot breath danced across me as he said, "Damn, Katie. Tell me I can have you tonight. In my bed."

My heart thumped as I tried to make my brain work. "Okay."

He kissed my back again. "Good. Now, I'd better leave or I might just risk people hearing you scream as I lick that pretty pussy."

"Is that supposed to be a threat?"

Nolan groaned and stepped away. "Not here. If I'm to get you for one night, I want you alone and to myself."

I watched in the mirror as Nolan left. As soon as the door clicked closed, I put a hand on the wall to keep my knees from buckling. Had any man ever affected me like him?

No, most definitely not.

Maybe no man ever would again.

But that was too damn depressing to think about when I had not only a surprise to look forward to, but also sleeping with Nolan. I wouldn't let anything ruin that.

When Jenn popped her head in to check on me, I learned that the salesperson still had to mark any alterations. I blushed as Jenn pulled the zipper back up, her eyes twinkling as she said, "Nolan's never been so horny that he'd undress a woman in public before. Well, at least to my knowledge."

My face heated. "Um."

"Hey, it's a compliment. You want a partner who

can't wait to rip off your clothes." She waggled her eyebrows. "Trust me, it can be fun."

Soon the saleswoman returned and stuck in pins to mark what needed to be adjusted. Once done, I found Nolan sitting in a chair outside the dressing room, looking at his phone, frowning.

But as soon as he saw me, he smiled and put his phone away. After standing, he took my hand and kissed the back of it. "Let's get something to eat and then it'll be time for your surprise."

"I'm starving and up for anything. All I had were some pretzels on the airplane."

He frowned and glared at Jenn. "You should've asked if she was hungry."

Jenn rolled her eyes. "I figured we'd go out to lunch after this. It's only noon."

I jumped in. "It's fine, Nolan. I was eager to see the dress shop."

He grumbled. "Well, still."

I placed a hand on his upper arm. "How about if you take me to one of your favorite spots? Maybe not a sit-down restaurant, though, because I'm impatient for my surprise."

Nolan smiled. "I'll save the best restaurants for later." He took my hand. "Come on. The car is outside and the ride won't be long."

After I waved goodbye to Jenn—she'd take the car we'd arrived in—we exited the shop and sat in the car. Like the other one, it had a driver, so Nolan and I were together in the back seat. I gestured toward the partition. "Can they see or hear anything?"

"Only via the intercom. Why? Do you have something planned?"

He waggled his eyebrows, and I grinned. "Maybe later."

Groaning, Nolan squeezed my hand in his. "For the first time in my life, I hate seatbelts."

"Why?"

"Because I want to hold you in my lap."

"Oh."

I shared a glance with Nolan, and the man looked at me like he couldn't wait to eat me up.

Since talking about tonight would only make us both flushed, turned on, and frustrated, I changed the subject. "So, what was your meeting about?"

He hesitated, and my mind turned to the worst—he'd had a hot and bothered reunion with his ex, had declared his undying love, and was thinking of ways to let me down gently.

Then I remembered Nolan unzipping me and decided that was ridiculous. I may not know the man as well as I wanted to, but I would never pin him as a two-timing bastard.

He finally let out a breath. "I run a charity, and they needed my help."

"Wait, what? You run a charity? Since when?"

"I've been doing it for years. I don't want or need the glory, though, so I keep my involvement a secret."

"Even from your family?"

"Yes, even from them."

Maybe it wasn't my place, but I couldn't help but

blurt, "Why do you keep so many things from your family? They love you, Nolan. You can't deny that."

"I know they do, but it's complicated." I raised my eyebrows in question, and he sighed. "Well, when I first started getting big roles and received the paychecks to match, I offered to help my family with things, such as replace the roof, upgrade the winery equipment, you name it. However, Beck got angry, saying he could make it work by himself, and that he didn't need my charity. I suspect he acted that way because he was young and out to prove something. But it still hurt. And even more recently, when I offered to pay for Abby's college tuition, she said she'd manage it on her own." He shrugged. "Over time I've learned not to offer them anything. And I guess my charity became just another secret, one they might resent me for."

I frowned. "Resent you? Why the hell would they do that?"

"I don't know. It was just a gut feeling."

Oh, Nolan. I squeezed his hand in mine. I wanted to shout that he was being ridiculous, and he should share with his family, and that everything would work out.

However, the Wolfe siblings were beyond stubborn. I'd known them my whole life, and their stubbornness tended to make them dig in when they shouldn't.

Besides, his family wasn't here—I was. And I wanted him to know he could trust me with anything. So I asked, "Why don't you tell me about your charity? Because now I'm extremely curious."

Nolan searched my gaze, and I let my curiosity show. Finally he looked at our hands, ran his thumb against my skin, and answered, "It has two main focuses. The first one is support for kids dealing with grief or family troubles."

"Much like you had to deal with it."

He nodded. "I was fortunate. Because despite all our problems, my family supported and loved me. However, not every kid has that. So I wanted to have resources available—hotlines, texting outreach, and counseling services to help them deal with their grief."

"Wow, that's amazing, Nolan. And yet there's still more. What's the other part your charity focuses on?"

"Well, mostly helping kids deal with grief, family troubles, and mental health in general through the arts. There are programs for acting, music, painting, writing, dancing, you name it. Mainly I have art centers and summer programs, although one day I'd also like to expand it to scholarships and grants." He met my gaze. "While my top charity directors know I fund it, along with Jenn and Tina, no one else does. If word got out, it could be a disaster."

I put it together. "People would find your programs and arts centers, wanting to catch a glimpse of you."

"Yes."

"And yet you told me. Why?"

His gaze searched mine. "I don't know. I just wanted to."

He trusts me. That realization made my heart rate tick up. Was it my imagination, or was our relationship growing deeper and more complicated by the day?

The car stopped, and I mentally cursed. I didn't want to stop talking about this.

However, once Nolan's driver asked what we wanted for lunch, Nolan released my hand and we ordered.

Then silence fell as we ate and made our way to some secret destination, both of us lost in thought.

Chapter Eighteen

Nolan

Aunt Lori: Tell me you're coming for West's birthday on the 12th, Nolan. We're having a party. <birthday cake emoji> <party popper emoji> <dancing emoji>
West: He doesn't have to come. I don't want a party.
Aunt Lori: Of course you do! It's the first time you'll be here to celebrate it with us in nearly two decades.
Zane: She's got you there, brother. Do you really want to make our dear aunt cry?
West: Stop guilt-tripping me, Zane. It won't work.
Zach: Well, West IS inching ever closer to forty, so you'd better come see him while you still can, Nolan. <old man emoji>
West: <middle finger emoji>

Beck: Don't worry, it's going to be low key, with just some wine and good food. I put my foot down about a grand party.
Aunt Lori: It's sweet how you think that worked, Becky. <laughing emoji>
Zane: I have your back, Aunt Lori. I wasn't here for my birthday, so we need to celebrate them both.
Abby: I'm staying out of this.
Beck: Coward.
Abby: <chicken emoji> <shrugging emoji> <dashing away emoji>
West: Don't come, Nolan. There won't be any party, if I can help it.
Me: I'll be there for your wedding next month, West. But why is this a group text?
Aunt Lori: I have all six of you back in my life, and I'll be group texting every day.
Me: Well, I have an appointment. Keep me updated.
Aunt Lori: I'll let you know when the party plans are finalized. <heart emoji>
Beck and West: <sighing emoji>

As my driver, George, parked the car, I tried my best to push aside the conversation I'd had with Katie. I still couldn't believe I'd told her about my charity. It hadn't been planned, and yet I'd *wanted* to finally tell someone about it.

I was a long way from blurting it out to my family,

but that was okay. There had been a lot of changes for the Wolfes over the last year, and they didn't need more disruption in their lives.

Once George turned off the car, I focused on my Christmas present for Katie. After removing a blindfold from the seat pocket, I held it up.

She raised an eyebrow. "Really? I have to be blindfolded?"

"Yes. Don't you trust me?"

I mentally cursed at asking that. We hadn't spent that much time together, after all.

However, she nodded. "Okay. Although if it's to bring me into a sex dungeon, I'm not sure I'm ready for that. I'm not saying I'm against it entirely, but a girl needs some time to prepare."

I snorted. "No sex dungeon today, I promise." I raised the blindfold again. "Now, let's get this on you."

She leaned forward, and I tied the fabric around her eyes, my touch lingering in her hair. Then I ran a finger down her soft, warm cheek, and Katie shivered. I imagined her blindfolded in my bed, as I teased her with a feather.

Calm the fuck down, Nolan. Right. Her present. "Wait here until I open your door." I raced around to the other side, pulled the door open, and took her hand. "Come on. I'll lead you inside."

Once Katie was on her feet, I put an arm around her shoulders and gripped her hand closest to me. The biggest independent bookstore in the city was in front of us. Even though the door sign said, "Closed," I knocked, and the owner opened it.

She smiled, stepped aside, and I guided Katie toward the middle of the large space.

I whispered, "Surprise. Have a look."

She tore down the blindfold and blinked. "A bookstore."

"Yes. And let me explain—you can get as many books as you want. Both the mystery and romance sections are some of the best, I've been told. Although you don't have to limit your choices to those two. Pick out whatever you want, with no limit."

She turned toward me and blinked her eyes rapidly, almost as if she was about to cry.

"What's wrong, baby? Did you want something else?"

Shaking her head, Katie replied, "No, it's perfect. But a few books will be good enough."

I placed a finger under her chin and stroked her soft skin. "Don't hold back. Let me give you this, Katie. Please."

She searched my gaze as I held my breath. To most, it wouldn't seem like a big deal—either she accepted, or she didn't. But to me? A man who had trouble spoiling or helping those he cared about? Her answer meant the fucking world to me.

Finally, she nodded. "Okay. But can I get some new bookcases as part of the deal? Because the ones at home are pretty full already."

I kissed her briefly. "Yes. As many as you need." I gestured around. "And I'll be your book carrying mule today, too. The store is empty of customers, except for us. So take your time and don't feel rushed. The owner has agreed to keep it open as late as we need."

She surveyed the space. "Is it truly empty?"

"Yes. That's why I couldn't easily reschedule it—it would've been unfair to the owner."

And it'd cost me a fortune twice over. But that was the lesser of my concerns. I didn't want the store to get a reputation for not being reliably open.

Katie threw herself against me and hugged me. I wrapped my arms around her and laid my cheek atop her head. "Merry Christmas, baby."

"Thank you, Nolan. This is probably the best present in my life. No, scratch that—it *is* the best present ever."

"Good." I kissed the top of her head. "Now, let's get started. I'm curious to see what you pick out."

Katie looked up at me. "Just don't be judge-y."

"I won't. Maybe I'll have to read some of them myself."

She grinned. "Then I'll make sure to pick out some scorching romances. Ones that make you all hot and bothered."

"Okay, color me intrigued."

She laughed, stepped back, and turned toward the romance section. "Come on, then."

I followed her, amused, as she ran her finger down the titles. She plucked one out. "This one I've seen around. He needs to marry in order to claim his inheritance. So he asks his executive assistant to be his fake wife for a year."

"Out of all the women in the world, he asks the one person who will probably disrupt his life the most?"

"Of course. That's the point. She hates him, he thinks she's a quiet mouse, and what do you know? Once married and stuck together, they let down their walls, have some hot sex they can't seem to avoid, and eventually fall in love." Katie sighed. "He even has a pet name for her."

"If you haven't read it, how do you know?"

"People love to share quotes. Especially the dirty parts."

I chuckled. "Of course they do."

"Hey, don't knock it until you've read a few. This one is supposed to have some deep character development, too."

I took it, noted the title, and added it to the basket I carried. "I'll get the ebook on my phone and start it as soon as possible. I like to read between down times at my job, when there's not enough time to nap or go for a run."

"Those are vastly different things."

"Both relax me, in different ways." I gestured toward the shelves. "You have one book so far. Pick out some more that tickles your fancy."

"'Tickles my fancy.' How old are you again?"

I winked. "I can be from any age, remember?"

A mischievous glint entered her eyes. "Which opens up lots of possibilities."

"Er, for what?"

She patted my chest. "We'll get to that. Now, let me pick out some more books."

As she rushed off, I followed and couldn't stop smiling. And as she picked out an interesting collection of romances—from ones about cowboys to people who change into dragons to adult-only fairytale retellings—I got a better glimpse into Katie Evans. She loved to read, didn't bat an eyelash to point out some of the hottest books and mention a scene or two, and most importantly—she had accepted my gift.

By the end, I didn't care how much I'd spent. Or that Katie would need five or six bookcases to hold them all.

No, because I'd received the most precious thing of all—time with a woman who treated me as just a guy. A woman who didn't mind teasing about hot sex scenes in a car or in a helicopter or even in some abandoned cottage in the mountains. A woman who teased me and didn't mind being teased in return.

And by the end, I was more than ready for our night together. Even if I suspected it would be a point-of-no-return for me when it came to wanting Katie, I didn't care.

First, though, I'd make her come so hard that she'd forget about all other men. Then I could start wooing her for real.

Chapter Nineteen

Katie

Abby: Nolan did what for your Christmas present???

Me: You truly didn't know about the bookstore shopping spree?

Abby: No. But it was an amazing present, for sure.

Amber: And so romantic. <smiling face with hearts emoji> Especially because Katie loves reading so much.

Emmy: I agree. First the vintage dress, and now an unlimited book shopping-spree. I think Nolan is spoiling you.

Me: Maybe. But the real test is yet to come.

Emmy: What, figuring out just how many blowjobs you should give him to say thank you?

Me: As if that would be a bad thing. <overheated emoji>

Abby: <puking emoji> That's my brother! Seriously, can't you guys find someone else to hook up with?

Amber: I'm dating outside your family.

Abby: And?

Amber: Um. We're taking it slow.

Abby: <sighing emoji>

Me: Hey, you could play the field, Abby. Then you can spill it all to us.

Abby: I'm off men. Maybe for good.

Me: Then I'll make sure to give you a new vibrator for your birthday.

Amber: Why do you keep giving us vibrators?

Me: Why not? Every woman should have a back-up plan and a guaranteed orgasm.

Emmy: You don't need to give me any more, though. West is very, very good at keeping me satisfied. <overheated emoji>

Abby: <puking emoji> x 3

Me (typed but deleted): I'm about to learn if another Wolfe brother is just as good, or if West is an anomaly.

Me (actual reply instead): Enjoy your man, Emmy. I need to dash. But I want all the details later.

Abby: Without me. Please.

Me: Fine, without you. <heart emoji>

As soon as we were back in the car, I took Nolan's hand. "Thank you. I mean it."

He smiled warmly, and it shot straight between my thighs. "You don't have to keep thanking me. Seeing you so happy is reward enough."

Nolan Wolfe was kind, funny, sexy, and so much more. Ever since he'd proposed a fake engagement, I'd wondered something. So I asked, "Why are you still single? Even before your nightmare ex, any lady would've been lucky to have you. And yes, I know you have your fame to worry about. But there are plenty of actors who find love and marry. It's not impossible."

"No. But..."

"But what?"

He sighed and ran a hand through his hair. "Well, it's going to sound stupid as I'm thirty-two years old and so much time has passed."

"You met the girls who bullied me. I'm not quite as ancient as you are, but I still haven't gotten over those memories completely. Sometimes things stay with us forever, no matter how hard we try to move past them."

He raised an eyebrow. "I'm ancient, huh?"

"Don't change the subject, Nolan. Tell me what still bothers you. Please?"

As he tapped his fingers against his thigh, I waited. I knew whatever it was, whatever his memories were, it would reveal a little more of the true Nolan Wolfe, the man who kept to himself more than anyone else I knew.

After what seemed forever, he replied, "Well, in high school I was hurt and betrayed by my best friend, and I guess I've never really opened myself up to anyone again."

I tried to recall who might have hurt him. But while our age difference didn't matter now, it had been a different story when we were younger. "Who? And what happened? If it's not too painful to talk about, that is."

"What, and ruin your night? That's probably not a good idea."

"No, tell me. I want to know. It won't ruin my night. I promise."

If anything, it'd probably make me fall a little more for the man.

Not that we were actually a thing. But a girl could dream a little.

After searching my gaze for a few seconds, he finally said, "After my dad died and West ran away and Beck shouldered the responsibilities of running the winery, I felt somewhat isolated. My older brothers were basically gone, and my younger siblings were still children. I ended up spending more and more time with my best friend, a guy I'd known since childhood. His name was Scott Allen."

A vague image of a boy with blond hair and fair skin flashed into my mind. "I kind of remember him. And yes, you two hung out a lot."

He nodded. "One way I coped with my grief was through acting, but the other was getting away from my home as often as possible so I could avoid the memories. Scott always invited me to his house after school, and hanging out with him helped me feel a little more like myself, like I'd been before everything had changed. But just as I was starting to feel a little hopeful about the future —I'd landed some roles both at school and for the Summer Star Festival—everything changed in the blink of an eye."

At the hurt in his gaze, I yearned to crawl over and hug Nolan. But I also didn't want to risk him changing the subject. Whatever he was about to reveal had hurt him deeply.

So I stayed put and asked, "What happened?"

"A girl. More specifically, Scott and a girl. And no, I didn't care if he dated and had a girlfriend. We'd both brought girls from the drama club to my family's orchard before. But this time was different. He betrayed me right after he started dating her."

I willed for him to keep going, and he did. "Scott had liked Cindy Davis for a while. But she was one of the more popular kids, and me and Scott were theater geeks. And since high school is full of drama and cliques, I wasn't sure he'd ever get a chance with her. So when he told me she'd agreed to go on a date with him, I was happy. While unlikely, I wanted to believe love could conquer all.

"Right after he told me the news, he invited me to a party at his place. Scott rarely held parties outside of get-togethers with the theater crew, but he finally convinced me to go, saying it'd be the best one that year for the kids of Starry Hills High.

"The party was inside the barn on his property, with a bonfire outside of it. I mostly stayed in a corner of the barn since I didn't know anyone apart from Scott. Then it happened."

He looked out the car window, and my heart thumped harder. His tone said it hadn't been good. And I wished I could spare him the pain.

But maybe telling me would help. So I said gently, "Tell me what happened next, Nolan. Please."

He tapped his fingers against the door's armrest for nearly a minute before he spoke again. "Cindy's older brothers showed up, found me, and hauled me over to the stand of trees near the barn. They stripped me bare except for my underwear, wrote 'Nerd' on my chest, and tied me to a tree. Then everyone came, taking pictures and making fun of me, all while my supposed best friend just stood there, doing nothing, as he held Cindy's hand."

Tears pricked my eyes as I imagined Nolan being humiliated like that, especially when he'd always avoided the spotlight, unless he was acting.

I curled my fingers into fists. "Why the fuck would they do that? You weren't the kind of guy to make enemies as a kid."

He finally met my gaze again, his expression unreadable. "I learned later that West had gotten one of the brothers kicked off the baseball team. And since they'd never been able to get back at him, they decided I was a good enough target instead."

"Oh, Nolan."

I burned to ask if he'd ever talked to West about it. However, Nolan spoke before I could.

"And it gets worse. Apparently, Cindy had only ever

agreed to date Scott so her brothers could get their revenge on me. He felt like a fool, tried to apologize, but I didn't care. He'd thrown years and years of friendship away for the chance to kiss a girl. To say our friendship was over was an understatement. Less than a year later, right after graduation, I took my first big job and left Starry Hills."

My heart ached for him. But there was rage, too, at someone hurting this wonderful man so deeply that it lingered all these years later.

Nolan resumed tapping his fingers again. "Once I'd made a name for myself and returned to Starry Hills, Cindy Davis tried to throw herself at me. She batted her eyelashes and somehow thought bygones should be bygones. It was my first wake-up call about how fame could affect one's life and their relations to people." He finally met my eyes again. "So I've kept my distance, always second-guessing what people really thought of me, or what they wanted from me."

Because they didn't want him for himself, was left unsaid.

A lot of things suddenly made sense about Nolan. He kept his distance from his siblings, not just because of time and living far apart and grief, but merely being West's brother had ended in humiliation. Also, he didn't like to let people close because the one person he'd trusted outside his family had betrayed him.

And then, as soon as Nolan was famous, that bitch Cindy had suddenly wanted to cozy up to him.

Add in his ex, Wendy, and more and more I started to understand how alone Nolan truly was.

As the car stopped and the driver said over the intercom we'd arrived, I released my seatbelt and crawled over to Nolan before he could leave. I sat on his lap and put my arms around his neck.

For a few seconds, we merely stared at each other. Hurt still lingered in his gaze, as did a flicker of vulnerability.

And I didn't like it. Not at all.

I kissed him. I'd only meant for it to be comforting, but soon he threaded his fingers through my hair, tilted my head, and took it deeper. As his tongue licked and stroked and explored, I moved to straddle his lap and pulled him even closer.

Kisses couldn't cure all hurts, but I was determined to let him know I was there, I cared, and he deserved so much better than what had happened to him.

Eventually, he broke the kiss and laid his forehead against mine. "I hope that wasn't a pity kiss."

I traced his jaw with my finger. "No. I've been wanting to kiss you ever since you unzipped my dress earlier today."

The corners of his mouth kicked up. "I can still feel your warm skin under my lips, your scent filling my nose, and your soft sighs as I kissed up your spine."

He arched up, his hard cock pressing against me, and I moaned.

He whispered, "I don't want to wait until after dinner. Tell me I can have you now, baby. I want to strip you, and worship you with my mouth, and watch you bounce on my dick as you ride me."

His words shot straight between my thighs. "I thought you wanted to know my fantasies."

As his hands caressed my back, my sides, my ass, he asked, "What do you want me to do to you, then?"

I bit my lip a second before replying, "I know you carried me to the clinic when I was sick. But..."

"But what?"

"I've been dreaming of you going all Highlander, tossing me over your shoulder, and whisking me to your bedroom to have your wicked way with me."

His accent was Scottish when he said, "If that's what my lass wants, that's what she'll get. Aye?"

I smiled. "Ooh, a man who can do accents on demand AND carry me up the stairs? I've hit the jackpot."

"I can even get costumes."

He waggled his eyebrows, and I laughed. "You're full of surprises, Nolan."

"The good kind, I hope."

"The best." I kissed him. "Now, take me upstairs and do dirty things to me."

After opening the door, he helped me off his lap, followed me up, and then without another word, tossed me over his shoulder.

I squealed as he lightly slapped my butt. "I didn't think you were serious."

His large, warm hand caressed my ass cheek. "What my baby wants, she gets."

With that, he ran up the stairs to the front door, dashed inside, and then up another set of stairs. I laughed the whole way. Here I was, in a mansion in

Malibu, with a bona fide movie star carting me up the stairs, just because I'd asked him to do it.

Sometimes life was stranger than fiction. But in a good way.

However, as soon as Nolan entered his bedroom, shut the door, and slowly slid me down his body, I forgot about everything except his hard chest pressed against me.

Gently brushing the hair off my face, he said, "Now's the chance to tell me if you want to back out, Katie. No pressure—this is entirely up to you."

A flash of insecurity rushed through me. "Why? Did you want to back out?"

He growled. "Fuck no. I'm dying to strip you naked, devour your pussy, and make you scream. But only if you want it. Not because of pity or scoring with a famous person or just to please me. I want you to want this for yourself."

"Have I ever treated you as some high and mighty movie star, or put you on a pedestal?"

"No."

"If anything, you were my best friend's annoying older brother for so long. But that's definitely changed." I stood on my tiptoes and whispered, "As for wanting you, why don't you see for yourself how wet and ready I am?"

He growled, moved my head, and kissed me. Not soft and slow, but hard and fast, as if he couldn't get enough of me. Every lick and stroke and nibble was another claim on me.

His hand didn't waste time unzipping my jeans. As soon as his rough, warm fingers caressed my belly underneath my underwear, I widened my stance. "Touch me, Nolan. Please."

Running his hand down, down, down, he finally stroked through my center and growled. "Fuck, you're dripping for me, baby. And if I don't taste you soon, I'm going to explode."

"Have a little problem, do you?"

His forefinger rubbed circles around my clit, and I had to grab onto Nolan's arms to remain upright.

"I think someone needs to suck my dick and see just how long I can last."

At the thought of looking up, Nolan's heated gaze burning into mine as his hand guided my head faster and faster, more wetness rushed between my thighs.

"Like that image, do you, baby?" I nodded. "Then strip, let me eat that pretty pussy, and then you can take my dick like a good girl."

"Only if you strip too."

Nolan removed his hand, and I felt a little cold. But then he tore off his shirt and bared his broad, muscled chest, sprinkled with dark chest hair. I vaguely noted a big tattoo on one of his upper arms, but then he shucked his pants. As he stroked his long, hard cock, my mouth went dry.

He growled. "You're still dressed, baby. Strip. Now."

Maybe if Nolan hadn't both told and shown me how beautiful I was back in the dress shop, I might've hesitated. But his dick was proof he liked what he saw, so I took off my sweater and then shimmied my jeans down. I hooked my fingers under my panties, took a deep breath, and then removed them. Next, the bra was on the floor.

I stood naked and tried not to fidget under Nolan's searing gaze.

Nolan released his cock, walked toward me, and kissed me again.

At the feel of his hot skin against mine, I moaned, ran my hand around, and grabbed his ass. His round, firm ass that I couldn't help but dig my nails into.

Before I knew it, something hit the back of my legs. Nolan broke the kiss. "Sit down and spread those thighs for me, baby. Show me my pussy."

His possessive words rolled over me, and my clit throbbed. I sat, spread my thighs, and waited.

Nolan's gaze trailed over me, full of heat and desire, and then latched onto my center. The longer he stared, the wetter I got.

"Nolan?"

He walked over, knelt before me, and then ran his hands up and down my thighs. "You have the prettiest pussy, baby. Now let me see just how sweet you taste."

After kissing my mouth, he trailed his lips down my neck, to my left breast, licked, and then kept kissing his way down my belly until his head was between my thighs. His hot breath against me made me squirm.

Pushing against my inner thighs, he widened them. With a growl, Nolan lapped at my pussy, fucking me slowly with his tongue, and I dug my fingers into his hair and cried out softly.

He stopped to whisper, "So fucking good. You taste so good, baby. I need more, much more."

I didn't know where it came from, but I said, "Then don't stop."

His gaze met mine before he licked my pussy again. Each stroke and tease made me dig my nails into his scalp. Then he circled around my clit without ever touching it, and I arched toward him, trying to move his head.

Nolan chuckled. "I won't leave you hanging, baby. I promise. But the wait will make it good, so fucking good."

He thrust a finger inside me, curled it, and I cried out. "Nolan."

"There's my name on your lips. Next time, I want it to be a desperate plea."

His tongue flicked against my clit, just once, and then he went back to circling around it, over and over. I tried to move his head, to get him to where I needed him, but Nolan slowly fucked me with his finger as he continued to tease with licks and hot breaths. Eventually, he leaned back, removed his hand, and sucked his wet finger into his mouth. He moaned, and the sight made me even hotter.

I could've reached down and finished myself off quickly, but I want to come from Nolan's touch. However, I wasn't above torturing him a little. So I pinched and rolled my nipples, arching as I did it.

"Fuck, baby. That's it. Show me what you like."

One of his hands moved mine away so he could pluck and roll and pinch my nipple.

I met his gaze. "Please, Nolan. I'm close, so close."

Leaning down, he took my nipple between his teeth

and tugged. I placed my hands behind me to keep from falling backward.

After suckling me for a second, he released me. "Look at how red that nipple is for me now. Let's see if your clit is just as swollen."

His hands caressed down my sides, over my belly, and then between my thighs. His thumbs pulled the hood of my clit back and the cool air only made me wetter.

Nolan's hazel eyes met mine. "Who's made you this swollen, baby? Tell me."

"You did."

"And do you want me to suckle that sweet clit between my teeth and make you scream?"

I gripped the blanket with my fingers. "Yes. Please."

Nolan lowered his head and murmured, "I can't wait to taste your orgasm on my tongue."

Before I could say anything, he suckled my clit and lights danced before my eyes as pleasure exploded throughout my body. Each spasm only made me gasp and scream and arch toward Nolan.

But he continued to suck and lap and tease me until he'd wrung every last spasm from my body. Then he moved his tongue to my entrance, lapped, and he groaned.

I finally couldn't remain upright and fell back on the bed, breathing hard.

Nolan rose and braced himself over me. "You're definitely the sweetest thing I've ever tasted, baby. Once will never be enough."

As I caught my breath, I stared at Nolan. His hair was every which way from my hands, and I smiled.

He nuzzled my neck, kissed it, and asked, "Is that smile because of me?"

"Yes and no."

He leaned back. "Oh?"

Raising a hand, I ran a hand back and forth over his chest, loving the springy hair there. "You should see your hair."

He nipped my bottom lip. "Just wait until you see yours, after I get you on your knees."

After moving my hand to the back of his neck, I pulled him close enough to kiss. "I can't wait."

"Fuck, Katie, you're going to kill me."

He pressed his body against mine, his hard cock pressing into my belly, which only made me hot all over again. "Let me return the favor, Nolan. I'm curious about how you taste."

"Only if you want to. If you're tired, I can wait."

My hand trailed between us, and I traced the length of his dick. As he moaned, I said, "Oh, I want to. I want to see you fall apart and come as hard as me."

"Fuck, baby."

He kissed me, taking it deep, his tongue claiming my mouth as his hand massaged one of my breasts. Even though I'd just orgasmed, my pussy throbbed all over again, eager for more, much more.

I hooked a leg around his hip and rubbed against him. Nolan broke the kiss. "I can feel how wet you are for me, baby. Does the thought of sucking my dick turn you on?"

"Yes."

He leaned back, helped me up, and then placed a pillow on the floor. "Then kneel and open that perfect mouth of yours. I'm clean, baby. I promise."

The fact he'd put a pillow on the floor, even now thinking of my comfort, warmed my heart.

But as soon as I knelt in front of him, his cock jutting long and hard in front of me, I forgot about everything else.

I bit my bottom lip, and I noticed a drop of precum appear. I quickly licked it off, moaning at his musky, salty taste.

Nolan's hand went to my head. "I want to see those pretty lips wrapped around my cock. Watch as you suck me deep until I coat the back of your throat with my cum."

Wrapping the fingers of one hand around his length, I stroked. Slowly. I swore he got bigger as I did it.

Nolan growled. "Take my dick, baby. Take it deep."

Remembering how he'd teased me at first, I ran my tongue along the underside of his cock, swirled around the head, and then went back. His grip tightened on my hair, but he didn't push me forward.

Time to make him squirm like he'd done with me.

I cupped his balls and fondled them as I stroked his dick. His head fell back as he groaned, his dick letting out more wetness.

After lapping it up, I teased the slit on his head.

"Baby, I'm not going to last if you keep doing that."

I smiled up at him. "I'm just giving you a taste of your own medicine."

Gently squeezing his balls, I took just the tip of his dick into my mouth, flicked my tongue underneath, and then retreated.

Nolan pushed against my head, and I met his eyes, full of heat and...longing. Had his ex never done this?

Jealousy raced through me, and I pushed aside thoughts of other women. All that mattered right now was me and Nolan.

I took him into my mouth, as far as I could, and took a second to breathe through my nose. Then I started to move. Slowly at first, taking my time to tease the underside with my tongue as I went. Nolan's restraint finally snapped, and he guided my head. I let him control my movement and raised my gaze to watch his face.

His eyes burned, and it shot between my thighs. I moved a hand to my clit and stroked as I continued to bob on Nolan's cock.

He growled. "That's right, baby. Take your pleasure too. It makes me so fucking hot to see how much swallowing my dick turns you on."

This man and his mouth. I stroked faster, just as Nolan guided my head quicker too. Deeper and deeper I took him, until he hit the back of my throat, and Nolan stopped. "Right there. I feel you. I'm so close, baby. Make yourself come, and I'll follow."

He moved my head again, and I stroked faster. It didn't take long before I cried out around his dick and Nolan stilled, hot jets of semen hitting the back of my throat. I swallowed every last drop.

Eventually, he pulled out, knelt down, and wiped

my chin. "Dip your fingers into your pussy and let me lick them clean."

I did as he asked. His gaze never left mine as he sucked and licked until every last drop of my arousal was gone.

After he pulled away from my fingers, he kissed me. It turned heated, his hands cupping my face as his tongue claimed my mouth.

I wondered if finally, finally, I'd feel Nolan inside me. But then my stomach rumbled. And again.

Nolan pulled back, but kept my face in his hands. I fought a smile at his cocky grin.

He said, "I think we need a break before we continue."

"Continue?"

"Oh, I want to feel that pussy grip my dick, baby. We're nowhere near done."

Apparently, I wasn't out of his system yet. Which was good, because he was nowhere near out of mine.

He stood, helped me up, and then pulled me flush against him. I laid my head on his chest, listened to his heartbeat, and he stroked my back in slow circles. His deep voice rumbled under my ear. "Part of me wants to keep you locked in here, all to myself."

My heart thudded. The wishful part of me wanted it to mean forever, here with this man. But rationally, I knew he just meant for sex.

Which I wasn't against, but I wished for more than that. Much more.

Stop it. Needing a distraction from my thoughts, I

finally glimpsed out the bedroom window and gasped. "That's the beach!"

He chuckled. "You knew I lived on the beach."

"Well, I thought near it. But it's right there. Is that your backyard?"

"Yes. I have a private beach." He leaned back. "Should we eat dinner outside, on the beach?"

I stroked his chest. "Could we? It'd be nice to relax outside for a while before we, er, spend more time inside."

He kissed my nose. "Tonight will be up to you. Did you want to come back to my bedroom after dinner?"

"Yes."

Maybe I should've hesitated, but screw it. Until I had penis-in-vagina sex, I would constantly wonder what it'd be like to be with Nolan.

I had no idea if the offer was beyond tonight. I'd probably want Nolan every day, if I could have him. But one night might be all he needed before he tired of me.

Don't think about that and ruin the day. Just embrace what you do have.

Nolan kissed me one last time before stepping away.

I nearly asked him to hold me in his arms again.

He gestured. "There's a bathroom in there. Your suitcase will be in the walk-in closet, which is that door." He gestured toward one off to the side. "I'll meet you downstairs, if you think you can manage it?"

"Of course."

He picked up his clothes, stared at me another second with an unreadable expression, and then left the room.

My clit was still sensitive as I walked toward the closet, a reminder that I'd actually been naked with Nolan. More than that, he'd made me orgasm harder than any man before in my life.

But as I opened the closet door and stepped inside, my jaw dropped. The "closet" was bigger than my bedroom back home. Hell, maybe two of my bedrooms put together.

Clothes hung from various bars, shoes organized, accessories too. And there sat my pink suitcase in a corner, somewhat dirty and battered from my trip here. It looked decidedly out of place.

Just like I was.

That realization helped bring my head back down from the clouds and reminded me this wasn't the life for me. Short, curvy, outgoing Katie Evans worked on a dairy farm. She didn't lounge on private beaches, have dresses that cost more than a month's salary, or mingle with rich and powerful people.

All I could do was enjoy the time I had, go on my trip of a lifetime, and return to Starry Hills.

Oh, and have sex with Nolan. I was curious about what that man could do.

However, I would never have a permanent life with him. It was time to stop wishing and hoping and dreaming, and instead do something practical, like come up with what I'd say to his ex when I finally met her.

Because it was only a matter of time before I encountered her in L.A., and there was no way in hell I'd let her best or bully me.

Chapter Twenty

Nolan

Jenn: She's your wolf mate.
Me: WTF are you talking about?
Jenn: Wolves usually mate for life. You're a Wolfe, and she's your wolf mate.
Me: How long have you been waiting to use that factoid?
Jenn: Years. I didn't want you to be a lone wolf forever.
Me: What if my last name was Fish?
Jenn: Some fish return home to spawn. And where did you find Katie? Back home.
Me: <sighing emoji> Do you have an answer for everything?

Jenn: Of course. It's why I'm the best assistant in the world.

Me: You are good. BUT, I'm not a wolf. Or a fish.

Jenn: No, you're just a sweet guy who needs to find his person. And I think you have.

Me (typed but deleted): I want to believe that.

Me (actual reply instead): Have you finished arranging that surprise for me?

Jenn: Nearly.

Me: Then work on that and stop looking up wolf-related facts.

Jenn: <wolf emoji> <heart emoji> <wolf emoji> Just saying.

Me: Work on the surprise, Jenn.

Jenn: <sighing emoji> On it, Mr. Killjoy.

As I cleaned up and dressed, with Katie's taste still lingering in my mouth, I kept reliving her coming apart on my tongue. Or kneeling before me, swallowing my cum.

All flushed and soft and beautiful.

Not claiming her straight away with my dick had been difficult. And yet, I wasn't about to starve the woman. Hell, I could do with some food, too. That way, I'd be at full strength and could make the night even more memorable.

Even if my plans had shifted and I wanted Katie for more than one night—I now knew I'd never get her out of my system—I had to be patient. Until Katie experienced what life with me would be like outside of Starry Hills, I could never ask her to be my girlfriend for real.

I could barely handle my fame some days, and I'd been dealing with it for years. The constant attention and Hollywood politics might be too much for Katie.

I hoped not, but she needed to see and experience it herself. The New Year's party event would give her a much-needed glimpse. After that, I could hopefully start making more long-term plans.

Once I was finally dressed again, I headed downstairs, put in the order with my chef for dinner on the beach, and waited for Katie. I checked my phone to see if there was any more Wendy drama, but there were only texts from Aunt Lori and Jenn.

I almost wished Wendy would act so I could react. However, maybe pigs could finally fly and she'd given up.

Hearing footsteps on the stairs, I looked up and watched Katie descend. She'd changed her outfit to a dark green sweater and dark jeans, probably to better handle the wind and cold on the beach.

Now that I'd seen her naked, it was easy to undress her with my eyes and imagine her walking down to me without a stitch on.

As my dick twitched, I mentally cursed and got myself under control.

When she reached the bottom of the stairs, I noticed the slight frown between her eyebrows. I asked, "What's wrong? Did you need something?"

She smiled—it seemed forced to me—and shook her

head. "No, it's just been a long day and I'm a little tired. And before you suggest I should retire for the night or something, don't. I *want* to see the beach and then your bedroom again. A walk and some food will give me energy. Going outdoors usually does."

I took her hand and threaded my fingers through hers. She squeezed me back, and I led her out the back door and down the path to the water. "I'm the same way. Beaches both relax and energize me. I've always wanted to live along the ocean, so it was the one indulgence I allowed myself, once I could afford it. It's not the rolling hills of back home, but the sound of the waves always calms me and helps me think."

We reached the sand. Even though it was in the low 60s, I removed my shoes and dug my toes into the somewhat warm sand. "And this. There's something about walking barefoot in the sand."

Katie eyed the water in the distance. "It's warmer here than back home, but I'm not sure if I'm brave enough to go barefoot."

I bumped my side against hers. "Try it. If you're too cold, you can always put your shoes back on."

She raised her brows. "Should I be worried that you're encouraging me?"

"Well, if you ever want me to chase you down the beach, barefoot is the better way to go."

She finally smiled—a real one—and it eased my worry a little. "I didn't know our walk included chasing."

Leaning down to her ear, I whispered, "Don't you want to have a little fun before dinner arrives?"

"Wait, arrives? Don't tell me—you have a chef."

"Of course. I thought I told you that already. Or at least, Jenn should have."

"We got distracted. But I like your assistant. She's nice."

Sensing Katie wasn't in the mood to play on the beach, I walked and she kept her shoes on and followed. "Jenn is a godsend. She's more than my assistant—she's my friend, too. Hiring her was one of the best decisions I ever made."

"When was that?"

"Five or six years ago now. She's the second cousin of one of Aunt Lori's friends back home, and I agreed to interview her. Jenn grew up in L.A., knows the area well, and even worked on some movie and TV sets in the past. How someone didn't swoop her up before me, I'll never know."

"Maybe it was destined to be. After all, she met her wife because of you."

"Yes. Although in the beginning, I wasn't sure if they hated each other or were crazy about each other. They bickered. A lot."

Katie chuckled. "Sometimes there's a fine line between love and hate."

"True. And it's a good thing you like Jenn. She's going to take you shopping over the next few days. Because while I wish I could stay with you, I have to leave town for a nonnegotiable business trip."

It was something I couldn't get out of—related to my production company—even if I wanted nothing more than to stick around and spend as much time as possible with Katie.

She frowned. "Did you tell me this before?"

I shook my head. "No, it came up today. And I'll only be gone for a day and a half. Besides, we learned today that if I go shopping with you, I'll want to see everything and things could get heated very, very quickly."

"That's not a bad thing."

I groaned. "Katie."

She laughed. "Hey, you're the one that has some kind of magical tongue. A girl could get used to that."

"I'm just glad you didn't mind me going down on you. Some women...don't like it."

"What? Since when?"

I shrugged one shoulder. "Everyone has their own tastes, and I don't shame them for it. But spreading you wide, tasting your sweet honey, and feeling you fall apart on my tongue turns me on."

She stopped and turned toward me. "Well, I won't complain. Feel free to do it whenever you want."

"Really?"

Katie bit her bottom lip, and my heart thudded. Was it just banter? Or did she feel the same intense attraction I did?

Facing forward, she started walking again. "I won't say no."

That wasn't the answer I'd hoped for.

We were nearly at the waterline when Katie released my hand and ran to the very edge, where the waves wouldn't reach her. Squatting down, she picked up a few seashells and stood. "I've always wanted to collect shells from around the world and display them on a shelf. It's one of the things I plan to do when I can finally travel."

Oh. She was thinking of when she'd leave me and be free again.

It shouldn't hurt. After all, that was the agreement we'd made.

But it did.

I'm not giving up. I had many months left yet to prove there was more to this than an agreement. "You haven't collected any seashells for your shelf yet?"

"I think we came to the beaches down here when I was really little, but I don't really remember it. This is the first time, as an adult, I've been to a sandy beach. The shoreline around San Francisco Bay isn't like this."

"Then if you could go to any beach in the world, where would it be?"

"Oh, that's tough. The beaches in Thailand are supposed to be beautiful. But even just going down to Mexico, to the Yucatan, would be nice. The latter also has some amazing ruins I'd love to see too."

"You'd choose the ruins over Cancun?"

She wrinkled her nose. "I don't need a place full of resorts. I like to go off the beaten path a little. I mean, I'm not about to hike through the jungle by myself. But I want to plan out my trips, find restaurants where the locals eat, and try the non-touristy places."

I crouched down and shifted through the shells in the sand. "That's one of my favorite things to do, actually. To find hidden gems."

"Really?"

"Yep. I avoid fancy restaurants, if I can help."

"Says the man with a private chef."

I chuckled. "Well, I can burn boiled pasta. But even my chef is from a little family Italian restaurant I discovered by chance. He was taught by his parents and aunts and uncles, and makes good food that some rich people might turn their noses up at."

Katie sat down, her legs crossed, and asked, "What kind of stuff?"

"Oh, you'll see soon enough."

She drew shapes in the sand with her finger. "I think you like giving chances to people who might not get a second glance from other famous people."

I sat, too, tossing a shell back and forth between my hands. "Someone gave me a chance when I was a completely unknown young actor. I'm just trying to pay it forward."

"How does someone as rich and famous as you remain so grounded?"

I shrugged. "I have Aunt Lori's texts to remind me I'm just Nolan Wolfe and not Nolan Drake."

"Haha, nice try. But it's admirable, really." She placed a hand on my upper arm and squeezed. "You're such a good man, Nolan."

I sighed. "This again? But bad boys have all the fun."

I winked at her, and Katie laughed. She then leaned her head on my shoulder, and I wrapped an arm around her.

For a few minutes, we sat in silence, watching the waves. Sitting there with Katie, combined with the sounds of the ocean, was peaceful.

To think, if I could just convince Katie I wanted her

as my girlfriend for real, I could have this all the time. And then I could just be a man with his woman, enjoying nature, as the rest of the world faded away.

Soon I heard people approaching and reluctantly turned my head. Antonio and his assistant came toward us. I waved, untangled myself from Katie, and helped her up. "Dinner's here."

As soon as my chef was close enough, I introduced him to Katie as Antonio's assistant laid out our dinner.

Katie said, "Nice to meet you! I've heard good things, and I can't wait to try your food."

Antonio smiled. "Well, if there's anything you want, just let me know. Even if I've never made it before, I can learn how. Considering how Nolan likes to eat a lot of the same things, it'll help break up the monotony."

I shook my head. "I've said a million times that you can surprise me whenever you want to."

"Yes, and then you don't eat it and instead get some fast food." The chef shuddered.

"It's one of my guilty pleasures. There's something about French fries and a burger from the Golden Arches that can't be beat."

Antonio merely raised his brows before smiling at Katie. "Anything in particular you want for breakfast?"

"Um, French toast and bacon?"

"Consider it done. Come visit me in the kitchen or my office anytime, Ms. Evans."

"Call me Katie, please."

"Katie then."

As Antonio flashed a smile—one that Katie returned—I clenched my fingers into fists. Even though I knew

Antonio had a fiancée and wasn't a threat, jealousy roared through me.

The sooner I could woo Katie for real, the better.

Once we were alone and both sitting on the blanket spread over the sand, I removed the dish covers and was instantly hit with the scent of lemon and garlic.

Katie gasped. "That's fancier than any pasta I've ever had in my life."

It was creamy lemon garlic shrimp pasta. "This was the dish that led me to hiring him. My guess is he wants to win you over, too."

After picking up a fork, Katie twirled the pasta and slid it between her lips. She closed her eyes, moaned, and my dick stirred.

Once she swallowed, she opened her eyes again. "That's so, so good. I could probably eat it every day for weeks and never tire of it."

"It's one of the dishes I eat every week, part of Antonio's so-called monotony."

"Well, I'm on board for that kind of monotony."

Katie picked up a warm breadstick covered in butter and garlic and took a bite. I merely watched, fascinated at how she took pleasure from the simplest things. Being with Katie was so different from my past relationships in L.A., when status and expensive trinkets had been way more important than anything else.

And as Katie continued to ooh and ahh over everything she ate, allowing me to even feed her the chocolate mousse for dessert, I thought about Jenn's words. Maybe this Wolfe had, indeed, found his mate.

Soon Katie yawned and cuddled against me as we

looked at the stars. Before long, she quieted, snored softly, and went slack in my arms.

I should be disappointed that she'd fallen asleep and we probably wouldn't be having sex tonight. But as I carried her home, nestled against my chest, disappointment was the last thing I felt.

No, it all just felt...right. Perfect, even.

And as I fell asleep with her pulled close—Katie still in her clothes since she'd been too sleepy to change—I smiled and dreamed of a future where I took my future wife to beach after beach, helping her to collect seashells, until she had shelves near to bursting from them.

Chapter Twenty-One

Katie

Emmy: So, how is Nolan's mansion?
Me: I don't care about the house. You should see his beach. I think Nolan needs to have a beach party here this summer.
Amber: I'd love to visit in the summer. Then I could also stop by some famous bakeries for research.
Abby: Really? You could lounge on the beach all day, but instead you want to visit bakeries?
Amber: <tongue out emoji> I have plans. Big ones.
Me: I vote for a girls' trip to Disneyland.
Emmy: Ooh, yes. But I'd probably bring the twins too. They've never been, and I'd like to take them before they become any more teenager-like.

Abby: <sighing emoji> Let me guess? I'll have to watch them while you and West go have sex in a bathroom or in a hidden corner of the park?
Emmy: Not everything is about sex.
Abby: Says the woman who constantly has to stop herself from gushing to me about what you did WITH MY BROTHER.
Me: Call me anytime, Emmy. I want the details. <heart eyes emoji>
Emmy: Only if you give me the same about Nolan. Something tells me the quiet brother will surprise us all.
Abby: No, no, JUST NO. Don't tell me. I don't want to know.
Amber: <laughing emoji>
Me: We'll talk later. I need to do some more shopping today. I promise to send pics of my dress on New Year's. <heart emoji>
Abby, Emmy, and Amber: <heart emoji> <blowing a kiss emoji>

I still couldn't believe I'd fallen asleep on the beach after dinner. Something about sitting with Nolan, his arms wrapped around me, had felt warm and safe and comfortable.

And I didn't even wake up as he carried me back to the house and tucked me into bed.

He'd been gone by morning, though. His flight had

been early, and I'd been more exhausted than I'd thought.

And now? I had to go shopping for hours and hours, getting everything else I needed for New Year's and a few events beyond.

I reached the bottom of the stairs and waved to Jenn. She returned the gesture and said, "Come on. If we stick to my schedule, you'll have tomorrow off to do whatever you want."

"Nolan won't be back until dinnertime tomorrow, though, right?"

"Yes. But tomorrow, we can go anywhere in the city, your choice. Living here, I sometimes take things for granted. It'll be nice to see it through the eyes of a tourist again."

A tourist. Yes, that was exactly what I was.

Then why did the term not sit right with me?

Because you want more of last night, more of quiet moments and cuddles and good food on the beach. And then maybe you could go looking for hidden gems together, whenever Nolan can get away from his job.

Jenn's voice brought me back to the present. "Hmm, I wonder why you have that dreamy-eyed look?"

I blinked. "What are you talking about?"

Rolling her eyes, she said, "The two of you are impossible, I swear."

"I don't follow."

"You'll figure it out soon enough. Now, we need to leave or my schedule will go to shit. First up: bra and panty shopping."

"Um, no one will see my underthings at the party, so why do I need new ones?"

"You really need to stop worrying about how much things cost. Besides, I'm sure someone will see you in them, and I want him to drool."

She waggled her eyebrows, and I smiled. I'd always wanted to have sexy lingerie to show off to my guy.

No, not my guy. Nolan wasn't mine. Not really.

Jenn added, "Besides, I got word this morning that Wendy will be at the same party. And the more armor you have, the better."

"So, what are you saying? That a thong will make me feel like a goddess?"

"Hey, you can wear granny panties for all I care, as long as it makes you feel badass. But I've found that when I feel gorgeous and amazing and kick-ass, it's easier to face the glitz and glamor of Hollywood. Even though I deal mostly with other assistants, some of them are major snobs. Being the girl who grew up in the cheapest apartment her parents could find, even with them both working two jobs? Well, I must smell, given how they hold their noses up sometimes."

"I grew up on a dairy farm, which is probably worse in their eyes." I hesitated to mention my past, but then said, screw it. "Even growing up, other girls teased me for it in Starry Hills. So no doubt, some hoity-toity people here will mention it."

"That's easy enough to counter, though—just mention your brother's name. Kyle Evans and his cheeses are famous and even trendy right now, which makes them hard to get. When it comes to popular, scarce items, the person who can hook other people up has all the power."

I laughed. "And to think, cheese might open doors for me. Who knew?"

Jenn snorted. "It's one of the many strange things about this city. Wine can do it too, but few people know Starry Wolfe wine is made by Nolan's family, even with him doing the ads for the brand now."

"In the age of the internet, how is that even possible?"

Jenn shrugged a shoulder and then shepherded me out the door and into the waiting car before finally replying, "Starry Wolfe wine is more for everyday people. It's good—I drink it all the time—but since it doesn't cost thousands a bottle, it hasn't reached 'must-need' status here."

I rubbed my forehead. "Equating worth with a price tag instead of the actual item doesn't make any sense to me."

Jenn patted my arm. "Don't worry, I'll help you navigate the rat race as best as I can. Maybe if I do a good enough job, I can get some of your brother's famous cheese?"

She put her hands together, complete with puppy dog eyes, and I laughed. "I think that can be arranged. I take it for granted since we always keep a decent amount back for our family. Plus, I always get to eat leftovers after the tours and tasting table."

"You're a tour guide, right?"

"Yes. People are going to laugh at me about that, aren't they?"

"Never to your face. And not all of them—many actors start off with waitressing or bartending until they get a break. Wendy, though, is a different story. She sees you as standing in the way of her happiness and will do whatever it takes to win."

"Which I don't get. He's not the only hot actor around town. She could be making waves with another popular one, right? Seems easier."

Jenn shrugged. "It's about status. Nolan's the most in-demand male actor right now. Add in his sexiness, and she probably thinks they can make and raise beautiful children to dominate the next generation."

"It seems cold and calculated to me."

"It is. But that's Wendy for you. However, men will do all kinds of crazy shit for a pretty face and a chance to fuck someone."

"But not Nolan."

Jenn smiled. "No. Nolan's different, for many reasons. And a marriage like that would destroy him, I think. He's lonely, more than he'll ever admit, and needs someone in his corner."

I could be that person. Easily.

But would he even want that?

Jenn touched my arm, garnering my attention. "For what it's worth, I've never seen him smile, growl, or whistle as much as he has since he's met you."

"Um, you're one of the few people who knows about our plan. It's just part of his act."

"Maybe." She opened her phone and tapped it. "We're nearly to the first store, and I'd like to go over your hair and makeup appointment for the New Year's party."

I blinked. "I have hair and makeup appointments?"

"Of course. Nolan arranged for you to have them. But only as much or as little as you want. How they style everything is up to you. Although your hair would look beautiful swept up with a few dangling curls."

As Jenn brought up some hairstyles on her phone, I tried to concentrate. However, I was still stunned by the fact Nolan had hired hair and makeup people for me.

True, I'd been a little worried. I was hopeless except for the most basic of styles and had planned to ask Jenn to make a hair appointment.

Even with the amazing dress and professional people dolling me up, would it be enough? At the thought of mixing with the rich and famous, my stomach churned into knots. Would I feel like a fraud? Make some kind of faux pas and prove that the small-town girl had no business mixing with the famous?

Stop it. I may not have dealt with Hollywood people, apart from Nolan. But over the years as a tour guide, I'd mixed with a wide-ranging group of people. I could do this. I *would* do this.

But finding some sexy lingerie to start building my armor couldn't hurt.

Chapter Twenty-Two

Nolan

Me: Sorry I had to stay away another day, baby. I'd rather be home with you.
Katie: It's okay. You're trying to learn how to be an executive producer instead of just an actor. And sometimes things don't go as planned.
Me: Still. I wanted to show you around and finally feel you fall apart around my dick.
Katie: <overheated emoji> Don't tease me like that!
Me: I still remember your taste.
Katie: Keep it up, and I'm going to have to remember to pack a vibrator next time.
Me: Only if I can watch.

Katie: Hmm, it'd be like watching your own secret porno, wouldn't it?
Me (typed but deleted): No, more like I want to know exactly how to please my future wife.
Me (actual reply instead): Should I arrive carrying a pizza box? Then you can say you don't have any money and want to pay me another way.
Katie: Maybe. If it's with pepperoni and extra cheese.
Me: I'll bring three of them.
Katie: Then I'll think of some creative ways to pay you. Hurry home. <heart emoji>

The heart emoji was innocent, and yet it made me smile every time I looked at it. I'd never had such an easy time joking via text with a woman before.

And if I had returned even a few hours earlier, I would've arrived with those pizza boxes. However, I'd been delayed four more hours and by the time the car pulled up to my front door, I barely had time to get ready and change for the New Year's party.

As I showered and dressed, I heard a commotion coming from down the hall. No doubt it was the team I'd hired to help Katie get ready. Jenn had said not to disturb them and that I should wait at the foot of the stairs.

So I did. I adjusted the bowtie of my tux yet again when voices traveled from the hallway above.

But then Katie appeared at the top of the stairs, and everything else faded away.

Her hair was swept up except for a few teasing curls, one of which bounced against her breasts as she walked. She wore the black dress from the shop, but the alterations now made it fit like a glove—snug against her boobs and abdomen before flaring out to land just above her shoes.

Her dark heels peeked out.

Ones I wanted her to wear as I finally thrust between her thighs and made her scream my name.

She bit her bottom lip, clearly nervous, and I snapped out of my trance. I met her and took her hand, bringing it to my lips and kissing the back of it. "You look beautiful, Katie. Stunning."

Her pale cheeks turned pink. "It's just the hair and makeup."

True, she wore more makeup than usual—somewhat more dark and smoky, as befitting a nighttime party. However, that wasn't it.

I traced her neck with a finger, over her shoulder, and down her arm, loving how she shivered at my touch. "No, it's just you, Katie Evans. You're the reason you're beautiful. Not because of anything else."

Her gaze met mine and time slowed as we stared at one another. She was two steps above me, putting our heads even. Heat and longing and something I couldn't identify flared in her blue-eyed gaze.

I leaned over and kissed her gently, which was a mistake. Because the quick peck only caused heat to rush through my body and straight to my dick. I wanted to say fuck the party and finally claim my fiancée upstairs. Where she'd dig her nails into my back as she moaned my name and spasmed around my cock.

That would be a much better way to ring in the New Year.

Jenn appeared and cleared her throat, breaking the moment. I frowned at her. "What?"

"Don't bark at me. You know we have to go to this party. If you two don't show up, Wendy will say it's because Katie's afraid of her. Then she'll make up more rumors, putting even more of a spotlight on Katie, and you don't want that, do you?"

Fucking Wendy Webster.

Katie spoke before I could. "And after all this work to get ready, I want to go. I've never been to a fancy party for New Year's before. Usually I hang out at a friend's house or go to the shindig at The Watering Hole."

I kissed the back of Katie's hand again. "If you want to go, then we will." I searched her eyes. "But if at any time you want to leave, just say the word and I'll get us out of there, ASAP."

She nodded. "Okay."

"Good." I guided her to the bottom of the stairs and took out a large, square box. "But first, this is for you."

She frowned as she took it, opened it, and gasped.

Inside lay a diamond and sapphire necklace. As soon as I'd seen the blue stones, they'd reminded me of Katie's eyes.

"Nolan, I can't accept this."

"Don't be silly, of course you can. What kind of fairy

godmother would I be if I sent you to a ball without a dress and jewelry befitting a princess?"

She laughed. "You're my fairy godmother?"

"Why not?"

"Then where are your wings and wand?"

Leaning over, I whispered, "I'm undercover and don't want to give myself away. Otherwise, everyone will start asking for wishes."

Katie snorted. "You're silly."

I winked. "I try." I took the necklace. "Will you wear it for me?"

After a second, she nodded.

"Turn around."

She did, and I laid the piece over her chest and brought the clasp to the back of her neck. Once I secured it, I leaned down and nuzzled her skin just above the metal. And again.

Katie leaned back against me, and I moved a hand to one of her breasts.

Jenn spoke up. "Ahem. Could you two at least wait until you're alone in the car? If Nolan starts shedding his clothes, I might be scarred for life."

She gave a fake shudder, and I shook my head. "You should've been an actor."

Katie walked away from me, and despite how it felt wrong, I let her. "Come on, Nolan. I'm curious to see everyone and get another glimpse of your life."

After threading my fingers through hers, we exited the house, and I helped her into the car. Jenn and her wife would arrive separately, so we were alone.

As soon as the car was underway and the partition

was up, I took Katie's hand again. She smiled at me and plucked at her skirt.

I studied her. "What's wrong?"

"I'm nervous. I shouldn't be, given how amazing I look. Seriously, whoever that guy was who did my hair, he can do miracles."

"Jorge is one of the most in-demand hair stylists in town. I met him while filming a movie a few years ago." I tugged the curled section over her chest and watched it bounce back up.

She swatted my hand away. "Don't do that. It takes more product that I'd like to get it to hold the curl."

"But it's just begging for me to tease it." I reached to tug it again, but Katie laughed and moved away.

"Stop, Nolan. You can do that *after* the party, and much more, but not before."

In our text messages, we'd danced around finally having sex after the party. "Provided you don't fall asleep again."

She stuck her tongue out at me. "We'll see. I'm used to country hours."

I raised an eyebrow. "Says the woman who spends a lot of Saturday nights at a bar with her friends."

"Hey, Sunday is one of my days off. And usually there's dancing and alcohol involved, which both keep me alert."

I reached for her curls again, but at her narrowed eyes, I grabbed her hand instead. "There'll be dancing and drinks at the party, so fingers crossed, it keeps you awake. Because I don't want to just dream about you tonight—I want to worship you in my bed for real."

Her gaze turned heated as she said, "Maybe on the way home, we can warm up for the main event."

At the thought of tossing up her skirt and eating her sweet pussy, my dick stood at attention. My voice was hoarse as I said, "Tease."

She grinned. "I'll take that as a compliment."

Laughing, I reached and tugged her curl. But I kissed her gently afterward to quell any protest.

I was about to haul her into my lap when someone rapped on the window. I sighed. "We're here."

"The wait will make it that much better, Nolan. Just keep remembering that."

"And I'm going to get you back for that remark, baby. You think you've seen me tease that hard little clit? You haven't seen anything yet."

She squirmed in her seat as her breathing picked up. "Now, who's being the tease?"

There was some more rapping, and I scowled. "I suppose we'd better get this over with."

But as I noticed the excitement in Katie's gaze, my frustration faded. This was Katie's first high-profile event. She deserved to enjoy herself and make memories she'd never forget, in a good way.

Once I exited the car and helped Katie out, cameras flashed and reporters asked questions. I tucked her arm into mine and whispered for her ears only, "It's best to stop and smile for the cameras a few times along the carpet. That way, we'll have flattering pictures. So when I stop, follow my lead. Okay?"

She nodded, and we walked down the red carpet.

Even if it wasn't a movie premiere, the host—and my friend—Zara Jones liked to make a statement.

When we stopped at a larger roped-off section set up for pictures, I smiled and Katie did the same. A reporter asked, "Is this your fiancée, Nolan?"

"Yes. But she's standing right here, so how about you ask Katie questions related to her?"

Jenn had prepared Katie for this, but I still held my breath when the reporter asked, "Katie, how does it feel being the fiancée of someone so famous? It's a long way from your family's dairy farm."

Katie's smile never faltered. "Well, remember, I've known Nolan my whole life. He's still just the boy who climbs trees and makes wishes, like when we were kids."

"Nolan, what did you wish for most recently?"

"Health, happiness, and the best for my family."

Another reporter shouted, "Katie, Katie! What will you say to Wendy Webster? She arrived a little before you."

I tensed and waited to see if Katie needed my help.

She shrugged. "I guess we'll see what happens, won't we? She can say whatever she wants about me, but I don't appreciate her harassing my future husband."

For a beat, I forgot that our engagement was all pretend. I couldn't remember the last time someone had wanted to protect me, at least not since I'd left Starry Hills.

And here was Katie, willing to suffer Wendy's nastiness if it was merely about her but not about me.

I started to fall for Katie Evans right then and there.

But as we started walking again, I tried to keep my

hopes to a minimum. Katie had no idea what we were about to face inside. I knew she could handle whatever they threw at her, but maybe she didn't want to face it constantly. And she would have to, if she agreed to be mine.

I'd just have to protect her like she said she'd protect me. If anyone tried to harm or humiliate Katie, they'd have to deal with me. Not just tonight, but in the future, too.

And soon we walked into the lion's den, together, ready to face what came next.

Chapter Twenty-Three

Katie

Me: Okay, here's a picture for you all.
Emmy: OMG, you look gorgeous! <heart-eyed emoji>
Amber: Soooo pretty! I wish I could get my hair like that.
Abby: That dress. <heart-eyed emoji> Maybe I should ask Nolan for a princess dress for my next birthday.
Emmy: And where would you wear it, hmm?
Abby: <middle finger emoji> Let's focus on Katie.
Me: <laughing emoji> Don't worry, I know I look fabulous. Nolan hired movie professionals to do my hair and makeup. And damn, I have to admit I like being spoiled a little.
Abby: You're going to rock the party, Katie. Just remem-

ber: Nolan picked you. Which makes you more special than any of them.

Amber: Um, I'm not sure that logic is sound. People are special in different ways.

Abby: It's not about logic. Katie is better than the rest of them.

Emmy: You do realize the person holding the party was our client? I like Zara.

Abby: Yeah, yeah. Zara's cool. Still, Katie is far better.

Me: Well, time to go. Wish me luck! It's been a while since I wore heels, and I hope I don't trip.

Amber: Good luck! You'll be fine. And don't worry, I know Nolan will be there to catch you if you fall. <heart emoji>

The entire walk down the red carpet, my heart pounded so loud I expected every reporter to remark on it.

Except they didn't, and I managed to stumble through every question and sound confident, which was the important part.

By the time we reached the entrance, I sighed and leaned a little into Nolan.

He squeezed my arm in his and whispered, "You did a great job, baby. Amazing, in fact."

"All those years of putting on a smile for my tours, no matter if I had to deal with assholes or not, paid off."

He kept his voice low. "Ready for the next round?"

"Is this a boxing match?"

"In a way, yes. But I put my money on you to win."

It was a simple, throwaway comment. And yet, it invigorated me with extra energy.

Standing up taller, I nodded. "Bring it."

He laughed softly. "I'll introduce you to my friend first. She's the party host, and then we'll make the rounds. And remember—"

"To let you know if I ever need a break. I know, Nolan. And I will."

With a nod, he propelled us toward a couple near the door—Zara Jones and her husband. Since Emmy had organized her wedding, I knew Zara wasn't snobby or thought she was better than everyone simply because she was a successful movie star. So when she smiled at me, I smiled back.

She had light brown skin, dark hair pulled back into a twist of some kind, and dark brown eyes. She also wore a dark blue gown decorated with shiny stones; it was also floofy enough to hide most of her obvious pregnancy. "That dress makes me think of a galaxy full of stars."

I mentally cursed. That wasn't exactly a polite, formal way to make an introduction.

But Zara laughed. "I thought the same thing. I love anything that sparkles."

The man with fair skin and blond hair at her side spoke up. "A little too much. You should've seen the comforter she wanted to buy. But I drew the line at sparkles that could end up on my ass."

Zara tsked and then said to me, "Hello. I'm Zara Jones, and this is my husband, Brody."

"Oh, hi. I'm Katie Evans. Nolan's fiancée."

Nolan placed a hand on my lower back. "Hey Zara, Brody. Thanks for inviting us."

"Well, of course. It's probably the last big event we can have until after the baby's born, and I was determined to make a splash."

Nolan said, "You definitely did. A red carpet?"

Zara laughed. "Well, why not? Everywhere who attends my party deserves it."

Zara's husband murmured, "Not quite everyone."

His gaze was off to the side, and I followed it to find Wendy Webster standing amidst a crowd of people. She wore a dark red dress that hugged her slight form, which matched the bowtie and cummerbund of the man she stood next to.

Zara lowered her voice. "Well, I invited her date, Bryan, and I had no idea he'd bring her. But everyone knows the rules—if she causes a scene, my bodyguard will toss her out. I don't care who she is."

Brody rubbed his wife's arm. "Calm down, honey. She's not worth distressing the baby."

Zara took a few deep breaths. "I know."

She shared a loving glance with her husband, the type which contained an entire conversation without words, and my heart ached with longing.

Would I ever have such a close relationship with someone? Have a man look at me like Brody looked at Zara, as if she were the most precious thing in the world?

Nolan said, "We'll do our best to steer clear of her. Katie and I just want to have a good time."

Zara nodded. "And you will. Go enjoy yourselves! I'll see if I can chat some more later."

Another couple came up, and Nolan guided me across the room to the bar. Once we both had our flutes of champagne, we walked to the perimeter of the big ballroom so we could talk.

After a few sips of fortification, I said, "Zara's nice."

Nolan nodded. "We worked on a movie together years ago and kept in touch. She worked her way up from nothing too, although her story is far more impressive than mine."

"Well, according to Emmy, she's a fantastic tipper, so that's a plus in my book."

The music changed to something slower. Nolan took my empty glass and placed both of ours on the tray of a passing server. "Will you dance with me, Katie?"

My heart thudded. "What, as in slow dance? I don't really know how, beyond swaying in place."

He put out a hand. "I can teach you. Do you trust me?"

Without hesitation, I answered, "Yes."

As soon as I placed my hand in his, he guided me to the dance floor. After putting a hand at my waist, he used his free one to take mine. Once I had my hand on his shoulder, he said, "We'll go slowly at first. Once you get the hang of it, we'll match our pace to everyone else."

He counted off and for a minute, I concentrated on following his movements. Soon we were gliding across the floor in time with everyone else, and I smiled up at him. "Handsome, rich, *and* an excellent teacher? Is there anything you can't do?"

"I suck at baseball. And I'm afraid of snakes."

"But didn't you star in that adventure movie, the one where you had to walk through a room of snakes?"

He shuddered. "Don't remind me. I nearly pissed myself when a scene required draping some across my shoulders."

I smiled. "So, the great Nolan Drake is afraid of snakes. I'll keep that in mind, in case I need to plot revenge."

I waggled my eyebrows, and he laughed. "Fair's fair —tell me something you're afraid of."

"Well, it's not so much an animal or insect, per se. But I'm afraid that I'll never figure out what to do with my life, or discover my purpose. I'll travel, yes. But after that? I don't really want to return to my family's farm and conduct tours again. But do what instead? I have no idea."

"You still have time to figure it out, baby."

"I'm nearly twenty-seven years old, Nolan. Shouldn't I know by now?"

"Not necessarily. Even if you had figured everything out by now, things could always change at the drop of a hat, no matter your age. For example, look at Emmy's brother. Rafe was a soccer star for nearly twenty years, and yet one injury ended his career and he now has to start over." He guided me through a difficult twirl before continuing, "I think for some people, it takes time and patience to know what you should do or where you belong. And it could always be more than one thing, changing as your life changes. What was fulfilling at twenty might not be the same as at fifty."

"Maybe. But my sister Cassie always knew she wanted to be a nurse, and Kyle's always loved the dairy farm. Sam likes the farm, but is excited to start working for Emmy's wedding and event planning business soon. But me? I sure as hell don't want to conduct tours forever. And yet, it's the only thing I seem to be good at."

He tilted his head, as if to study me. "Have you written a list of things you like to do? Or are good at? Don't hold back, write everything down, no matter how far-fetched. Then you could see where they overlap and maybe find a new path. There's a perfect job out there for you, baby. I just know it."

It was something so simple, and yet I'd never really tried that approach.

And the fact Nolan was encouraging me didn't hurt either.

"It's definitely something to think about."

He tightened his hold on me. "Even if you don't have it all figured out straight away, it might plant a seed that will take root. One that, during your travels, might finally grow and spark a new passion or dream."

The music started to wind down, and I wished we could dance forever. "Do you have an answer for everything?"

He chuckled. "Not even close. I'm just observant. Sometimes I'm wrong, but not often."

He winked, and I laughed. "We might have to test that theory."

"Any time, baby. Any time."

The music stopped, and Nolan guided me off the

dance floor. He waved at someone and I asked, "Is that another friend of yours?"

"Yes. Dylan Murphy and I worked together in a few movies. We played best friends in one and hit it off in real life, even if our schedules rarely match. Plus, his family runs a ranch in the same town where my aunt lives—Sun Falls. It was quite the coincidence."

I was about to ask more about his family in Sun Falls when something tugged at the back of my skirt. Hard.

Then there was a loud ripping sound, and cold air blasted my ass and thighs.

A familiar voice said, "Oh, I'm *so* sorry. I didn't mean to step on your dress. But there's just so many people here." Wendy raised her voice. "Give us some space! Now!"

The last thing I needed was space, but soon the noise died down. Well, apart from my thudding heart, Nolan's growl, and the sound of cameras clicking.

Ones probably taking pictures of my ass encased in shapewear.

For a few seconds, I couldn't think above the roar in my ears. The night had been going so well, to the point I'd thought maybe I could fit into Nolan's life.

But then his damn ex had gone and ruined everything.

And now I'd be the laughingstock of the internet by morning.

Nolan tried to pick up my ripped skirt, but I pushed him away. "Don't."

His gaze turned concerned, and I looked away. Once

I had my skirt in my hands, covering my butt as much as I could, I turned toward Wendy.

Wendy and her self-satisfied smirk.

I want to cuss her out. Yell, scream, and tell her she was a piece of shit.

And yet, I knew that was what she wanted—for the country girl to show she didn't belong in the big city, let alone among the rich and famous.

Tears heated my eyes, but I took a few deep breaths. I could cry later, but I'd be damned if I did it in front of *that woman.*

Meeting Wendy's gaze, I said calmly, "Of course it was an accident. If you'll excuse me."

Keeping my head high, I strode from the room and down the hall to where the private bathrooms were for the guests.

As soon as I entered one, I locked the door, sat on the closed toilet lid, and put my head in my hands.

Unbidden, taunts from my childhood came racing back to me:

Look at Fat Kat! Why does she wear skirts? I've never seen the top of someone's legs be so much bigger than the bottom.

Did you hear? Fat Kat asked Toby to the dance! Like he would ever do that—he's going with me. Together, he and I have a chance at being crowned king and queen.

Do you smell that, girls? Cow shit. It must be Fat Kat stinking up the hallway.

. . .

This was like middle school all over again, but a million times worse.

Tears finally fell, and I sobbed, quietly. No matter how old people got, they still had cliques and taunts and put others down to feel better about themselves.

Except this time, it'd been in front of Nolan's friends and colleagues. It'd also be in front of the entire world by tomorrow, if not already.

I could handle the Mean Girls of Starry Hills as an adult. But this? The world and the internet making fun of and judging me? Complete strangers tearing me down, laughing the whole time, and forgetting I was a real person?

I didn't know if I was strong enough to deal with that.

Someone knocked at the door, and Nolan's muffled voice came through. "Katie? Baby? Are you okay?"

Calm down and get home. Then you can break down again.

Sitting up, I did my best to dab my eyes with toilet paper and blow my nose. "Just a minute."

Going to the mirror, I sighed. My makeup was smeared, and my hair was starting to slip.

Almost as if midnight approached, and I'd soon turn back into the dairy farm version of Cinderella.

Nolan knocked again. "Katie, please. Open up."

After a few last dabs to erase my tears, I put my shoulders back and unlocked the door.

Nolan rushed inside, shut and locked the door, and reached out, as if he would cup my face.

I put my hands up. "Don't."

Maybe if I weren't so worked up and emotional, I would've noticed the hurt in his eyes and been nicer.

But it barely registered as I said, "I want to go home, Nolan. Home, home, as in Starry Hills. Can I go tonight?"

He searched my gaze for a few beats before nodding. "Of course. I have my car out back. Zara told me a discreet way to leave so we can avoid any reporters or cameras."

My first thought was: *even Nolan is embarrassed by me.*

I nearly started sobbing again, but managed to hold back. I needed to get home. Soon. Or I might embarrass myself further. "Then let's go."

On some level, I registered how Nolan kept his distance, never touching me like he had in recent weeks. But since it took everything I had to keep my tears at bay, I couldn't concentrate on anything but following his directions and fleeing the scene.

Even in the car, I sat as far away from Nolan as possible and laid my cheek against the cool glass of the window, watching the lights as we drove back to Malibu.

All my dreams of being able to handle Nolan's fame were gone. Maybe if I could've said screw the world and been outrageous, I could've survived better. Or, I could've come out on top, with Wendy being the laughingstock instead of me.

However, I hadn't wanted to embarrass Nolan like that.

Of course, I had in the end, anyway. But at least this way, it wasn't my fault.

But was that any better?

My eyes heated again at the thought of what the world was saying about me. I was so lost in my thoughts that I nearly missed Nolan's soft voice as he asked, "Do you want to end our agreement?"

I should say yes and be done with it.

And yet, I couldn't bring myself to do it. Not tonight, at any rate. It would give Wendy the win, and I'd be damned if I let that happen. If we did end it, then it would be on Nolan and my terms, no one else's.

I replied, "I don't know. I need some time to think, Nolan."

From the corner of my eye, I saw Nolan clench his fingers into fists. "I'm going to make her pay, baby. You'll see."

I finally met his gaze and blinked at the rage there. "Don't get yourself into trouble on my account, Nolan."

He grunted. "You're worth any trouble, Katie Evans."

My throat tightened. "I don't know about that."

So I didn't have to talk any more, I put my cheek back on the cool glass. Thankfully, Nolan didn't push me.

Which was good, because any more nice words and I would've started crying and crawled into his lap at the first opportunity.

But I wasn't going to be clingy or make Nolan feel as if he had to comfort me. He was a nice guy and would do it, anyway. However, I wanted it to be because he cared for me.

And now you might never get the chance to tell him how you feel and learn his feelings in return.

Somehow I kept myself together, and Nolan respected my wish for silence. And in less than two hours, I was packed, changed, and on Nolan's private plane back to Starry Hills.

Alone, like I'd asked for.

I even told the flight attendant to leave me be. And the entire way, I cried silently, wondering what the hell I was going to do now about Nolan, let alone how I'd face the morning and the world's mockery.

Chapter Twenty-Four

Katie

Nolan: I wish you'd either call or let me visit.
Nolan: She won't get away with this, I promise.
Nolan: I can send Antonio up to Starry Hills, if you want?
Nolan: Please, Katie. Just talk to me.
Nolan: If you want some space, I'll give it. But I'll be in town for West's birthday. Let's talk then.
Nolan: I miss you, baby. And once I figure out how to get back at her, I'll let you know.
Me (typed but deleted): I miss you too, Nolan. I wish you were here right now and the rest of the world would just fade away.

. . .

The next afternoon, I lay on my side atop my bed with my eyes closed and a pillow hugged to my chest. My three best friends sat around my room with me.

Despite it being New Year's Day, my three best friends had come at the crack of dawn and refused to leave.

After not talking about the night before long enough to down some coffee, I finally asked them to see what the world was saying about me and my ass.

Abby asked, "Are you sure you want us to tell you what we find? I still vote for ignorance and alcohol."

Amber patted my arm. "Maybe you should wait, Katie."

I shook my head, still not opening my eyes. "If I cower and pretend nothing happened, Wendy wins. And while my chances of besting her aren't great, I need to try." I finally sat up and opened my eyes. "But I'm not quite brave enough to do it alone."

Emmy smiled and hugged me. "Well, that's why you have us."

My eyes pricked with tears, but I held them back. "Thanks. And sorry for my weepy outburst when you all first arrived."

Abby waved a hand in dismissal. "If you can't cry with us, then something is wrong with the world."

I couldn't quite smile. "I know. My sisters kept asking through the door what had happened, but I couldn't face them. Not yet."

Amber nodded. "I get it. I love my brothers, but I would rather shave my head than spill my secrets to them."

I hugged the pillow against me again. "Okay, enough stalling—tell me what people are saying about last night."

I'd managed to avoid opening any of my apps on my phone or checking social media since leaving the New Year's party.

And yet, I needed to learn what was being said to see if I could salvage this.

If I wanted to try to salvage whatever I had with Nolan.

Don't make any hasty decisions or run away, Katie. Maybe it's nothing with Nolan, but you can at least fulfill the agreement and see the world.

Abby spoke up. "Well, there are pictures, of course, and even a few videos. I don't think it's too bad, though. I mean, look at your sexy ass! Mine is too flat. I wish I had some curves like you."

I raised an eyebrow. "I doubt everyone is saying, 'Wow, look at that butt! I want one just like it!' So stop stalling. What are some of the captions and comments?"

Abby sighed. "Fine. But I wasn't lying. Flat butts are completely overrated."

Emmy rolled her eyes. "Since Abby's hung up on her genetics, I'll tell you one: Hot star's date strips for guests."

I suspected that was one of the kindest ones. "And the comments?"

Amber shook her head. "Internet comment sections

are the worst places in the world, and you should avoid them at all costs."

"I need to know, Amber. Tell me."

She bit her lip for a second before replying, "Fine. It's what you'd expect—some people are objectifying you and wanting to do things like smack your butt. Others are making not-nice comments."

Amber was often the peacekeeper, the one who didn't like to rock the boat. As much as I loved her for it most of the time, I needed more of the truth.

I looked at Abby and raised my eyebrows.

She nodded. "I'll do it. There are derogatory comments about your appearance, your size, and, er, something I'd rather not repeat."

"Tell me."

Abby cleared her throat. "That one day, you'll crush Nolan to death while having sex."

Pain lanced my heart.

But I'd asked for it. And no doubt, Wendy would use every single thing against me. So I needed to listen and toughen up. "What about Wendy? What did she say?"

Emmy's gaze turned wary, which was never a good sign.

"Tell me."

Emmy shook her head. "She's a vicious cow. I want to state that for the record."

"Noted."

"Fine. Well, her post says that after you left the party, her and Nolan met up later to ring in the New Year. And also to celebrate their wedding, which is back on."

I growled. "It was never on in the first place. And seriously, what is wrong with that woman? Does she think humiliating me would win him back?"

Abby shrugged. "My guess is that she thinks it shows she'd do anything to get her man, and Nolan would like that."

I muttered, "The last thing Nolan wants is to be the focus of scandal and drama."

Something that would always continue, as long as Wendy thought she had a chance with him.

Was there even a way out of this where Wendy left him alone and I could have a chance to date Nolan for real?

I rubbed my eyes with my fists. "I think I need a nap to recharge my brain."

"Are you sure?" Amber asked. "I thought maybe we could open some wine and plot how to get back at that lady. I've been listening to a lot of true crime podcasts lately and have some good ideas stored up."

I opened my eyes and blinked. "Who are you and what have you done with sweet-tempered Amber King?"

Amber smiled. "I'm sweet to a point. But after that, the gloves come off." She mimed taking off her gloves and then made fists. "I don't have many people on my shit list, but Wendy Webster is one of them."

Abby nodded. "Mine too."

Emmy said, "Me as well."

I looked at each of my friends and smiled. "Thanks."

Amber spoke again. "That's what the BFF Circle is for. Zach always teases we could take over the world if we put our minds to it, and I agree. Somehow, some way, we'll deal with Wendy Webster. Just wait and see."

My phone vibrated again on the nightstand, and I didn't bother to look. It'd be either my sisters or Nolan, provided the latter hadn't given up on me. Considering I hadn't replied and had all but ghosted him, I wouldn't fault him for it.

Emmy asked softly, "What are you going to do about Nolan?"

Sighing, I plucked at the comforter. "I don't know. He's such a sweet guy, and I love being around him. But this?" I gestured toward all the cell phones. "This would only be the beginning. And so the question becomes: could I handle this sort of criticism and harassment day in and day out? To be honest, I'm not even sure how he does it, and he's had years of practice."

Emmy said, "You should at least talk to Nolan about your feelings and worries before making a decision. Trust me—hiding everything from those you care about only tortures yourself and keeps you from ever finding happiness."

She would know. Emmy had only recently shared with us how she'd blamed herself for the car crash that killed her parents when she was ten.

Taking her hand, I squeezed. "I know you're right, Emmy. I do. But he's done so much for me, spoiled me, and it seems like I should just buck up and handle it myself."

Abby grunted. "No fucking way. You tried that in middle school and were miserable. I would've kicked the asses of those bullies if I'd known about them. My height would've been an advantage for once."

Abby was nearly six feet and had been the tallest girl her age in Starry Hills until junior year. None of us had known how much it'd bothered her until high school.

Each of us had kept secrets, it seemed.

And right then and there, guilt crashed over me. I was keeping a major secret from them—that my engagement was fake. I burned to tell the truth. And yet, I couldn't do that without talking with Nolan first.

Damn. It always came back to talking with Nolan, didn't it?

With a sigh, I rubbed my forehead. "I need to act like a grown-ass adult and talk with him, don't I?"

Emmy nodded. "It's not easy. Trust me, I know. But if I'd never opened up to West? Then I definitely wouldn't be getting married next month, maybe not ever."

More guilt hit me. "Your wedding, Emmy! I completely forgot it's next month. And here I am, complaining about some mean comments from strangers. We should be gushing over the bachelorette party and working on party gifts for the reception."

Emmy shook her head. "I'm a wedding planner, so it's not as exciting for me as it is for other people. I'd be okay going to Vegas and getting a quickie wedding. However, I know it's important to West, Avery, and Wyatt that we all do it together, with family here in Starry Hills." She shrugged. "Plus, I can show off my skills for my own wedding. That way, you won't complain when I say I'm planning all of yours in the future, when you're ready."

Amber laughed. "You're oh-so subtle, aren't you?"

Emmy winked. "I'm more excited to plan weddings for you ladies than myself. No rush, though. I want you all to find love, too."

Abby grimaced. "I told you—I'm off men."

Amber patted Abby's shoulder. "Date or don't, it doesn't matter. Just don't let that jerk rob you of happiness forever."

Abby put up a hand. "We are not talking about the Douchebag Disaster. No, we should be focusing on Katie. And, well, I may know how you can sit down and have a chat with your man in private."

I studied Abby. "What have you been up to?"

"I'm not even going to pretend to deny it. Nolan asked me how you were doing, and I told him not good. He wants to see you, Katie. Not here, or in L.A. He wants to take you on a trip, just the two of you, away from prying eyes so you can talk."

"Even if I agreed to that—which I haven't—a trip isn't going to help. I already know I love being with him when we're in Starry Hills or alone. It's in public, outside of our little bubble, that I'm not sure I can handle."

Emmy said, "Then tell him that, not us. Don't let your life become like one of the books we keep yelling at because the main characters never talk with each other."

I snorted. "The miscommunication trope sucks ass."

Amber nodded. "Right, so don't live it in real life."

Abby smirked. "Or I may call you a TSTL heroine."

I tossed a pillow at her. "Don't even dare. I'm not too stupid to live."

Abby caught it and laughed. "Normally, I'd agree with you. We're all pretty fabulous. Most days. But even if you decide to end it with Nolan, go enjoy a free vacation. It's not like he's going to take you to Fargo, North Dakota, in January. He'll probably whisk you away to some place warm."

Emmy said, "Hey, Fargo could be fun. Snowed in, bundled up in bed, with a fire blazing..."

Amber shook her head. "They need to talk before any of that could happen."

Abby waggled her brows. "Or maybe they could bang it out first and then talk after."

My cheeks heated, and I mentally cursed. For years, I'd been teasing my friends with outrageous sexual innuendos. Now I was on the receiving end, and it wasn't quite as fun.

Still, they were right. I knew they were. I couldn't hide forever.

And yet, I didn't want to text with Nolan or even talk on the phone. I wanted to see him in person before I said anything. So I replied, "Abby, tell Nolan I'll go. But let him know I won't text or call him between now and then. It'll give me space to think."

"I'll tell him. And I'll hint—heavily—that he needs to take you someplace warm. So dust off your razor and get ready to show off that sparkly bathing suit you have."

I loved my black tankini suit with fake white stones. But what if someone caught me on camera and this maelstrom started all over again?

Don't think about that now.

"And tell him to make sure it's remote because I don't want to deal with crowds of people until we figure things out."

Abby saluted. "Of course. Let me get on it. You have a passport, right?" I nodded, although I'd never used it. She continued, "Just give me a sec, then."

Abby typed on her phone, and I itched to see what Nolan replied.

But no, it was for the best to wait and talk in person. The line had blurred between our deal and my heart, and I needed to see if Nolan's feelings had shifted like mine. If so, then maybe, just maybe, I'd risk facing the world and the internet again.

He could say he doesn't feel that way about you.

True. But I needed to know, even if his answer ended up crushing my heart.

A heart that wanted Nolan Wolfe but wasn't sure it could handle Nolan Drake.

Chapter Twenty-Five

Nolan

Abby: She's agreed to go on a trip with you. But it has to be remote. And I vote for warm.
Me: I already know where I'm taking her.
Abby: Details?
Me: Nope. I'll pick her up in two days. Tell her to pack for at least four.
Abby: Optimistic, aren't you?
Me: I can't fuck this up, Abby. I need to make it work.
Abby: It's not going to be easy. Maybe you're used to all the attention and criticism, but Katie's not. Hell, I wouldn't be, either.
Me: I know. But that's a conversation between me and Katie.

Abby: Fine. But brother or not, if you hurt her, I will kick your ass. Maybe break your nose, too, for good measure.
Me: I don't plan on hurting her.
Me (typed but deleted): I'm falling for her. I want more. So much more.
Me (actual reply instead): I'll treat her like a queen, I promise.
Abby: I saw the necklace you gave her. That was a good start.
Me: I'll send the final details later today.
Abby: <sad face emoji> You're blowing me off now, huh? Rude.
Me: Love you too.

Two days later, I paced inside the Sonoma County airport, waiting for Abby to drop off Katie. I'd offered to pick her up, but Abby had insisted it would be better for her to drive Katie and let us have the plane ride to talk.

While I'd calmed down a little since the night of the party, just thinking about Wendy Webster and what she'd done to Katie made me curl my fingers into fists. What should've been a magical night had turned into a nightmare.

I still didn't know how I'd deal with Wendy. I had to be careful and do it in a way that highlighted her jealousy and instability without making me look like a complete asshole.

Regardless, that could wait. Seeing Katie, talking with her and convincing her to give us a chance, was my priority.

So when I saw Abby's tall, dark head in the crowd, I walked toward it. Soon, I could see Katie walking next to her, a roller bag suitcase behind her.

She was wearing stretchy pants, a long sweater, and had her hair tied back—and she'd never looked more beautiful.

Damn, I'd missed her.

I reached them, smiled at Katie, and said, "I'm glad you came."

Her lips moved a fraction, but didn't quite smile. The dark circles under her eyes were like a stab to my heart.

Because I'd caused that—me, my fame, and my crazy ex.

She shrugged. "I'm trying to be an adult and not run away from my problems."

It was a long way from: *I missed you and love you and can't live without you.* But it was a start.

I gestured. "My jet is this way. Can I get your bag?"

She allowed me to take it and then turned to give Abby a hug. "Thanks, Abby."

"No problem. Just keep me updated. I'm dying to know where you're going." Abby looked at me and mouthed, "Meanie."

I shook my head and waited. Once Abby waved and

disappeared into the crowd, Katie turned toward me but didn't meet my gaze.

Another knife to my heart.

Clearing my throat, I gestured. "Come on. The sooner we get settled, the sooner I can tell you where we're going."

"It's not Fargo, is it?"

I blinked. "As in North Dakota? Um, no. I like a little snow, but not that much."

She smiled. "Good. Abby kept teasing you'd take me there just to be contrary to her suggestion."

"I might try to needle my sister when it concerns her, but not you."

Silence fell, and I itched to reach over and take Katie's hand.

But we reached the gate for my jet and went outside to climb the stairs. Once inside, I gestured to a seating area with a table, the seats facing each other. It'd be easier to talk without temptation sitting next to me.

Once buckled in, the flight attendant did the mandatory spiel for Katie's sake, and then we were soon in the air. After the flight attendant gave us drinks, I said, "Leave us for now, please. I'll press the button if I need anything else."

"Of course, Mr. Drake."

When alone, Katie asked, "He doesn't use your real name?"

"No. In the beginning, I was trying to keep Nolan Wolfe and Nolan Drake separate. And even if Drew knows the truth by now, I haven't had the heart to correct him."

Katie tapped the side of her Cherry Coke can for a few seconds before meeting my gaze. "So."

"So. How are you? Truthfully?"

She sighed, and yep, more pain.

"It's been brutal, if I'm honest. I've had to turn off my phone most of the time, or at least turn off the internet so I can still text. People from high school have been giving me a hard time again, too."

I crushed the paper coffee cup in my hand, which was thankfully empty. "Is it those bullies again? They're easier to deal with than Wendy. Say the word, and I can ruin them tomorrow."

She blinked. "What? How?"

"I know some powerful people. More than a few would give me a favor."

Maybe call in a loan that was due at a bank, or get clients to stop investing in the hedge fund of one of the mean girls' husband.

Yes, I'd done my research after the Christmas market.

Katie shook her head. "No, don't do that. I don't want to sink to their level. Although it's tempting to do that for your ex, for sure." She tapped the can again. "How do you handle it, Nolan? You've been famous for nearly a decade now. And even a sexy, charming guy like you has to have haters."

I pushed aside that she thought I was sexy and charming for the moment. "You're right—not everyone loves me. But I mentioned before how Jenn helps with all my social media. Even so, stuff still slips through and finds its way to me. I just have to remember those people are commenting on a fantasy about some guy called Nolan Drake, who they've put on some sort of pedestal. Some idolize him, some sexualize him, and others feel insecure and try to tear him down. But it's the work I love—acting and now, also producing. So I just think of it as having a lot of crappy coworkers that I need to ignore if I want to keep my dream job."

"Hmm. Crappy coworkers. I'd never thought of it that way."

I nearly reached for her hand, but instead crushed the paper cup some more. "It's different for you, Katie. Fuck, I know it is. Maybe if you actually cared for me, it would be different. But..."

"But what?"

My heart tightened, but I knew what I had to say. It didn't mean the end of us forever, just for now. "You don't have to stay with me just to get a trip. You've more than earned one, and I'll pay whatever you want. So if you want to jilt me now and end the nightmare, you can."

Her eyes searched mine, and I took a risk. I allowed my feelings for her to show through—about how much I'd miss talking with her, laughing with her, and even her mouth around my cock as I fucked it hard.

How she meant more to me than simply a way to deal with my ex.

How she'd wormed her way into my heart.

How I wished to claim her as mine for real.

She sucked in a breath. "Nolan."

I finally released my cup and put my hand out, palm up. "I needed to lay that out for you and release any obligation. Because here's my truth: I want to date you for real, Katie Evans. To call you my baby, and spoil you, and finally have you naked and all to myself, with no interruptions. To laugh about the little things, or sit in silence on the beach and watch the stars. To hold close the one person who actually sees me and not my fame." I took a deep breath and added, "I want a chance with you, baby. Do you want the same, knowing that a future with me might be tough?"

For a few seconds, she bit her bottom lip and stared at me. It felt like years, but could only be seconds before she finally placed her hand in mine. I curled my fingers around hers and then brought it to my mouth so I could press my lips to her skin. "Is that a yes?"

"Yes, for now."

"For now?"

"Well, I-I care for you, Nolan. I do. And not in a brotherly way. But it's still a lot—your ex, your fame, being the focus of the world. I'm used to being fairly invisible outside of Starry Hills. And at home, I can be outrageous and funny and find ways to take the attention off my appearance and move it to other things. But doing that elsewhere will embarrass you, and I don't want to do that."

I sat, stunned, as I tried to process her words. "Wait, you've been trying to hold back for my sake?"

"Well, yes. I know you don't like to be the center of attention in your personal life. It's why I held my tongue with Wendy on New Year's and didn't stand my ground with her."

I rose, released her hand temporarily, and sat across

the aisle, in a seat without a table. I patted my lap. "Come here."

She didn't hesitate to walk over, and I pulled her down. Once I had my arms around her waist and she put hers around my neck, I leaned my forehead against hers. "Don't ever try to hide yourself, Katie Evans. Not for me, not for anyone. I like the woman who teases me about sex dungeons or being a sparkly vampire. Or, the one who dances with abandon at The Watering Hole when you've had a little too much to drink. Or, the woman who will do battle to win her family's Fourth of July baseball game just to have bragging rights for a year." I searched her lovely blue eyes. "That's the woman I like. That's the woman I want everyone else to see, too."

"Even if it embarrasses you?"

The corner of my mouth kicked up. "Have you met my Aunt Lori? When it comes to people I care about, it takes a lot to embarrass me."

Love. I wanted to say loved. But it was too soon. Right?

She replied softly, "I want to be me—the real me—but I'm not entirely sure who that is anymore."

I rubbed her hip and leaned back to better watch her face. "What do you mean?"

"Well, for so long, I acted out to distract people and to help stop the bullying. Some of it is me, I think, but some of it is for show. I just don't know what is or isn't real, if that makes any sense."

"Yes, I think I get it—the public act and the true you. I know a little about that myself." I moved a hand and brushed some hair off her cheek. "But don't hold back for any reason, baby. Say and do whatever you want. Think of this trip as a test. There won't be many people around, so it's the perfect chance to test the waters and figure out exactly who is Katherine Something Evans. What even is your middle name?"

She snorted. "Ruth."

My lips twitched. "Ruth?"

"Hey, it was after my great-grandmother. If my dad would've had his way, it would've been my first name."

"Then everyone would've called you Baby Ruth."

She stuck out her tongue. "You're so much meaner than everyone says."

I chuckled. "Like you wouldn't tease me about my middle name, which is Hank."

"Was that a family name, too?"

I raised an eyebrow. "You're not going to tease me?"

"Hanky Panky comes to mind, but that's too easy. I'll have to think on it."

Squeezing her side, I replied, "You do that. But no, both my first and middle names are taken from famous baseball players—Nolan Ryan and Hank Aaron."

"But wasn't Nolan Ryan's first name Lynn? You could've been Lynn Hank Wolfe, and that would've sucked for you."

"And how do you know that factoid about my namesake?"

Katie shrugged. "I was into baseball when I was little, mostly so I could try to figure out how to beat my brother on the Fourth of July. He's so much older, and I needed every advantage I could muster for the annual family game."

I imagined Katie as a child, studying baseball games and looking for tips on how to win. I kissed her nose. "You're adorable."

"Not sure anyone's ever said that about me before."

"Well, you are to me."

"Hmph. Well, seeing as I'm so adorable, will you finally tell me where we're going?"

She batted her eyes.

I laughed. "You might want to save that move for when you really need it, because it might just work on me."

After lightly swatting my chest, she asked, "Where are we going, Nolan?"

"South."

"That's not very helpful. I mean, an entire continent is south."

"It's a surprise. And I thought you liked surprises?"

"I'm starting to reconsider that when it comes to you."

I kissed her gently. "I'm not going to budge. Since we have hours and hours until we get there, what do you want to do? I brought cards. Or..."

I stroked her cheek with my thumb before trailing it to her bottom lip.

Her breath hitched. "Or, what?"

"We could join the mile high club."

I grinned, and she laughed. "There's the flight attendant and the pilots. They'll hear us."

"Oh, they'll leave us alone unless I call. And I doubt they'll hear anything. The pilots are behind a door, and

Drew will no doubt be working on his latest screenplay attempt."

She narrowed her eyes. "You seem to have everything planned out. Have you had sex with a woman on your jet before?"

"No, never. I'm usually not that risky. But when it comes to you, Katherine Ruth Evans." I nuzzled her cheek. "Well, you make me want to be wild and crazy and take risks like never before."

She traced my jaw. "And believe it or not, you make me want to take risks too, Nolan Hank Wolfe."

As she wiggled in my lap, my dick turned to stone. My voice was husky as I asked, "Is that a yes?"

"It's a yes. But how is this going to work, exactly? And please don't say we're doing it in the bathroom. Those things are tiny."

I chuckled. "No, not in the bathroom. I was thinking of bending you over that table and fucking your sweet pussy from behind."

Her pupils dilated. "Oh."

I nipped her bottom lip. "But before that, I'd strip you bare, spread your thighs, and make sure you were nice and wet and swollen for me. With my tongue."

She swallowed. "The mouth on you, Nolan."

Leaning over, I whispered, "I bet if I touched your cunt right now, you'd be dripping, wouldn't you?"

"Yes."

I worried her earlobe and loved how she moaned. "Then strip and show me, baby. Show me that pretty little pussy and let me worship it."

She glanced at the open windows, and I laughed softly. "No one can see us up here."

"True."

After nipping my bottom lip, she stood. I watched as she moved to the aisle and fisted the bottom of her sweater. When she hesitated, I rubbed my dick through my jeans. "Don't tease me, baby. The faster you're naked, the faster I can taste you."

The corners of her mouth kicked up. Then she took a deep breath and removed her sweater.

Underneath, she wore a lacy black bra, one that was sheer enough to show her hard nipples.

My restraint snapped. I strode over, took one of her hard buds into my mouth and suckled through the lace.

Katie's hands went to my shoulders, and she moaned as I sucked and nibbled and lightly tugged with my teeth. Desperate to see her with nothing on, I dragged the cup down and groaned. "So red and hard and wet from my kisses. But I need another taste. I'll always need another taste."

After taking her taut bud into my mouth again, I teased with my tongue and teeth and loved how she arched toward me, as if needing more. Much more.

Releasing her nipple, I tortured the other one, too. All while massaging her free breast, plucking her hard little peak, and reveling in the pure sweet scent that was Katie Evans.

When my dick was so hard it hurt, I released her nipple and breast to kiss her mouth. I moved her back toward the table, until she hit it. Then I threaded my fingers through her hair, tilted her head, and took the kiss deeper. Fuck, every lick and lap and tease of tongues drove me wild.

But it wasn't enough, not nearly enough. I ran my hand down her front, over her soft belly, and beneath the elastic waist of her leggings. Down, down, until I reached between her thighs.

"Fuck, you're so wet already."

"And what are you going to do about it?"

At her saucy tone, I met her gaze and asked, "What do you want me to do, baby? Tell me."

She ran a hand up under my shirt. Each pass of her fingers against my chest only made me harder. "You mentioned something about worshiping."

"I did, and I pride myself on being a man of my word."

I picked her up and set her on the table, and she squealed and then laughed. "What is with you always picking me up or carrying me?"

After removing her bra, I fondled her breasts as I replied, "You mentioned the Highlander fantasy. You like when I carry you. Admit it."

As I rolled both her nipples, she moaned. I asked, "Don't you?"

"Yes. Oh, yes."

I ran my hands down her sides, to the waist of her leggings. "Help me get these off."

It wasn't sexy and seductive, but it took a mad, frustrating minute to get the leggings, shoes, and underwear off.

Note to self: See if she doesn't mind me ripping her clothes off next time.

But as soon as she was naked, I spread her thighs and stared at her glistening slit. "So fucking perfect. Look at you weeping for me, baby. Say it's for me."

"Yes, it's because of you, Nolan Wolfe."

It was a small thing, her using my real name. And yet, it was yet another thing that made me love this woman.

Because, fuck it. I didn't care if it hadn't been long. I'd never felt so at ease as when I was with Katie. She tried to get to know the real me. She even let me spoil her, and I'd never been so attracted to anyone in my life before.

Katie was it for me.

Time to show her with actions what I couldn't say with words just yet.

I knelt and didn't waste time lapping her pussy, moaning at her taste, and spreading her even wider.

Each lick and swipe and nibble only made Katie lean back on her hands more and cry out as she arched her hips toward me.

Wrapping my hands around her thighs, I kept her spread wide as I teased her clit. Slowly circling her hard little bud, making the scent of her arousal grow stronger, and reveling in her cries. When one of her hands tugged at my hair, I looked up.

Her heated gaze shot straight to my dick, as did her breathy voice. "Nolan, please."

I stopped long enough to ask, "Please, what? Tell me what you want, baby."

"Please make me come."

Never taking my gaze from hers, I suckled her clit

and lightly bit her. She screamed my name, and I thrust a finger into her pussy as she spasmed around me. I never let up, drawing out the orgasm, trying to see just how long I could pleasure her.

When she finally slumped and stopped, I kissed her clit, removed my finger, and lifted it to her nipple. After coating the hard bud, I suckled her, lapping and licking her clean.

"Nolan. Damn, are you trying to kill me?"

I released her and took her mouth in a long, lingering kiss, wrapping my arms around her and holding her close. Eventually I slowed until I could pull back and said, "I'm just getting started, baby. Now you're wet enough to take my cock."

She rubbed against my jean-clad cock, and I groaned.

Katie said, "I can't tell if you're hard enough or need a little encouragement. So strip and show me."

I kissed her again before finally releasing her. The second I let go, I felt too fucking cold. I needed her in my arms again. ASAP.

So I removed the condom packet from my pocket and stripped as fast as possible, uncaring where my clothes landed, until I stood naked. I stroked my dick and as she stared at it, licking her lips, I let out a drop of precum.

I held up the condom. "Maybe you could help me. Then you can check to see if I'm hard enough for you."

Her gaze burned hotter as she motioned for me to come closer. Once she had the packet, she said, "I hope you have more than one."

"Baby, I have two boxes in my carry-on."

"Optimistic, weren't you?"

"Optimistic would've been five boxes. Two is the bare minimum of times I want to claim you in four days."

Her cheeks turned red. "Oh."

"Yes, 'oh.' And after the first few times, we're going to try out a few more of those fantasies you mentioned." I nodded toward the forgotten condom packet. "Are you still going to help me?"

She tore it open and swatted away my hand. Just watching her slowly roll on the condom made me even harder.

Everything about Katie Evans fucking turned me on.

Once done, she tilted her head. "Now, what?"

"Now you stand up, turn around, and bend over that table. I want to feel that sweet ass cushioning me as I claim your pussy." Running the back of my fingers over her cheek, I added, "I've dreamed about taking you this way for weeks. Tell me I can have you that way."

"Oh, you can have me any way you want, Nolan. My hard-no list is very, very small."

Dirty images of how I could fuck her—against a wall, tied to my bed, blindfolded, and hell, even riding me in the middle of a field at night with only the stars for company—rushed through my mind.

"Then let's get started. Turn around and bend over, baby."

She scooted off the table, turned, and leaned over the table, showing off her incredible ass.

I ran a hand over one cheek and then the other. I

lightly smacked her, and she arched and moaned. "Like that, do you, baby?"

"Yes, oh yes. Do it again."

I kissed the slightly pink spot, nipped her, and then smacked her lightly again. One cheek, then the other, and then I soothed it with my mouth and tongue.

By the time I ran my fingers through her center, she was even wetter and dripping down her leg.

Fuck. I couldn't wait any longer. It was time to claim my woman.

Chapter Twenty-Six

Katie

I still couldn't believe I was tens of thousands of feet in the air, bent over a table, about to be fucked by Nolan Wolfe.

Oh, I'd dreamed about this for weeks. Months, even. Pretty much since he first asked me to be his fake fiancée.

But to have his hands slap my ass and then soothe the slight sting with his tongue? Damn, I moaned and arched and nearly begged for him to fuck me.

And yet, Nolan being Nolan, he ran his dick through my center and lightly teased my still-sensitive clit. I gripped the edges of the table and pushed back against him.

He chuckled. "And I thought I was impatient."

"Stop teasing, Nolan. I want you inside me."

His lips brushed my back, and I shivered as he teased my skin with his tongue. His hot breath danced against me as he said, "What my baby wants, my baby gets."

Then he pushed inside me, slowly, inch by inch.

I knew he was thick, but damn. He stretched me, in a good way.

By the time he was fully inside me, I wanted—no, needed—to feel more of him. So I reached back and dug my nails into his thigh.

Nolan moaned. "Fuck, baby. Do that again. Make your own claim on me. One I can look at and instantly remember having you spread out like this for me, wet and swollen and so fucking beautiful it hurts."

I wasn't a virgin, and I knew some guys would whisper anything during sex and not mean it.

And yet, something about Nolan's words rang with the truth. As if he truly thought I was beautiful, even leaning over a small table inside an airplane and displaying my big ass.

Definitely a good guy. One who really was mine now. Finally.

"Tell me I can move, baby. I don't know if I can be gentle this first time."

A good guy with a dirty mind and mouth. Even better.

I dug my nails into his skin again. "Don't you dare hold back."

He ran a hand up my spine, to my head, and gently tugged my hair. The slight sting only made me wetter.

After he released my hair, he gripped my hips and thrust, hard and fast, to the point I had to let go of him and hold on to the table. I arched into his movements, loving how full I felt from behind. He went harder and faster, until I forgot all about the pilots or flight attendant, and moaned. Loudly.

Then one of his hands moved around until it found my clit. He lightly toyed with me, and I laid my forehead on the table, trying to make this last longer.

But then he pinched me and lights danced before my eyes as pleasure exploded throughout my body. Wave after wave, and I soon recognized that Nolan had stilled inside me and moaned, too.

I eventually came down from my high, and Nolan kissed my shoulder, my neck, and then my other shoulder. "You feel even better than I imagined, baby. So tight and perfect."

Turning my head to lay my cheek on the table, I sighed. "You're not too bad yourself."

He nipped my earlobe. "I was expecting, 'Oh, Nolan, you're the best I've ever had and no one could ever compare.'"

At his higher pitched voice, I giggled. "That's not what I sound like."

"That's not what I sound like," he mimicked in the same voice.

Laughing, I tried to get up. Nolan pulled out, gently lifted me up, and turned me until he could hold me against his chest. I sighed and nuzzled my face against his chest hair, breathing in the heady mixture of male and sex. "You'd better not ever use that voice during sex.

Otherwise, I'm going to stomp off and dust off one of my toys."

He hummed, the vibrations under my cheek relaxing me further.

"I'm curious about these toys of yours, baby. Did you bring any of them with you?"

"Sadly, no. I wasn't sure what would happen, and I guess I wasn't as optimistic as you were."

As he stroked my back in slow circles, he said, "Well, next time, bring them. Watching you fall apart as I teased you with a toy would definitely be worth seeing."

"Well, you are over thirty. So I guess you'll need that extra time to recover."

He lightly smacked my butt. "I'm not pushing sixty. And besides, when it comes to you, it doesn't take long."

As he arched his hips against me, I sucked in a breath. He was already getting hard again.

Leaning back, I asked, "Then what's next? I mean, you did say we have hours to kill."

His smile, joyful yet cunning, made me catch my breath.

"Well, maybe we can try the bathroom. And before you protest, the one on here is about five times the size of a regular airplane bathroom, complete with a shower."

I blinked. "You have a shower on here?"

He laughed. "Of course. Sometimes I have to fly halfway across the world and be ready to go as soon as we land."

"Well, if there's a shower, having sex in the shower is definitely something I like."

"Doesn't everybody?"

I shook my head. "Sadly, no."

I had an ex who'd refused. We didn't last long.

Nolan gently raised my head and kissed me. His tongue slipped inside my mouth before licking and stroking and devouring me until we were both out of breath again.

He put his forehead against mine. "Well, my hard-no list isn't very long either. And sex in the shower is a hell yes for me. I mean, I need help reaching my back, after all."

I rolled my eyes. "Uh-huh. Sure."

"Hey, it's true. And I know you'll be very, very thorough. You'll make sure to caress and wash everywhere." He whispered into my ear, "Maybe even using your mouth. I still remember you sucking my cock dry."

Despite my two orgasms already, my clit throbbed. "Where's that shower?"

Grinning, he took my hand and guided me to a door. Inside was a small-ish bathroom, but it had a shower stall, a toilet, and a sink.

Nolan removed and tossed his condom, only to take out another one from a bag on the sink counter.

He held it up. "Ready for me to fuck you against the wall and make you scream my name?"

I shivered, in a good way. "Well, we don't want the condoms going to waste now, do we?"

Soon we were in the shower, me up against the wall with my legs wrapped around Nolan's waist, as he indeed made me scream his name as I came.

Chapter Twenty-Seven

Katie

Abby: Well? Where did he take you?
Me: I'm not sure I should say.
Abby: Hey! I helped put this all together for you, remember?
Me: Hmm....
Abby: Katherine Evans, tell me.
Me: Woah, you must be irritated if the full name comes out.
Abby: Do I need to dust off the middle name too?
Me: No, don't. Please.
Abby: Katherine Ruth.
Me: Noooooo. Not fair, Abigail Marie. So not fair.

Abby: Yes, yes, my middle name is better. But I'm dying here! Please? Tell me. <pleading eyes emoji>
Me: Fine. Let me send you a pic.
Abby: Oooh. Lucky! I've always wanted to go there.
Me: Well, I have a sexy guy waiting for me. More later. <heart emoji>

After the shower sex, I was sore and ravenous. Nolan, of course, had amazing meals waiting for us. And after eating, I dozed against him for the remainder of the flight to our mysterious destination.

I was just dreaming of Nolan and me having sex in the ocean when something jostled me gently.

"Wake up, baby. We've landed."

Blinking slowly, I nuzzled against the warm, solid form at my side. "I don't want to move. I'm comfy."

"I know, baby. But trust me—it'll be worth it. We have a pit stop to make before we go to our accommodations."

That piqued my curiosity, and I sat up to stretch. "What kind of pit stop? Wait, scratch that. Start by telling me where we are."

He opened the window shade. "See if you can guess."

Leaning over, I looked outside. It was an airport—much bigger than the county one back home—and there were big and small planes everywhere. I also noticed all the signs and company names written in Spanish—even my high school Spanish self could tell that. I also spotted a familiar flag. "Mexico?"

"Yep, we're in Mexico. Cancun International Airport, to be precise. But no, we're not heading to Cancun. That's the opposite of where I plan to take you."

"Mexico." I sat back in my seat. "It's my first passport stamp, you know."

He smiled. "The first of many, I'm sure."

I wiggled in my seat. "When can we get off so I can get my stamp?"

He laughed. "Soon, baby. I promise. I'll even let you go first, so you don't have to wait another minute."

It took far too long to disembark and go through customs. But when the worker finally stamped in my passport for the first time, my chest tightened. I'd waited so long, and after twenty-six years, I was finally getting to travel outside the US.

Nolan frowned as he watched me, but went through his interview and waited until we were walking away to claim our luggage. He wrapped an arm around my shoulders. "Are you okay, baby?"

"Yes." I sniffled. "It's just...such a big thing. Something I've dreamed about doing for so long, you know? And it's finally come true."

He kissed the top of my head. "Is it everything you thought it'd be?"

"Yes and no. I mean, I'll be staring at that stamp for a long, long time. But I'm eager to see more than the airport. After all, it doesn't count until you set foot outside of it."

"Well, lucky for you, I have a car waiting. The first surprise will take less than twenty minutes to get to. The drive to where we're staying will be an hour and a half after that, but it should be worth it."

"Okay, now I really want to know where we're going."

"Nope, I'm not telling you. It's a surprise. I'm even going to blindfold you when we get close and guide you out. That way, I can watch your face when you see it."

"Part of me loves that you've planned this all out. And the other part is annoyed because I want to know everything right now."

His eyes twinkled with mischief. "I plan to surprise you a lot, so you'd better learn to be a little more patient."

"Or, imagine this—you could just tell me upfront and I could plan which thing is better and should be done first."

"Then I'd have no say in it. And that's the fun of surprises—catching people off guard."

"Hmm. I guess that means I'll have to tease you even more than you do me, when it comes to surprises. Mine won't be as grand as an impromptu trip, but I'll come up with a few things."

He stopped to kiss me. "As long as it's from you, any present will be the best one of my life."

"Nolan."

He smiled. "It's true, baby. Because each surprise will also reveal a little bit more about you, which will not only help you figure yourself out, but it'll also make me happy. Because I want to know every little thing about you."

As I stared at him, it was hard to believe that only a little over two months ago, Nolan had proposed a fake engagement to me. Out of the blue, at a children's birthday party, no less.

And now? It was starting to feel more and more like we were a couple. And not just because of the sex, although that was definitely a perk.

Nolan Wolfe, sex demon. Who would've known that under his quiet exterior was so much more?

But it was more than that. He listened and teased and encouraged me when I needed it. Hell, he'd brought me to Mexico and made one of my dreams—to travel outside the US—come true.

Yes, I still had to sort out my feelings about the paparazzi and fans and all that came with dating a famous actor. But for now, I just wanted to spend time with my boyfriend.

Just thinking of Nolan as mine made me smile.

Nolan traced my mouth. "What are you thinking about?"

"You. Me. Us. And how much I want it to work."

"We'll take it as slow or fast as you want, baby. But for the next four days, let's just have fun and get to know each other, okay? The rest of the world can wait."

Delaying problems had never ended well for me before. And yet, I couldn't resist the sexy man next to me.

My sexy man.

"Okay, I'll try my best. Now, let's hurry and grab some coffee on our way out. Because I'm eager to see what else you have planned for me."

He kissed me. "Then let's go, baby." He moved to my ear to whisper, "Because I'm already thinking of more ways to take you later. Maybe on a beach or in a pool."

"That doesn't really reveal anything, does it? There are tons of beaches and pools in Mexico."

"Yep." He put a hand on my lower back. "Come on. The car should be here by now."

Nolan guided me out of the airport and to the car and driver he'd booked. Once we were settled in the backseat, I was torn between laying my head on Nolan's shoulder or looking at the window.

After interlacing his fingers with mine, Nolan said, "Go ahead and look. I want you to see as much as you can until I have to blindfold you."

"You're really doing that, aren't you?"

He grinned. "You bet. And don't worry, the area will be clear for us, so there's no chance of some random person taking pictures."

I suspected he'd paid a small fortune, again, to do something private for us.

At some point, we'd have to talk about that. I didn't mind being spoiled sometimes, but I also didn't want him to waste so much money on things for me. There was a line, and besides, I wanted him to have more funds for his charities.

Maybe he'd even take me to one of his centers and let me help out.

That's in the future. Take the next few days to get to know Nolan and really decide if you can handle living in the spotlight.

Not wanting to ruin my first international trip, I pushed my worries aside and watched as the airport and buildings faded and soon morphed into a thick jungle.

I wondered if you could hear the birds and what it'd be like to walk through it, so much so I jumped when Nolan touched my cheek.

Blinking, I met his gaze. His eyes searched mine. "Sorry to interrupt, but we're nearly there." He held up a long strip of black material. "Time to put on the blindfold."

I gave the window one last glance before turning toward Nolan. I'd have plenty of time to look at the scenery later. I knew how much this meant for Nolan—to treat me in a way his family rarely let him do.

Closing my eyes, I leaned forward. "Go ahead."

His strong, warm fingers caressed my cheek a second before a soft fabric wrapped around my eyes and head. He tied it—I could tell by the slight pressure on my face—and then he kissed me. Not just a peck, but his tongue seamed my lips, and I opened.

As he stroked slowly and tangled with my tongue, there was something about not being able to see anything that made his heat and taste and touch that much more intense.

When he finally broke the kiss, I sighed and said, "I definitely want to keep this blindfold for later."

His voice was husky as he replied, "Oh, that can be arranged. Maybe you'll let me tie you up as well."

The thought of being tied to a bed, blindfolded, as Nolan teased and stroked and played with me sent a rush of wetness between my thighs. Squirming in my seat, I said, "Don't tease me like that until you can see it through."

He cupped my face, his thumbs stroking back and forth. "Hmm, so you do want me to tease you later. I'll remember that for when you beg for me to hurry up."

As I tried to think of how to respond to that, I heard a car door open and a warm, light breeze caressed my skin.

"Wait here until I get you." I felt Nolan leave, but within seconds, my door opened. A hand found mine, and he said, "Let me help you out and then I'll guide you. It won't take long, I promise."

I didn't hesitate to allow Nolan to assist me. Even if being a real couple was new, I trusted him. He'd never done anything to make me doubt him so far, and I hoped he never did.

With him behind me, his hands on my shoulders, he gave gentle commands, and we walked. It could only have been a few minutes before he stopped. "I'm going to take the blindfold off now."

His fingers worked, and the material fell away. I blinked a few times against the bright sunlight before everything came into focus, and I gasped.

In front of me was a huge Mayan temple. A kind of step pyramid, with a large rectangular shape at the top. The sun was just starting to set, making the sky a beautiful blend of pink, red, orange, and purple.

"It's like something from a postcard. What is it?"

He squeezed my shoulders. "We're at Chichén Itzá, and that's the Temple of Kukulcán."

It was only then that I noticed the other stone ruins surrounding the area. An area that was empty except for what looked like staff. "You did this for me?"

He turned my head and kissed me. "For you, I'd do anything, baby."

Tears stung my eyes. "More and more, I wonder how you're real."

He moved to stand in front of me and searched my gaze. "Are you going to cry? Why? Did I do something wrong?"

I placed my hands on his chest and shook my head. "No, of course not. This is quite possibly the most amazing surprise I've ever had in my life. Well, maybe it ties with the bookstore shopping spree. But still, I can't believe you went to all this trouble. For me."

He cupped my cheek, his gaze intense. My heart thudded as I tried to deal with an onslaught of emotions—happiness, excitement, vulnerability, uncertainty, and something close to love.

Which was impossible. After all, I hadn't known Nolan very long.

It had to be the gifts. Yes, that was it. Maybe expensive surprises made me think I loved him.

His voice was low as he said, "I would do anything for the chance to see you smile, baby."

My throat closed up as I took in Nolan's tender expression. No man had ever looked at me like that before.

As if I were precious. Treasured. Loved.

Then he broke the moment and tickled my side. I squealed and laughed, and Nolan pulled me close to kiss me quiet.

And so we stood there, devouring each other like it was the first time all over again, in front of a Mayan temple at sunset.

More and more, my life started to feel as if it were a book or a movie.

Nolan's kisses slowed until he finally pulled away and asked, "Did you want to walk around a little and see some more of the site? The place is ours for the hour."

He put out his hand, and I wrapped mine around his. "Let me guess—Jenn booked this all for you."

"Yes. And according to her, it wasn't easy."

"She deserves a raise, for sure."

"Hey, I already pay her a small fortune. But maybe she and her wife deserve a vacation too, all expenses paid."

"Whatever it takes, don't lose that woman. She's a miracle worker."

"I'm glad you like her. I've never had a happy girlfriend *and* a happy assistant before."

Even if it was a little childish, I stood a little taller knowing that Jenn liked me better than the others before me.

How many had there been?

Nope. Not going down that road.

I tugged our clasped hands. "Come on and show me around. I need to stretch my legs before we get back into the car again."

As Nolan guided me around Chichén Itzá and told

me about the various structures—he had an interest in history—I couldn't stop smiling like a fool. I had an amazing boyfriend who was smart and kind and funny. And sexy. Couldn't forget sexy.

The only downside was still a big one, though—his fame and all that came with it. However, I planned to enjoy our little vacation to its fullest before dealing with the real world again.

Yet I was thinking more and more I could face anything if it meant Nolan Wolfe was mine. Maybe even for forever.

Chapter Twenty-Eight

Nolan

Aunt Lori: Where did you rush off to? <dashing off emoji>
Me: How do you even know I've gone anywhere?
Aunt Lori: Oh, come on. You were seen with Katie at the airport. Did you rent a little love nest somewhere? One to make her fall even in more love with you? <heart-eyed emoji>
Me: ...
Aunt Lori: Ooh, maybe you're planning a destination wedding and are doing some research? I've always wanted to go to one of those. Make sure it's somewhere with lots of sightseeing things nearby.

Me: Shouldn't you be focusing on West and Emmy's wedding?
Aunt Lori: Pshaw. That's in about six weeks and is mostly planned. Now that I've helped with one, I want to plan the rest of my niece and nephews' weddings.
Me: Go bother Beck.
Aunt Lori: Oh, that one will come soon enough.
Me: Did he propose?
Aunt Lori: Not yet. But I know it's going to happen. Then your wedding. And after that...hmm. I have work to do.
Me (typed but deleted): Sometimes you scare me.
Me (actual reply instead): I'm going out with Katie. Don't expect to hear from me for a few days.
Aunt Lori: <winking emoji>

By the time we finally reached our rented house near Tulum—a place with lots of beautiful beaches nearby—it was dark, and Katie couldn't stop yawning.

So after changing clothes, we merely crawled into bed and fell asleep.

Waking up with Katie in my arms the next morning made me smile. She slept on her side, her mouth open a little, with a little bit of drool on her pillow. It was just so...real.

And I loved it. Just like I loved her.

But before I could say those words, I needed to make

sure she felt the same. I didn't want her to feel pressured or obligated. I had some actor friends who'd used the L-word too early, and their partners had blurted it back, only to break up not long after the news had spread all over the internet.

It was hard enough making any kind of relationship work, but it was a million times harder when so many people cared and gossiped and analyzed everything you did.

Maybe when I finally transitioned into mostly just a producer role, I could get a little peace. I'd thought about it for years, about when I would only take roles I really wanted instead of taking one after another to fill my time and keep from getting bored.

Something Aunt Lori had said to me during the holidays came back to me: *It's hard for your siblings to really get to know you, Nolan. I think you've worked so hard over the years to try and get over your grief. However, your absence only pushed your siblings away and created distance. Slow down a little, enjoy life and your family, and I bet you'll be much happier.*

Aunt Lori always liked to give advice. Some of it was silly, of course. But sometimes she was pretty fucking smart.

And she'd been right—avoiding my family had helped put distance from the pain of remembering my mom and dad when they'd been alive. But it'd been years and years of me staying away. Maybe I needed to start closing the gap again.

Katie stirred in my arms, and I snapped back to the present. I watched as her eyelids fluttered open. She blinked and then instantly smiled at me. "Good morning."

Everything faded away except for the warm, beautiful woman in my arms. "Morning, baby."

I moved to kiss her, and she turned her head. "Ugh, I have morning breath."

"And I don't care. Because so do I." I turned her head and kissed her.

Soon I had her rolled onto her back, her hips cradling me, and my hard dick pressed against her sleep shorts. "I definitely think you should sleep naked from now on. Tell me I can rip them off."

She ran her hands down my back to grip my ass.

Bare, of course. I didn't sleep in clothes.

"I've always wondered what it'd be like."

"What?"

"To have a guy want me so much, he'd rip my clothes off."

Growling, I sat up. Taking her shorts, I ripped them up the side seams and finally got them off. But seeing her glistening slit wasn't nearly enough. So I also ripped her tank top right down the middle, exposing her full breasts and soft, round belly. "You're so fucking beautiful."

While rocking my hips against her center, I cupped her breasts and leaned down to take a nipple into my mouth. Her hands moved to my hair, and I loved how she dug in her nails, holding me close, as I tortured her taut little bud.

Her hips ground against mine. "Condom, Nolan. Now."

One day, I would take her with nothing between us.

But for now, I grabbed one from the box on the side table —I'd been optimistic last night about this morning— ripped open the packet, and rolled it on.

Then I positioned my dick at her entrance and paused. "Look at me, baby. I want to watch your eyes as I claim you. As you take my dick into that sweet little pussy and moan my name."

She obeyed. "Hurry up, Nolan. Please."

Never taking my gaze from hers, I thrust into her and Katie cried out as she arched toward me, her breasts wobbling in a way that made me want to pull out, hold them together and fuck them with my dick.

Later.

I pushed up her legs and began to move. Slowly at first, taking my time to brush her clit each time I thrust, loving how her face and chest flushed pink.

Then I hooked one leg over my shoulder to free up my hand. I tugged one nipple and then the other before I trailed my hand down, down, down to between her thighs. I lightly circled her clit, loving how she tried to move her hips so I'd touch it. But I kept teasing her, reveling in how she moaned and groaned and begged me to make her come.

Pressure built at the base of my spine, and I slowed my hips. Katie needed to come first. Always.

So I finally pressed against her clit. Hard. She cried out my name as she spasmed around my cock.

One, two, three pumps and I groaned as I came, each pulse of my dick sweeter and more intense than the one before.

I slumped over Katie, held her close, and rolled to my back so she was on top of me, my cock still inside her.

She braced her hands on my chest and pushed up. At her well-pleasured look, I smiled smugly.

Running her hand back and forth through my chest hair—the engagement ring on her finger winking in the light—she said, "I have to say, that's almost better than waking up to fresh coffee."

I raised an eyebrow. "Almost?"

She grinned. "Yep. You relax me, but coffee gets my butt going to face the day."

Brushing the hair off her face, I said, "What happens if you don't get any?"

"What? Sex? Or coffee?"

I lightly smacked her butt. "Coffee."

"I can get grumpy." She traced shapes on my chest. And even though it was innocent, my dick stirred again.

"I get the same way without coffee. I also get hangry if I don't eat."

"That's the case with anyone in your family."

"And now you know why we fight for the biggest cuts of meat at the table."

My siblings and I often played a game when we got together for dinner. Beck deliberately cut the meat into different sizes and it became a battle to get the bigger pieces. Because once it was on your plate, no one could touch it.

Just remembering the last time we'd done that made me realize how much I missed those kinds of silly games.

"What is it?" Katie asked.

"Hmm? Oh. I was just thinking of the last time I had dinner with my family."

"They miss you when you stay away, you know."

"I know."

She remained quiet for a few beats as she continued to stroke my chest. Then she said, "Well, West and Emmy's wedding is coming up. Do you think the reception dinner will be the same way?"

I laughed. "I don't know if Emmy would like that. Knowing my family, they'd end up tossing food and her dress would be ruined."

"Then maybe a wedding where everyone wore jeans and T-shirts, in case of a food fight, would be fun."

Was she talking about if she ever got married?

If we got married?

Since pressuring her was the last thing I wanted to do this early into our little vacation, I distracted her with a kiss. When we were both breathless, I finally rolled her over and sat up. "If I stay in bed any longer with you, we'll never leave it. And I have one more surprise for you."

"Nolan. You spoil me too much."

I shook my head. "This one wasn't expensive at all." I put out a hand. "Come on. We'll get ready, find super strong coffee just for you, and have some fun in the sun."

It would be in the 80s today, so taking her to the beach was perfect. For many reasons.

And soon we were ready, armed with a giant bag of necessary beach stuff—according to Katie—and I guided her down the private path to the beach.

When we finally broke through the trees, the view of the sandy beach and rolling waves made Katie gasp.

"A beach!"

And she ran down toward the water. I followed close on her heels.

Chapter Twenty-Nine

Katie

Me: You won't believe what Nolan did for me. Look at the pics!
Cassie: Woah, a temple at sunset AND the beach?
Sam: He really does love you, doesn't he?
Me (typed but deleted): I think so. Or, at the very least, I want to believe so.
Me (actual reply instead): Going home will be hard. But at least this has given me a taste of travel and I'm itching to do some more.
Cassie: Lucky for you that you have a rich fiancé with a private jet.
Me: <tongue out emoji> There's more to Nolan than that.

Sam: Like sexy? Tall? Probably a god in bed?
Me: You're fishing there.
Sam: Hey, it's a sister's prerogative.
Cassie: So?
Me: It's good.
Sam: Good? Oh, no, that's bad news.
Me: <tongue out emoji> It's hot and sweaty and dirty and amazing. Better?
Cassie: Much, much better. And just how dirty are we talking?
Me: Oh, look. It's time to go out. <heart emoji>

As I watched the rolling waves, it was hard to believe I was standing on a beach in Mexico.

Yes, a lot of people came to the Yucatán Peninsula for the beaches and sightseeing. But it was more than that—Nolan had listened to me. Truly listened.

And when he came up beside me and held out a seashell, my eyes pricked with tears.

He said, "Maybe you can add this to that shelf you want to create, the one for shells from all over the world."

As I gingerly picked it up, a tear rolled down my cheek.

I tried to brush it away, but Nolan beat me to it, wiping it away with his thumb. "What's wrong, baby?"

I laughed. "Nothing's wrong. You're just too wonderful, is all. And..."

"And what?"

I bit my bottom lip. I hadn't meant to add the "and" part. Because it would reveal too much about how I felt, about what I wanted, and about the future.

"Tell me, baby. Let's not keep secrets from each other, even if we have to keep a few from the rest of the world."

I cleared my throat a few times until I got my emotions under control. Then I said, "And well, sometimes I wonder, 'why me?' When you can have any woman in the world, why are you doing all of this for me?"

He cupped my face. "Because I care for you, Katie. It's going to sound silly, but let me try to explain, okay?" I nodded, and he continued, "I've spent nearly twenty years of my life mostly alone. The death of my dad really splintered my family, and I didn't have a sibling to be close to. Then I was betrayed by my best friend, and I had no one. And despite getting a break early in my acting career, I was even more isolated. Yes, there were and still are fans and actor acquaintances. But my colleagues are all busy themselves, and some view me more as a rival than merely another actor; true friendship is difficult. And fans only have a rosy view of me with no desire to know the shy guy who likes to read books and travel off the beaten path."

Oh, Nolan. Just thinking of all the years he'd been lonely, I ached for him even more.

His gaze became more intense. "But from the beginning of this fake engagement idea, you were different. You didn't treat me as some hero, as a man supposedly above others because of my fame. No, you treated me like any other guy, talking to me about the small things instead of constantly quizzing me on the latest Hollywood gossip. And if that wasn't enough, I've never felt such a pull toward another woman as I do with you."

His words were a lot to take in. It almost sounded like... "You think I'm your person?"

He tilted his head. "Your person? What do you mean?"

Even though my cheeks heated—maybe I was wrong—I answered, "You know, the one you can always turn to, rely on, and be yourself with. Even if you're in a shitty mood or sick as a dog or about to fall apart, you turn to that one person because they will be there for you, through thick and thin. More so than anyone else in the world. They will always feel like home."

He smiled. "I like that—you being my person. Although you forgot a very important thing."

"What?"

As he leaned toward me, his scent and heat distracted me. But somehow I focused on his words as he said, "You're all of those things to me, Katie. But you're also so fucking beautiful and the best sex of my life."

"You're just saying that."

He shook his head. "No. Anytime I'm away from you, I long to laugh with you over dinner, or I think about pinning you against the wall to fuck you, or even holding you in my arms as we fall asleep. I want all that, and so much more, baby. With you."

My heart thudded as I tried to process his words. "With me?"

Nolan nuzzled my cheek before whispering into my ear, "Yes, because I think you *are* my person, Katie Evans." He leaned back to meet my gaze again. "And I'll prove it to you, no matter how long it takes."

Before I could reply, he closed the distance and kissed me.

Even though we'd kissed plenty by now, this time felt different. Wrapping my arms around him, I pressed as close as possible and simply met his tongue stroke for stroke. I licked and explored and let him know how much I wanted to be his person. How much I wanted him to be mine.

How, despite the odds, I wanted this to last.

But dealing with his ex and social media and everything else could wait.

Right now, right here, being with this man was all that mattered.

Because Nolan Wolfe had stolen my heart.

I only hoped he wouldn't end up breaking it. I wasn't sure I'd find someone like him again. Someone I didn't need to impress. Someone who just wanted to spend time with me because it made him happy.

After finally breaking the kiss, he said, "I'm tempted to fuck you in the ocean. If you don't want to, tell me now."

"Well..."

He released me, and I quickly added, "I want it. But first? You need to catch me."

I dashed down the beach, laughing as Nolan came

after me. He could've easily caught me, but he allowed me to dodge and run away again.

Eventually, I took off my swimsuit dress cover and ran into the water.

As soon as it reached just above my breasts, Nolan caught up with me and tugged me close. He murmured, "Got you, baby. You're mine now."

"Good. Because I don't want to be anywhere else."

He growled and then kissed me.

And yes, soon he held me against him and fucked me right there in the ocean, pulling out before he came.

I didn't like it.

I'd been on the pill since I was eighteen, and maybe once I could finally confess my feelings, I'd ask him to come inside me.

But then Nolan kissed me and started playing chase in the water with me and I forgot all about the future.

I planned to make the most of the vacation with my boyfriend. Once we were back in California, back in reality, I'd finally try to be myself and see if this could work long-term.

Only then would I tell him how I felt.

How I loved him.

Not before.

Chapter Thirty

Nolan

Me: I can't wait to have you in my arms again tonight. It's been too fucking long.

Katie: I hope more than just in your arms.

Me: I still have that blindfold, and I promised to use it.

Katie: Mm, yes, please. That's what I want after the wedding.

Me: While I'm happy West made all his brothers groomsmen, it means more time apart since you're a bridesmaid.

Katie: We'll see each other during picture time. <heart emoji>

Me: But I can't muss your hair, or risk kissing you because of smearing your makeup. Maybe we can sneak

off and I can make you come with my mouth, if I can think of a way not to wrinkle your dress.
Katie: <overheated emoji> I wish. But just looking at this dress makes it wrinkle. <crying emoji>
Me: Just think of all the ways I'll wrinkle it later.
Katie: Meanie.
Me: You know you love it.
Katie: Maybe. <tongue out emoji> But it's time to help Emmy. I'll see you as soon as possible. <heart emoji>

After my trip with Katie to Mexico, my life became hectic.

First, I had a high-profile benefit coming up for my charity. But since it wasn't public knowledge that it was mine, there were a lot of hoops to jump through to get everything planned and the word out.

Then there were some screen tests as producers tried to find the perfect woman to play opposite me in an upcoming role.

If that wasn't enough, I had some production meetings for my company that I couldn't put off. I was on the cusp of signing a deal and had to schmooze and dazzle when needed.

All of that meant I didn't have time to visit Katie in Starry Hills. And every day that passed without seeing her was like a stab to my heart.

Oh, we texted and talked on the phone. But it wasn't

the same as having her in my arms or in bed or underneath me.

The constantly busy schedule I'd once embraced now felt more and more like a prison of my own making.

But I had a plan for that. One that I couldn't really focus on until after West's wedding and my charity's benefit party. Then I'd make Katie my top priority.

Just thinking of having her back in L.A. and chasing her on the beach instantly lifted my mood. And considering it was West's wedding day, I needed to be supportive. Emmy was good for him, and she didn't deserve me being grumpy.

I finished getting ready and went to find my brother. Or brothers, since all of them were inside West's bedroom.

I waved. "I didn't realize I was late."

Zach shook his head. "You aren't. But some of us don't get distracted sexting with our girlfriends and got here early."

He waggled his brows, and I smirked. "Sounds like someone is jealous."

Zach dramatically placed a hand on his chest. "Moi? Never. I can play the field, and you can't."

Zane snorted. "The field? Ever since I got back, you have yet to get a woman into bed."

Zach narrowed his eyes. "Yes, let's share that with the whole fucking world."

Zane shrugged. "It's a small town. I'm sure everyone knows."

Beck nodded. "The women all know to keep away."

Zach asked, "Why the fuck would you say that?"

Beck replied, "You know why, even if you're too fucking stupid to realize it."

West grunted. "Amber King."

"Amber is barely a friend anymore," Zach grumbled.

I said, "Maybe. But until she truly moves on, no one else will touch you. Everyone likes Amber more than you."

Zach growled, "Asshole."

I snorted. "I'm the nice one."

Beck sighed. "So you want everyone to think, Nolan. Why did you ask Aunt Lori about me and Sabrina getting married? Now she won't leave me alone."

"Because she was trying to plan my wedding, and I wanted to distract her," I replied and shrugged. "Not like you wouldn't do the same thing."

West glanced over at me. "Unless you want tacky tourist mugs at the reception and everyone wearing fairy tale costumes, make sure that doesn't ever fucking happen."

Zane frowned. "Costumes?"

West nodded. "Aunt Lori wishes she could've had medieval dresses, or some such shit, at her own wedding. So she's determined to get one of us to have costumes at ours."

Zach smirked. "Nolan would be the perfect person to do that. He dresses up for a living."

I flipped him off. "That's what I think of your idea."

Zach laughed, and I did too. Even West and Beck chuckled, along with Zane.

I thought maybe, just maybe, I was making progress

with my brothers when someone knocked on the door and broke the spell.

As Rafael "Rafe" Mendoza walked in, we all quieted, and West narrowed his eyes. "What the fuck do you want?"

Since West was marrying Rafe's sister, he should be nice to the man. But apparently, there was some sort of beef between the pair. Which was strange considering they'd been best friends as boys.

Rafe crossed his arms over his chest. "I'm only here because Emmy made me come. Something about getting to know all her new brothers-in-law, or some such shite."

West shook his head. "You're not in the UK any longer, Mendoza. Shit is the word we use here."

Rafe clenched his hands around his arms, almost as if resisting doing something stupid, like punching West. "I don't do it on purpose. When you live somewhere as long as I did, then sometimes words get swapped out without even realizing it."

Zach smiled. "Hey, maybe I should try learning a British accent. Maybe that will help with the ladies."

I switched into one. "It might finally make you sound clever."

Zach gave me the double bird. "Fuck you, Nolan."

But as we grinned at each other, I knew we'd reached a comfortable level of shit-talking with each other. Like all brothers should have.

Beck—who, despite being the second oldest, had spent many years acting as the head of the family—went over to Rafe and put out a hand. "Well, I'll welcome you to the family, even if West is being a stubborn asshole right now. He'll come around eventually."

Rafe looked skeptical, but shook Beck's hand. I went over and offered mine. "To be honest, I'm surprised we haven't met since we were kids. We support some of the same charities. I saw your name, but you never showed up at the benefits."

The man had been a world-famous soccer player before an injury had ended his career earlier in the year.

Rafe shook my hand and dropped it. "I didn't come stateside much until recently. I'm going to one of them in a few weeks, though. For the Creative Arts Haven charity."

My charity.

I nodded. "I'll be there with Katie. Make sure to say hello."

"I will." He walked over to West and put out a hand. "At least for today, let's call a truce. For Emmy's sake."

Tension built in the room as West stared at Rafe. I was debating how to get the stubborn fool to be nice for his wedding day when West finally shook Rafe's hand. Barely for a second, though, before he dropped his arm.

"For Emmy. But don't think we're fucking best friends again."

Rafe clenched his jaw, and I wondered what was being said without words. "Wouldn't dream of it."

I cleared my throat. "Good. We should probably leave soon for pictures."

Zach sighed. "Provided Aunt Lori didn't convince the photographer to change the shoot until after the wedding."

West grunted. "It'll be dark then. Besides, I've basically lived with Emmy for months now. It's not like she's a blushing virgin."

Zach raised his brows. "What about it being bad luck to see the bride before the wedding?"

West rolled his eyes. "It's a stupid superstition. I didn't see the bride for my first wedding and look at how that turned out."

West had married young, to a woman he'd knocked up after a one-night stand. His life had quickly turned to hell. In the end, his first wife died in a car crash while out with another man.

I said, "Emmy is different. And I'm sure the two of you will be so fucking sweet and happy it'll make Zach want to puke."

Zach sighed. "I'm not against affection. But, really, finding Beck and Sabrina that one time has scarred me for life."

He shuddered, and we laughed. Beck said, "That's what you get for coming back early from a business trip and not telling me."

Zach grunted. "I live here, too."

Before Beck could reply, there was a knock on the door, and West's two kids rushed into the room. Avery wore a pale pink dress, one with a puffy skirt. She twirled. "Isn't it pretty, Daddy?"

West squatted down and pulled his daughter into a hug. "You look beautiful, love."

Avery squirmed. "Don't wrinkle my dress, Daddy. I want to look nice for the wedding pictures."

West chuckled and released his daughter. "Then I

won't ruffle your hair." He turned toward his son and straightened Wyatt's little tie.

As West chatted with his kids, longing surged inside of me. Having children had always been in the abstract. But watching my grumpy older brother melt for his little boy and girl showed me more of the future I wanted—with Katie as my wife and mother to our children.

Don't get ahead of yourself.

I was still waiting for the right moment to confess my feelings to her, and then hopefully not long after proposing to her for real.

Maybe after the charity event in a few weeks.

But for now, I pushed all that aside and simply shot the shit with my brothers until it was time for pictures.

And when I finally saw Katie? My heart skipped a beat.

She wore a dark blue dress like all the bridesmaids did. But Emmy had been smart and let them each choose a style in the same fabric that flattered their figures. Katie's gown hugged her breasts tightly and then flared out in a loose skirt. The type of waist name escaped me. But I didn't fucking care.

I strode over to her, took her hand, and kissed the back of it. I whispered for her ears only, "You look beautiful, baby. And I can't wait to see that dress on the floor and you in my bed."

She laughed. "I've missed you, too." After running a hand down my jacket lapel, she smiled. "You look pretty sexy yourself."

"You like a man in a tux, then?"

"I like anything you wear," she purred.

Zane's voice broke the spell. "Speak a little louder. I don't want to miss the good stuff."

I flipped him off, and Avery clucked her tongue—sounding a lot like our Aunt Lori as she said, "That's not very nice, Uncle Nolan."

I bit my lip to keep from laughing, rearranged my face into a solemn expression, and turned toward my niece. "I apologize, Avery. I'll be on my very best behavior today, I promise."

She nodded. "Good. I want the best day ever for Emmy. Well, I always want her to have good days and be happy. But especially today because she becomes our mom for real."

I smiled at her. "That she does. And we'll *all* be on our best behavior for today, won't we, guys?"

I glanced around at my brothers and Rafe, and they all grumbled their assent. Abby, Amber, and Katie all looked as if they were trying not to laugh.

Before anything else could ruin the peace, Aunt Lori finally showed up with Emmy.

West's jaw dropped as he took in his bride, and I couldn't blame him. Emmy looked nice in her off-white dress. One that hugged her slight frame.

Aunt Lori stood between West and Emmy. "You might have to see and touch her for pictures, but no kissing, unless the photographer tells you to. You need to keep something special for the ceremony, after all."

West shook his head. "You already made me sleep at the house with you all last night."

Aunt Lori raised an eyebrow. "One night away won't make your cock fall off."

West rolled his eyes as my brothers and I snickered.

Thankfully, Avery was too busy whispering in the corner with her brother to make a comment.

I went over to Emmy and kissed her cheek. "You look beautiful, Emmy. Take care of my brother, won't you? He's not the easiest person to get along with, I know. But he does love you."

Emmy smiled. "Oh, don't worry, I've gotten him figured out. Mostly."

She looked over at West, and at their shared loving glance, jealousy shot through me.

Which was ridiculous. Katie was my girlfriend in truth. But suddenly, that didn't seem like enough.

Later. You can talk to her later.

Within minutes, Aunt Lori marched us to the cars, and we drove over to Emmy's place for pictures and the wedding.

The only time I was able to touch Katie was for pictures and walking her down the aisle.

But after the ceremony, I swept her off her feet at the reception and danced with the woman I loved, happy to have her in my arms again.

Chapter Thirty-One

Katie

Me: Don't go near our secret hideout tonight.
Cassie: Hmm, I wonder why? <winking emoji>
Sam: That only makes me want to go.
Cassie: OMG, are you a voyeur and never told us?
Sam: I'm not saying anything.
Me: Ew, but I'm your sister.
Sam: I wouldn't be looking at you, would I? But Nolan? <overheated emoji>
Me: No. He's mine. Eyes off.
Sam: <laughing emoji> Okay, okay. I'll stay away. But I think you need to invite me to some fancy premier party in exchange.
Me: <middle finger emoji>

Sam: So, that means you'll think about it?
Cassie: Ignore her. Enjoy sexy times with Nolan. I expect a full report later. <heart emoji>

As I danced with Nolan and he held me close, I couldn't stop smiling.

He chuckled. "The pictures are long over, you know. You don't have to keep smiling."

"I can't help it. I'm happy."

He kissed me softly. "Oh? What, may I ask, has you so happy?"

"You're fishing, aren't you?"

"Maybe." He moved a hand down to quickly squeeze my butt before moving it back to my waist. "But I'm also so fucking happy right now, baby. And it's because of you."

I played with the hair at the nape of his neck. "I wonder if we'll be this happy and smiley at your fancy charity event."

He frowned. "Are you worried? Jenn and I are doing everything we can to keep Wendy from showing up."

"I know. But I have a weird feeling, is all. Like, our future will be decided that day, or something."

"Woah, that sounds ominous."

"Well, you have to admit that Wendy has been super quiet and hasn't been stirring up more trouble. Her fans still post about my ripped dress, but not her. And I would've expected it. Part of me wants to believe she's finally given up."

"Only part?"

I sighed. "Well, the other part of me says she's playing the long game and I'm going to end up crying in a heap on the floor afterward."

He growled and pulled me closer. "No fucking way. I can't challenge her to a fight like I would with a guy, or simply call her a jealous cow—that will only garner her sympathy. My best bet is uncovering something to damage her brand. That will hurt her more than anything else because Wendy lives to be worshipped and be the center of attention."

"But you haven't thought of anything yet?"

He shook his head. "I'm still looking for proof. It's frustrating as hell, but I'm not giving up. Until I have something, I'll just have to do my best to keep her away from us."

"That may not be possible. And if she does show up? Maybe if I provoke her, her bad behavior will make directors think twice about working with her."

"Maybe. But I wouldn't ask you to do that."

I smiled at him. "Which is exactly why I'm offering."

"Do your worst."

I chuckled. "I'm not sure about that. But I won't back down next time. With you at my side, I'll feel invincible."

"I'll be there." He kissed me quickly. "You're so fucking amazing, baby. I sometimes can't believe you're mine."

At being called his, I melted a little. "Ditto, Nolan. But enough about Wendy fucking Webster. Do you think we've put in enough of an appearance for tonight and could slip away?"

He raised his brows. "Why? What do you have planned?"

"Hey, it's my turn to surprise you."

His gaze turned heated. "Will you end up naked and riding my dick by the end?"

The thought of the last time I'd done that, back in Mexico, sent wetness rushing between my thighs. "Maybe. Or not. You'll just have to trust me and see."

Nolan glanced at the table for the wedding party. "I think we've been around long enough. It's been hours, and everyone will be watching the happy couple dance soon. It's the perfect time to slip away."

A quick glance revealed West guiding Emmy to the dance floor. "We'd better hurry. Follow me."

I took his hand and tugged. Nolan moved quietly with me—past the area where I could grab my coat and change my shoes—and we exited the barn Emmy used for weddings on her property.

My family's dairy farm was next door, but it was still a bit of a hike. Once we were well clear of the reception, Nolan asked, "Are you going to blindfold me?"

Smiling, I shook my head. "Not this time. It takes a little maneuvering to reach our destination, and I'm not strong enough to pick you up."

"Pick me up? Color me intrigued. Are you sure you won't give me more clues?"

I raised my chin. "Nope. It's time for you to see how it feels." He sighed dramatically, and I laughed. "That won't work on me, buddy. Sorry."

"Doesn't mean I won't try."

He winked at me, and it sent a rush of heat between my legs.

I picked up my pace, eager to get to our destination, and changed the subject on purpose. "It's not as warm as Mexico, but at least it's well above freezing."

He didn't bat an eye at the change in topic. "Although being snowed in together—in what was it? Oh, Fargo—has its perks. Just saying."

I laughed. "One day, we'll go somewhere buried in snow. But today is not that day. Besides, where we're going is special to me. Someplace only me and my siblings know about."

"Not even the BFF Circle knows?"

I shook my head. "No."

He smiled. "Then, lead on."

We hurried in silence. Not strained, but comfortable, as if simply being together was enough.

Which was yet another thing I'd never had with another guy before. Just Nolan.

Soon we reached the secret path up a hill. I took a flashlight from my coat pocket—I'd come prepared and hopeful about tonight—and clicked it on. "This way."

After a few minutes, we reached the top, where a little shack was hidden amongst the trees. I gestured toward it. "Here it is."

"Was this always here, or did you all build it?"

"It was here, although we've fixed it up over the years." I unlocked the door and went to the side, where the small generator was. "Normally, I'd do this myself. But with my dress and nails done, could you start it?"

"Sure."

Nolan surprised me yet again by quickly getting the generator going. At my look, he explained, "My dad took me, West, and Beck on a few fishing trips when we were little. Usually the little cabin ran on a generator and was heated by a fireplace."

"A man full of surprises." I gestured. "Come on. I'm freezing."

Nolan followed me inside. I switched on the lamp and small heater.

He whistled as he looked around the one room space. "What's all this?"

The walls were covered in pictures from magazines, printed ones from the internet, actual photos, and little bits and pieces nailed or superglued on, creating a giant collage.

"We each decorated a wall—four siblings, four walls. Can you tell which is mine?"

He walked over to the one plastered with nature scenes, castles, seashells, and faraway places. "This one."

Warmth spread through me at the fact he knew me so well. I walked over to him, took his hand in mine, and nodded. "And you see this one?" I pointed to a picture of Chichén Itzá. "You helped me mark off the first one."

After squeezing my hand, he replied, "I'll need to take a picture of this, or several pictures, so I don't miss anything."

"Why?"

He smiled at me. "Because I plan to take you to each and every place on this wall, baby. One location at a time."

"Oh, Nolan. You don't have to."

He turned and placed his hands on my waist. "I don't have to, but I want to. I want to make as many of your dreams come true as possible."

My heart swelled as I stared at the man I loved. He was so sweet and sexy and surprising. Yes, surprising.

And mine.

Not tonight. It wasn't time for love declarations. Especially when we still hadn't sorted out his ex.

But as I ran my hands up his chest and back down again, I leaned my hips against his and smiled at his erection. "While not featured on my wall, I've always wanted to bring a boy here."

As he nuzzled my neck, he whispered, "I'm not a boy, though."

He pressed his hard cock against my belly, and I sighed. "No, thank goodness, you're not."

Chuckling, he moved his head until he could stare into my eyes again. "I want to strip you naked and kiss every inch of your skin. But..."

"But what?"

He glanced at the other three walls. "I almost feel like we should cover them, or something."

Laughing, I shook my head. "They're just pictures and can keep secrets. They won't talk about any of the dirty things you'll do to me here."

"Dirty, huh? And what does my baby want tonight?"

"Hmm." I ran my hand back and forth against his dress shirt. "It's too cold to do what I really want—for you to tie me up and tease me."

He groaned. "Now I'm going to be imagining that until I can do it."

"Good. Then you won't forget."

He rocked me against his dick. "Never." He kissed me. "Tell me something else, then."

"Do anything you want to me, Nolan. I just want you inside me. Now."

With a growl, he kissed me. Our tongues tangled as he guided me back toward the small table in the room. He lifted me and sat me on it, spreading my thighs and standing between them. "Good. Because I've been hard all night, watching you sway your hips and strut around in that dress. Teasing me the entire time."

Wetness rushed between my thighs. "You've been watching me all night? And I've just been walking, nothing special."

He ran his hands up my thighs and back down again, each time making my skin heat and pussy throb.

He shook his head. "No, you've definitely been swaying and teasing me, knowing I couldn't do anything in a room full of friends and family."

I tilted my head. "Well, you could, though. If you discreetly made me come with your hand, under the table, and no one would be the wiser."

He moaned. "Fuck, baby. The thought of you trying not to cry out as you drip down my hand and your greedy pussy milks my fingers makes me so hard."

"Then we'll have to try that someday. Maybe not with family, but in public somewhere."

With a growl, his lips crashed down on mine, and I

opened to his tongue. As he stroked his against mine, he ground against my pussy, making me even hotter.

My hand went to his fly, and I undid the zipper until I could reach into his boxers and stroke his cock. I rubbed the tip, groaning when I found the drop of wetness.

He was just as ready as I was.

And I decided tonight, here in my special place, was the night. I broke the kiss to say, "Please, Nolan. Take me without a condom. I'm clean and on the pill."

"Are you sure?"

For a split second, I wondered if I'd pushed too soon.

But Nolan added, "I'm clean too, and the thought of feeling your hot pussy around my cock makes me even harder. However, I never want to pressure you."

And just like that, I knew my decision was the right one. "I want you inside me, Nolan. Now. Bare."

With a growl, his hands went to the waistband of my pantyhose, and he ripped them off.

I'd barely blinked at the feat before he undid the top button of his trousers, took out his cock, and ran it through my center, up to my clit, and back down again.

I gripped his upper arms to keep from falling back as he continued to tease me. "Nolan. Please."

He growled. "I love it when you beg. Tell me you want me, and then beg again."

After another brush against my clit, I moaned. "I want you, Nolan Wolfe. Please."

He then thrust inside me, and I arched toward him. He was so big and hard and warm. And as he moved his hips, his eyes never leaving mine, the pressure built little by little.

I didn't care about the table creaking, or that we were mostly still dressed, or what might happen outside of these four walls.

No, all that mattered was me and Nolan and how amazing it felt to have him inside me.

Add in the intense heat and caring in his eyes, and I nearly blurted out that I loved him.

But then he snaked a hand between us, flicked my clit, and I forgot about everything but the building orgasm. He teased me with slow circles, and I started to see dots. One last pinch, and I screamed his name as I came, digging my nails into his arms, riding wave after wave of the most intense pleasure of my life.

Nolan stilled, leaned over, and groaned against my neck as he came inside me.

I didn't know how long we breathed heavily, saying nothing. But eventually Nolan lifted my face and kissed me. Once, twice, three times. "That was quite possibly the best orgasm of my life."

I smiled. "And I'm sure you'll say that the next time."

"Yes. Because each time with you is better than the last, baby."

I should tell him to stop teasing. But I simply grinned like a fool and melted against his chest. Nolan's arms came around me, and his heart beating beneath my ear made me sleepy.

He kissed the top of my head. "I should get you home."

Shaking my head, I said, "No. Take me to your place. I know you have to leave tomorrow afternoon, but I want to spend the night with you."

He chuckled. "Am I going to get lucky?"

Swatting his chest, I said, "Maybe. But first, I want to get warm and take a shower."

As he stroked my back, I struggled to keep my eyes open. "Tell me there's a car at your house we can use. I don't want to make you walk all the way back to Emmy's place."

"Yes. I have a tiny car I share with my sister, Sam. But she won't need it tomorrow."

"Good. Then let's clean up and I'll carry you to the car."

"No, you don't have to. I can walk."

"I want to, though. I want any excuse to hold you close to me and my heart."

Part of me wanted to read into his words—did he mean love?—but I was too tired to deal with a heavy, emotional conversation. "Fine, you can carry me. This time. Don't even think about doing it at the charity benefit, though."

"Of course not, baby. But even if we do our best to blend in with the crowd, we'll be noticed." He traced my cheek. "Will you be okay? Because I won't be able to divert all the attention, no matter how much I try."

"I know. And I can handle it, I promise."

More like I *had* to handle it, no matter what. Because being with Nolan meant accepting all of him—both the shy, sweet, and dirty guy I had now, but also the famous movie star who always had the world's attention.

He kissed my nose. "Just remember that you don't have to face it all by yourself. I'll be right by your side, ready to help whenever you need it, baby."

"I know. I trust you."

His gaze intensified, and my heart raced.

But before I could ask anything else, I yawned, and it spurred Nolan into action. As soon as we were cleaned up, he carried me down the path and to the car I shared with Sam. He insisted on driving, and I didn't fight him.

And by the time we made it to his house, I was barely awake. Once we were in bed and my head hit the pillow, I passed out, dreaming of my wedding and the future I was starting to think was possible.

Chapter Thirty-Two

Nolan

Abby: Just an FYI: I'm going to be at your charity event.
Me: Um, okay. Not that I don't want you there, but how did you get invited?
Abby: Why? Because I can't afford the astronomical price to attend?
Me: It IS for charity.
Abby: Whatever. Emmy asked me for a favor, and I'm going with Rafe.
Me: As in Rafe Mendoza?
Abby: <eye roll emoji> No, as in Rafe Smith Jones. Of course Rafe Mendoza.
Me: No need to get snippy.
Abby: <sighing emoji> Sorry. I didn't want to go, but

Emmy was worried about her brother. I don't know about what exactly, but she said he needed to be around a friendly face.

Me: Not Emmy?

Abby: Gee, thanks, Nolan. You really don't want me to come, do you? <tongue out emoji>

Me: <eye roll emoji> That's not it, and you know it. I mean, aren't the siblings still working things out?

Abby: Yes. But West and Emmy are still newlyweds, and well...

Me: West didn't want her to go.

Abby: I think so, but he never said anything. However, Avery has a swim meet and Wyatt is working on a kid's photography contest, and Emmy is trying to help them all.

Me: She's too good for West.

Abby: You've got that right. Anyway, I owe Emmy, big time. So I'll be there.

Me: Make sure to say hello. And I can put you and Rafe at my table for dinner, if you want.

Abby: Perfect. I don't want to turn into a feather-brained idiot sitting at the table with someone famous. Well, famous and someone I haven't known since the day I was born.

Me: Consider it done. See you then.

Since I had a few behind-the-scenes things to sort out, I arrived several hours early to the benefit location. By the time guests were due to arrive, I checked my phone and saw Katie's text that she was on the way.

I smiled. Jenn had found another amazing dress, apparently, and said I would "drool at the sight of Katie."

I couldn't wait. Because tonight was about more than earning enough to fund my charity for another year and maybe expand it. No, tonight was also when I wanted to tell Katie I loved her. In private, of course. Later. Much later.

Another mini-emergency came up, and I focused on calming the caterer down, saying it was okay to substitute one type of salad for another.

Soon, people began arriving. Some were my colleagues from past movies. Others were from the tech and banking industries. And others were directors and even studio executives.

Between me, Jenn, and Tina, we'd managed to pull this off.

Then I finally spotted Katie standing with Abby and Rafe, and I managed to excuse myself and stalked toward her.

Yes, stalked. Because she was in a stunning black dress, wearing the necklace I'd given her, and was already attracting attention from other men.

But she was mine.

I did everything not to be rude, but somehow got across the ballroom in less than five minutes. As soon as I stood in front of Katie, I took her hand and kissed the back of it. "Hello, baby. You look gorgeous tonight."

Her pale cheeks flushed, and it took everything I had to keep my dick under control.

She smiled. "Another tuxedo in less than a month. Maybe next time, you should try something else for variety. Hmm, maybe a dress kilt?"

I chuckled. "Maybe." Never letting go of Katie's hand, I turned toward Abby and Rafe. Neither of whom looked happy. Abby's jaw was clenched in annoyance, and Rafe had his arms crossed over his chest.

I nodded at both of them. "I'm glad you two could make it."

Rafe grunted. "We barely did, thanks to Abigail."

"It's your fault, *Rafael*. Not mine."

Rafe opened his mouth, as if to argue, but I stepped in. "Well, you're here now, and that's all that matters. Maybe a drink would help? There's champagne and an open bar." I waved in the direction of it.

Abby sniffed at Rafe and then smiled at me. "An open bar sounds perfect. I'll see you at dinner?"

"Yes. We're at the same table."

After nodding, Abby headed toward the bar, but Rafe stayed behind. I studied him for a second, and as he tapped his finger against his arm, I could tell he was still agitated.

But I didn't know him well enough to pry. The man was older than me and had left Starry Hills to play soccer in England when I was still in middle school.

However, Katie smiled at Rafe and said, "Thanks for walking me in. I know even fewer people than you do at this event, so I might have to seek you out later. Maybe even for a dance."

Even though it was irrational, I nearly growled at the thought of her dancing with Rafe.

Get a grip, Nolan.

Rafe shrugged. "It was nothing. And there's another footballer here somewhere. Er, I mean soccer player. It's going to take time and practice to switch back to that phrase after so many years in the UK."

I shook my head. "Don't worry about it. I've worked with a lot of British actors over the years, so no need to explain."

Rafe almost smiled. "Thanks."

Silence fell, and he nodded and excused himself. Once alone with Katie, I whispered, "Will they survive the night without killing each other?"

"I don't know. It's weird, though. Because for years, Abby always gushed about how well Rafe did in this game or that one. But ever since he showed up in Starry Hills again, she's been constantly irritated with him."

"Hmm."

She glanced up at me. "What is that supposed to mean?"

"Nothing." I wrapped an arm around her waist. "Are you up for some introductions? I want to show off my girl."

She smiled. "Just guard the back of my dress, okay? I don't need a repeat of last time."

"I will be your dress's bodyguard." I raised my arm and then three fingers. "Scout's honor."

"But you were never in the scouts."

Leaning down, I murmured, "Then I swear on your perfect, spankable ass that I'll protect your dress."

She sucked in a breath. "Nolan, behave."

Chuckling, I stood up again. "Fine. Now, come on. I want to introduce you to a few people."

And so I took her to meet some of my fellow co-stars, a director, and even a baseball player.

Katie charmed them all, easily. And as the minutes ticked by, my tension eased. Maybe, just maybe, without Wendy around, things would go smoothly.

Katie would finally see she could fit into this part of my life, too.

My hopes of telling Katie how I felt and her feeling the same increased by the second.

Chapter Thirty-Three

Katie

Abby: We're going to be late. Rafe got lost.
Me: Oh no! Are you on the right track now?
Abby: No. He accidentally pulled out to the wrong side of the road and we got pulled over. Luckily, he got off with a warning, but he still won't let me drive. Stubborn ass.
Me: Okay, that's a lot to take in. You'll have to explain later. He should let you drive.
Abby: I know! But he won't. I'm working on it, though. Come hell or high water, I'm going to this damn event.
Me: Be safe. I'll wait out front so we can go in together.
Abby: You don't have to do that!

Me: Nolan is probably running around with his head cut off. I'll wait, and we can make a grand entrance.
Abby: If you're sure.
Me: I am. Now, convince Rafe to let you drive. And let me know when you arrive. <heart emoji>

Walking in with Rafe and Abby had been intense. I couldn't ask Abby for details until later, when we were alone, but clearly getting lost, pulled over, and finding this place had caused some major friction between the pair.

And judging by how many drinks Abby was downing, I'd have to check on her soon and make sure she was okay.

But as Nolan guided me around and introduced me to some people, I forgot about Abby and Rafe. Unlike his ex, they were nice to me. They smiled, made small talk, and the baseball player even offered free tickets to Nolan and me for his next game in L.A.

It was nearly dinnertime when Jenn and Tina found us. At Jenn's forced smile, my stomach dropped.

Nolan asked, "What's wrong?"

Jenn kept her voice low. "Matt Bellis is here and demanding to see you ASAP."

From Nolan, I knew he was on the verge of signing a deal with the man.

Nolan frowned. "Here? Why? Our meeting is the day after tomorrow, and there's nothing that can't wait for a couple of days."

Jenn shook her head. "He texted me up a storm, then had his assistant do it too, and finally he hunted me down."

Tina scowled. "I offered to kick his ass out of the event, but Jenn told me no."

Jenn smiled at her wife. "It's nothing I can't handle, love."

Tina shrugged, and Jenn turned back toward Nolan. "I think he might cancel the whole deal if you don't meet him now, Nolan. But it's your call. What do you want to do?"

He looked at me, and I said, "Go. I know how important this deal is for your production company."

"Are you sure, baby? I don't want to leave you alone with so many strangers."

I gestured toward Jenn and Tina. "I won't be alone. Besides, Abby is here too, remember?"

As he searched my gaze, I could see how torn he was. I patted his chest. "Go. If I can't survive a short while by myself at this event, then we have bigger problems. I'll be fine."

He kissed my cheek. "If you're sure?"

"I am."

Nolan said to Jenn, "Watch out for her. Both of you. Okay?"

Tina rolled her eyes. "We'll be fine. If nothing else, few people want to upset me. Not if they ever want to hire me as their lawyer. And I'm the best, so they want to."

Nolan smiled. "True." He cupped my cheek. "I'll be back as soon as possible, okay?"

"Okay. Now, go."

After one more long look, Nolan asked Jenn for Matt's location and left.

Jenn threaded her arm through mine and then her other one through Tina's. "Now, ladies, there's a bar with our name on it. Dinner will start soon, and I don't know about you, but I haven't had a drop tonight and could use some relaxation juice."

I snorted. "Relaxation juice?"

Tina shook her head. "Don't even try to argue how stupid it sounds. It only makes her dig in deeper."

Jenn stuck out her tongue. "Says the woman who calls Parmesan spaghetti cheese."

"Hey, that's what my mom said growing up. And you get the point."

As the two women bickered, I smiled and relaxed. And after a few sips of wine, I relaxed a little more.

Before long, it was time to round up a slightly tipsy Abby and head inside the room being used for dinner.

Rafe already sat at the table, nursing what looked like a whiskey. He barely grunted a hello before downing his drink and crossing his arms.

Even though Abby had to sit next to him, they ignored each other.

I chatted with Abby, Jenn, and Tina—Rafe made an occasional comment or grunt—until dinner was placed in front of us.

Nolan still hadn't returned.

Jenn whispered, "He'll be back as soon as possible. Bellis isn't the easiest guy to charm, but Nolan has a way with him."

"I still think it's odd he demanded a meeting now." I speared a piece of steak. "Does this kind of thing happen often?"

Jenn shook her head. "Not really. Yes, people make connections at these events. But most want to enjoy the booze, food, and entertainment and save business for later."

I swallowed and drank some more wine. "I hope Nolan's back before the music and dancing starts."

But as the minutes ticked by and the servers started clearing the dinner plates and placing dessert in front of everyone, I wasn't so sure.

Regardless, as long as Wendy didn't show up, it'd be a success in my books.

Then a familiar voice came over the speaker system. "May I have your attention, please?"

What the hell? I searched and found her—Wendy Webster stood on the small dais at the front of the room, where charity employees had made their speeches during dinner.

My heart raced as I met her gaze.

A gaze full of malice and satisfaction.

Oh, shit. What was she going to do now?

My first instinct was to run. Then I said screw that. If Wendy tossed shit at me, I'd fight back this time. Nolan was my man, not hers.

I was done running away or fearing her.

After smirking at me, Wendy looked around the rest of the room. "I have two important announcements to make tonight, ones I wanted you all to be the first to hear." Murmurs rose up before Wendy continued, "The first is that Nolan Drake and I have signed a deal with Matt Bellis for an adaptation of Jessie Donovan's Stonefire Dragons series. It's going to be the next bingeable, must-watch show and will start airing early next year."

Even though I knew the series—it was about people who could change into dragons—I focused more on what she said about Nolan. There was no way he would've signed a deal to work with Wendy on anything.

But the woman in question spoke again before I could further process the news. "And the second announcement is that Nolan grew tired of lying to everyone and asked me to clear the air. You see, he was upset with me for always taking him for granted. So, to make me jealous and teach me a lesson, he hired a girl from his hometown to be his fake fiancée for six months. And the girl in question? Why, Miss Katie Evans."

She pointed at me, and you could hear a pin drop, it was so quiet.

Although my heart pounded so hard, I was surprised it didn't reverberate inside the room.

This couldn't be happening. Could it?

And where was Nolan?

As if reading my mind, Wendy spoke again. "But during our talk this evening with Matt, Nolan confessed he still loved me and said the fake engagement was done." She held up her hand to show off a ring with a giant diamond. "He wants me and always has. And my last piece of news is that our marriage will be streamed online for all to see!"

For a few seconds, I sat, stunned.

Then my brain started working again. Nolan would

never agree to marry Wendy. He couldn't stand her. Something else was going on.

You can look into that later. For now, Wendy's here. So deal with her.

I stood and strode toward the dais, all eyes on me.

However, I didn't care. With each step, rage churned in my belly as my heart raced and palms sweated. By the time I reached the dais, my entire body was shaking with anger.

Wendy merely raised an eyebrow and still spoke into the microphone. "Yes? If you need your payment for services rendered—I can't remember how much Nolan promised you for this little job—I'll take care of it later."

Before I could stop myself, I slapped her. Hard enough that she stumbled backward.

Commotion stirred behind me, but I ignored it and stalked toward Wendy. She instantly backed away from me, her expression uncertain.

I knocked the microphone from her hand, leaned in, and growled, "You're lying, and I know it. You're just making a fool of yourself."

Wendy stood tall again and looked down her nose at me, her composure regained. "Oh, am I? And where is Nolan, pray tell? Not here. No, he's waiting for me at my place in Beverly Hills, no doubt naked and impatient to celebrate our engagement."

Where *was* Nolan?

For a split second, my insecurities rushed forth, and I wondered if he really had been playing me all along.

But then I remembered his thoughtful gifts, his

heated looks, and how he always made me feel special, treasured, and desired.

No. My gut said something bad had happened to him. I didn't know what, but he sure as hell wasn't waiting to hook up with Wendy.

My fingers curled into a fist, and I barely restrained myself from full-on punching her lying face. "You're going to regret this day, Wendy. Just wait and see."

Tired of her vitriol, I turned and stalked back down through the tables and out the door. I didn't stop until I reached the cloakroom, got my coat and purse, and found a corner to lean against the wall, close my eyes, and catch my breath.

What the fuck had just happened?

And where the hell was Nolan?

Jenn's voice reached my ears. "Katie, are you okay? Don't believe a word that bitch says."

I opened my eyes to find Jenn, Tina, and Abby standing in front of me.

Abby spoke next. "Kudos to you for slapping that cow. Seriously, I wonder if she's ever been told no in her life."

I tried to smile, but failed. Instead, I let out a long sigh. "It doesn't matter. The world is going to laugh at and judge me for the rest of my life now."

Abby frowned. "Why?"

I bit my lip for a second. Tina and Jenn knew the truth, but not Abby.

Guilt swirled in my stomach as I said, "Nolan asked me to be his fake fiancée back in October."

She blinked. "What?"

"It's true."

Abby stared a second, then shook her head. "I call bullshit. That man adores you, or I'll eat my best pair of shoes."

"Well, it started out as fake. But I thought maybe..." I swallowed and added, "But he's not here now, is he?"

Abby's phone buzzed. She glanced down and then looped her arm through mine. "The valet brought round the car, and Rafe's waiting for us. He's the only one who's under the legal limit right now, so we're going to have to suffer his terrible driving."

I barely paid attention to anything as Jenn, Tina, and Abby guided me out of the hotel and into Rafe's car.

Once inside, I checked my phone. But there was nothing from Nolan. So I texted him:

Me: Nolan, what happened to you?
Me: Can you just let me know you're alive?
Me: You're starting to worry me.
Me: Okay, now I'm getting mad.
Me: Did you know what Wendy had planned? Are you really working with her?
Me (typed but deleted): Nolan, please. I need you right now.
Me (actual text instead): Call me as soon as you get this message.

I stared out the window, not really seeing anything as I kept reliving my encounter with Wendy. Rationally now, I knew slapping her probably hadn't been the best choice. But I still couldn't seem to regret it, even if it would make my life hell from now on.

Still, where was Nolan? Given how extreme Wendy had been with me, would she be the same with Nolan? Was he in danger? Hurt?

Or had he really ditched me at the charity event to hang out with that Matt Bellis guy? That seemed more reasonable. But even two hours ago, I would've expected a message from Nolan, at the very least. But now? If he'd read about my showdown with Wendy, maybe he was in damage control mode and avoiding me.

Maybe I imagined him having feelings for me.

Maybe I would never see him again, unless I ran into him by accident in Starry Hills.

Stop it. I needed to avoid thinking about maybes and what-ifs.

Which was easier said than done.

Eventually, Rafe pulled up to a hotel, and Abby bumped her shoulder against mine. "You're staying the night with me."

After glancing at my phone one last time—still nothing from Nolan—I shrugged. "Okay."

Jenn was also in the back seat with me and Abby. "And I'm going to locate Nolan's ass and see what the hell is going on."

It was either shrug or cry, so I shrugged again.

Maybe once the shock of the evening wore off, I'd worry more. Nolan didn't seem the type to just disappear without a word to his assistant. After all, Jenn and Tina handled damage control for him. Surely he'd reach out to them, if not me.

And yet, how well did I really know him? It could've all been fake. A mere fantasy I'd built up, one that had finally fallen to pieces, with reality now closing in and nearly drowning me.

One where Nolan didn't smile at me, or kiss me, or even text me constantly because he said he missed me.

And one where I most definitely would never have him above me, crying out as we both came, and cuddling in bed afterward.

I would go back to being Katie Evans, the dairy farm tour guide, with the man I loved probably out of reach forever. Because even if he was angry about Wendy's performance, mine hadn't been any better.

Being with me would be toxic for his career. I was sure of it.

Tears pricked my eyes, and I willed them away. I might start crying, but not before I was alone with Abby.

Rafe glanced at us in the rearview mirror. "As soon as I drop off Tina and Jenn, I'll be back. I'll text you, Abby."

My friend nodded. "I'm not sure what the plan is for tomorrow, but I'll let you know."

Thinking about tomorrow was too difficult. And not just because maybe Nolan would tell me things were over now. Even without that, the fallout from tonight would be monumental.

I'd probably have to disappear from social media completely, just to keep my sanity.

Tomorrow. I can think about all of that tomorrow. After releasing my seatbelt, I opened the door and got out. I made the mistake of looking back inside the car, and all the pitying glances only made my eyes heat with tears all over again.

"Abby. Can we hurry inside? Please?"

My voice cracked, and Abby kicked into overdrive. She was out of the car, herding me through the lobby, toward the elevator. With each step, my chest tightened, and my throat grew thick.

The elevator doors opened just as we arrived, and I ran inside, losing one of my shoes in the process.

Abby bent to pick it up, but I tugged her inside and hit the Close button. "Leave it."

"Okay."

She reached to hug me, and I shook my head. "Not yet." I whispered, "I'm going to fall apart soon, and I want to do it in private."

Biting her bottom lip, Abby nodded.

We rode the elevator in silence, and thankfully, no one else got in. I took off my other shoe, and as soon as the doors opened, I rushed out and followed Abby to her room.

I checked my phone one last time as Abby tapped the keycard, but Nolan hadn't responded. There were a million notifications from other people, but I didn't dare check them. Not yet.

Once we were both inside the room, I plopped down on the bed and put my head in my hands, doing my best to breathe and not cry.

I'd been right about one thing—this night had determined my future. Just not in the way I'd hoped.

Nolan was AWOL, Wendy probably had everyone's sympathy after my slap, and instead of falling asleep in the arms of the man I loved, I was about to cry inside a hotel room with one of my best friends.

And as soon as Abby asked, "Are you okay, Katie?" I let out a sob.

The floodgates opened, and I broke.

I cried for a lifetime of wondering if people were judging me for what had happened tonight.

I cried for never telling Nolan how I felt, or even being strong enough to ask him if he felt the same.

I cried for the future I finally knew I wanted, but would never have.

Twenty-four hours ago, everything had been perfect.

And now?

Well, now I loved a man who didn't feel the same way, thousands of Wendy's fans would probably bully me for the rest of my life, and I could even face an assault charge, if she pursued it.

But Nolan, Nolan was the part I missed the most. He'd listened and understood me and made me laugh. Not to mention he'd given me the best sex of my life, too.

And that didn't even touch on his kindness or hard work or loyalty to his family.

Yet, he was nowhere to be found. Not one word, either.

Maybe, just maybe, he was at Wendy's place and celebrating with her after all.

At that thought, I cried and cried, until I started hiccupping and feeling sick.

Somehow, Abby helped me change clothes, washed my face with a cool cloth, and assisted me into bed.

Then she sat next to me, silent but supportive, until I finally fell asleep from exhaustion.

Chapter Thirty-Four

Nolan

When I opened my eyes to brightness, I groaned and instantly shut them again. My head pounded and my mouth was as dry as a desert.

Not to mention my entire body ached.

What the fuck happened? I racked my brain, trying to remember, all while slowly opening my eyes.

Once they adjusted, I looked around the sunlit room, but nothing was familiar. It was a bedroom of some sort, with a twin bed, lamp, a bottle of water next to me, and a large bucket in the corner. The walls were bare and white, and the one window was small and had bars on the outside.

This was most definitely not my place, or that of anyone I knew. How the hell had I ended up here?

All I remembered from the night before was meeting with Matt Bellis, sharing a drink with him as we talked about our deal, and then nothing. Until now.

I tried to get up off the bed. However, the pain of a thousand pins and needles piercing my brain made me groan, and I laid back down. As I breathed and calmed down, I managed to check my pockets. But, of course, everything was gone.

I closed my eyes and tried to remember anything else, anything that might be a clue. But nothing came after that drink.

Could I have been drugged?

And if so, why?

Ransom seemed unlikely, given how many people knew I'd gone to meet with Matt. And if he thought this stunt would get me to concede on the finer details of his demands, he had another thing coming.

Then I remembered how last night had been about more than a deal with Bellis.

Katie. Where was she? Had they taken her too? Was she okay?

And if they hadn't snatched her, was she worried? Or, worse, thought I'd left her to fend for herself among the wolves?

I needed to get out of here, stat. If only I could stop the ache in my head and stand up.

Something was slipped under my door, and I craned my neck. It was a stack of papers, but I couldn't read what they said from the bed.

Which meant I needed to get my ass up and see what they were. Because until I had more information, I couldn't plan shit.

Gritting my teeth, I sat up, inch by inch, until I was upright. By then, I was sweating, my heart thudded, and I was far too weak.

Fucking hell. I must've been drugged.

It took far too long, but I eventually stood and wobbled over to the door. A quick check proved what I suspected—it was locked.

While supporting myself with the wall, I picked up the small stack and made it back to the bed. Only once I was sitting again did I glance down at the papers. They were articles printed from the internet. I read the first headline:

Slap Heard Round the World: Small-town Girl Attacks Wendy Webster

Frowning, I scanned the article. It was obvious whoever wrote it idolized Wendy and portrayed Katie as some money-grubbing, violent, unstable woman jealous of Hollywood's darling couple.

It took everything I had not to crumple the paper. How the fuck could people still think Wendy and I were a thing? I knew people could be delusional, but this was a whole different level of fucked up.

I kept reading and reached a section that made my stomach drop:

. . .

At last night's charity event, Wendy revealed Nolan's elaborate plan to make her jealous, one that involved hiring Katie Evans to act as his fake fiancée. Now that the gig is up, will Nolan finally be truthful and declare his undying love for Wendy Webster?

All I could think about was Katie, alone among people she mostly didn't know, having to suffer Wendy's lies. I wanted to cheer for Katie standing up to Wendy and slapping her, but I was too worried about the aftermath.

I knew just how brutal the internet and social media could be. And Katie most definitely didn't deserve that kind of hell.

Which would be all the worse since I hadn't been there to support her. And now? There was no way to reach her, either. Not while I was stuck in this room.

However, I *would* get out and do everything within my power to help her. Just as soon as I had a plan.

But first, I needed to know as much as possible about the night before. Then I could maybe use the story or facts to my advantage.

So I scanned the rest of the papers. Some were posts by Wendy, some by mutual acquaintances who said they knew all along I couldn't have fallen for the small-town girl when the hottest female actor in the world loved me.

And then I came across a picture—one of Katie standing outside a hotel at night, her expression sad and broken and lost.

Oh, baby. I'm so sorry. I traced her cheek, wishing I could've been there.

I crumpled the papers and threw them across the room with a roar. My woman was hurting, and people needed to pay for it.

Scanning the room, I took stock again of what I had. If I were at full strength, I could probably break the door down. But that was hours away. Provided they didn't try to drug me again.

No, I had to use what was available now.

After sliding to the floor, I looked under the bed. Nothing.

Then I took a closer look at the floor lamp. It was a cheaper one, the type that you had to screw together to finish. After testing the base, I took apart the lamp, until I had the base and lifted it.

Yes. It was heavy and should be solid enough to help me break the window. Then, if I was loud enough, it might get someone to open the door and I could hit them with it too.

I stood, and even in my slightly weakened state, I could easily heft the base and walk to the window. I could see a small yard and a fence. There were other homes beyond it, too.

And being Southern California, it was one of the 1960s neighborhoods with mostly one-story homes. Which would be easier to escape.

Taking a deep breath, I stood to the side of the window, swung the base at it, and turned my head and closed my eyes. It shattered—clearly it was the same age as the house and not double-paned—and I opened my eyes again.

Yep, the window was mostly gone. Maybe if someone didn't come check on me and I regained enough strength, I could test the bars. If they were loose at all, I might be able to knock them out. Or, I could take apart the bed frame and use a metal side to pry it off.

However, when I heard the door lock turn, I rushed right behind it, out of sight.

It opened, and a man said, "What the fuck is going on here?"

I didn't recognize him. Regardless, I swung at his head—but not too hard, because I didn't want to kill him —and made contact. He dropped like a stone.

Thank you anal former director for making me learn how hard to swing for unconsciousness instead of death. I'd have to send him a gift later, or something.

But for now, I searched the guy and found a wallet, cell phone, and some keys. Since it would take too much time to search for something to tie him up, I merely shut the door and locked it.

With adrenaline pumping in my veins, my tiredness was forgotten, and I searched the small house. However, no one else was inside.

Maybe later I'd be insulted that whoever had orchestrated this plot thought one guard was enough. But for now, I tried the cell phone I'd found. And with the security code being 1234, I quickly pulled up a map.

I was in Orange County, south of L.A. After memorizing the address, I called Jenn. Even though I wanted to call Katie first, Jenn would be able to get me picked up and ask Tina what to do about the whole kidnapping thing.

Because I wasn't taking any chances that they'd go after Katie next.

If they didn't have her already.

She picked up on the second ring. "Where the fuck have you been? Do you know the hell Katie and the rest of us have been through?"

"Katie's all right?"

"Yes. What the hell happened to you?"

At least Katie's safe. I explained what I could remember and then recited my current address before continuing, "I need someone to pick me up and for you to talk to Tina about the guy currently locked in a room. I wasn't sure if we should involve the cops or not."

"Hmm. I'm still mad at you, but I'll get it all done. Can you hang tight, or do you think it's wiser to move?"

"I'm going to walk around the neighborhood and remain in public, just in case someone else returns here. I doubt they'll drag me down the street by force. However, I'll stay nearby. Have the driver call this number." I paused and then blurted, "How is Katie?"

"That is a conversation we should have in person. And don't worry, I'll assign a few of your private security guards to watch her from afar. For the moment, let's concentrate on getting your ass back home and putting Tina's favorite P.I. on the case. We'll keep the cops out of it for now, unless Tina says otherwise."

After clearing up a few more details, Jenn hung up, and I went out the front door.

While I wanted to check online to see just how big

the damage was—to better know what Katie was facing—I had to keep an eye out for any other threats.

Luckily, no strange van pulled up and whisked me away. By the time my usual driver called and I got into the backseat, the adrenaline had faded and exhaustion set in.

But I didn't let myself fall asleep. While, yes, me not being a prisoner any longer was good, until I held Katie close and told her I loved her, I wouldn't be able to relax.

And given everything that I already knew about the night before, I wasn't sure if Katie was going to run into my arms anytime soon.

However, I didn't care. I would do whatever it took to win her back.

And I would also find a way to destroy Wendy Webster once and for all.

Chapter Thirty-Five

Katie

The next morning, I shut off my phone. It kept beeping with notifications, and when I'd first opened it, I'd accidentally tapped one and it brought me to a post where Amber defended me against Wendy. The comments were a mixture of support and full-on hatred. But, of course, it was the negative ones about me that I still remembered:

She's always been out of control. She's probably a danger to us all.

I knew there was something about her. If she enters The Watering Hole again, I'm leaving before she hits me too.

Of course, Nolan never wanted to marry her. I mean, Fat Kat? She was probably just after his money.

Definitely a gold digger. Nolan must've been desperate to ask for her help.

Once my phone was off, all I wanted to do was to crawl into my bed back home and hide from the world.

Abby and Rafe arranged it all—Rafe even insisted on renting a private jet—and we were on our way early in the morning.

At some point, Abby received word that Nolan was safe and wanted to talk to me. While I mentally breathed a sigh of relief that he was okay, I wasn't ready to talk. Abby made excuses for me, bless her.

Before lunchtime, Abby pulled up to my parents' house and turned to me to say, "I wrote down all of our numbers. Seriously, call me or just show up anytime. Any of us—me, Emmy, or Amber—will come at the drop of a hat. Are you sure you don't want me to stay?"

My throat tightened, and if I hadn't cried most of the night and morning, I probably would've started again. "No, I really just need some time at home and to get back into a routine. But thanks for everything, Abby."

She reached out and hugged me. "Anytime, Katie." She leaned back. "And as soon as I hear from Nolan again, I'll let you know."

I shrugged, too tired and emotionally exhausted to do anything else. "Whatever. I'll see you later."

Ignoring her look of concern, I stood and walked to

the door. It opened before I could grab the handle, revealing Cassie and Sam.

Cassie asked, "Are you okay, Katie? You never replied to our calls or texts. We've been so worried."

"I know, but..."

As if sensing I didn't want to talk about it all just yet —they had to know what had happened with Wendy— Cassie hugged me and then Sam did too.

Sam said, "Come on. It's time for coffee, cookies, and to lock ourselves in your room until you tell us everything."

I tried to smile, but failed.

Cassie pushed against my back. "Come on. We're not taking no for an answer."

I could've fought them, but right now, cookies with my sisters sounded perfect.

Once they fetched the coffee and cookies—and some chocolate too—we all sat on my bed.

Cassie said, "No matter what, we're on your side, Katie."

Sam nodded. "That witch always looked too smug and fake to me anyway. She deserved what she got."

Sighing, I shook my head. "You're in the minority. I barely looked online, but I saw enough before I disabled all my accounts and shut off my phone."

Cassie paused and then finally asked softly, "And what she said about you and Nolan? Was it really all a sham engagement?"

I sipped my coffee and ate a whole chocolate chip cookie before I replied, "It started out as an agreement, almost a business deal. But then, well, I..."

Sam said, "You fell in love with him."

My gaze shot to hers. Abby had said the same thing during our flight. "How does everyone seem to know this?"

"You're not good at hiding your emotions. Oh, you think you are. And sometimes, you can manage it for a short while, like with the bully mean girls. However, we know you well, just like the BFF Circle. Your feelings for Nolan Wolfe were as plain as the nose on your face."

I sighed. "Not that it matters. The world probably hates me—most of it, anyway—and if I thought I'd struggle with all the attention from merely being Nolan's girlfriend, now it's ten times worse. I don't see how it could work between us."

Cassie said, "But Katie..."

"No." I paused, swallowed, and said the part out loud that I hadn't been able to say to Abby. "The best thing for me and Nolan is to stay away from each other. With me out of the picture, maybe the scandal will die down, to the point people start forgetting about me."

"Are you sure that's what you really want?" Cassie asked.

"Yes, I'm sure. Can we drop it for now, please?"

My sisters looked like they wanted to say a lot more, but reluctantly nodded.

"Thank you." After taking a deep breath, I stood from the bed and walked to my closet. "And the best thing for me to do right now is keep busy. So I'll do the afternoon tours."

Sam blinked. "What? Are you sure?"

"Yes."

"But people will probably stare or ask questions. Or, worse, hurl insults at you."

I shrugged. "It gives me a chance to test out explanations and discover which one will shut people up the fastest."

Cassie searched my eyes. "Maybe you should wait a day or two and get some rest. Sam can do them for today, at least."

"No. I'll do the tours. Otherwise, I'll just sit here, under a blanket, and wallow. And I don't want to wallow any longer. But there is one thing you can do for me."

"Name it," Sam stated.

"If Nolan shows up, tell him to go away."

"What? Why? Don't you want to talk to him?"

So he can let me down gently, be nice about it, and probably offer me something in exchange for all my pain? No, thank you.

And because I loved him, I knew what I had to do.

"No. Him associating with me will only drag down his image and maybe tank not only his career, but his fledgling business as well. And I can't do that."

They tried to argue, but I shut them down quickly.

Sensing I needed a bit of normalcy, my sisters chatted about what had happened over the last two days. Their presence, plus the sugar and caffeine, helped my mood a little. But only a little.

Because I kept thinking of Nolan, Wendy, and how messed up everything had become.

How getting over Nolan might take a lifetime. Because I'd never find someone as kind and sexy and thoughtful.

How Wendy had won, in the end. And I would be the one picking up the pieces.

How even showing my face in Starry Hills was going to take more courage than I had at the moment.

Strangers, though, from out of town would be a good distraction.

By the time two o'clock rolled around, I was showered, dressed, and in my Starry Evans Dairy Farm uniform. In it, I felt a little more safe and protected, as if the polo shirt and khakis were a type of familiar armor.

Besides, if I were lucky, no one would ask me anything about Nolan or Wendy.

I went downstairs and to the side room used for admin duties. My brother Kyle sat there, saw me, and stood. He grunted. "Say the word, and I'll give Wendy Webster a piece of my mind. I don't give a fuck who she is. She messed with my little sister."

I shook my head. "She's not worth it. But maybe refuse to sell your cheese to any of her friends, and it'll make me feel a little better."

"Consider it done." He shifted from foot to foot and pulled me into an awkward hug. Yeah, Kyle usually wasn't a hugger.

But my tall, strong brother's arms were warm and safe and always felt like home.

When he finally let me go, I smiled up at him. "Thanks, Kyle. For having my back."

"Any time, sis. Any time." He glanced at the clock. "Are you sure you want to run the tour?"

"Yes. I need to keep busy."

"Well, I'll be within earshot. If anyone gives you trouble, holler and I'll come running."

"Thanks."

After a little more coffee, I put on a smile and went out to the main reception area, where my two o'clock group waited.

But as soon as I saw some familiar faces, my stomach dropped.

The Mean Girls of Starry Hills—Kristina, Jordan, and Lydia—were here.

Kristina smirked at me. "And look who showed up. Well, Fat Kat, it seems you have some claws after all, don't you? Too bad you used them on the wrong person. Wendy Webster will destroy you."

Jordan nodded. "She definitely will. And Nolan only dating you because of a deal makes a hell of a lot more sense. Why would he pick you when he could have Wendy?"

Lydia added, "I hope the rumor of Nolan and Wendy's wedding being streamed is true. No doubt it'll be magical. And soon they'd take over Hollywood."

I curled my fingers into fists but bit my tongue as I counted back from ten in my head.

There were other customers in the group. And the last thing I needed was to feed the rumors about me being some uncontrollable, violent female with mood swings.

My voice was steadier than I'd thought as I asked, "Shall we begin the tour?"

Kristina whispered with her friends, but surprisingly, the trio kept mostly quiet as I went through my spiels.

By the end, I was calm and grateful that the other five tour members were polite and friendly. No one else mentioned Nolan, Wendy, or what had gone down.

But the peace was too good to be true. Because once the nice people left, it was just me and the Mean Girls.

One took out her phone and pointed it at me. I tensed, wondering what the hell was going to happen now.

Lydia had her hand inside her large purse. When she pulled it out, she had on a glove and a pile of fresh cow shit.

I tried to back away, but Lydia ran up and smashed it into my cheek. "That's for Wendy Webster. And a reminder of where you truly belong."

The three laughed at me.

Probably like the world did right now, too.

Tears pricked my eyes, so I ran all the way to my room and shut the door. I wiped off my cheek with a shirt, and then sat on the floor, propped against the wall, and did my best not to cry.

And failed. Laying my head on my knees, I sobbed. Quietly at first, but soon I couldn't stop.

At some point, my brother came into the room, sat next to me on the floor, and held me against his side.

I had no idea how long we sat like that. But when I finally quieted down, my brother growled and said, "I'm going to fucking kill Nolan Wolfe."

"Don't, Kyle. Please."

He grunted. "We'll see. If he doesn't fix this, then

yes, I'm going to kick his ass into next week. I don't care if he's Beck's brother or not. Any guy who abandons someone when they need them the most, well, they're fucking heartless."

Too exhausted to argue when Kyle was worked up, I sighed and sat a little longer on the floor with my brother, wondering if my life could get any worse.

Chapter Thirty-Six

Nolan

Me: Katie, baby, are you there? I can explain everything, but I need to talk to you.
Me: Do you even have your phone on? Please, baby. Don't ignore me.
Me: I tried calling your parents' house, but was told you weren't there. Where are you? Abby won't tell me.
Me: I promise I never would've left you alone at the charity event by choice.
Me: All of your social media accounts are gone too. Am I texting into a void?
Me: Even if I am, I miss you, baby. I want to hold you, talk to you, and kiss you. I need you.
Me: Well, I'm in Starry Hills now. Aunt Lori told me

you're in town, so I'm going to find you. We need to talk. I miss you.

Me (typed but deleted): I love you, Katie. Life is empty without you. Together, we can figure this out. Just let me in.

Me (actual text instead): No matter what, I'm not giving up on us. We need to talk, and I'll do whatever it takes to make that happen.

The last few days had been hell. Not because of the media or the paparazzi stalking me and shouting questions, or even because Wendy kept posting shit about our fictional wedding.

No, it was because no matter how hard I tried, I couldn't get to Katie.

She was in Starry Hills. I suspected at her family's house, but her sisters, brother, and parents kept saying she wasn't home. Kyle's glare, in particular, told me Katie wasn't happy.

I even checked the little shack she and her siblings used, but she wasn't there either.

So now I paced inside the apple orchard on my family's land and debated making another wish on the Wishing Tree—I would take whatever help I could get at this point—when Abby showed up.

The very sister who had been missing for a few days. Aunt Lori had said Abby was safe, but not much else.

I blinked at her sudden appearance before rushing

over to her. "You know I didn't leave her there by choice, Abby. Tell me you believe me."

Abby studied me for a few seconds and then crossed her arms over her chest. "So you said in your texts. But what you shared seems kind of far-fetched. I mean, a kidnapping, Nolan? Really?"

I ran a hand through my hair. "It's true. As we speak, my lawyer is getting a signed confession from the guy who did it. He also revealed how it was Wendy who hired him. You can talk with Jenn or Tina if you need to, but I swear it's the truth."

Abby studied me for a few seconds and sighed. "I think I believe you." She then narrowed her eyes. "But that fucking bitch. Seriously, I want to kick Wendy's ass. And since I'm taller and stronger than her, I bet I could, too."

"While I appreciate the sentiment, you doing that will only give her another win in the court of public opinion."

"I won't stir shit up for you, Nolan. But I hate having to worry so much about what the world thinks. How have you dealt with it for so long?"

I shrugged. "It wasn't hard most of the time. Being a reclusive actor has its perks." I placed a hand on the nearby Wishing Tree. "If only I could go back and tell my agent no fucking way would I ever date Wendy, my life would be so much easier."

Abby moved to lean against the Wishing Tree, facing me. "But if you'd done that, would you have ever approached Katie?"

"I'd like to think yes, but probably not." I glanced at

my sister. "I love her, Abby. Truly. But I can't even talk with her, let alone explain things and tell her that."

Tapping her fingers against the tree trunk, Abby said, "Normally, I'd offer to help my big brother without any sort of conditions. But I'm in a bit of a sticky situation right now and might need your help soon. Can I call in a favor later and you'll be discreet?"

I searched Abby's face, and only then noticed the dark smudges under her eyes. Something wasn't right. But judging by the stubborn set of her jaw, she wasn't ready to reveal her troubles. Yet, anyway. "Whatever you need, Abby, just say the word, and I'll be there."

"Truly?"

I smiled wryly. "It's something I've tried offering to you all for years, but pride and ego seems to make us all stubborn asses."

Abby's mouth twitched. "We are that." She sobered. "I'm sorry if I've been extra distant the last year or so. I don't have an ex that'll go as far as orchestrating a kidnapping, but I have my own ex-asshole issues."

She must mean whatever had happened in San Jose during her student teacher internship.

However, Abby could close herself off when pushed, so I merely said, "If you ever need to talk, I'm here. I'll even jump on a plane, if I need to."

"Thanks, Nolan. I'll remember that." She cleared her throat. "Now, about you and Katie. I'm willing to help, provided you finally declare your undying love and sweep her off her feet."

I nodded. "If she'll talk to me, and if she doesn't hate

me, I'm going to offer my heart, my future, my everything to her."

"Why are all the good guys related to me?" She sighed. "I'll round up the BFF Circle, and we'll hit The Watering Hole for drinks. And don't worry, I'll figure a way to get Katie out of the house. She hasn't stepped off her family's property since returning to Starry Hills, but it's high time she does."

I frowned. "If she's truly not ready, don't force her, Abby."

She smiled. "Despite all your fame and fortune, you're still such a nice guy." She looked away and muttered, "Unlike some other guy I know."

I had no idea what she was talking about. But before I could ask, Abby took out her phone and typed. She must've got a reply straight away because she nodded and smiled at me. "Emmy's onboard, and Amber will be, I'm sure of it. We'll be there by 8pm."

I nodded. "That gives me enough time to get everything ready."

Abby tilted her head. "Ready for what?"

"Nope, I'm not saying. It's part of me offering Katie everything, and it's a surprise."

"You always were good at keeping secrets, so I won't even try badgering you. Although I have one thing you might want to add."

As she explained, I had to admit it was pretty good.

Once I said I'd do it, Abby yawned. "Awesome. And if I'm going to be on my A-game tonight, I'd better go home and take a nap. I'll text you about any changes."

Abby waved goodbye and dashed off. The dark

circles under her eyes, her yawning, and her brief disappearance made me wonder what she'd been up to.

But Abby was a grown woman now and not the nearly defenseless baby sister from when we were kids. I had to trust that she'd ask me for help if she truly needed it.

With a sigh, I looked up at the Wishing Tree—tall, solid, and one of the few constants in my life. Thinking about that helped ground me a little, and I whispered, "All I want is a chance to talk with Katie. If you make that happen, I'll ensure you're taken care of and pampered for all time."

As the breeze blew, I laughed at myself. I was now talking to a tree.

And yet, as I left the orchard, I felt more optimistic than I had in days.

Chapter Thirty-Seven

Katie

I didn't want to go out, but Abby, Emmy, and Amber didn't give me a choice. When they threatened to tie me up and toss me into the car—we had an inside joke about friendly kidnapping each other, and it seemed to be my turn—I caved.

As Kyle drove to the bar so he could drop us off, I resisted sighing. Because given my shitty luck lately, everyone would stare and laugh the second I stepped foot inside.

Amber bumped her shoulder against mine. "It's going to be fine, you'll see."

"Of course you'd say that. I've never met a more optimistic person in my life."

"I think you underestimate the people of Starry

Hills. The Mean Girls are their own unit and are pretty much considered outsiders now. Everyone else knows you, Katie. And they're on your side. I should know, as I've heard it a lot in the bakery lately."

"Great," I grumbled. "People are gossiping about me."

Amber rolled her eyes. "It's a small town and people gossip about everyone. Even me."

"You? What do they say about you?"

"Oh, just that I'm the quiet one who seems to always keep herself together. Not that I do, but that's the public face I show at the bakery."

I searched her gaze. "Is something wrong, Amber?"

She shook her head. "Nothing I can't handle. Besides, tonight is all about you."

"Are you sure?"

"It's fine, I promise. Now, are you ready to have some fun? I even agreed to dance tonight."

Amber scrunched her nose at the thought of dancing, and I laughed. "You agreeing to do that *is* a pretty big deal. What was it the bartender said that one time? Oh, that you looked as if you were trying to do the Robot and failing miserably."

She stuck out her tongue. "I never said I was good at it."

Emmy—who'd been in a deep conversation with Abby—caught that last part. "Dancing is about having fun, nothing else."

Amber snorted. "Says the woman who actually has rhythm."

"Hey, I just listen and move to the music. Try not to overthink it and just go with the beat."

Amber shook her head. "Going with the flow is not my strong point. I like plans and rules and instructions."

I said, "Hmm, maybe we should try blindfolding you. That way, you'll have to really listen to the music and feel the beat."

"Maybe in private, but not in a bar. Promise me you all won't do that tonight!"

Abby and Emmy laughed and promised. But my mind caught on the blindfold part, and I instantly thought of Nolan and the promise he'd never see through.

Stop it. If I kept thinking about Nolan, about how most things came back to him, then I'd never be able to move on.

Not that I wanted to. But there was no future for us. I accepted that now.

The car stopped, and Kyle turned in his seat. "I'll be up until one. After that, you're on your own."

I stuck my tongue out at him. "So much for being there whenever I need you."

"Hey, a guy's got to sleep sometime."

He winked, and I smiled. Leave it to my brother to treat me as if the whole blow-up with Wendy had never happened.

Abby opened the door and got out. "Come on. I'm more than ready for a drink."

We all climbed out and headed inside the bar. People waved or nodded in greeting as we entered. None of their expressions held pity or disgust or amusement. No, they were just being friendly, like they'd been my whole life.

Amber whispered, "See? I told you."

I rolled my eyes. "Fine. Maybe Starry Hills is safe. As long as I never leave, life will be good."

Abby shook her head. "I can't see you staying here forever. But enough about the future—tonight is all about drinking, dancing, and having some fun."

So we ordered drinks and sat at a high table off to the side. After my first margarita, I started to relax. Just as I sipped my second, music started playing. However, it wasn't anything I'd ever heard at the bar before.

In fact, it was vaguely familiar. Then it hit me—it was the exact song Nolan and I had danced to at Emmy and West's wedding.

A mixture of longing and sadness crashed over me. I missed Nolan, every second of every day. And this song? It was like twisting a knife in my heart.

I stood so quickly that the bar stool fell over. "I-I can't stay. I need to go."

Turning, I was about to rush toward the door when he was there, in front of me.

Nolan Wolfe.

Looking as sexy as ever, dressed in a...kilt.

He took a step toward me, his hand raised. "Please, Katie. Don't run away. Dance with me, and we can talk."

I wanted nothing more than to run into his arms, hug him, and never let go.

But Wendy's threat—one of her bodyguards had shown up the day before to issue it—bounced around my head: *Get back with Nolan, and I'll not only press assault charges but I'll also sue your family for every penny they have. But that's not it. No, then I'll destroy your brother's reputation and ensure no one ever buys his cheese again. So it's your choice: stay away from my man or I'll make your family homeless, penniless, and humiliated. If I get a whiff of you sharing this, I'll start taking apart your happy family piece by piece. And that's not an idle threat. And if Nolan finds out and confronts me? I will destroy you, country girl. I promise you that.*

If it were just me she threatened, then maybe I would've risked it. But I couldn't chance destroying my family as well.

"I-I can't, Nolan. I'm so sorry."

Tears threatened to fall, so I dashed out of the bar and into the parking lot. The cool air felt good, and I looked for a spot where I could hide until I could get a ride.

However, Nolan must've run after me, because he easily found me.

At his concerned expression, I swallowed and did my best not to cry.

"Katie, baby, please just talk with me. I'm so fucking sorry you had to face Wendy on your own that night. I didn't leave by choice, I promise you."

I blinked at his words. "What do you mean, it wasn't by choice?"

He put out a hand, palm up. "Won't you at least sit in my car and talk? I can see you're shivering, baby, and it kills me."

Rationally, I should say no. I should run far, far away and never see Nolan again.

But as I stared at his outstretched hand, at the man wearing a kilt because I'd mentioned once how I'd like to see him in one, reason went out the window. I desperately wanted to know *why* he'd left me at the charity benefit. Surely one conversation wouldn't get back to Wendy and start her rampage?

"Please, baby. Just let me explain."

Before I could change my mind, I placed my hand in his. As his fingers curled around mine, some of the weight I'd been carrying lifted from my shoulders.

He brought my hand to his mouth and kissed the back of it. The press of his warm, soft lips against my skin made me shiver, in a good way.

"Come on. This way."

We walked in silence to his car, although I kept stealing glances at his profile and his bare legs as the kilt swayed as he moved. Before I could think better of it, I blurted, "Isn't that cold?"

The corner of his mouth ticked up. "Let's just say my balls have nearly ascended back into my body. Women in skirts have my respect now, for sure."

I smiled and was about to make a joke about the plus side of skirts and kilts—easy access—when I caught myself. We weren't dating, we weren't anything but exes at this point. And I needed to guard my heart and steel my resolve if I wanted to spare my family any pain.

He opened the door for me, and I slid into the seat. Once he was also in the car, he turned toward me. "I'll get straight to the point—the reason I wasn't there when Wendy made her announcements was because I'd been drugged and kidnapped."

My jaw dropped. "What?"

"It's true." He explained about waking up in a strange house, finding a way to get free, and how Matt Bellis and Wendy had worked together to make it happen.

When he finished, I blurted, "Why aren't they both in jail yet?"

"I'm working on it, I promise. Tina wants an airtight case and to do some digging without Wendy catching on. But none of that matters right now. I would've been there for you, Katie, if I could've been. I promise you. And the fact I wasn't? It kills me."

I couldn't get my head wrapped around everything. And yet, I liked to think I knew Nolan well enough to know he told the truth.

Even so, that didn't change anything. Maybe if Wendy went to jail, she couldn't hurt my family. However, it wasn't a guarantee.

Nolan moved to take my hand, and I inched it away. Hurt flashed across his face, and the knife in my heart twisted a little more.

He asked softly, "So you can't forgive me, then?"

I should say no, I couldn't. That would make everything easier.

And yet, I didn't want to lie to Nolan. Not about this. "It's not that. I just...can't do this, Nolan."

"Why?"

Such a simple question, and yet the answer was so damn complicated.

He continued, "Is it because of my fame and the attention? If so, there's something I haven't told anyone, not even you, because I needed to sign a few things first."

My curiosity got the better of me. "What is it?"

"Well, after this last movie role, I plan to wind things down and focus primarily on my production company."

I frowned. "Why? I thought you loved acting."

He shrugged. "It was an escape, one I needed for a very long time. But it was just another form of running away from my past and pain, no different than West leaving town or Zane joining the Navy." He searched my gaze and said softly, "But I don't need to run any longer, baby. And a big part of the reason why is because of you."

I melted a little. "Oh, Nolan."

"It's true—without you, I'm not sure I would've tried to talk and mend things with my family. Oh, I'm far from done. But it's a start. And that's just the beginning—you see me, accept me, and I hope, even care for me. Not because I'm famous or rich. No, you like plain old Nolan Wolfe, the shy guy who is often the nice one. And you've taught me that being the nice guy isn't a negative, either." He leaned forward. "I love you, Katie Evans. With my whole heart. I was drifting before I met you, trying to figure out where I belonged. But now I know—it's with you. You're my person, my place, my home. I know asking for your forgiveness is a lot, and it might take some time, but tell me you'll at least give us one more chance? That you'll let me show how fucking good we are together?"

A tear rolled down my cheek—one of happiness—

and I wiped it away. I wanted to scream yes, of course I'd give him another chance.

And yet, I couldn't. Not as long as Wendy was a threat to my family.

Shaking my head, I fumbled for the door handle. Once I found it, I opened the door and whispered, "I wish I could, but I can't, Nolan. I'm so sorry."

And with that, I dashed out of the car, back into the bar, and into the women's restroom. Inside the stall, I put my head in my hands and cried.

Cried for the man I loved but couldn't have.

Cried for the future I'd always wanted but could never have.

Cried for the pain I knew I'd cause him when I loved him, too.

Soon, Abby's voice filled the space. "Katie? What's wrong? Why are you crying? Did Nolan botch things?"

After a few deep breaths, I calmed down enough to open the stall door and walk out. "No. He was rather wonderful."

"Then why the hell are you crying?"

I shook my head. "If I tell you, if I tell anybody, it could hurt my family."

She searched my gaze for a few seconds. Then she took out her cell phone, shut it down, removed the battery, and put a hand on her hip. "See? There's no way this will get out to anyone. So, spill. You know I can keep your secret."

As I searched Abby's green-eyed gaze, I wavered. She could keep secrets. And even if she wanted to, she wouldn't confront Wendy if I asked her not to.

I also remembered all the years I'd kept being bullied a secret and how miserable I'd been. This would be a million times worse.

I sighed. "This can't get out to anyone, Abby. I mean it."

"Cross my heart and hope to die, it won't."

So I explained Wendy's threats. By the end, Abby was cursing up a storm. When she finally calmed down —I sometimes thought she had the worst temper of all the Wolfe siblings—she said, "We're going to find a way to solve this, Katie. You and my brother make each other happy. Well, when that cow isn't interfering. There has to be a way for you to get your happy ending."

"I wish there was. But she's a millionaire many times over, with powerful connections. How can we compete with that?"

"There has to be a way. We should tell Amber and Emmy, too."

"But will Emmy keep it from West?"

Abby waved a hand in dismissal. "She will, if revealing it will end up hurting you. She's kept plenty of secrets of mine."

Normally, after that hint drop, I'd prod for more information. But a flicker of hope had lit in my chest, and it made me overly optimistic. "Well, just us four, and no one else. Most especially not my sisters."

"Whatever you say. We'll think of something." Abby nodded. "We have to. I can't stand seeing my best friend and my brother so unhappy."

"Thanks, Abby. But if we're going to scheme, we need to do it somewhere private."

"Emmy's barn should work. Come on. Let's round up the troops, and I'll book a car. We can't have Kyle getting suspicious."

Soon we were out the door, piled into a car, and heading back to my place. We'd walk from my land to Emmy's, to keep West from seeing her and asking questions.

I hated how my friends had to keep sneaking around. And yet, if we could think of a way to deal with Wendy and I could be with Nolan, I would ask for West's forgiveness later.

For now, I had to think of the future I wanted. And maybe, just maybe, Wendy Webster would lose this time.

Chapter Thirty-Eight

Nolan

As Katie ran from my car, I tried to process everything.

Her gaze had been a mixture of love and regret. As if she'd wanted to say yes to us but couldn't.

But why?

Especially since her heart had been in her eyes after I said I loved her.

Something else was up. I wish she'd talk to me, but maybe there was a reason she couldn't. My best guess was Wendy had threatened her, or some such bullshit.

I placed my hands on the steering wheel and tightened my fingers. If I rushed back into the bar and demanded to know what was wrong, I doubted Katie would tell me. No, I needed to sort out this shit with

Wendy first and then try even harder to win back my woman.

What I needed more than anything was a way to destroy Wendy in the court of public opinion. Until that happened, her superfans would continue to do her bidding and stand by her. But how?

With a growl, I started up my car and turned onto the road, with no real destination in mind. Something about driving on autopilot helped me to think.

I was no more than a mile from the bar when I remembered something about the last joint interview I'd done with Wendy, one we'd done to promote the film we both starred in.

The one where the mics and cameras had still been on when she trashed her fans and most of the big-time directors in town.

If I could get ahold of that footage, it would reveal her true colors to the world. It might not solve everything, but it was a good fucking first step in bringing her down.

Since my phone was connected via Bluetooth, I dialed Jenn. As soon as she picked up, I said without preamble, "I need you to contact someone who has access to cut footage for the show, *The Stars Behind the Movies*."

Used to my sudden calls, she merely asked, "Why?"

"Wendy had a hot mic when she thought the cameras weren't rolling any longer."

"Ooh, I like where this is heading." After a quick recap of the content, Jenn added, "I'll have it by tomorrow, come hell or high water. What do you want me to do with it?"

"Leak it anonymously, on the condition they'll share it in full."

"I'll make it work. There's someone who owes me a favor." She paused and then asked, "And Katie? Any progress?"

"I'm still working on it."

"See that you do. I like her. And she's good for you."

"Trust me, I know. Make sure to send me a text when the leaked file goes live."

"Of course. Anything else?"

"Yes. I think Wendy threatened Katie with something. See if you can find that out for me, too."

"Gee, you don't do small requests, do you?"

"No, and I have one more." After I described it, I finished with, "Help me pull all this off, and you'll definitely get a raise."

"Hmm. I'd almost do it for the sheer joy of seeing Wendy taken down a few pegs. But I won't pass up extra cash."

I smiled. "Thanks, Jenn. I do appreciate you."

"I know. Otherwise, I wouldn't stick around. I'll text you updates."

After she hung up, my mood lightened a little. Not much, but the first step of my plan was in motion.

Now, I just had to get the others in place, too.

Chapter Thirty-Nine

Katie

The next morning, I was still sleeping when someone pounded on my door, and I jolted awake. "What the hell?"

Cassie's voice came through the door. "I'm coming in, so cover up." And then she barged into my room.

Rubbing my eyes, I asked, "What's so important that you have to wake me up at the crack of dawn?"

She sat on my bed. "Katie, you have to see this. It's about Wendy."

I rolled over. "Ugh, no. If I don't hear anything about Wendy fucking Webster ever again, I'll die a happy woman."

"No, trust me—you want to see this."

I pulled a pillow over my head. "Go away."

"Fine, we'll do it this way."

Her phone soon blasted at full volume, and the voice of the woman who'd ruined my life now echoed around the room.

"Thank fuck you nixed the idea of having some fans interview us."

An unfamiliar female voice said, "I still think it would've been a nice touch."

"No. The less time I have to spend with those cretins, the better."

Cretins?

I removed the pillow and sat up as Nolan spoke. "You should appreciate your fans, Wendy. They make your career possible."

It was such a Nolan thing to say.

Ignoring the pangs of my heart, I sat up and Cassie turned the screen toward me.

Wendy, Nolan, and a woman famous for interviewing actors were on the set of a show I vaguely recognized.

But I didn't have time to note anything else before Wendy said, "No, *I* made my career possible. They're just a nuisance I have to deal with. Luckily, social media makes it easy to fawn over them while I'm secretly gagging at home."

I blinked. What the hell?

Nolan frowned. "But I thought you adored your fans."

Wendy waved a hand in dismissal. "No. I wouldn't get within a hundred feet of most of them. But I need them to promote my movies. And to have leverage. I mean, having tens of millions of followers gives me social proof with directors. Who are another bunch I can't stand."

I sucked in a breath and asked Cassie, "Where did you get this?"

"It's online. Now, shush. It gets better."

The interviewer asked, "Why is that?"

Wendy shrugged. "They all have god complexes. I really struggled with it until I learned how to stroke their egos. Now, I have most of them eating out of my hands. And let's just say that with the right type of *persuasion*, I've advanced my career much faster than most."

By persuasion, she had to mean sleeping with directors to get roles.

Holy shit. Even though this was a train wreck about to happen, a thrill of happiness and relief threaded through me. Would this be enough to take Wendy down a notch, to the point she'd leave me alone? Or, at the very least, leave Nolan alone?

Nolan stood there, frowning hard. But the interviewer merely tilted her head and asked, "Did they pressure you to do it in exchange for a role? Because if so, you need to speak up."

"Oh, nothing like that. I pursued them. Sometimes relentlessly." She winked. "I have my tricks."

Nolan stood open-mouthed, reacting like most of the world probably would.

Where had this come from? And how had Nolan gotten hold of it? Because I knew, in my gut, he had something to do with this leaked video.

The audio slowly died out, and the video ended.

Turning toward Cassie, I said, "Tell me everything about this video. When did it show up? Where? What's the reaction?"

"When I checked my phone while making coffee, it was already everywhere. The show, *The Stars Behind the Movies*, denies any responsibility. So I don't know where it came from. But the world has completely turned against Wendy, that's for sure. There was even an announcement about her no longer having the star role in an upcoming movie."

"Let's check. I need to know it's bad enough that maybe..."

"Maybe what? What haven't you told me?"

I sighed. "Well, I suppose it's probably safe now since Wendy won't be thinking of me in the middle of this shitstorm."

And so I explained her threats. When I finished, Cassie lightly shoved me. "You shouldn't keep secrets like that from us!"

"I know, and I'm sorry, Cassie. Last night, the BFF Circle talked with me and we were thinking of ideas. But now, maybe, just maybe, this scandal will overtake mine."

"I should think so. Wendy's been cultivating her fans for years and years. And now? When they learn she can't stand them? They're going to turn on her, if they haven't already."

"Does it make me a horrible person to want to see how bad it is?"

"Of course not. Wendy deserves everything she

sowed. Let's check the latest and then figure out a way for you and Nolan to talk."

A flicker of hope flared in my chest. "Maybe. Let's just make sure things are bad enough that Wendy won't be thinking of destroying us."

Cassie gave me a one-armed hug. "No matter what happens, we'll get through this. Now, let's see how much Wendy is suffering."

The more we looked, the worse it got. Maybe I was an awful person because it made me smile to hear her fans say, "Wendy is a vile, manipulative narcissist. She's enemy number one, and she doesn't know what the hell we're going to rain down on her."

But as happy as Wendy's demise made me, I kept looking at my nightstand drawer, where I kept my phone. It was turned off still, but I was tempted to turn it on and reach out to Nolan.

However, it was mere hours since the video had leaked. I needed to be sure Wendy couldn't talk or charm her way out of this first. Only then could I see Nolan, tell him about her threats, and say how I truly felt.

Although waiting was pure hell. Everything I wanted was so, so close.

Chapter Forty

Katie

Two days later, things hadn't improved for Wendy Webster.

Her former followers had made good on their threats. Post after post, video after video, they all shouted and cried and asked how they could've been duped for so long. Her term of "cretin" had become their new rallying cry, turned into a positive. Almost as if saying they were cretins was spitting in Wendy's face.

Because of the posts and the negative PR, all of Wendy's signed movie deals were canceled. The growing list of directors who refused to work with her grew. Her endorsement deals ended. She'd even deleted all of her social media accounts.

Apart from a few blurry paparazzi pictures, the woman had vanished.

Not only that, but thanks to the new scandal, my own had been forgotten already.

It was a relief, for sure. And yet, as I held my still powered-off phone in my hand, my heart raced and my palms sweated. I needed to call Nolan and see if he'd forgive me.

However, it was easier said than done. I was afraid he'd tell me to fuck off.

He wouldn't do that.

Or so everyone said.

But it was time to stop being a coward. I powered on my phone and waited for it to load. The main screen had just appeared when the doorbell rang. Ignoring it, I opened my texts. It took forever to scroll to find Nolan's. And as I read his pleas to contact him, my eyes heated with tears.

When I reached the most recent ones, from the night he told me he loved me, I had to reread them a few times:

Nolan: I meant it. I love you, baby. So much. And if I didn't think you felt the same, I wouldn't be bothering you now. But I saw the look in your eyes. When you're ready, I'll be here waiting for you.
Nolan: SHE is taken care of and should leave us alone. I'm here and ready to listen when you want to talk.
Nolan: I'm not sure if your phone is still off or if you want nothing to do with me. But no, I don't believe that. We'll talk soon, baby. I love you.

Nolan: PS—I found a beautiful shell on my beach, and I'll save it for when I see you.

I kept reading the words, "I love you" over and over again. Yearning rushed forth. I wanted Nolan Wolfe as mine. I wanted him forever.

Then call him already.

Just as I hit Dial, Sam knocked and barged in. "Someone's at the front door for you."

"I'm busy."

"I think you want to take this one."

Nolan's phone went to voicemail, and my stomach dropped. Was he avoiding me?

I didn't want to do this via a message, so I clicked End and looked at my sister. "Why?"

"Just trust me."

She winked and walked away.

After tossing my phone on the bed, I headed toward the front door. Maybe it was just Abby, Emmy, or Amber coming to check on me.

But as soon as I reached the front door—still closed—and saw the hallway was empty, I looked at Sam. She gestured. "Open it."

With that, she left me alone.

I wasn't in the best mood for games, so I yanked the door open. On the other side, Nolan knelt on one knee with a high heel shoe in his hands.

My shoe.

The one I'd lost the night of the charity event.

He smiled at me, and all my anger and frustration and worry melted away.

"Nolan. You're here."

He didn't get up, but held out the shoe some more. "I've come for the woman I love. She wears this shoe and lost it on the night I should've been there for her." I tried to say it wasn't his fault, but he pushed on before I could utter a word. "She makes me happy and completes me in a way I never thought I'd find. I love her teasing me about being a vampire or that I have a hidden sex dungeon. I love when she falls asleep in my arms under the stars, trusting me to take her home. I love how kind and funny and perceptive she is." He smiled. "You're my person, my place, my everything, Katherine Ruth Evans. I love you. Will you be my girlfriend, knowing everything that comes with it?"

I did my best not to cry. Although Nolan Wolfe kneeling on my front stoop, holding up my lost shoe and declaring his love for me was quite possibly the most romantic thing I'd ever seen in my life.

I took the shoe, placed it on the entryway table, and offered my hand. "I love you, too, Nolan Hank Wolfe. Now, get up and kiss me."

With a grin, he rose, pulled me close, and pressed his lips to mine.

As I opened and his tongue twined with mine, I forgot all about the hell caused by his ex or the heartbreak at having to push him away.

He was warm and solid and safe. I loved him more than anyone in the world, and as he kissed me, I knew there would never be any other man for me. Nolan was it.

He was my happy ending.

Eventually, our kisses slowed, and he laid his forehead against mine. He murmured, "Come back to my place and let's finish celebrating."

I smiled. "Hmm, and what would this celebrating entail? More kissing?"

He brushed his lips against my cheek. "Definitely kissing. But not just your mouth. I want to kiss every inch of your body. While you wear a blindfold."

Heat rushed between my thighs. "I might be open to it."

He chuckled. "Your breathless reply tells me you're more than open to it." He nipped my earlobe. "I bet if I ran my fingers through your pussy, you'd be wet and swollen for me already. Wouldn't you, baby?"

"Maybe."

He nipped my ear. "Come with me. Let me fulfill one of your sex fantasies tonight."

"It's yours as well."

After brushing hair off my face, he replied, "Which is why it's perfect. So, what do you say, baby? Will you come stay the night with me?"

"Yes. A million times, yes. Let me just grab a few things."

"I can help you."

"If you 'help' me, we'll never leave."

Nolan winked, and my heart skipped a beat at how handsome he was. "We could start our celebrations here."

"What, and have someone walk in on us? Um, no." I kissed him. "I'll be back in a few minutes."

Nolan took my hand, brought it to his lips, and then said, "I'll be here for you. Always."

My heart thudded again at the truth behind his words. "I'll be right back."

After one last kiss, I grabbed my shoe, rushed upstairs, and threw a few toiletries and clothes into a bag. I was just rushing back down the stairs again when Cassie and Sam blocked the bottom of the stairs. "Get out of the way. I'm in a hurry."

Cassie smiled. "I bet. So you and Nolan are back together?"

"Yes. Now, move."

Cassie laughed. "Only if you share the details later."

Sam waggled her eyebrows, and I sighed. "Fine. Now, will you move?"

They each hugged me quickly and got out of the way. Sam said, "Don't do anything I wouldn't do!"

Nolan waited in the entryway, his lips twitching. He said, "I hope her hard-no list is as small as yours."

Sam's voice boomed down the hallway. "Smaller!"

With a groan, I opened the front door and tugged Nolan. "Come on, before my parents investigate and things get embarrassing."

He laughed as we headed toward his car. "I imagine your dad would just get up and leave without a word."

"Probably, but I'd rather not find out."

Nolan opened my door, and I smiled at his now-familiar gesture. After I slid into the car, he rushed to his side. Once seated, he leaned over and kissed me gently.

I sighed. "I'll never tire of that."

"Of what, me showing up with lost items and saying I love you despite your forgetfulness?"

I lightly smacked his arm. "Meanie."

He grinned. "Hey, it could be a game. You lose things on purpose, I have to find them, and then you come up with creative ways to thank me and celebrate."

I couldn't hold back my laugh. "That's almost tempting."

"Well, we'll talk about it. But not tonight." His gaze smoldered. "All I want is you naked and at my mercy."

I pressed my thighs together. "Then stop talking and start driving."

Once Nolan was on the main road, he laid a hand on my thigh and squeezed. "Has your online harassment stopped?"

"I haven't checked too deeply, but from what my sisters and the BFF Circle have shown me, everyone's talking about Wendy and her betrayal."

He nodded. "That's what I've seen as well. Word is that Wendy's going to leave the country for a short while and live incognito."

"Do you think it'll be a case of she goes away for a few months, the world forgets, and she comes back to an adoring audience again?"

He shook his head. "I don't think so. Because if she does, I have a signed and recorded confession from Matt Bellis that will get her arrested. I told her about it, too." He glanced at me and then back at the road. "She won't be bothering us anymore, baby. We're free. Well, as free as being with me can be, at any rate."

Relief flooded through me. "Is it true? She won't ever bother us again?"

"I can't guarantee it 100 percent, but it's very unlikely. I can't imagine Wendy would enjoy going to jail." He squeezed my leg again. "Our life is our own, Katie. Yes, I'll still get some attention, especially with this last movie I'm working on. But with time, it should get easier. I'll focus more on my production company and my charities, and while people will probably often still recognize me, we can always get creative and give them shows."

"What, of the sex-related variety?"

He laughed. "No. But maybe we can show up at certain events in historical dress. Maybe I'm a Highlander and you're my rival's sister I stole to be my bride."

"Maybe. Or, we can be fae royalty, complete with pointy ears and fancy clothes. Or, you can put on some pale makeup and sparkles, and you can be the vampire and I'll be the human you can't resist. Or..."

He patted my thigh. "We can come up with as many ideas as we like. As long as you're having fun and are happy, that's all that matters to me."

Silence fell a few beats and then I blurted, "I hope you know I forgive you for that night."

He grimaced. "Maybe, but I still blame myself."

"Don't, Nolan. I mean, you were literally kidnapped. That's one of a handful of acceptable excuses for ditching me at the charity event. Right alongside picking up a magic-filled artifact that sends you back in time, rescuing kittens from a burning shelter, or accidentally falling down a well."

"A well?"

"Hey, you're older than me. I'm sure you watched old *Lassie* reruns as a kid."

"I'll try my best not to fall down a well, baby. That should be easy."

"You say that, but you never know..."

He tickled my side briefly, and I laughed.

Nolan said, "Life will never be boring with you, which is another thing I love."

I touched his hand. "You didn't exactly have a boring life before, though."

"Maybe boring isn't the right word. No, I was lonely." He glanced at me with love in his eyes. "But never again."

"No, never again."

We smiled at each other and then Nolan had to concentrate on the winding road leading to his house. As soon as we arrived, he helped me out of the car, and we walked up the front steps. I said, "You really should bring your family here. Well, here and to your place in Malibu."

"I'm working on it. But I'm rather grateful they don't know about my home in Starry Hills right this second. That means we won't be interrupted."

He stopped me from entering the house. "Let me carry you, baby. I want to start out the way I mean to go on—supporting you when you need it, and loving you so much I want to be as close as possible to you whenever I can."

"I'll be here for you too, although don't ask me to carry you. I'm not sure I could manage that."

"Maybe you could if they invent super exoskeleton armor like in the superhero movies."

He winked, and I giggled. "I wouldn't mind seeing you in tights."

He nipped my bottom lip. "I love you, Katie."

"I love you, too, Nolan."

Then he scooped me up and carried me up the stairs. My heart pounded for so many reasons. Not just because I was going to have sex with Nolan again, although that was definitely a plus. No, it was because I was going to do it with the man I loved.

Blindfolded.

I could hardly wait.

Chapter Forty-One

Nolan

Aunt Lori: You're in town and didn't stop by? <crying emoji>
Me: I see the gossip chain is working.
Aunt Lori: Don't change the subject. Where are you, Nolan?
Me: I'm winning Katie back.
Aunt Lori: Oh, well carry on. Come see us when you get a chance. I won't go near your secret hideaway in the meantime.
Me: Wait, how do you know about that?
Aunt Lori: I know everything that goes on in this town, lad. The woman you bought the house from was my friend's niece. I expect an invitation soon.

Me: Er, okay. In a few days.
Aunt Lori: I'll give you a week. If we don't see you by then, I'm storming the castle.
Me: It won't come to that. I'll contact you soon.
Aunt Lori: Can't wait. We can have a big family dinner at your house for the first time. <heart emoji>

As I carried Katie up the stairs, I could barely believe she was here. Not only that, but Katie loved me as well.

Holding her close, her heat and scent surrounding me, I burned to claim her. As mine. Forever.

I strode into the bedroom and laid Katie on the bed. After caressing her cheek, I kissed her and said, "Strip for me, baby. I'll get the blindfold."

She reached out and stroked my erection through my jeans, and I groaned.

"I want you naked, too. Even if I won't be able to see you, I want to be able to feel your skin against mine."

With a growl, I kissed her. Not gentle and soft, but hard and possessive. By the time I pulled away, we both were breathing heavily. "I'll be right back. And yes, I'll be naked."

Katie didn't waste time stripping off her leggings and long sweatshirt. I watched her wiggle and arch until she wore nothing.

"You're so damn beautiful."

I wanted to walk back and caress every inch of her soft, warm skin.

"Clothes, Nolan. Why are you still wearing them?"

I undressed quickly and casually stroked my dick as I memorized Katie's body. "Time to play."

After grabbing the blindfold from the dresser, I went over to her and quickly tied it. I moved to her ear and whispered, "Ready for me to tease you, baby? To tease you until you're begging for me to make you come?"

"Yes, please. Hurry up."

"Lay back for me." Once she did, I lightly traced the curve of her breast. "Did you bring any of your toys with you?"

"Ugh, no. And now I wished I had."

Leaning down, I licked her nipple and then blew on it. She arched her back a little toward me. "Luckily for you, I ordered a little something once you mentioned toys." I opened the nightstand and took out the vibrator. After turning it on, I lightly circled her nipple and Katie cried out.

I teased around and around, never quite touching her taut peak. Then I removed it and Katie growled. "Why did you stop?"

"So I could do this."

I took her nipple into my mouth and licked and nibbled and sucked until Katie's hands were in my hair, holding me close, and her legs had fallen open.

Running my hand through her pussy, I said, "You're wet but not wet enough, baby. Let's see how drenched you can get for me."

"Nolan."

I moved the vibrator and circled around her clit, without ever touching it. Every moan and groan and cry of Katie's only made me harder.

The urge to plunge into her tight, wet heat was overwhelming. To fuck her so hard she'd forget about everything but me. To come inside her, claim her, and then hold her as she fell asleep in my arms.

I would do all of that. Eventually. For now, I wanted to play some more and make it that much better for my woman.

For my future wife, even if she didn't know it yet.

Moving the vibrator down, I teased her pussy. One side and then the other before I thrust gently, with just the tip, and she spread her legs wider.

Her voice was breathless as she said, "I'm not sure how much more I can take of this, Nolan."

"Oh, you can take more, baby. I know you can. I'm just getting started."

And I smiled as I debated what to do next.

Chapter Forty-Two

Katie

From the moment Nolan had tied the blindfold, every touch, caress, or kiss was that much more intense.

Him just teasing my nipple, sucking it, and then playing with my pussy made me wet and hot and desperate.

But then he removed the vibrator, and I barely suppressed a whimper. Part of me wanted to reach out, pull him close, and tell him to make love to me already.

And yet, I liked not knowing what came next. Not seeing Nolan's intention in his eyes.

Just wondering what he would do made me wetter.

"Why aren't you doing anything? You can't be done."

"Oh, I'm far from done, baby. You're not leaving this bed until you come. Several times." He lightly fingered my entrance and then coated my clit with my wetness.

Even with just the brief brushing of fingers, I felt my orgasm building.

"We can play with the toy some more later. Because if I don't taste you soon, I'll die."

His hot breath caressed my pussy, and I opened wider to him. As his warm hands rubbed my thighs, my heart raced and I throbbed everywhere.

One second, then another. Just as I was about to growl at him again, Nolan licked my clit slowly. It was brief, and yet pleasure shot through my whole body. The touch wasn't enough to orgasm, but damn, it felt good.

His hot breath danced against my center as he said, "You taste so fucking good. But I need more, much more."

I waited, breathing hard, my every nerve at the ready. Then his tongue lightly fucked my pussy, and I moaned. Each lick and lap and light nibble made me grab the blanket with my fingers harder.

But I didn't want the blanket. I wanted—no, needed—to feel Nolan. I fumbled around until I found his head and dug my nails into his scalp. He growled loudly and fucked my entrance harder.

I arched and moved my hips, wondering if I could maybe come this way. Because if I didn't orgasm soon, I might cry.

Then his touch was gone completely. I reached around, but didn't find him. "Nolan? Where are you?"

"Here."

Then his hands pulled me down the bed and my legs went over his shoulders. His hot breath danced across my center.

I didn't have time to protest as he teased my clit with his tongue. Fast, then slow, and fast again. Always changing the tempo to keep me guessing, making me hotter, and I arched. "I'm close, Nolan. So close. Please."

"Please, what? Tell me what you need, baby."

"Make me come."

Then I felt his lips around my clit, and he suckled. The pressure built even more, to be almost painful, and then he lightly bit me and I screamed his name as pleasure rushed through me. Wave after wave as he continued to suckle me and draw out the orgasm.

Once I finally relaxed against the bed, spent and boneless, Nolan lapped at my pussy a few times and hummed. "You taste so fucking good, baby. I'll never get enough of your honey."

"Mmm." That was all I could manage.

He chuckled, moved, and then suddenly the blindfold was gone and I had to blink my eyes against the lights.

Nolan's smug expression came into view, and I smiled. "Someone's proud of himself."

He kissed me slowly, and I could still taste myself on his lips. When he broke it, he said, "Not proud, just so fucking happy and lucky that you're mine." He caressed the side of my breast. "You're so beautiful, baby. And I love you so much."

Tears unexpectedly sprung to my eyes, and I tried to blink them away. Nolan sat on the bed and pulled me into his lap. "What's wrong, baby? Did I say or do something I shouldn't have?"

I shook my head. "No, no, you did everything I wanted. And more." I smiled at him. "I'm just so happy, Nolan. And it's still hard to believe this isn't a dream and that you'll still be here when I wake up."

He cupped my cheek. "I'm not going anywhere." He kissed me softly. "To prove how real this is, I think it's time I give you another orgasm."

"How does that work, exactly? I mean, some people can come in their sleep."

"Never as hard as when I'm with you, baby. Ever."

His gaze smoldered and I wiggled on his lap. Yep, his hard cock was more than ready for me.

Running my hand up his chest, I played with his chest hair and moved to straddle him. "Then let's see if you're truly awake, shall we?"

He chuckled, but as soon as I moved to my knees and took hold of his dick, his laughter died. I never broke eye contact as I positioned him and slowly slid down his cock. Once he was in to the hilt, I hooked my hands behind his neck, kissed him gently, and said, "I love you, Nolan Wolfe."

"I love you too, Katie Evans."

With a growl, he kissed me again and guided my hips.

As we moved, I broke the kiss so I could stare into Nolan's hazel eyes. The mixture of heat and love warmed my entire body. I clung to his shoulders and moved my hips faster, loving the combination of his adoring gaze and his bare cock inside me.

Since I was still sensitive, it didn't take long for the pressure to build again. And when Nolan circled my clit, I cried out. "Nolan."

"Baby, I love you. Tell me the same."

"I love you."

"Good girl."

He rubbed my clit firmly, and I stilled as another orgasm crashed over me. Nolan clung to my hip with his other hand and stilled as he cried out, too.

When we'd both come down from our highs, I laid my forehead against his shoulder and hugged him close. "Mmm."

He laughed. "I take it that's Katie code for, 'That was the best sex of my life, Nolan.'"

I snuggled more against him. "Maybe. Mmm."

His arms wrapped around me, and he kissed my forehead. "I could sit like this forever, baby, and still never have enough of you."

"Now you're being swoon-y."

"Swoon-y? What's that?"

"When you say stuff that makes me sigh and want to swoon with happiness."

"So I should aim for it all the time?"

"Most definitely."

"Then I should start now." He hugged me tighter against him. "I love you, Katie. So much. I never imagined I could be this happy, and yet here we are, just getting started."

I leaned back until I could see his gaze. "We are. Although we still have a lot to discuss and talk about.

Because once we leave Starry Hills, the real world will intrude again."

"I know, and we'll face it together. But regardless of any future discussions, there's one thing that's nonnegotiable."

"And what's that?"

"I'm going to take you to every place on that wall collage of yours, no matter how long it takes me."

I smiled. "That might take a lifetime."

"And I couldn't imagine a better way of spending it."

My heart nearly burst with feelings for this man. "I love you, Nolan."

"I love you too, baby. Now, let's rest a little and then we'll start round two."

After Nolan cleaned me up, we cuddled together under the blankets. I asked, "And how many rounds will there be?"

"As many as we want. We have a week."

"Why a week?"

He stroked my back in slow circles, and it took everything I had not to fall asleep. "Aunt Lori knows about my place, apparently. She gave us a week before she stops by."

I chuckled. "I had a gut feeling she knew. There's nothing in Starry Hills that she doesn't know about." I paused and then added, "Do you think she knew about our arrangement in the beginning?"

"Maybe. But she's also perceptive and probably kept quiet to see how things played out."

"Why?"

He kissed the top of my head. "She wants me and

my siblings happy. Beck and West found love and have turned into sappy bastards. Well, compared to before. I think she wants that for us all and is willing to do anything to make it happen."

I snuggled more against his side. "Three down, three more to go."

Although as we joked about which Wolfe sibling would fall in love next, deep down, I worried Abby might never risk her heart again to find it. She'd been hurt so badly by that asshole in San Jose, had vowed to never let her walls down again with a man, and had even started researching foreign countries where she could get a work visa to get away from the USA.

Maybe it's just a knee-jerk reaction to her pain, and she never follows through.

Of course, she might also be serious.

But soon I couldn't keep my eyes open any longer, and I fell asleep to dreams of a future with Nolan.

Chapter Forty-Three

Nolan

S*ix Months Later*

Abby: I wish we could be having dinner at your place, Nolan. It's so peaceful.
Aunt Lori: That would ruin his plans.
West: Why are we being included in this?
Aunt Lori: Because Nolan needs help setting things up. And we always help family.
Abby: Exactly. We helped you, West. And you too, Beck.

Beck: I proposed alone, thank you very much.
Abby: And who helped with the string lights?
Beck: Fine, whatever.
Zach: I'm still up for helping you, Nolan. I wish you'd let me bring a speaker and playlist, though.
Zane: Your music would ruin the mood, asshole.
Zach: Hey! I can pick romantic stuff.
Zane: You say that, and the lyrics would be about a dead soulmate, or something.
Zach: That can be romantic.
Me: No music. Stick to the plan.
Beck: Don't worry, I'll make sure Zach doesn't even have his phone.
Zach: I am a grown man, brother.
Beck: Sometimes.
Zach: <middle finger emoji>
Aunt Lori: Now, now, behave, boys. Or I'll start sending quotes from the latest racy book I'm reading.
Me, Zach, Zane, Beck, and West: <horror face emoji>
Abby: <laughing emoji> You guys are so easy to manipulate.
Aunt Lori: So, everyone is still on board?
Everyone else: Yes, Aunt Lori.

Six months flew by, and my love for Katie only grew. Despite me having to spend a lot of time on location for my last movie, she was always there for me. We called, texted, video chatted whenever we could. And I flew her out when she had the time.

No, not because she was still doing her family's dairy farm tours. Katie had fallen in love with the Starry Arts Haven Center and months ago had switched to working there. While she volunteered with as many of the kids as she could, she particularly focused on children who had been bullied or verbally abused.

She felt like it had always been her destiny to work with kids who went through similar events as her own. Even if being bullied as a kid had been hard, she used her experiences to bond and help others.

Not that she'd ever have to worry about her Mean Girl bullies ever again. I'd called in a few favors and all three of them were now divorced and not even speaking to each other. Thankfully, the kids had all been allowed to stay with their fathers. They weren't much better, but that was still saying something.

But as much as I loved acting, I was glad to be back in Starry Hills and done with filming. Any roles in the future would be ones that called to me. It was nice to have that to look forward to.

However, I was more excited about asking Katie to be my wife.

And so I'd asked my siblings to help me set up the apple orchard. It was a family tradition to propose there. West had done it last year. Beck had done it the month before. And now? It was my turn.

I asked Katie to meet me there instead of at the

airport. So after quickly changing at our place—we'd lived together for the last five months—I rushed over to my family's winery. I pulled into a spot close to the orchard, and no sooner had I stepped out of the car than Beck found me.

At his grimace, I laughed. "Tell me they didn't veer from the plan."

"A little. Trying to get Zach and Zane to follow a plan is like herding cats, I swear."

"Well, I appreciate all your help and the headaches it caused."

Beck slapped my back. "No worries, brother. I've dealt with far worse. At least your ex didn't try to kill people like Sabrina's did."

"No, mine just tried to publicly humiliate the love of my life and turn the entire internet against her," I drawled.

Beck snorted. "We do have a track record. West's story almost seems tame by comparison."

"Let's hope it's that way for the twins."

Because Abby was already in the middle of her own weird, unpredictable story. One that I didn't quite know how would turn out.

Although I constantly wished on the Wishing Tree she'd get her happy ending, too.

I cleared my throat. "Tell me everything's ready? Abby should be bringing Katie by soon."

Beck nodded. "It should be. Come on. The sooner you say it's good, the sooner I can send Zach and Zane home and spend some alone time with my fiancée."

Seeing Beck's smile made me do the same. "Let's hope they don't want a double wedding."

"No, I want Sabrina to have her own special day. I like Katie, I do. But my Sabrina deserves to be treasured and admired and the sole focus of her own wedding."

Sabrina's childhood had been shitty—full of verbal abuse and poverty. Katie had convinced Sabrina to volunteer a few times with children at the Starry Arts Haven Center who'd had similar experiences. The two had bonded over their work, and Katie even had plans to expand to Sonoma. That way Sabrina could help out closer to home, since her business and life were based in Starry Hills.

I squeezed Beck's shoulder. "Don't worry, I want Katie's day to be special, too. Although our wedding will probably be sooner rather than later since Katie wants a big family."

"You're going to end up with ten kids, aren't you?"

"Maybe not ten. But a few, yes." I smiled. "The thought of parenthood is both fucking scary and amazing."

"Well, we're going to wait so Sabrina can build up her business. I'll leave the baby making to you two. Sabrina and I will just practice a lot in the meantime."

He winked, and I laughed. After throwing an arm around my brother's shoulder, we headed into the orchard. It didn't take long to reach the center, where there was a stone bench and the Wishing Tree.

And just like I'd asked, they'd decorated it perfectly. "She's going to love this. Thanks, everyone."

Aunt Lori walked over, and I hugged her. She said,

"Anything for my lads." She leaned back. "Abby will be here any minute, so let me round up the gang and we'll get out of your hair."

I leaned down and kissed her cheek. "Thanks, Aunt Lori. I'm glad you could be a part of this."

She lightly swatted my arm. "Of course I'd be here." Her expression softened. "All I ever wanted was for you six to find love and happiness like I did with my Tim."

"Thanks, Aunt Lori. For everything."

She patted my arm. "It was nothing." She eyed Zach, who was tying a speaker to the tree. She walked toward him. "Hey! I see you, Zachary Wolfe! No speakers."

As she got Zach to take it down—and look sheepish—West came up and nodded. "Good luck. Even though I'm sure she'll say yes, it can be fucking nerve-racking."

"Thanks. And thank Emmy for helping to keep Katie occupied long enough for you all to do this."

"I will. She's already planning weddings for Sabrina and Katie. Don't even think of hiring anyone else."

I laughed. "Noted. Besides, she *is* the best wedding planner I know. I'd be a fool to go anywhere else."

West nodded. "Right answer."

He winked, and I said goodbye to all my brothers and Aunt Lori. It wasn't long before I heard Katie and Abby's voices in the distance.

"Do we really need to stop by the orchard and make a wish right now? Nolan should be here any minute. It's been a week, and I've missed him."

Abby replied, "We'll be quick. I promised Rafe I'd make a wish for something today. So I have to do it because I always keep my promises."

It was still hard to believe Abby had married Rafe. They bickered a lot, and I sometimes had my doubts, but Aunt Lori said not to interfere and so I didn't.

Sure, I kept a close watch and an ear to the ground. But for now, I was letting them figure things out.

However, as soon as Katie entered the orchard, I forgot about everything else. It was show time.

Chapter Forty-Four

Katie

Nolan: I have a list of things I want to do to you tonight.
Me: Tease. <tongue out emoji>
Nolan: Ice cubes will be involved.
Me: Oh, so I can shrink your dick?
Nolan: I thought you'd want my dick as big as possible.
Me: Hmm. But then you'd have to use your mouth. I've missed your mouth.
Nolan: I planned to have the ice cube IN my mouth when I teased you.
Me: <overheated emoji> That will take some skill.
Nolan: I've been practicing. I have it down.
Me: What, did you pretend your pinky was my clit and teased yourself?
Nolan: Er, not exactly.

Me: But then you'd make sure to have the right balance of hot and cold. I don't want to freeze.
Nolan: You won't. A little cold with a little heat is perfect. You came hard when I froze that glass dildo and played with you.
Me: I almost forgot about that. You are getting creative. <heart emoji>
Nolan: I'm just getting started, baby. <winking emoji>

I loved Abby, but I really didn't understand why she had to go make a wish on the Wishing Tree right now. I mean, she and Rafe had a place in town. They could stop by anytime.

However, she swore it was urgent. Something to do with a big decision they had to make. And since Abby rarely asked for favors, I couldn't say no.

We entered the orchard and memories of us playing here as children rushed into my mind. "We should all pick apples together this fall and make pies, like we used to."

Abby smiled. "That would be fun. And yes, Amber, the master baker, will win. But I'd like to make mine bad on purpose and make Rafe eat it."

Their Vegas marriage had surprised us all. And secretly, I hadn't been sure it would last. However, Abby seemed happier and lighter than she'd been in over a year. So much so, I might have to wish on the Wishing

Tree that she and Rafe were meant to be together forever.

Before I could reply, we reached the center of the orchard and my jaw dropped open.

Seashells were tied to various branches and hung everywhere. Little glass balls also twinkled in the sunlight. The reflections danced off Nolan, who stood near the stone bench, his hand outstretched, wearing a tuxedo. "Hello, baby."

Abby hugged me and then dashed away. I barely paid attention as I walked toward him and took his hand. "What's going on, Nolan?"

He kissed me quickly before he gestured toward the bench. "Sit down, first."

I did, rearranged my skirt, and then found Nolan kneeling in front of me, holding two rings—the sapphire one from our fake engagement and a new one with an amethyst.

Sucking in a breath, I placed a hand over my mouth. "Nolan."

He smiled. "Our story began with an agreement. We were basically strangers playing roles, trying to fool the world. However, it didn't take long for me to notice just how special you are, Katie Evans. You're funny and kind and have a bigger heart than most people realize. You're also strong, determined, and adventurous. There's nothing I can't tell you, nothing I can't share. I know you'll listen and talk with me. Not because I'm famous or rich. Simply because you like me, love me, see me. I love you for all those reasons, and so many more. I want to spend the rest of my life making your dreams come true, making you laugh, and being your home. Will you marry me? For forever this time?"

A mixture of pure joy and love rushed through me. "Yes, Nolan, I'll marry you. For forever this time."

He slipped a ring on each hand before cupping my face and kissing me. I pulled him close and reveled in his heat and scent and familiar taste. When he finally broke the kiss, he sat on the bench, moved me into his lap, and kissed me some more.

Eventually he stopped so we could catch our breaths. I laid my head on his shoulder, hugged him close, and said, "So, does this mean we're going to give Aunt Lori the theme wedding she always wanted?"

He chuckled. "Only if you want it, baby. The sky's the limit. I only have one condition."

I lifted my head. "Which is?"

"You let me take you for an extended honeymoon. Now that I'm done filming, I plan to take you any and everywhere you wish to go. I want to help you fill up your passport, get extra pages, and keep going until you're ready to come home."

I traced his jaw. "Home is with you, Nolan."

He nuzzled my cheek. "You know what I mean."

"I know. And I'm sure at some point, I'll want to settle down. Especially since I don't want to abandon the children at the center. I'll have to find a really good replacement for when I'm absent. We can't go before then."

"Of course not, baby. We'll make sure the kids are taken care of. Then we're off to see the world."

"Together. Forever."

He nodded. "Yes, for forever."

As we sat kissing and murmuring about the future, the stars came out and the moon shone brightly. However, I didn't need to stare at them to help calm down my worries about the future. No, this time they shone down on me, sitting in the lap of the man who was my future, twinkling their congratulations, eager to see where our lives led us next.

Epilogue

Nolan

Just Over Three Years Later

Aunt Lori: I can't wait to show off my dress tonight!
Me: I'm sure it's nice.
Abby: <laughing emoji> You need to do better than that.
Zach: Even I know that. Aunt Lori, you'll be radiant.
Zane: Unlike you. I swear, you can't tie a bowtie to save your life. You're going to embarrass Nolan.
Zach: <middle finger emoji> I'll ask Amber to help me. Maybe. If Luna will ever let her out of her sight.
West: You are paying for dinner later, right, Nolan?

Me: Er, yes. I said I would. I mean, you all are staying in my house. It's not like I wouldn't feed you.
West: Good. Children are expensive. Especially when you have a teenage boy. Wyatt alone eats enough for three people.
Me: You can have Wyatt visit me anytime to eat me out of house and home.
Abby: Another reason I'm waiting.
Me: You're married to a millionaire, Abby.
Abby: Still.
Beck: I thought tonight was supposed to be a grown-up night out? I miss those.
Me: The movie is kid-friendly, though. So if you've changed your mind...
Beck: No! I love my daughter. But seriously, I need a night off.
Me: Don't worry, our nanny is the best. Maybe in the country. She'll take good care of them all.
Aunt Lori: And we're getting a family photo taken together, too, no matter if I have to ask some stranger to do it. Now, finish getting ready. I can't wait to see you all. <heart emoji>

I held my one-year-old son, Bowen, against my hip and kissed his cheek. "We'll be back later. You'll be good for Maria, won't you?"

He nodded and then laid his head on my shoulder and sucked his thumb.

I hugged his little body close and breathed in his baby scent. It was never easy leaving him, no matter how many times I'd done it to go to work.

I whispered, "I love you, Bowen. And I'll make sure to get you one of the stuffed dragons for your bed."

He nodded again.

Just as I debated whether or not to see if he'd call me Daddy again—he was a champ at Mommy but saved Daddy for rare occasions, which made Katie laugh—Katie came down the grand staircase.

My jaw dropped. She wore a dark blue gown, complete with the sapphire necklace I'd given her during our fake engagement and the little tiara I bought on a whim a few years ago. "You're beautiful, baby. So beautiful."

Katie smiled, smoothed her dress, and asked, "You can't tell I'm pregnant again, can you?"

She was only three months along but carried twins this time. Tonight we'd planned to tell our family the news. "No, you look just as stunning as normal."

She walked up to me, laid a hand on Bowen's back, and kissed our son's cheek. "You'll be a good boy, won't you, Bowen, for Maria?"

Bowen removed his thumb and nodded. "Good boy, Mommy. Me good."

Katie smiled. "Of course you are, love." She raised her face, and I kissed her. She murmured, "You look sexy yourself."

"You always did have a thing for a guy in a tuxedo."

"Not any guy—just you."

I kissed her again. But before I could say another word, the nanny came to retrieve Bowen.

With her dark hair streaked with gray and smile lines around her mouth, Maria looked the part of a kind nanny. Jenn even said she could've been from central casting. With the salary to match. However, she was rumored to be the best in town and I didn't care how much it cost when it came to my kid's happiness.

Once Katie and I kissed Bowen and said goodnight, we were alone in the main entryway of my Malibu mansion. I offered my arm, and Katie wound hers through it. She asked, "Ready for the big night?"

"Mostly. I know all the test audiences went great. And yet, critics can be brutal."

She patted my upper arm. "It's the kids and families who matter. You made a wonderful Christmas movie, Nolan. One that will become an instant classic. I'm so proud of you."

It'd taken some work and a lot of revisions, but I'd finally written a cute, heartwarming Christmas movie about dragons. It took my production company, some investors, and a director I had worked with before to make it happen. Tonight was the premiere.

"I hope so."

Katie replied, "I know so. And look, here come more people who'll agree with me."

All of my siblings and their spouses came down the hall, including Aunt Lori and her fiancé, Fernando. Everyone wore either tuxedos or fancy evening gowns. I'd insisted they let me buy everything for the premiere.

After years of them refusing everything, they'd slowly started to say yes.

Aunt Lori spoke first. "Agree with what?"

Katie replied, "That Nolan's movie is going to do amazingly well and become a yearly favorite."

Aunt Lori nodded. "Of course it will. Anyone who says otherwise, well, they'll have to deal with me."

My aunt was barely five feet tall, and yet her expression said she meant it.

I nodded to Fernando and then kissed Aunt Lori's cheek. "Thanks, Aunt Lori."

I looked at each of my siblings and their spouses. "I'm glad you could all be here tonight. I know you're all busy."

Beck shook his head. "Of course we'd be here, Nolan. This movie is special to you, which makes it special to us."

Zach nodded. "Besides, my daughter loves dragons and if I don't get one of those special stuffed toys they're handing out, I'll never hear the end of it."

Amber rolled her eyes. "You want the dragon, not Luna."

Zach looked sheepish. "Maybe."

West grunted. "Can we get going? The longer we stay here, the longer I expect to hear Ben calling for his mother, and I want Emmy to myself tonight."

Emmy shook her head. "Stop worrying. It's just a phase he's going through, West. Ben loves you too."

I said, "I feel you, brother. Bowen's first word was 'Mama' and it took him months to say 'Dada.'"

Abby sighed. "I thought this was an adult night of fun?"

Rafe hugged her close. "It will be. Come on. The limos should be here by now. Nolan and I each ordered one because as much as I love your family, there's no way I want to squish fourteen people into one car."

Abby laughed. "I'd like to see us try. Then we pull up to the red carpet, we all come out, and the press will think it's like one of those clown cars."

Katie looked up at me. "Can we try that?"

"Next time, baby. My company has a lot riding on tonight."

She nodded. "I know, and don't worry, I don't want to have Zach elbow me in the side, or for one of you tall people to accidentally kick me with your long legs."

I pulled her close. "I'd protect you."

"Oh, so now you're arguing for us to ride together?"

"Er, no. Not exactly."

Katie laughed and patted my chest. "Don't worry, I also don't want to wrinkle my dress. Now, come on. We don't want to be late. If Jenn and Tina have to wait too long for us, we'll never hear the end of it."

So we piled into the two limos and headed for my movie premiere. It was weird and wonderful to be surrounded by most of the people I loved in the world tonight. It was still hard to believe that I'd not only grown close to my family again, but had also found the love of my life, my person, my home.

And with Katie at my side, I could face anything. What had started out as a plan to free myself had ended up bringing me the one person I never wanted to let go.

Bonus Scene 1

Nolan

A Month After Nolan's Real Proposal

Abby: I can't believe we're finally going to see your big house, Nolan!
Me: Um, it's just a house. With a beach.
Zach: A private beach. I bet you and Katie swim naked sometimes, don't you?
Me: It's not a private island. I have neighbors.
Zane: It's not like he'd tell us, anyway.
Beck: I'm more interested in the huge outdoor barbecue setup you have.
West: I just want to eat and watch Emmy walk out of the water. Slowly.
Abby: Er, was that supposed to be private, for Emmy

only? I love you, but I don't want to hear about your *Baywatch* fantasy role-plays.

West: ...

Me: I didn't think I'd have to say this, but bathing suits are required. Do what you want in your rooms—I spaced us all out—but not on my damn beach.

Zach: <sighing emoji> Makes me wish I had someone I could test how soundproofed your walls are.

Abby: <puking emoji> I don't want to hear your sex noises.

Zane: Cheer up, Zach. Maybe we'll meet someone on the beach.

Me: Another rule - No hooking up and ghosting my neighbors or their friends. I have to live here.

Zach: As if they really even know who you are. They're all mansions with a shit-ton of land.

Beck: Don't worry, Nolan. I'll help monitor the children and make sure they behave.

Zane and Zach: <middle finger emoji> x3

Me: I wish Aunt Lori was coming, too. And not just because she'd help keep you all on your best behavior. But she has that girls' trip with her friends, with nonrefundable tickets.

Abby: She wants us to bond. So let's bond, all. Wolfe Siblings Unite. <wolf emoji>

Me: That depends on whether Zach can keep it in his pants or not...

Abby: Why didn't I have sisters instead?

Me: Love you too, Abby. <heart emoji>

I tried to focus on whatever was on the TV, but I kept glancing toward the hall. My siblings should be arriving any minute.

Katie patted my knee. "Don't worry, they'll be here. And it'll be a great long weekend."

I'd offered to host them for Labor Day weekend, and they'd all said yes. They'd even let me send my jet to pick them up. "Maybe I should've gone to the airport."

"You had that video conference you couldn't miss. Don't worry, Jenn will charm them, I'm sure."

"Still."

Katie leaned against me and hugged me. "It'll be fine, Nolan. I promise. Especially since I helped you decorate all those empty rooms so they had places to sleep. Although I still wish you would've let me buy a few sexy surprises to 'accidentally' leave on their beds."

I smiled. "It was tempting. But I *do* want them to come back again."

She patted my chest. "They will. I mean, you have your own beach. That's more than enough."

I narrowed my eyes. "You just wanted me for my beach, didn't you?"

Katie winked. "It was definitely a plus. But of course, that's not the only reason." She kissed me. "Now, I can think of other ways to distract you until they get here." She climbed onto my lap and wiggled. "Like this."

I groaned as my cock started to harden. "I would normally jump at the chance, baby. But I don't want to meet my brothers with a hard-on. I'll never hear the end of it."

She traced my jaw, which didn't help in the control-my-dick situation. At all.

Katie said, "Do you want me to dump ice cubes down your pants, then?"

I snorted. "That would work. But then it'd look as if I pissed my pants."

"Oh, I know! I can get a bag of peas, hold it over your crotch, and that should make you shrink."

Just the thought of ice-cold peas instantly tamed my dick. "That image alone is enough." I kissed her and then maneuvered her to sit beside me. "Now, we need to behave. Just for a little while." I nipped her earlobe. "I'll make it up to you later."

"Well, there is that item on my list I've been dying to try..."

"Consider it done."

She beamed at me. "You do spoil me."

"Well, I am your fairy godmother, remember?"

We both glanced at the shoe on the mantel; I'd had it mounted inside a glass case. I'd worried about it being too cheesy. However, Katie had kissed me and rewarded me many times over for the gesture.

Just as I was about to suggest waiting on the back porch, the doorbell rang and I heard the door open. Jenn always did that when she was expected. The house was enormous, and otherwise, she'd have to wander for a while to find us.

After standing, I offered my hand to Katie. "Ready, baby?"

She put her hand in mine, and I helped her up. Katie

replied, "Yep. Come on. This weekend will be fun, you'll see."

With Katie's hand in mine, some of my nervousness faded. We made it to the entryway, which was full of all my siblings, plus Jenn, Sabrina, Emmy, Avery, and Wyatt. Rafe was mysteriously absent.

Jenn waved toward the crowd. "Here they are, all safe and sound! Now, I need to dash. If that's all right?"

"Of course. Thanks, Jenn. Add it to my list of favors I owe you."

"Well, I'm about to go to Paris for a week with Tina, courtesy of my employer. So I think we're good for now." She winked. "Have fun and don't let the house burn down."

I waved and Jenn left. Silence fell for a few seconds and then Abby bounced on her feet. "Where's the beach?"

Chuckling, I went over and hugged my sister. "You can leave your luggage here for now."

Zach asked, "What, you don't have a butler?"

"No. A chef, housekeeper, and a gardener, yes. But until recently, I didn't really have a need for a butler."

Zane gestured around the room. "We might come visit you all the time now, so you should hire one. And make sure they're British."

Zane shook his head. "Not even that will help your attempt at a British accent."

Zach flipped off his twin. "It's worth a shot."

"I'll think about it. Now, who's ready to see the beach?"

Katie squeezed my hand, and I squeezed back. As I

guided everyone to the sliding back door and down the path, there were tons of questions about my place, my neighbors, and how many rooms I had.

By the time we reached the sand, Abby squealed, took off her sandals, and raced for the water. Emmy, Sabrina, Zach and Zane followed her—Zane slowly, as he was still healing—and Katie glanced up at me. "Will you be okay if I join them? I want to splash Abby when she's not looking."

I chuckled. "Go have fun, baby. I'll be fine."

I kissed her, and then she raced down to the water. A scream from Abby told me she'd been successful.

West and Beck stood on either side of me. Beck spoke first. "It's nice here. Even if you do have a huge-ass mansion that's a little intimidating."

"It's just a house. And I need a mansion so that I have enough room for all my siblings and family to stay."

West grunted. "It's definitely a long way from that cabin we went to with dad, for fishing."

"Yeah. Although maybe the three of us can go fishing one weekend, if you're free."

West smiled. "I'd like that. Wyatt would rather study the fish than catch them. And Avery thinks they're gross."

Beck said, "I haven't been fishing in years. Once the season winds down in a few months, maybe we can go together."

"Then let's make it happen. Tell me where you want to go, and I'll arrange it."

For a second, I thought maybe my brothers would

protest yet again, be stubborn, and refuse to let me treat them.

But West slapped my back. "Then I'm going to pick somewhere fancy."

Beck nodded. "Maybe ice fishing. I've never done that."

"Hmm, ice fishing. I'm sure we can find a good place in Canada. Make sure to have your passports ready."

My brothers and I hashed out the details of our winter fishing trip until the women convinced us to play in the water.

And as I splashed everyone I could manage, my nervousness completely forgotten, I simply enjoyed spending time with my brothers and sister. I suspected this was the first of many visits from my siblings, and I couldn't wait for the day when they just showed up unannounced, annoyed me, and then we laughed later over drinks.

Bonus Scene 2

Katie

Six Weeks After Katie and Nolan say, "I love you" to Each Other

Cass: I'm bummed we can't go to Disneyland with you for a few more weeks. I miss you.
Me: I know, I miss you both, too. But I'm always here via text, video calls, you name it.
Sam: I'm still trying to convince Kyle to come with us.
Cass: Why? He's grumpier than usual. He'll probably scare the children.
Me: Is he still complaining about the woman who runs the diner?
Sam: Yeah. And yet, he constantly goes to fix things for her. I think he likes her.

Cass: Except she wants nothing to do with men. I can't blame her, considering what her ex-husband did.
Me: Yes, that had to be a nightmare. Still, I hope he figures it out.
Sam: Me, too. I still have to live with him, and I'm tired of his barking.
Cass: I'm thinking of finally getting my own house. And no, I'm not sharing with you, Sam.
Sam: <pleading eyes emoji> Pretty please?
Cass: No. I love you, but I'm over thirty and want a place to call my own.
Sam: <crying eyes emoji> Meanie.
Me: When I visit, I'll see if I can get to the bottom of Kyle's moods. That should make things better for you, Sam. <heart emoji>
Sam: That's why I love you most, Katie. <heart emoji>
Cass: <middle finger emoji> for you Sam
Me: I really do miss you both. Play nice because I have to go.
Cass: Enjoy your visit. I'm sure you'll love Nolan's charity center.
Sam: It might even change your life. <heart emoji>

Nolan's driver stopped in front of a large building that probably had been a warehouse at some point. There was a big sign that said, "Starry Arts Haven Center."

After weeks of trying to find time, Nolan had finally brought me here. He squeezed my hand. "Ready?"

"Yes! Er, sorry to shout. But I've just been so curious. I scoured the website and social media pages, but there's only so much you can glean from it versus being here in person."

"Well, then let's not keep you waiting any longer, baby. Let's go."

He disembarked first, opened my door, and helped me out. I glanced up at him. "This is the first time you've been here without a disguise or at night, isn't it?"

"Yes. Once I finish filming my current movie, I hope to be able to spend more time here."

I tugged his hand. "Come on. I want to see what you created."

He nodded, and we went inside. A woman in her forties, with tan skin, black hair, and dark brown eyes, greeted us. "Hello. I'm Sarah Nguyen, the director of this place. It's an honor to have you visit us, Mr. Drake. I'm sure the kids will love to see you. That superhero movie franchise you're in is really popular with them."

Nolan smiled. To a stranger, that might be all they saw. However, I noticed him shift his feet a little—he didn't want to focus on himself. I may not be a movie star, but I could help shift the attention away from him. "Hello, Sarah. I'm Katie Evans. I mentioned how I might be interested in volunteering here."

"Oh, yes, sorry, Ms. Evans. Welcome! And we're very happy about your interest. If you have any questions, let me know. Now, come on. The acting class should just be finishing up and you can chat with the children."

Once Sarah turned and walked, Nolan mouthed, "Thank you."

I squeezed his hand in reassurance.

There were lots of rooms for the various classes, events, and even counseling services. This was Nolan's flagship location. Or, he hoped it would become that once he launched a second location sometime next year.

Sarah cracked open a door, nodded, and motioned for us to follow inside.

I whispered to Nolan, "Showtime," before we followed her.

The kids in the room ranged from ages ten to eighteen. An older man and woman were at the front, talking with two of the older students.

However, within seconds, silence fell and everyone stood staring at Nolan.

Wanting to put the kids at ease, Nolan bowed and said, "Hello, everyone."

Noise erupted, and the teachers slowly calmed the chaos. The woman said, "Yes, Nolan Drake has come to visit us. He promised to answer some questions. And maybe if you all behave, he'll even take a few selfies."

Nolan had already said he'd take them, but it was the sort of trick my teachers had done in the past. And it worked—the kids all stood quietly in a group.

Nolan answered some questions, and most of the class was star-struck. However, a girl of about thirteen sat by herself in the corner, reading a book.

I quietly went over to her and whispered, "Can I sit next to you?"

She glanced up and back at her book. "If you want."

After a few seconds, I asked, "You don't have any questions for Nolan?"

She bit her lip before nodding. "Yes. But I know not to ask them."

"How come?"

She shook her head. "It's not important."

I sensed she didn't want to talk about it, so I gestured toward her book. "What are you reading?"

"It's a play we're studying. I want to try out for a part since it was one of my mom's favorites, but I'm scared. The last time I was in a play..."

Her voice trailed off, and she glanced down back at her book.

I'd caught the "was" part of her words. Something had happened to her mother.

Best to get her thinking about anything else. "Well, I've never seen that play myself. Maybe you could practice for me? We could wait until the others are gone, if you want. I have no other plans for the day."

She glanced at me and then back at the book. "Are you sure? I want to practice, but I'm new and don't know any of the other kids. And I don't want them to laugh at me if I freeze."

"Why would they laugh at you?"

For a minute, I thought she might not answer. But then she whispered, "Because I might be cursed. Last time I was in a play, my mom died coming to see it."

Oh, honey. My heart ached for the girl.

"I would never laugh at you. But it's up to you if you want to practice or not. I know losing someone you love is hard. And sometimes it takes time to do some of the things you used to enjoy, especially if it reminds you of them. But if you ever want to practice in front of someone, I'm going to be volunteering at the center. And I'll make sure to be here during the acting classes."

She played with the edges of the book. "Maybe. If I see you next time, I might. I need to practice, though."

"Of course you do. I'm Katie, by the way."

"Oh, I know who you are! You're Nolan's girlfriend. Nice to meet you. I'm Chantel."

"Well, Chantel, I look forward to watching your practice when you're ready. And I promise not to tell Nolan how much better you are than him afterward."

I winked, and she smiled. "I'm not better."

"But you could be."

She fidgeted with the book in her hands. "I'll look for you next time, Katie."

Sensing she wanted to be alone, I nodded and stood. "And I look forward to it, Chantel. I can't wait!"

The teen smiled again and then focused on her book. As I walked over to Nolan, a sense of rightness settled over me. In all the years I'd been trying to figure out what I wanted to do, I'd never felt as good and determined as I did right now.

It'd been a long, bumpy road, but my gut said this center and Nolan's charity were the purpose I'd been waiting for.

As I watched Nolan pose with the students—sometimes in ridiculous superhero stances—I smiled. Not only did I have the kindest, sexiest man on the planet to call my own, he'd also helped me figure out what I wanted to do with my life.

And later, when I told him, Nolan supported my desire to volunteer and work with his charity.

Chantel eventually got the lead role, and Nolan and I went to opening night. She also later became a famous movie star, just like I'd hinted she could be.

Author's Note

I hope you enjoyed Katie and Nolan's story! I had a lot of fun with them, but also connected with the pair on a lot of levels. Every book of mine has a little of me in it (with a lot of make-believe), and this one was no different. I both suffered a little bullying about my appearance like Katie and have buried myself in work to hide like Nolan. Even if Nolan is a billionaire movie star, I'd like to think there are levels to him a lot of people can connect with. Don't tell Beck or West, but he's probably my favorite so far!

I dropped a few hints and it should be no surprise that Abby and Rafe are next. Their story actually starts during the last few chapters of this one and overlaps. They drink too much one night and wake up married in Vegas. Whoops! But Rafe has a deal—stay married for a year to avoid bad PR and he'll help Abby get revenge. Like with Nolan and Katie, there will be a little drama. I have a weakness for British soap operas (*Coronation*

Street and *EastEnders*, thank you, BritBox) and like to add a dash of it to my stories. I can't wait to start their book!

As of writing this, I am contemplating a short novel about Kyle Evans (Katie's older brother). But we'll see what happens. :)

I want to thank Ashley, Iliana, and Amy — three great beta readers who help me find typos and minor inconsistencies. Thank you!

And to all of you who've read this far, thank you from the bottom of my heart. Being an author is both the best and hardest job in the world, and it's only possible because of you all. I hope to see you in Starry Hills again, and if you want to make sure you never miss a release, then please join my mailing list at:

kaylachase.com/newsletter

Until next time, happy reading!
~Kayla~

Trust Me With Forever

Starry Hills #4

He's a former pro soccer player struggling after a career-ending injury. She's his little sister's best friend who no longer trusts men after being conned. But after drinking too much and waking up married to her in Vegas, he makes a deal—stay married for a year to avoid bad PR and he'll help her get revenge. However, the more time they spend together, the harder it is to remember it's not real...

This will be Abby Wolfe and Rafe Mendoza's story. More detailed synopsis to come.

TRUST ME WITH FOREVER will release later in 2024.

About the Author

Kayla Chase writes sexy, feel-good romance full of laughter, friendships, and family. Her stories usually include crazy get togethers, fun festivals or events, and communities you want to be a part of. She also writes happy endings because real life and adulting can be way too hard.

She lives near Seattle but also grew up in California, which gives her lots of beautiful places to include in her stories (such as Sonoma wine country). While she's also lived in Japan and England, she has yet to figure a way to get her characters to those places. (But she does travel on a shoestring when she gets the chance!)

When not writing, she loves to read, jog on her treadmill, fit in some yoga, or try new recipes in the kitchen. More often than not, her cats derail her plans and make things, er, interesting.

facebook.com/kaylachaseauthor
instagram.com/kaylachaseauthor

www.ingramcontent.com/pod-product-compliance
Lightning Source LLC
Chambersburg PA
CBHW060215030726
47499CB00004B/1055
9798891560130